THE *PROMISE* OF *ZACCARIAS*

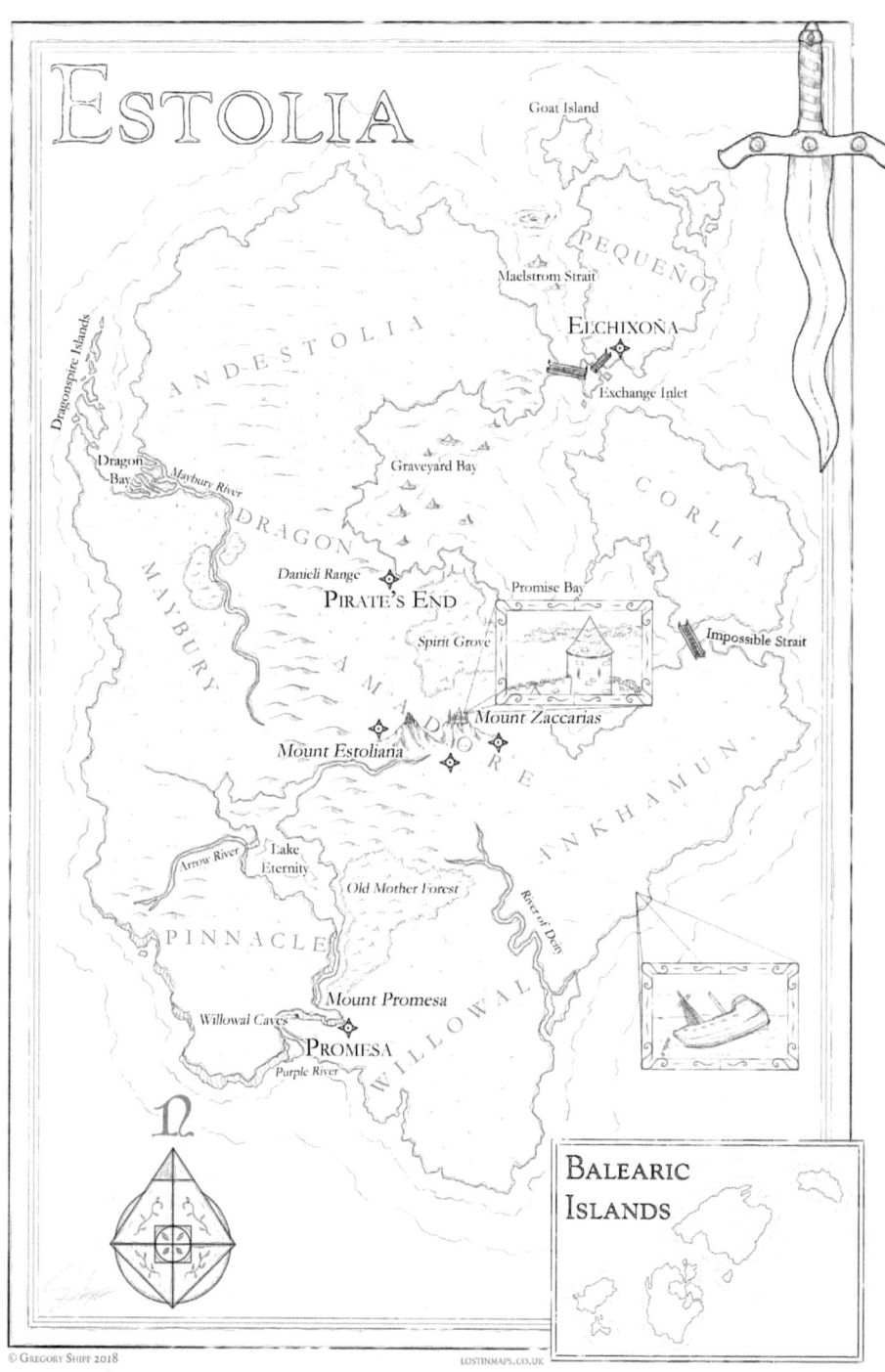

ESTOLIA

Goat Island

PEQUEÑO

Maelstrom Strait

ELCHIXOÑA

Exchange Inlet

Dragonspire Islands

ANDESTOLIA

CORLIA

Dragon Bay

Maybury River

Graveyard Bay

DRAGON

Danieli Range

PIRATE'S END

Promise Bay

Spirit Grove

Impossible Strait

MAYBURY

AMADORE

Mount Zaccarias

Mount Estoliana

INKHAMUN

Arrow River

Lake Eternity

Old Mother Forest

River of Deen

PINNACLE

WILLOWAL

Willowal Caves

Mount Promesa

PROMESA

Purple River

BALEARIC ISLANDS

© GREGORY SHIPP 2018

LOSTINMAPS.CO.UK

THE PROMISE OF ZACCARIAS

Sasheena Kurfman

TALES OF ESTOLIA 1

ESTOLIA PRESS

Tales of Estolia Volume 1 is a collection of short stories about the fictional island nation of Estolia. Estolia does not actually exist, and all the stories within this volume are a work of fiction. Some of the stories in the Tales of Estolia take place in Halloween County, California; in the townships around Hallow's End; and in the nation of Hath. All these locales are fictional and everything within: names, characters, businesses, events and incidents are the products of the author's imagination. Any resemblance to actual persons, living or dead, or actual events is purely coincidental.

Cover, Interior Design & Title Page Illustration by Sasheena Kurfman.

Map Design by Gregory Shipp **www.lostinmaps.co.uk**

Cover Model: Kelsey King Lecky

Author Photograph by Aubrey Say;

Hair Color & Style: Dezzi Anderson;

Beauty Salon – Pretty Drama – Chasity Rasdal;

Copyright © 2018 by Sasheena Anne Kurfman

Estolia Press
PO Box 571
Keno, OR 97627
www.estolia.com

ISBN: 978-1-949376-00-5 (Paperback)
ISBN: 978-1-949376-01-2 (Large Print)

First Edition
10 9 8 7 6 5 4 3

THE PROMISE OF ZACCARIAS

dedicated to

Abi

you've enriched my life

TABLE OF CONTENTS

Part 1 – The Promise of Zaccarias

✖ Cast of Characters ✖

Alanis – One of the participants in the Grand Design. *Deity* for Hath

Amadora – Zaccarias' mother

Amadore – The second born son of Estoliana and Zaccarias

Ascelina – The bride of Zacarian. Rescued by Zacarian from a pirate ship

Caylaria – One of the overseers of the Grand Design

Conara – One of the participants in the Grand Design

Elora – One of the participants in the Grand Design. *Deity* for Estolia

Estoliana – The daughter of a minor landowner

Ezekias – Zaccarias' father

Falloran – One of the participants in the Grand Design. *Deity* for parts of China

Khrynos – One of the overseers of the Grand Design

Miriam – Zaccarias' oldest daughter

Nefermari – (Mari) Wife of Qi – Slave – Half Nubian, Half Egyptian

Paldiya – One of the participants in the Grand Design. *Deity* for Anoxes

Phineas – Zaccarias' older brother

Qi – Royal Scribe, developer of the Estolian written language, inscribed Zaccarias' words in the stone walls of the caverns in Mt. Estoliana

Qimarian – Oldest son of Qi and Mari

Sapphira – Zaccarias' middle daughter

Sebastian – A religious man who helps found the Estolian religion

Talitha – Zaccarias' youngest daughter

Tarritray – Male *Deity* not part of the Grand Design

Zacarian – The first-born son of Estoliana and Zaccarias

Zaccarias – Hired muscle from the *Ankhamun*, a merchant ship headed for Egypt

Zenta – One of the participants in the Grand Design. *Advisory Role*

Prologue – Conference of Deities

Very few of my protégés ever realize the critical purpose built in to the different iterations of The Grand Design. Those who do, like Khrynos and I, come to cherish that moment when it is time to start afresh. Wherein ten of the most refined and advanced beings convene and embark on the journey together. The participants come from each of the five dimensions of reality, matched and paired, refined and readied for that one pulsebeat of existence in the Great Cycle when it is time to begin again. What better way is there to travel through Infinity towards that elusive goal of Eternity? Who, having been a part of The Grand Design, would turn down the chance to be both guide and guardian when the cycle starts again?

~Caylaria, 'Musings on Eternity'

ELORA HEARD the chimes and felt the thrill of accomplishment. It was time for the inception of the Grand Design. She swept her hand downward and then stepped through the black portal that appeared before her. She was in a forest meadow and sweet birdsong punctuated the crisp air.

She saw only one other individual in the glade. "This is a pleasant glade, Alanis," Elora said.

Alanis preened. She worked on the forest glade for some time to make it just perfect for this meeting of *Deities*. She walked over to the circle of boulders and sat on one of them. Elora sat on another, and as the others arrived, they each chose a boulder until ten *Deities* were sitting in one large circle.

The ten *Deities* leaned forward, heads bowed, when Khrynos and Caylaria stepped out of nothing and into the center of the circle.

"Today we begin the Grand Design," Caylaria said. "Each of you will impact the lives of a limited region. Give edicts to your charges and guide them. Follow up on the promises you make. You may have as large or as small a connection to your charges as you wish. The only thing you cannot do is eliminate their free will."

"While each of you will work to impact your chosen realm of influence, other *Deities* from alternate cycles will be working on their own Designs," Khrynos cautioned them.

Khrynos and Caylaria spoke for the next few minutes – or it could have been an eon or two. When finished with instruction, they stepped to the side and in the center of the glade a small globe now floated representing the planet upon which they would exercise limited influence.

In turn, each *Deity* selected a small region of the planet within which they would hold sway and could make their presence felt. Their influence could extend from their selected regions only if they could successfully influence those who were tied by blood or faith to their sphere of influence.

When it was her turn to select, Elora chose a small island in a vast in-land sea. The people living on an island would be easier to influence than their landlocked counterparts. Her Grand Design required her subjects to maintain a certain level of isolation.

After Falloran selected an isolated region in the largest land mass, Khrynos looked around the circle of *Deities*. "Zenta, what region do you select?"

Zenta did not hesitate. She approached where Khrynos stood next to the spinning globe. The nine selected regions each pulsed with the colors of their respective *Deities*. "I choose to forego the role of *Deity*, and in-stead take an Advisory Role. Here, in this region. I will help shape events to promote the goals of the subjects that come within my influence. I know my direct influence will be held in abeyance for thousands of years." She settled her hand over a small region on the west coast of the northern of the pair of smaller connected continents. "This region of the globe will, in time, bring together a concentration of people from other parts of the Grand Design. I feel constrained to influence events rather than individuals."

Alanis and Elora both stepped forward. Elora glanced at Alanis and with a smile took one of her hands before both women set their hands on Zenta's shoulders. "I knew," Alanis said, "the instant you touched the globe, that my citizens, and those of Elora, would both come to this region, and that together, our three-fold influence will be an integral part of the Grand Design."

Elora felt the solemn weight of responsibility as she looked from Alanis to Zenta, then towards Khrynos and Caylaria. "There will be a nexus in this region, tying together our diverse religions, and bringing the purpose of the Grand Design to fruition."

Caylaria intoned, "Let it be so recorded: the selection of region and influence has been made. We shall reconvene at the appropriate time." The pulsing colors on the globe stopped pulsing and glowed fiercely with the respective colors for a moment, before fading to the natural colors. The colors faded along with the conference; each participant began the critical preliminary work for their Grand Design.

The Grand Design

721 BCE

The children of Zaccarias will never be asked to do more than they are capable of doing.
~Hieronymus Jeremiah, Capitulo 2

THE ISLAND ELORA CONSTRUCTED from an idea was beautiful. Nothing in her existence prior to the Grand Design prepared her for this moment. This was the substance of her dreams, flavored by her imagination, augmented by her individuality. She compared it with the other lands in the Grand Design. None came close to her creation in style, beauty, or grandeur.

Among the fine details put together for the island destined to hold her people, she was proudest of the two mountains at the center of the island. both had lengths and lengths of caves throughout. The first mountain was much taller, split into two peaks.

The second mountain, on the other side of the narrow valley, was about a third shorter, and what was left of the peak looked more like a bony hand reaching up through the ground to grasp the peak, only to discover it was missing. There was a small plateau in the very center of the fingers of stone. Halfway between the truncated peak and base of the mountain the eastern side spread out in a grand plateau. Where it met the sides of the mountain her people would discover the entrance to the network of caves.

The south-western quadrant of the island was itself another large plateau, higher than the rest of the island, with an impressive waterfall leading into a central lake.

Two large bays dominated the east. Three separate ocean channels led to the bays, but only the middle channel held a safe approach through the many submerged rocks surrounding the island. The main island was ringed by hazardous waters, making it unappealing for those who would invade.

The flowering fruit tree peppering the island was one of her gifts for the faithful; with unique species of butterflies and bees to pollinate the plentiful blossoms.

Her most critical achievement was the way inhabitants of the neighboring islands saw the island as unimportant, uninspiring, small, and therefore not worth the effort to explore. Particularly when they considered the potential risks to their ships.

Once it was fully prepared, she needed to find the right sort of people for the island. People to accept her as *Deity*, who would live the edicts she would give them. Without that, it was all for nothing. And it had to begin with a single man. A man willing to agree to the requirements placed before him.

Finding a man to bestow her blessings upon was harder than she expected. So many of the men she happened upon were coarse, intemperate, motivated by sexual allure, and untrue to their word.

She walked unseen through the markets in many of the bustling population centers ringing the inland sea. The dark souls of the seething throngs of people buffeted her from all sides. This interaction with humanity was a hazard she did not consider when she fought so hard to be part of the Grand Design. It was, however, a critical step. Her design could not move forward without the perfect man for her purposes.

The man she was following impressed her with his intellect and insight. Just as she considered selecting him for her Grand Design she was halted by what she saw within him. His thoughts shifted towards sex – she could work with that – but as they grew specific, she was repulsed. No, this man would *not* work as the one to begin her experiment!

She had time before she had to settle on one man for her Grand Design. But it was discouraging when finding the right man seemed impossible.

"Perhaps you want more than any man can give?"

Elora turned and saw it was Zenta walking next to her. Zenta who had no people, no part of the Grand Design for many more human generations. They walked next to one another through the shopping district. "Maybe you're looking in the wrong place or for the wrong type of man?"

Elora stopped and gestured to another man she had considered much earlier – and discarded. "See this man? He is strong of body. Intelligent. But he will not work in my Grand Design. He lacks the qualities of character necessary for success."

"What is it you need or want then?"

"Intelligence, strength, bravery, loyalty and above all other things, integrity. He must be capable of the necessary belief to follow my commandments," Elora said.

"Perhaps your search is too far from where you wish your progenitor to flourish? It may be the compatibility you seek requires proximity in addition to those other things."

Elora looked from the bright colors of the fabric vendors to the vendors of metals. Perhaps she *should* look closer to her land. "You are wise." Elora thanked Zenta before moving her awareness from the eastern city to the region which held her island in the western half of the sea. She would choose one of the cities near her land. Anoxes, or Chellah, or Palmara.

She was immediately aware of a ship passing close to her island. The ship was a merchant vessel, heavily laden with cargo and livestock. The *Ankhamun*.

She explored the hearts and minds of each man toiling on the ship. Most were unsuitable to her design. In addition to the men, a stowaway was hidden among the livestock – a woman. She was ready to move on when she realized there was one other man who remained unexplored on the ship.

He was high up in the rigging, probably on the lookout for pirates. He called himself Zaccarias, and was a large, imposing, physical man. He was illiterate like most of the people of this era, but quite intelligent. She took the time to read from his mind his story. He was the second son of a wealthy landowner north of Anoxes. His older brother was to inherit the land and wealth of their father. He left his home to find his fortune and future.

What caught her attention more than anything else was his unswerving devotion to what he perceived as right. He was exactly what she was looking for: a man of great physical and moral strength ruled by loyalty and guided by intelligence. He would serve her Grand Design if he was willing. He had the qualities she wanted and needed. But he had to agree. Her design required compliance or it would never work.

She needed more than one man willing to promise her allegiance. The female stowaway was from south of Anoxes, fleeing a destiny she was smart enough to realize would not suit her – as third wife of an abusive older man. She wanted something more from her life than to merely be the object in a barter. She could serve Elora's needs. She felt the tingle of excitement and anticipation. This was it, then, the inception of her Grand Design. If she could obtain the rights from the *Deity* or *Deities* responsible for them.

Once she decided these two could beget the dynasty necessary for her Grand Design, her attention then turned to the other souls on board the ship. She could not meddle with the followers of any of the other *Deities* – not without a polite request at the very least. She composed the request to lock this couple in as her chosen progenitors. If it was permissible. One last peek into their minds decided her, and she sent a request for all *Deities* who held sway over this ship, her crew, and this region to come to a conference.

A rumble of thunder in the wake of a lightning strike just off the bow heralded her request, and then the scene froze amid the sound and fury of the sudden storm. On the storm-racked deck of the *Ankhamun* three *Deities* stepped through portals into the conference she convened. She waited a moment longer to see if any other *Deity* would manifest, but none did.

She brought forth an image of the two individuals from the *Ankhamun*. "I am Elora. This island is my domain." She pointed to the shadowy outline of the island off the bow. "I wish to begin my Grand Design with these two individuals. If there are no objections, I would have this ship wreck upon the rocky shores of my land, with only the cargo and my chosen subjects able to make it to shore."

The male *Deity* stepped forward. He took in Elora's petite frame, short stature, golden hair, and small breasts before looking at the other two *Deities*. They were both more beautiful than Elora.

"Tarritray," he introduced himself. He was as impressive a physical entity as

Zaccarias, the man Elora wanted for her Grand Design. "I control this sea. All upon it are within my authority. I enjoy the occasional shipwreck in the pursuit of a good cause. I'm sure I can find an incentive to cooperate." The way his eyes roved over the breasts and bodies of the female *Deities* made it clear he was looking for sexual favors to provide the incentive.

Elora recognized the two female *Deities* as participants in the Grand Design. The first to speak said, "I am Paldiya. The two you wish to adopt are from Anoxes, the region over which I hold complete authority." She moved closer to the image Elora called up, studying the two. "Both left Anoxes with no intention of returning. Neither are critical to my Design. You may have them." She then turned to Tarritray, looking him up and down. She curled her lip in disdain. With a swirl of her skirt she stepped through the portal, quitting the conference.

The third *Deity* was looking at Tarritray with speculative interest. A slow smile grew on her face when their eyes met. "This ship, and her fate is immaterial in my part of the Grand Design." She glanced towards Elora only a moment. With a wave of her hand, an image of two dark-skinned nearly identical boys from the *Ankhamun* coalesced in front of her. "These brothers *are* indispensable to *my* Grand Design. I have read the future, and they cannot perish in this shipwreck," she said. "I am Conara."

"Perhaps a compromise." Tarritray's eyes traveled over Conara yet again, his sexual attraction obvious. "I can wreck the ship, with the loss of all hands to the sea. Your subjects," he said with a gesture towards Elora, "will be swept to your island." He stepped closer to Conara. "While your two will be swept away from this island on the wild and wicked currents which abound here. We can guide them to Palmara, and from thence influence events to produce the outcome you desire."

"Your offer intrigues me." She moved towards him, one hand reaching up to caress his chest. "Shall we make it happen?"

Tarritray covered her hand with his own and the two of them faded out. Time resumed flowing and the ship started to fight the strength of the wind in the sails, heading towards the edge of the land Elora had so carefully prepared.

3

The First Vision

Obedience is the first lesson we learn within the temple as Acolytes. We learn the virtue in following directions that seem unimportant so we will give greater attention when we learn what is required of us as the sons of Zaccarias.

~Timoteo Salazar; Capitulo 48

ZACCARIAS AND THE first mate both watched as the newly hired seaman helped the invaders tie their small vessel to the *Ankhamun* and climb aboard. They spoke softly in one of the Moorish tongues, and then moved away from the rail and towards a small pile of supplies. One crate was partially opened, and Zaccarias could see the glint of gold within. Zaccarias looked at the first mate and nodded. They silently climbed down from the rigging, beckoning to the other guards to be prepared.

The fight, when it came, was short. The pirates had no chance against an organized repulsion. Zaccarias focused his attention on the new man while the others took on the pirates. Zaccarias felt his sword sinking into the gut of the new seaman and hid the shudder of distaste. His eyes met those of the man who thought him a fool, before the soul inside fled. Zaccarias lifted one foot and pushed against the man's chest, disengaging him from the sword, and throwing him overboard to feed the sharks already awaiting their meal.

When he turned to see how the rest of the fight was going, he saw the seven pirates were trussed up on the deck of the *Ankhamun* and the captain and first mate were deciding their fate. Two of the pirates looked like they had not yet reached puberty. A couple of the pirates cursed long and fluently when the captain decided to secure them to the deck of their small pirate ship and then sink it.

The leader of the pirates begged the captain of the *Ankhamun* to spare his two youngest sons, twins, not even men. Zaccarias felt the flush of destiny, as he liked to call it – that prickling of the skin that told him something monumental was being decided. He was proud to serve on the *Ankhamun* when the captain agreed. At their request, the two boys watched as the pirate ship sank rapidly. Afterwards, the Captain led them over to one of the jobs that needed doing.

Zaccarias looked towards the dark horizon, said to the First Mate, "The weather looks to be turning. I'll go aloft, keep an eye out for those who would target us in foul weather."

Once he was at his post, Zaccarias scanned the horizon, looking for additional pirate vessels. All he saw was the dim iron-gray background of the sea and sky merging with one another, brooded over by the lowering clouds. It was a fast-approaching, unpredictable storm typical for this region.

He heard the uncomfortable whinnies of the horses and the cries of his shipmates to each other. These sounds were muted when a blast of lightning was punctuated by a roar of thunder. A second bolt of lightning was accompanied by a deafening roar, and a massive jolt that almost threw him from his perch in the rigging. The sharp crack of wood splintering and sudden dramatic listing to the side had him hanging on the rigging, grappling for a more secure hold.

The high-pitched scream of a woman drew his attention. He saw her struggling to swim beneath where the mast overhung the seething sea. He dove into the water but realized his mistake instantly. His sword was dragging him into the depths. He could not surface with it strapped to his side. He would have to offer it as tribute to the *Deities* of the water and hope they accepted the offering and allowed him to live. All these thoughts rushed through his mind in the moments before he unfastened his scabbard and released it. He shot to the surface and gulped in a deep breath before beginning his search for the woman.

A desperate spluttering cry oriented him. He saw the flash of her face before the water dragged her down once more, threatening to consume her as it had just consumed his sword. He dove after her, reaching her in moments. He wrapped his arm around her ribcage and pulled her with him back to the surface of the water. Once he was on the stormy surface of the water, he searched but couldn't find the *Ankhamun*. What he did see was welcome – the bulk of land.

Zaccarias dragged the unconscious woman onto the stone-riddled beach. Water poured down his face as he looked back the way they came. There was no sign of the ship. It either sank or was pulled away by the fierce currents.

Where did she come from? There weren't any women on the *Ankhamun*. He thought she was young and beautiful. He would have heard if any of the men had a young beautiful woman on board.

He was distracted by the unseasonable heat of the winter sun beating down on him. Standing upright, he looked around with a frown, and saw that streamers of once-ominous clouds were rushing away, leaving the bright blue of the sky.

Much of the cargo from the unfortunate *Ankhamun* was washing up on the beach. The ship was fully laden, heading to Egypt to deliver the cargo to the Pharaoh of Egypt. He knew the cargo was extraordinarily valuable. His height, broad shoulders, and skill with weapons meant he was an asset in defense of the ship.

He looked around but couldn't see any place more comfortable than the rocks he was already standing on. The girl at his feet was breathing easily. His medical knowledge was limited to the ways to tend a wound in battle and how to breathe life into someone who drowned and was no longer breathing. But she was breathing already.

Since he couldn't help her, he opted to move her away from the swirling waves. Stooping, he picked her up, groaning at the effort it took. Normally he would have no issue in lifting a woman of her height and weight. He took a deep breath and focused on a small tree, ignoring his physical discomfort.

He carried her above the high tide mark. She would have to wake on her own. The tree he aimed for turned out to be pleasant-smelling, with beautiful unseasonable lavender-colored blossoms. He was breathing heavily when he laid her gently in the shadow of the tree. He leaned against the tree, catching his breath.

He looked back at the shoreline. He couldn't see any of his companions from the *Ankhamun*. All he could see were dozens of crates, large and small, washing up onto the rocky shore. The ship was a victim of the sea.

When he got his strength back, he decided to secure the crates. The inhabitants of the island might be hostile. He could bribe them with cargo originally destined for the Pharaoh. If the island was uninhabited, then he might use the cargo to obtain a berth on a passing ship. Aside from those considerations, he was not an idle man. He could not relax while some of the cargo was about to be swept back out to sea.

During a pause in his work dragging crates out of the water, he looked over to where he left the girl and saw she was sitting up and looking around. He waved in her direction before moving to the next crate.

He was trying to move a huge crate but it kept stubbornly hanging up on rocks. On his next effort to shift the crate, he finally got it moving. It was only as he succeeded in moving it above the high-tide-mark and towards the tree-line that he saw a pair of shapely hands had joined his, providing the extra man-power necessary to move the crate. He wiped the sweat and salt off his brow and turned to look at the woman.

"What language do you speak?" he asked. He used the dialect from a coastal region of Anoxes, hoping she would understand him.

"I speak several languages," she said in the same dialect.

"I am called Zaccarias."

"Estoliana." She looked up and down the rocky coast. "This is Pequeño. It is tiny to those passing it in ships, and large to those walking her shores."

He tried to judge the size of the island from what he could see. "It doesn't appear very small to me."

"Of course, it doesn't. That's part of the charm."

"How do you know so much about it?" he asked.

"I heard this ship would be passing near Pequeño. I hoped it would be close enough so I could swim ashore."

Not sure how to respond to that assertion, he straightened up and looked away from her. He saw several other crates the tide would likely reclaim if they were not moved out of the reach of the waves. He returned to his job.

When she joined him and continued to help him with his self-imposed task, he asked, "Why would you want to come here?"

"My father wished to wed me to the Captain of the Guard at Anoxes. A cruel man known to beat his wives. I left. I am *not* a dutiful daughter."

"Yes, but why come *here*?"

She looked around. "Who would not wish to live their life in paradise?"

For a while they worked together in silence, moving the smaller crates well beyond high tide, pushing the larger heavier crates as far up the shore as they could.

"What sort of people live here?" Zaccarias asked.

She cocked her head to the side, looking at him as if he was peculiar. With a small smile tilting the corners of her mouth, she said, "The Legend of Pequeño says it will not be inhabited until..." Her voice suddenly changed.

"Until those who are worthy walk upon her shores." The voice superimposed over Estoliana's voice echoed like the sound one heard when listening to a seashell; Zaccarias could feel the voice to the very depths of his marrow. He turned and saw a woman in a robe standing just above the high-water mark. Her hands were clasped and she had flaxen hair and large unfathomable gray eyes. She had the same petite build as Estoliana.

"This is your island?"

"No, Zaccarias, son of Ezekias and Amadora, this is *your* island if you are willing to accept the charge I shall lay at your feet."

"Who are you?" He felt a thrill of excitement at the thought of this land being his.

"I am *Deity*. Those who live in this region believe the island is small, unimportant, and unworthy. This is my influence." She moved closer, her eyes locked with his, and continued, "Battles, wars, struggle and strife will periodically come to the islands in this region. A land *must* be blessed to avoid being torn asunder by those conflicts. This land, Zaccarias, *will* be blessed. Both for you and your children, and their children, until time itself ceases to be."

Zaccarias was well-traveled and fascinated by stories of divine favor granted to regular mortals. He did not recall ever seeing any proof of divine intervention in his travels. "Blessings are easy to give. Many of the people I have encountered in my travels faithfully follow the dictates of their *Deity*, giving great devotion, but in the end, their god or gods do not provide the substance of the promised blessings."

"I am very simple, I shall give very few commandments, with tangible, specific blessings and promises. Behold the woman Estoliana." She pointed to the woman he rescued.

Zaccarias looked at her, realizing she was not taking an active part in the conversation. In fact, she had been speaking when her voice changed and became the deeply resonant voice of this woman who claimed to be *Deity*. She stood silently, as if unaware of the conversation taking place. She wasn't quite frozen, but he sensed she was disconnected from time. Or perhaps he was the one no longer connected to the regular passing of time.

He noticed how beautiful she was. Her hair was almost dry, a rich honey-gold, similar in color to her eyes. She was much shorter than he was, but that was not unusual since he was a very large man with a wide frame and musculature in keeping with his size. She had broad hips and beautiful breasts that were the perfect size to balance out her looks. Her features were pleasant; she was a desirable woman.

"If this island was to become yours, what blessings would you wish?"

"Are you certain you wish to know? I have an active imagination and could easily wish for more than any *Deity* might want to grant me."

She laughed. Her laughter was, he thought, like the music of angels singing, or the sound of bells ringing. "Zaccarias, your imagination, your intellect, your personality and character, all these I knew before I chose you to be the founder of a nation, a dynasty, and a religion. Speak aloud your dreams. What do you want for your land, your kingdom? I promise to listen to your dreams, to grant everything you request that is within my power, if you are willing to do what I ask in return."

Her expression and body language communicated sincerity and a deep and abiding belief in what she was offering him. He would lose nothing by voicing his deepest desires and his fondest wishes. If she was insincere, he wasted only his breath in sharing his dreams and aspirations. If she *was* sincere and capable of granting him his wishes, he would gain by sharing. There seemed no reason to remain silent, and every reason to share.

"To always be prosperous," he began, thinking of some of the less prosperous people he saw in his travels. "And for my children, and their children to have the same prosperity." He did not wish for any of his sons or daughters to be forced to seek their fortune far from family.

When she urged him to continue, he did, "I would want my people to be protected from famine, disease, and disasters.

"I would need to know we were safe from the lawless and merciless pirates who roam these waters, and from those who might become envious of our prosperity.

"It matters to me that my children, and their children, and so on would all know they have the same assurances. I would wish for a *Deity* who can give simple, easily-kept guidelines and not require an obscene level of worship."

He looked again at Estoliana and added, "My children and their children will need to be able to find worthy mates willing to perpetuate the faith I will establish."

"I like you Zaccarias." She smiled, and he felt a rush of warmth and approval which did more to convince him of her sincerity and power than anything else she did or said. "I influenced you both to come here to this island. Name it Estolia, after her." She moved closer to him, her gray eyes meeting his, her expression inscrutable. "I shall give you promises the likes of which no other man has ever received from *Deity*. Only *you* can decide if you are willing to believe in the promises I will give you. Only you know if you will be willing to do what I command to secure those blessings."

Deity moved even closer to where he stood. She lifted one hand and placed it over the abdomen of Estoliana, the other hand taking his. "You turn thirty tomorrow, Zaccarias. On your birthday, you will exchange with Estoliana her most valuable possession, for yours. What I command of you, I command of your descendants. Inasmuch as your posterity keeps your promise to me, I will keep mine – until time ceases to be."

"What *could* I give Estoliana? I have nothing but the contents of these crates from the *Ankhamun*." He didn't even have his sword.

The voice of *Deity* responded to his question, her voice settling deep into his marrow, as before, chilling him with the impact of her words, the meaning behind them. "You will give your soul into Estoliana's keeping, Zaccarias. The substance of your soul will be the exchange you will make. That is what she will take from you when you take her purity on your thirtieth birthday. When she does, you will be pledged to her forever. If she were to reject and leave you, you would die."

Zaccarias felt his skin prickle as her words hit him.

"No man can live without his soul. The promise I give you today, Zaccarias, is that you and your nation will know great prosperity. None of those who will fight and battle on these turbulent seas will see in your land anything of value. It will be unremarkable to all who see it, and left to grow in prosperity into eternity, so long as you and your male descendants keep to the constraints I will set you."

"If no man can live without his soul, how can I enjoy prosperity?"

She continued as if he did not speak. "Estoliana will conceive a son as a result of the extraordinary exchange you will make with her. This is my gift to both of you, for taking part in the exchange."

"But to exist without my soul?"

"You cannot exist without your soul. Once you give it into Estoliana's keeping, you must not try to exist without her. Too much time apart will grow acutely painful. You will measure your lifespan by the lifespan of your wife. Part of the prosperity you and your people will know will be a longevity and health unheard of in this world."

He wanted to believe. If she spoke the truth, he intended to pin her down and list what he had to do to obtain the blessings she was promising. "To get all you promise, what must I do?"

"What I promise to you, I promise also to your male descendants from now until time ceases to matter. They are to do the same as you: Find a woman pure of heart and body in their thirtieth year, wed her within seven days, and remain faithful to her for the entirety of their lives. Like you, they will give their soul into the keeping of their wife, and I will gift them a son in return. As long as you, Zaccarias, and your male descendants fulfill their part of the bargain, your nation will enjoy never-ending prosperity. If you or your descendants fail to wed the woman within seven days, your nation will fail before one full cycle of the seasons can pass. This requirement I give unto all your male descendants; the heir to your title must take it seriously."

"Every son I have, their sons also, for all time, must keep this promise, or the nation fails? It sounds like there is at most only a few generations where this will happen. If we have longevity, prosperity, many children, then the number of descendants constrained to follow your dictates becomes vast." Not that he wouldn't grasp hold of the promised blessings for himself. He felt a surge of disappointment in the future, it would not be sensible to expect every descendant to keep the promise he was willing to make.

"Have I said, yet, how much I like you Zaccarias? You will be Sovereign, King of Estolia. Your firstborn will be your heir. *He* is constrained to adhere to my commandment, in his thirtieth year to find a woman pure in body and mind, and then wed her within seven days of intimacy. If he cannot fulfill this promise, then your second son, or the second son of the monarch at the time, will, as a Last Resort, take on the burden of compliance. I shall gift your male descendants, especially those required to keep your promise to me with the ability to see the soul of the woman capable of keeping their soul. They will see it as an aura of great brilliance confirming her purity and suitability as their partner in this world."

She stepped towards him, her eyes boring into his. "You, Estoliana, and your posterity will be blessed with long lives; freedom from regional disputes; and granted guidance as a nation, so long as you and your heirs keep your promise to me. Your nation will never fail!"

He didn't respond right away. He looked away from those fathomless gray eyes and down at the beautiful woman standing mute and unaware of the conversation. "What of Estoliana? Does she get no choice? Is *this* what I am to teach my sons – to find and take the woman of their choice, regardless of her wishes?" As much as he desired the woman he rescued, he didn't wish to be like the men he met in his travels – taking without asking. He wanted for himself what his parents enjoyed – a partnership. This *Deity* could strike him dead, but he would *not* agree to a one-sided arrangement favoring only him.

When she didn't respond to him, he finally looked at her, expecting to see anger or disdain. Instead he saw approval.

"When I first noticed you, Zaccarias, I could tell you were a man of great character. *Ask* Estoliana to be yours, you will discover that she is as attracted to you, and to the concept of permanence, as you are to her. Be certain the wishes of the daughters of your land are honored by the men who will call themselves Estolian."

"You have my promise that I will do as you have asked, and I will teach my children so they will know what they are constrained to do from now until time ceases to be time." He felt the weight of the promise he was making, as if it was molded out of the stuff of his soul. "If Estoliana will have me," he added under his breath.

"Do not forget what you have promised me this day, Zaccarias, son of Ezekias and Amadora."

4

Purple River

To follow the urging of Deity and subsequently feel the promised rewards is itself one of the greatest blessings in this life.

~Amadore, First Consul to Zacarian; Capitulo 1

I N A FLASH OF LIGHT, *Deity* was gone and Estoliana continued speaking as if the entire conference he had with *Deity* never took place, "...until those who are worthy walk upon her shores."

Zaccarias looked at the beautiful woman whom *Deity* proclaimed would be his wife, who would keep his soul safe and protected. He could think of no woman more beautiful than she was, especially with the golden shimmering glow of the aura he could now see.

"You are correct. *Deity* looks out for this land and brings us here together." He smiled at her. Turning he looked at the crates strewn up and down the rocky beach. "We should focus on the smaller crates. The larger ones are less likely to be swept out to sea."

While they worked, he wondered if the crates of materials bound for the Pharaoh were evidence of how *Deity* would provide for them.

The sun was dropping toward the west when Zaccarias said, "We must find a good location to spend the night."

She pointed toward a mountain peak in the distance. "Let's go in the direction of those mountains."

"First, we should see what things the crates hold that might improve our comfort." One of the crates had several large bags used as padding for some sculpture in gold within. He went to the crate and pulled out the bags. Estoliana joined him and looked in at the golden cat statue partially visible.

She lifted her skirt, which was encrusted with salt and stained by seawater and joked, "I never thought I could wish for something other than a gold statue. I would prefer some clean clothing."

"One of the crates contains garments. They might work for you." He pulled several bags out of the broken crate and handed them to Estoliana before picking up a couple of his own.

He spied several overlooked crates half submerged in the waves and pulled them to higher ground. Soon they were at the collection of crates he remembered were partially damaged. He pointed to one crate and told her the contents appeared to be feminine garments.

She started to move toward the crate he indicated but then paused, looking at him with a slight frown. "What about you, Zaccarias?" Her hand reached out and touched the shredded shirt hanging off him, brushing the caked sand off his exposed ribs.

He had to contain the shiver of reaction to her touch. "Perhaps we should look together," he suggested.

She laid several of the cloth bags on the rocks and started pulling garments out of the crate. The first item she pulled out was a jewel-encrusted sheath of a dress. Her lips parted and she exhaled sharply. One delicate hand brushed over the intricate beadwork. "This is a work of art," she whispered. She carefully set the dress down on the cloth bag, smoothing it with one hand. A soft sigh punctuated the moment when she turned her attention back to the broken crate.

The next item was a simple creamy-colored sheath. She held it up in front of her body and then beamed a happy smile in his direction. "This will work."

She pushed several additional items into one of the cloth bags until she came to some that were undeniably masculine.

As with the dresses, the first was elaborate. The tunic did not boast the same type of beadwork, but the embroidery was intricate, in bright primary colors. Without asking his opinion, she pushed it into a second cloth bag. The next item she pulled out was as simple as her own outfit, an off-white tunic or overshirt and a sturdy set of workmanlike breeches. She held the breeches against him, tilting her head to the side before her lips curved upward in a smile of pleasure. "These look like they were made for you, Zaccarias."

He took the proffered items and then glanced down at the clothing he was wearing and the skin showing through the rips. His clothing was ruined, and he was filthy.

"I saw a small stream near those two trees. We could rinse off and then change into clean clothing," she observed. A rose-colored flush on her cheekbones emphasized the beauty of her bone structure.

He followed her to a warm hollow filled with sluggish water. Soon they were both submerged, still wearing their clothing. He wished he could just strip off to better clean himself before he dressed.

"I will bring you some more of those sacks – you can dry yourself with them and then dress. You should undress and wash properly." Her blush was even rosier at that statement. She didn't wait to hear his response.

He pulled the ruined clothing off, piling it on the bank of the stream nearby. When Estoliana returned, her eyes were fixed on the clothing and cloth sacks in her hands, not looking at him. "Here," she said softly. She set the items down within his reach and then turned hurriedly. Speaking over her shoulder, she said, "Let me know when I may return and do the same thing."

Once he left her bathing in the stream, he moved towards the broken crates he thought held some food and other delicacies. He packed a few things in the sacks methodically, but his thoughts weren't on what he was doing. Several times he stopped to feel the fabric of the breeches. They were a higher quality weave than he had ever worn, and he felt pleasure in the feel of the fabric against his skin. His right hand raised to the lapel of the shirt and he rubbed it between thumb and forefinger, feeling the richness of the fabric.

He felt as if he'd suddenly risen in rank from mere hired muscle to the nobility. That was when it struck him, like the coldest mountain stream water rushing down his spine. *Deity* proclaimed him a King over this land. Did he really have a conversation with a goddess? He could feel an echo of confirmation, as if she listened in on his thoughts and answered his question. He tied the last sack closed and then knelt on a broad rock. He closed his eyes and focused his attention inwardly, towards *Deity*. He promised to keep his word to *Deity* for the entirety of his life. He would have faith in her promises.

When he got to his feet, he felt renewed and invigorated. At a sound behind him, he turned and saw Estoliana coming towards him. She was now a stunning vision of loveliness. She wore jeweled sandals and the cream-colored sheath dress. Her hair was pulled back and fastened away from her face. She held a couple of the large bags stuffed full of items. A wide plank stuck out of one bag.

"Are you ready?" he asked her.

She nodded and then followed him as he struck out towards the distant mountain peak. They were still within sight and sound of the inrushing tide when he noticed a thick line of trees and foliage off to their left. He gestured towards the greenery. "The water in the stream was not very fresh." He wrinkled his nose in a grimace. "I am hoping we can find some fresh water. That looks a promising direction."

She didn't argue. Instead she just walked the way he indicated. It didn't take long to reach the thick line of trees. The purling sound of water over stones reached them. He led the way through the trees. They both came to a sudden halt at the vision presented to them. There *was* a river paralleling the thick stand of trees. It was purple. "I've never heard of a purple river," she said.

He set his bundles down and moved to the edge of the water. Up close the purple color was not obvious. He pulled off his sandals and waded into the water. The water was soothing against his skin. He looked back to the bank of the river where Estoliana was watching him. "Is it okay to drink?" she asked.

He bent over and scooped up some water in his hands. It looked clear, without color, like water should look. The first handful leaked out of his hands while he studied the color. He scooped up a second handful and brought it to his nose to smell it. It seemed to smell exactly as water should smell. With one more glance at Estoliana, he scooped up a third handful of water and took a sip. It tasted like water should. Fresh and delicious. He grinned at Estoliana and scooped up another handful. "It's delicious," he told her.

When she joined him, he stepped closer to the bank, ready to assist her if she needed it. He felt something break under his foot and glanced down curiously. A dark burst of color in the water near his foot alarmed him. When he moved his foot, he saw there was still a rapidly spreading plume of purple spreading from where he crushed something. It wasn't blood, as he thought to begin with. When the water cleared, he saw a half-crushed snail.

"I think the purple comes from the snails that appear to be quite common here." There were dozens, perhaps hundreds of the snails in the water.

Estoliana sat on a large rock and began unlacing her sandals. He moved closer to the edge of the river, watching as several other snails were crushed underfoot and left behind the burst of thick purple color. He was almost to the shore when he heard a deep voice proclaim behind him, "Willowal!"

He pivoted rapidly, his hand slapping his hip, regretting the loss of his sword more now than ever. He crouched slightly, ready to defend Estoliana with his bare hands if needed, and scanned the vicinity, looking for the new threat. Nothing. Large clumsy birds were standing on the far side of the river, and a few were floating on the surface of the water near him looking at him curiously.

He shifted his stance, preparing to look around more carefully for whoever called out to him.

"Willowal! Willowal!"

He swiveled back around, knowing the sound was extremely close. It was only then that he realized what was happening. He looked at Estoliana. She was holding her sides and laughing.

"It is the bird themselves who speak," he said. He could feel his face warm with a blush. When her laughter spent itself, he said, "The water itself is most refreshing. The snails make it purple."

She stepped carefully into the water and drank for some time. When she finished drinking, she picked up a half-crushed snail, looking at it curiously. She crushed it in her hand and they both stared at the purple which colored the water in her hands. When she dipped her hands in the water, she rubbed them together to get the purple color to wash off.

On the far side of the river were hundreds of the birds. They were ugly birds, he thought. Big bulky bodies, clumsy when taking off or landing. Brown, grey and white feathers. The only redeeming feature was that some of them had purple beaks and feet, and some had yellow beaks and feet. Despite the ugliness of most of their plumage, they had tufts of green, purple and yellow feathers on their faces that were as bright as the rest of their plumage was dull. The accent feathers gave them a comical appearance. Especially when they made their peculiar sound in a deep masculine human-like voice.

The beach on the far side of the river was the first sand beach he had seen on the island, and it was teeming with the Willowal birds. There were a few large caves in the side of a massive butte or plateau which marched alongside the Purple River as far as he could see upriver. He considered trying to cross the river to make use of the caves, but the buzzard-sized birds seemed to be quite numerous, living in the caves, and there was no clear vegetation on that side of the river. Just sand, caves, and birds.

Once they were both fully refreshed by the purple river water, they continued upstream. For a while the plateau on the other side of the river paralleled the course of the river. Then it started to angle towards the water. Ahead of them, it looked like the jut of the land pushed out at right angles to the river, cutting it off.

It was only as they neared the impressive plateau with, at the end, the stump of an old mountain, that it became apparent the river flowed through a tunnel in the plateau. They could see the glint of sunlight off the water in the depths of the tunnel. The spit of land in front of them must not be very wide.

A second stream of water trickled down along the edge of the plateau, and they turned to the right to follow it towards the crumbling remnants of the old mountain. The distance was not great, and they discovered the stream they were following seemed to bubble up from the base of the weathered stone mountain.

Estoliana went up to the edge of the pool of water and knelt on the short grass ringing the pool. She dipped her hands in the water and raised it to her mouth, sipping the water and then drinking deeply. When she was done, she brushed the excess water from her mouth and said, "I've heard of springs like this, where the water itself is a gift from *Deity*."

"It is clear, Estoliana, *Deity* is with us, guiding us." He didn't know how to share with her what he learned from *Deity*. He knew what he wanted to do. But she needed to be an active participant, choosing to be a part of the future *Deity* promised him. He could not expect blessings from *Deity*, if he did anything against the will of this woman.

His eyes met hers and for several heartbeats they were looking at one another. Finally, he broke the connection and looked around. The features of the location seemed to be ideal for a settlement. He set his burdens on the ground and walked up to the pond at the base of the small rocky outcrop. He tasted the water and found it to be even more pleasant than the Purple River water.

Estoliana set her bags at her feet and look around also. She was looking to the south, back the way they came. Scattered around the hulk of the mountain was a field of rough stones which looked like the remnants of the mountain which once towered over the land but was now only a large outcrop of stone. He imagined a once-grand mountain shaking off the rocky façade of its youth before relaxing to enjoy the weathering of old age.

Beyond the tumbled stones was a grassy plain, the sort which might take to the production of crops of grains and other foods. The trees he recognized along the watercourse were olive and almond trees. The last place that the *Ankhamun* took on cargo

– the island of Izquierdo – he helped bring the cargo on board, lashing it to the top of other cargo. Bundles of sticks that the first mate said could be planted and would produce a wide variety of fruit trees. He would have to see if he could locate the bundles and plant them properly.

"I believe we should stop here. This looks safe and well placed for us," he told Estoliana.

5

Keeping the Promise

In the ancient world, romantic tales were usually the stuff of legends only, and family units were nearly always fashioned out of expediency and familial loyalty. But in Estolia, the concept of love took on a much deeper meaning. The rich soul-to-soul connection between the two halves in a marital partnership in Estolia simply defied description. The keeping of the soul was, in truth, the greatest of the gifts from Deity to the sons of Zaccarias. Even in our modern world, the most extravagant tales of romantic love come nowhere near what Estolians not only expect, but also experience.

~Fernando Gilmar Zacarian; Capitulo 75

THE MAN WHO PULLED Estoliana from the sea reminded her of the statues created by the palace artisan in Anoxes. Tall, well-defined muscles, broad shoulders, and slender hips.

During the battle against the pirates, she watched from her hidden position among the bales of hay. He was such a large man, yet he moved with extraordinary grace. At the time, she thought he was the type of man a maiden would wish to have as a protector. As *more* than a protector. If her father had decreed that she was to be *his* wife, she would *not* have rebelled.

His instinctive reaction to a perceived threat, when the Willowal bird startled him, revealed his character. Willing to protect the woman who was with him, even though she was a stranger. She felt safe knowing he was with her on the island.

Thinking about safety reminded her of her reasons for fleeing Anoxes. She was gathering eggs in the fowl yard and searching out one of the nests of a secretive hen when she heard her father speaking. She remained where she was, invisible to the men but able to hear their words. The Captain of the Guard, Standish, was speaking with her father. She listened to their discussion idly at first. Standish was expounding on the virtues of two of the larger forest horses he was selling her father. They discussed the likely characteristics of the foals they were carrying, since the sire was his massive warhorse. It was only when Standish started to speak of the nuptials that she was shocked rigid. They expected her to marry Standish at the winter festival!

Bitterly, she realized she was worth nothing more to her father than a pair of horses. She would be turned over to Standish, regardless of her feelings. Regardless of his record with women. She wouldn't do it. Couldn't do it. Using the artifice her mother taught her, she hid her beauty and ran away, traveling rapidly toward the sea.

At the seaport, she bribed a young matron to allow her to sleep in the hay loft over the stable. During the days she spent time in the markets, disguised, listening carefully to passing conversations, trying to find a place to go where she would be safe. That was the first time she heard of the legend of Pequeño.

A few days after she hid in the loft, the oldest daughter of the matron visited her. "Mother is worried about this winter. The harvest was poor, and we won't have enough to see us through. She is considering returning you to Standish."

Estoliana could understand the trials faced by a woman whose husband was away on a military ship, struggling to feed her four daughters. She could no longer stay.

"I have a solution," the girl said. "There is a place you could go where you would be safe. An island between Izquierdo and Palmara. Pequeño."

"I've heard of it," Estoliana admitted. "Isn't there some legend about Pequeño?"

They spoke for some time, discussing the legend. When they were done, Estoliana had a plan. She would wait until dark, and then she would sneak aboard a merchant vessel bound for Egypt. It would stop at Izquierdo and then head to Palmara, passing close enough to Pequeño for her to swim there. "I can get you onto the *Ankhamun*, Estoliana, but only *you* know if it's worth it to you."

It was worth it. She would take the risk of being found, the risk of the unknown over submitting to Standish and his vile temper.

Her attention snapped back to the present. She was now alone on Pequeño with a man she admired.

He began to pull supplies out of the cloth bag he carried with him. He spread out the rich bedding he told her was once destined to grace the bed of a Pharaoh. The location he selected was in a slight depression thick with grasses which would make soft bedding. He made only one bed.

She turned away from where he was preparing their bed and started to rummage in one of the bags she brought from the damaged crates. She had fruit, bread, cheese, olive oil, and wine. She found a couple of boulders at almost the same height and perfectly placed so she could lay the one plank she'd brought with her. It made a serviceable table. She spread a couple of the cloth bags onto the plank, making a tablecloth. Upon the makeshift table, she placed the container of wine and the two wine glasses. Setting the loaf of bread to one side, she poured some of the rich olive oil in a broad shell she'd collected from the rocky beach. She placed the fruit and cheese near it. This was a feast fit for kings, she thought. They might not dine as well in the future, but they would dine well tonight.

They ate the meal quietly while the sun dropped below the horizon. When they were done eating, she asked him to share his story with her.

When he smiled in response to her request was when she noticed just how good looking he was. He had gray eyes, dark hair and a beautiful arresting face. He looked like he worked with his hands every day of his life.

"My father is very healthy. Our family are long-lived, and he will be active farming the land for another twenty years. But when he is ready to pass the land on, it will go to my brother." He shrugged, as if what he was saying wasn't hurtful. His voice didn't seem to hold any edge of hurt. "My brother is the oldest. It is right that it will go to him. I had two choices. I could stay and work the soil by my brother's side. Or I could seek my fortune and my future in foreign lands."

"You are not bitter?" she asked him.

"No, Estoliana. My brother Phineas knew I wouldn't return. My father said I would need to journey until I found myself, and when I did, I would know it and remain there. I've been traveling for nearly ten years, working as a hired sword. I feel as if I *have* found myself." His hand swept in a wide gesture, taking in the beautiful island surrounding them, his voice rich with pleasure, "This land has taken ahold of my soul."

This was *her* destination. She wanted to make this place *her* home. She did not know how to respond to his assertion.

When she didn't respond to his words, he said, "*Deity* sent us *both* here, blessed this land for *our* use." She wished she could see his face, see the underlying meaning behind his words. They did not have a fire, and the last vestige of the sunset was now flickering away in the night sky, making it impossible to make out his features.

The yawn that punctuated the indigo darkness didn't require light to see, it was loud, and she immediately yawned in response.

"Come." He held his hand out to her. "Let us rest, Estoliana. It has been a most adventurous day, first the wreck, then the gathering in of supplies, and then preparing this place to sleep."

He sounded as deeply weary as she felt. She remembered that he began the day by fighting off pirates. He must be exhausted to have done so much in so short a time.

She placed her hand in his and allowed him to lead her to the luxurious bed he spent so much time making. Once they were next to the bed, he stopped and turned her so she was facing him. His hands settled gently on her shoulders. She could feel the heat emanating from his body. She wondered if this was the point where he would assert his right to her body in the night.

"I will be honest with you, Estoliana," he said. "You are extraordinarily beautiful. I desire you. You may even feel the reaction of my body to yours. But I want you to know I will never do anything without your permission. You are *safe* with me."

She believed him. She closed the gap between them and wrapped her arms around his waist, resting her head on his chest. "Thank you," she told him. They stood together for several heartbeats before she pulled away from him.

She bent down and slipped her sandals off. She didn't have anything to wear to sleep in, so she decided to remain in the soft dress. The bedding, once she settled down into it *was* comfortable enough for a King or a Pharaoh. She saw Zaccarias start to prepare for bed, but she fell asleep almost instantly.

Estoliana woke to the sound of an owl hooting. A bright full moon was shining down on the clearing where she and Zaccarias were lying next to one another. Zaccarias' arms were around her. When he moved, she realized he was awake, probably awakened by the same owl.

He propped his head on one hand and looked at her, the moon glinting off his eyes slightly. "You are an incredibly beautiful woman, Estoliana," he repeated his earlier observation.

"You are quite attractive as well, Zaccarias."

"Estoliana," his voice was gruff, thick. "*Deity* brought us here to be together. To establish a nation... together. I wish to follow the dictates of *Deity* and make you mine."

She would have pulled back away from him if he wasn't holding her so closely. And she didn't want to pull away from him. She wanted him. But she couldn't say that. "Zaccarias, I have heard men say many things to try to get me to couple with them. Why should I believe your words mean anything more than any other man?"

He was silent for some time, as if searching for the right words to say. He sighed, and he sounded almost defeated. "I don't know how to convince you of my sincerity." He brushed her hair out of her face, smoothing it back and gently caressing the skin of her face with his thumb. "I have traveled for ten years in search of my destiny. I did not know when I was hired to guard the *Ankhamun* that I would be presented two of my dreams at the same time. I wish to make you mine, Estoliana. Not for tonight, or until we are rescued, but for all time. I wish to remain here, on this island, with you, until the day I die. And, if you are willing, when the first opportunity presents itself, I wish to marry you. From the moment I really saw you, I knew I had discovered my destiny. Here. With you."

"Here?"

"Yes, *here!*" he was emphatic. "*Deity* has given the two of us this land, to rule over, to fill with our children and their children. It is our land. We have but to fulfill the dictates of *Deity*, and we will be blessed all the days of our life. Together."

"You wish..." She couldn't figure it out. He was not going to do anything without her permission. But he was asking permission to possess her.

He leaned towards her and kissed her, his lips alive on hers, the warmth of his breath feathering on her face as he pulled back. His hand did not stray; she felt it resting on her hip.

"Estoliana, *Deity* has promised us prosperity. Together. This land is ours to rule. I have never wanted anything as much as I want to claim you in my life. *As* my life. Say you will be mine. My lady, my Queen, the Keeper of my Soul. Create with me, here, on this island, our very own nation."

"Here? On Pequeño?" she asked again. She reached up to caress his face. She was tempted to give in to this man, to believe his outrageous claims about the island, about *Deity*, about her.

"We will name our land, our nation, Estolia," he said.

She was swayed by his words. Did he really mean to keep her, claim her, and name a nation after her? "Forever?" She could hear the wistful longing in her voice. She did not wish to be a transient part of his life, of the nation he claimed he would be creating on this island.

"Forever, Estoliana," he whispered, "until time itself ceases to be." He kissed her again, his hand on her hip moving to the small of her back, pulling her body closer to his. She could feel the hot rigidity of his desire against her flesh.

"Zaccarias." She accepted him, and she knew he could hear it in the way she said his name. The hand on her hip slid lower, to the hem of the dress she was wearing. He pulled it up, his rough calluses rasping over the skin of her thighs and hips.

She sat up and pulled the dress over her head, pivoting her body to place it next to their bedding. He pulled his shirt off, and then lifted his hips to push his breeches off. When he pressed the hard length of his body against her, her heart began to race.

She touched him freely, marveling at the masculine body that was, to the touch at least, far more impressive than the stone statues she used to admire as a young girl. She memorized his shape and his texture while he ran his hands over her body doing the same.

His fingers fluttered over her ribcage, while his mouth explored hers. She caressed his face as his hips slid between her legs and then she gasped when his body claimed her. They were perfectly matched, their movements in tune with one another as if they shared the same mind and soul.

Her body arched under his, and she felt emotion flooding her body. She felt his emotions, his satisfaction to feel her body enveloping his, her soul consuming his. His voice complemented hers as they both cried out at the culmination of their coupling. A flood of warmth rushed up her arms and legs. She pulled him close, wrapping her arms and legs around him, pulling him tight.

Just as she needed to know she would always be with him, from now until time was no longer time, she sensed his own desperate need for reassurance, that *she* would never leave *him*.

For the next couple of days, they spent time transporting the smaller crates to the clearing and discussing how they could make this place into a home.

On the third morning, they woke to find half a dozen mares watering at the spring. She approached the mare nearest her, catching hold of a halter. Zaccarias did the same with another mare. From the bulge of their midsections it was clear that the two they held, and the other four were all pregnant.

"I forgot about the horses on the *Ankhamun* bound for the Pharaoh," Zaccarias said. "I spent time caring for them."

"I watched you caring for them," she admitted. "I hid among the livestock on the

Ankhamun. They are beautiful. Do you think we could use one of the chariots we discovered to bring the largest crates here?"

The day before, they discovered several chariots, half assembled, laced together and resting among the seagrasses. Zaccarias had pounced on the several packages of bound sticks they also found. He explained that the sticks were fruit tree starters and if they could get them planted, they would improve the variety in their diet. Once he set aside the precious bundles, their roots in a small stream making its way to the ocean, he helped Estoliana pull the chariots well above the high-tide mark. They left them since they were irrelevant without horses to put between the traces.

He fondled the ears of the mare nearest him and answered, "Yes, I think we could bring the rest of Pharaoh's crates here to the clearing if we used the power of these animals."

The next several days they retrieved the remainder of the cargo from the *Ankhamun.*

They opened each crate they brought to their settlement, investigating the contents, hoping to find items that would be useful to them. A few crates contained delicacies capable of withstanding a long journey. Their diet was a peculiar mixture of the humble foods gathered by the couple and delicacies only the Pharaoh could afford to eat. Most of the crates did not contain food and Zaccarias carefully sealed the crates that held only jewels and precious metals unnecessary to their survival.

On the seventh day they watched the sun rise from their comfortable bed. Once the last glimmers of dawn had faded into daylight, they dressed.

"Tomorrow..." Zaccarias began. Before he had a chance to explain what they would do on the next day, they heard a voice calling out to them. Estoliana moved close to Zaccarias before they both turned to see who was hailing them. Zaccarias' hand was on the fine sword they'd discovered among the crates.

Establishing Estolia

The great bounty of Deity in the earliest years has never been adequately recorded by the men who make the safety and future of Estolia their primary concern. We could never have survived without the small and seemingly insignificant blessings that spiced our lives and enhanced our comforts. As a mother cares for all aspects of her child's needs at a young age, and smiles upon independence at a later age, so too, did Deity see to our needs with abundance in the infancy of our nation.

~Ensayo of Estoliana

ZACCARIAS LOOKED AT the mounted man who was approaching. He was astride a magnificent pure black stallion. Noblemen and marauders alike preferred the medium-boned animals that were smaller than the large workhorses farmers used for plows and raw power. This animal had power, and stamina. An ideal mount for many purposes. The six mares they had in their herd were a cross between this type of animal and the fine-boned speed-focused breeds of Araby.

Once he dismounted, the robe he wore reached his ankles. It was a thick weave of dark brown, resembling the tree bark of the needle-leaved trees prevalent inland. It reminded him of the robe worn by *Deity*. It was unpretentious with two exceptions. The first was the sleeves. Each had a teardrop shaped opening that fell almost to the hem of the robe. When the man clasped his two hands together, the sleeves created a chevron pattern that pointed to the earth. The only other extravagance was a braided rope around the man's waist, fastening the robe closed. Each end of the rope had an endcap of metal worked to a fine point. He looked like he was a man who communed with *Deity*.

The man walked towards them with a sure and confident step. He led the stallion casually, as if the two were close friends. When he reached them, he bowed low. "Greetings," he said. "I am Sebastian." He used a dialect they could both understand.

"I am Zaccarias and this is Estoliana. Welcome to Estolia." He hugged Estoliana to him. "This is *our* land."

"I'm blessed to have discovered your unique island. I am a humble man with a sensitivity to *Deity* and felt my skills were needed here."

This was how *Deity* was providing him the chance to marry the woman who had taken hold of his soul. "We do require the services of a servant of *Deity*. Estoliana and

I have been waiting for the opportunity to wed. Will you do that service for us?"

"I would be honored to formalize your union." Sebastian said.

Estoliana excused herself. When she returned she was wearing the jeweled dress she discovered in the crates on that first day, for herself, and holding the fancy embroidered tunic out to him. When he took it from her, he was reminded that they were only together seven days. It seemed remarkable that he could be so close to a woman who was unknown to him eight days ago. Now he truly could not survive without her.

Throughout the ceremony, Zaccarias felt as if *Deity* herself was present, sealing their union with her holy approval. Once Sebastian was done with the service, Estoliana invited him to join them for some of the last of the delicacies from the *Ankhamun*.

During their meal, Sebastian learned their story and shared his own. Zaccarias felt compelled to share his vision and discussion with *Deity*. Estoliana had heard the entire story on their second day on the island. This was a test for Sebastian. Would he accept what he was told?

Sebastian's expression was not easy to interpret once Zaccarias finished speaking. Finally when he spoke his voice was barely above a whisper, "Few men are as blessed as I am, Zaccarias, to be directed by *Deity* to find acceptance and purpose. I hope you will accept me as a citizen of your nation and allow me to serve you and call this nation my own."

Zaccarias felt peace sweep through him; he heard a whisper of a feminine voice telling him, "This feeling, Zaccarias, is the way I will confirm your choices are right."

The whisper was still echoing round and round in his mind when he stepped towards Sebastian and embraced him. "I have need of permanent guidance. You are welcome to stay here. Forever."

⟨⟩ 715 BCE ⟨⟩

Over the next five years, they were blessed, just as *Deity* said they would be. Sebastian became Zaccarias' closest advisor. A steady stream of people came to Estolia. It was clear to Zaccarias and Sebastian that *Deity* was influencing individuals to settle in Estolia who would be willing to embrace the faith and follow the dictates of the religion Zaccarias developed.

It was almost two months after the marriage ceremony when the first settlers arrived, guided by *Deity*. The man couldn't speak. Dark-skinned and bald, he had an ageless quality – as if he had lived several lifetimes. His near-black eyes were eloquent, and his vivacious wife had a way of understanding what he wished to say and speaking for him. She was as talkative as her husband was silent. She introduced herself as Mari and her husband as Qi.

A few minutes after the introductions, Mari suddenly announced that Estoliana was pregnant, and that she would be available to help her give birth, explaining that she could sense when a woman was expecting a child, and how to help them; that she was a gifted midwife.

Their numbers steadily increased after Qi and Mari joined them – people brought to them by *Deity*; swelled with people who chance, circumstance, and the urging of *Deity* brought to their land. They were very busy in those early years, building stone dwellings against the base of the mountain. Sebastian, Qi, and Zaccarias spent much of their time together discussing *Deity*, and their plans for the future of Estolia.

Sebastian prepared two special cleansers he said were inspired by *Deity*. Qi added a third, and Mari explained how all three cleansers were to be used. A specific order of use was critical, she said, so the spirit of Anubis couldn't contaminate and claim the life force of a woman and her newborn child.

Mari and Sebastian were able to help Estoliana give birth to her first child, a son she insisted on calling Zacarian. He was barely a month old when Estoliana helped Mari give birth to Qimarian. Zaccarias and Sebastian gave each child a blessing on their seventh day of life.

Qi inscribed their words during the blessings. Zacarian's blessing stated that his direct male descendants would be King of Estolia far into the future, even beyond a thousand years.

Qimarian's blessing was of great interest to Zaccarias. He spoke the words, but, as with Zacarian, he felt as if they came direct from *Deity*. Qimarian, the blessing predicted, would find the love of his life on the island, and his choice to work with the horses of Estolia would bring great fortunes to the inhabitants.

Qi quickly found a place within the developing society. His role was that of royal scribe. He recorded Zaccarias' words on the sides of the aged and crumbling tower of rock from which the freshwater spring welled.

They named both the crumbling mountain, no more than a pillar of rock, and their settlement Promesa, after the promise Zaccarias made to *Deity*.

After the birth of Zaccarias' first daughter he learned why Sebastian was content with his role as celibate spiritual advisor.

"Your daughter is healthy and vigorous. Mari tells me your wife came through the birth safely, quickly, without any damage. *Deity* smiles upon you and Estoliana," Sebastian told him.

The two men were silent, the sounds of the women in the other room, the squalls of the infant, everything was a familiar augmentation for the young community. Sometimes, Zaccarias felt as if the only purpose behind their efforts was to be a nursery for the rapidly expanding population.

Zaccarias saw a wistful expression on Sebastian's face. "What is it, Sebastian?"

Sebastian looked like he was going to brush off the question. When he spoke, his voice was thick and emotional. "I envy you, Qi, and all the other men. The pride you must feel when your boys begin speaking our language, walking to you, everything there is to enjoy in your progeny. It is the only emptiness in my own life."

Zaccarias was quiet for a while before he finally asked, "Why have you never asked *Deity* for a woman to ease your loneliness, even if you cannot find one to keep your soul?"

Sebastian's eyes were mournful, damp when he admitted, "As a young man, I seduced more than one innocent, and ultimately I was made to pay for my crimes." He reached towards his groin and admitted, "I was unmanned and turned over as a slave when I survived the punishment. I was to serve the family most injured by my crimes."

Zaccarias knew there was some deep secret his advisor kept from him. "How did you come to serve *Deity*, and make your way here to Estolia?"

"I believe I was changed by the punishment that rendered me incapable of being a father. I sought to reach out to *Deity*, serve *Deity*, and find my future in the spiritual realm."

"And *Deity* answered?"

"Oh yes," Sebastian said, his voice full of the marvel of speaking with *Deity*. "The family I served was vacationing along the coast and their oldest grandson was swept out into the sea. I didn't think; I acted. I jumped into the sea, doing my best to rescue young Corlian. I didn't know if I would reach him in time. I did not even know if I would be able to rescue myself. But I was determined to return with Corlian or die in the attempt.

"I was almost out of breath when I reached him, pulling him to the surface. He was blue, and I could hear his parents sobbing in despair. I believe *Deity* inspired me, and I was able to give my own breath to young Corlian, and by the time I made it back to the shore he was breathing and crying. I gave him to his mother and wept and thanked *Deity* for helping me save him."

"This experience led you to *Deity*?" Zaccarias could see on his friend's face the reflection of a spiritual transformation akin to his own.

"Yes, Zaccarias, it did. The family I served, having seen my transformation, and out of gratitude for the way I saved their grandson, gave me my freedom."

"And how did you find Estolia?"

"I traveled for five years, acquiring Migo, my stallion. I became widely schooled in my travels, learning about the soaps of cleanliness, and other medical techniques, and how to commune with *Deity*. I took the position of horse handler on a ship traveling from Araby to the southwestern shores of the sea. I learned the shipmaster pocketed most of the money he was given to feed the horses. I tried to insist we dock in another port and take on sufficient feed to keep my charges alive. I was whipped for my temerity. By the time I recovered from my wounds, several of the horses were dead. I felt the whisper of *Deity*, telling me I must leave the ship, my charges with me. In the night I urged the half-starved horses to jump into the water. The captain saw what I was doing but said nothing. It was only when my stallion and I were the only two left that he insisted I feed myself to the sharks of the deep, as he put it."

"This was off the shores of Estolia?" Zaccarias asked.

"I thought we were near a different land. Once I realized we, the horses and I, were on an uninhabited island, I named it Corlia. There was much the horses could eat, and soon those who survived their travails grew fat. I asked *Deity* about my future. I was told I should travel across the nearly impossible rocky strait south of Corlia and continue west along the southern shore until I came to a purple river. I was told I would encounter those who had a need of a servant of *Deity*."

"Who told you this?"

"*Deity*." Sebastian's voice was matter-of-fact. "I knew with the sharpest clarity, that I would be needed. That I would find my destiny. I heeded *Deity*'s urging Zaccarias."

"Are you happy with us here, Sebastian?" Zaccarias asked softly.

"Yes, I'm happy here. I've found my purpose in life, and I believe I'll achieve a type of immortality in the impact I'll have on your children and on the children of other Estolians who have joined us, and who bring life to our nation. Truly, I would not exchange the life I know now for that which I had in my youth."

Two months after the birth of Zaccarias' daughter Miriam, He and Qi were sitting on the stone bench near the fount of *Deity*, as Estoliana named the small spring bubbling forth from the base of Mount Promesa. Sebastian joined them. "Karna brings forth twin boys. Mari says they are sturdy, healthy, and will make fine men."

"You predicted she would be carrying twins," Zaccarias said.

"The second generation numbers forty souls," Sebastian said. His voice was full of the satisfaction Zaccarias was feeling.

Zaccarias turned away from the large stone building and looked towards the north. In the five years they lived in Estolia, they developed the settlement on the southern shore of the Willowal region. The only exploration they did was shortly after Sebastian joined them. They rode the horses on the rocky beach towards the east. They slept under the stars on the two nights they spent traveling away from Promesa, and on the third day discovered a marshy region at the mouth of another river. Just beyond the river, they came upon a massive ship keeled over on the sand just below the high-tide mark.

It was the *Ankhamun*. He could still see the ankh symbol within the cartouche even if the rest of the stylized name was obscured by wind, weather, and tide. It was responsible for bringing him the greatest happiness of his life. "This region of Estolia will be named after the *Ankhamun*," he declared.

The only cargo remaining were several ingots of gold. They returned to Promesa with what they could carry. Sebastian made a few more trips to first secure the rest of the gold, and later with some of the men to disassemble the ship and store the wood in one of the Willowal caves. A large pillar of rock stood sentinel in the surf, and Qi inscribed Zaccarias' declaration about the *Ankhamun* on its sides.

Aside from the one trip of exploration, they were so busy creating the settlement they had never yet ventured towards the mountains.

"I believe," Sebastian said, looking with him towards the mountains. "*Deity* wished for us to wait until the time was right to explore this land."

"When will be the correct time?" Zaccarias asked.

"Now, Zaccarias, I believe *Deity* speaks to us and urges us to explore the heart of Estolia. Our crops are abundant, our livestock is plentiful, and we have loyal strong men to watch over Promesa while Qi, you and I travel north. I feel the pull of *Deity* to explore."

"You should travel north, my love," Estoliana said.

He looked at her. Their daughter was suckling at her breast, and his two sons held onto her legs. "You are sure?" Time spent apart from her could become painful.

"If *Deity* asks it of us then *Deity* will also comfort us." Her faith was an example to all Estolians, simple, straightforward, matter-of-fact. One could not know Estoliana and remain unmoved by the purity of her faith.

7

The Temple

One of the great debates the elders indulge in, while studying in the temple, is the influence of Deity in the formation of the land of Estolia. Some elders insist Deity formed the caverns of the temple, and the bones of the palace, so the sons of Zaccarias could easily create the marvels of architecture we now enjoy. Other elders argue that Deity's influence was in the way the creativity of the early generations was enhanced so they could see how to use the natural formations and create those fabulous structures. Regardless, it is certain we are all blessed by the beautiful constructs of our earliest generations here in Estolia.

~Thomas Harrison Zacarian; Capitulo 71

LATE THE NEXT DAY, Sebastian, Qi, and Zaccarias reached a verdant valley that stretched to the northwest. The two mountains which guided them in their journey stood sentinel over the valley. The taller mountain was on the southwest side of the valley; they could not make out the features as well as they would like. The sun was setting behind it, and it was thrown into darkness. On the northeast side of the valley was the second mountain, as impressive and unique as the first. For Zaccarias, it felt like he was home. Truly home. He would live and die here. He gave silent thanks to Deity for her wondrous influence over his life, and prayed his children, and their children would always be true to the promises he made.

The mountain to the northeast had a greater girth at its base, but was shorter and looked like it was once the more impressive peak. The flat top of the mountain was two-thirds as tall as the other peak, but enormous bony fingers of what looked like pure stone thrust up like the fingers on a man's hand, as if the mountain itself was reaching to grab a handful of sky. About halfway down was a broad plateau that stretched for some distance. He could imagine horses grazing on the nearly flat plain.

He wondered if, like much of Estolia, there were caves leading into the mountain from the plateau. He looked at the nearly flat top and could envision a grand structure built within those grasping fingers of stone, using the structure of the mountain itself to lend it stability. A project his sons, and their sons might work on. A fitting legacy for the promised longevity of Estolia.

The mountain to the southwest was really two peaks, a shorter one nearest the valley. Perhaps a little taller than the flat peak of the northeastern mountain. Hulking behind the shorter peak was the larger mountain. A ridge ran down from the larger

THE PROMISE OF ZACCARIAS

mountain around the southern side of the smaller mountain, as if the bigger peak was embracing the smaller peak, like a mother holding her child. Thrusting out of the peak of the larger mountain was a massive buttress of stone that dwarfed the flat-topped eastern peak. The shorter peak looked like it was easy to climb, even by a man on horseback. Perhaps he would lay out a trail and bring his sons to the peak to look over all the land that would be theirs.

"I feel the pull of *Deity*," Sebastian finally spoke into the long stretch of silence that settled between the three men after their arrival. "It is clear to me we must concentrate our attention on the smaller peak of the mountain to the southwest."

Zaccarias and Qi both reined their horses in the direction Sebastian indicated. They traveled into the valley, heading between the two mountains. Zaccarias felt the strength of *Deity*'s guidance in the form of a deep and abiding warmth. He was grateful *Deity* did not expect them to make their way in this world without guidance.

"I knew it!" Sebastian exclaimed. He gestured towards the smaller peak and said, "See, a cave!" He urged his horse forward at a faster clip, and the others followed him towards the dark opening at the base of the mountain.

The three men on horseback reined to a halt at the entrance to the cave, just within the shadow of the mountain. "We should make our camp here," Sebastian said, "and once we have done so, and made a fire, we will bring torches with us, and explore the cave." His expression was full of boyish enthusiasm.

Qi gently touched both Zaccarias' and Sebastian's arms, and when he had the attention of both men, he indicated his disagreement. Qi was probably the most eloquent man Zaccarias knew, especially considering he was incapable of speech.

Sebastian looked from Qi, to Zaccarias, and said, "If Qi thinks we should wait until the morning to investigate, then we will wait."

That night the three men lay on their bedrolls, staring at the brilliant star-spattered sky. Zaccarias thought about the past. "Brother," Phineas, his older brother said to him, "I know you will be successful in your quest." They were standing next to the remains of his farewell bonfire.

Zaccarias felt a great fondness for his brother. For Zaccarias, he had to make his fortune, since he would not inherit it. "Do you think we will meet again?" he asked Phineas.

Phineas looked up at the sky. Zaccarias followed his example and the two brothers watched a shooting star crease the sky. Only after the image faded from their night vision did Phineas answer, "No, Zac, we won't meet again. Mother and father know you will find your own future, your own path. I'm certain we will meet in the *life-after-this-life*; we'll speak with each other about our adventures. Will you promise to seek me out?"

Zaccarias hugged his brother, thumping him on the back, conveying the depth of his love. When he pulled away, he vowed, "There is no barrier in the *life-after-this-life* which will stand between the two of us. I will seek you out, and we will share our adventures with one another."

As Zaccarias' thoughts returned to the present, he saw another streaking light across the sky and felt as if *Deity* was confirming his promise to his brother. He *would* be able to meet him in the *life-after-this-life* and he would have the grandest adventures to share. As he drifted to sleep, he smiled at the thought of that future reunion.

The next morning, the three men approached the symmetrical entrance. They climbed up a short slope of debris and stood in front of the cave. The entrance was wide and welcoming. Once inside, they paused. The cave was large and spacious and it split in three directions. Directly ahead of them was a small roughly rectangular opening, while there were larger openings to right and left.

"I feel like we should explore the opening ahead of us," Sebastian said. When neither of the other two men objected, they moved toward the opening. Once they entered, they stopped and looked around in awe. It was as if an immense spherical bubble of air was captured inside the mountain while it was formed, creating a perfectly spherical or egg-shaped chamber.

The sides of the chamber sloped up gently in all directions. The ceiling wasn't visible to them by the light of their torches. The most remarkable feature of the entire cave was a single immense stalagmite rising from the far side of the chamber and not quite meeting a matching stalactite dropping down towards it.

As they approached the immense rock formation, Sebastian said, "I believe this room could be adapted for religious ceremonies."

Zaccarias paused and closed his eyes, trying to feel with his heart and soul what Sebastian was suggesting. He imagined rich-looking tiles, crisp lines, and an ambiance filled with the presence of *Deity*. When he opened his eyes, he felt the shiver of celestial forces touching their mortal lives.

Qi led the way around the rock formation to an opening on the far wall. Once they stepped through they could see the glint of light ahead of them. The three men moved towards the light and saw there was another entrance into the cave, they could see a little burbling brook and a nearly vertical wall of rock beyond it; the stone rose to impossible heights only a dozen feet on the other side of the brook.

"This is between the small forward peak, and the larger peak towards the back," Zaccarias noted. He paused to inhale the scent of the blossoms on a couple of trees on either side of the small brook. He closed his eyes and inhaled the fragrance for several minutes before turning to the two men with him.

"I can imagine," he said, "we might create a place here where a newly attached couple might go to be alone, secluded, away from the never-ending requirements of real life, so they might spend a week with each other to solidify the most critical connection they will ever make, two souls merging to become one."

They turned their back on the sunlight shining down into the garden crevice and saw there were two caves branching off to right and left. They took the passageway to the right side, moving deeper and deeper into the cave complex. Qi began to lead the way, his motions sure and steady, until they were in a narrow passageway about as wide as a man was tall. At times they seemed to be climbing, as if they were approaching the very heart of the larger mountain.

"It appears to be a labyrinth from this point onward," Zaccarias said. He worried they would become lost if they traveled much further.

"We should return to the horses," Sebastian suggested. Qi reluctantly agreed and led them back the way they came, he looked back several times, though there was nothing to see in the darkness.

By the time they left the cave, Zaccarias was feeling a strong sense of *Deity*. He turned to Sebastian, and asked, "What is your impression?"

"This cave complex will become a great temple," Sebastian retorted without pausing to think about it. "I am certain of it."

Zaccarias' eyes fell on the other mountain and he asked, "And that mountain?"

"The palace will go there," Sebastian said. "There the future King of Estolia will live, rule, and reign. Here will be the seat of power of the religion."

It felt as if Sebastian's proclamation about the cave complex behind them was stated with the overtones of the voice of *Deity*. Zaccarias had no doubts left. This cave complex was critical to the religious future of his nation. "Will we relocate?"

Qi answered him, in his typical silent method. He touched both men, and it was clear what their future held. Sebastian, translated, "Qi states it would not be possible to relocate while your wives have children still to bear. But it will be the correct time to have some of us relocate here within five years. By then there will be enough Estolians to create two settlements. You, Qi, and I, Mari and Estoliana will all come here, and begin the process of developing this region. There will be many years, many generations of hard toil before these mountains have realized the promise so potently within them."

All three men were solemn and pensive during the journey back to Promesa. Each thinking their own thoughts about the visions that were theirs in that holy valley between two unique mountains.

When they relocated to the valley, Qi and Mari chose to live within the Temple mountain. The small group who relocated discovered the spacious plateau halfway up the northeastern mountain was perfect in many ways. It had only one entrance or exit, which was easy to fence off, and there were multiple caves into the mountain. They settled easily within those caves, building smaller structures at the entrance to each cave-home.

Young Zacarian and Amadore were Zaccarias' true delight, along with their three sisters. Zacarian declared when they arrived in the valley that the entire region was to be named Amadore, after his brother. Amadore, for his part, challenged his brother after that declaration, "And what will we call the two mountains?"

Zacarian said simply, "They shall be named after mother and father."

Amadore got that look that Zaccarias felt was indicative of a connection to *Deity* his oldest son did not possess. His second son turned to look at the mountain with the temple. "That is Mount Estoliana, and like a mother grasps her child, the larger mountain is embracing the smaller." His eyes met his father's and he turned to look at the less impressive mountain, and he said, "And that is Mount Zaccarias."

"This then," piped up Miriam, their oldest sister, "Must be the Zacarian plateau." She was indicating the place where they established their home.

Estoliana looked down at her daughter with a pleased smile. "Will we name anything after you, Talitha, or Sapphira?"

"Perhaps the next three settlements will be named after us?" Miriam said. She was, Zaccarias thought, her mother in miniature.

Zacarian was the one to respond to his sister, "It makes perfect sense to name places after the three of you."

Qi, with the help of Mari, spent long hours writing the words Zaccarias shared with him. Zaccarias wanted the breadth of his experiences transcribed, his promise to *Deity*, and *Deity*'s promises in return. Qi recorded all Zaccarias' words in the stone walls of the natural chambers of Mount Estoliana, the same words he once unhappily inscribed on the sides of Mount Promesa. Sebastian, Amadore, and several other apprentices soon joined him, and as they came from a variety of cultures, soon a written language was developed unique to Estolia.

"Egyptian writing, which Qi learned as a young man," Mari explained, "can be written vertically or horizontally." She showed them examples of both. "The writing of the Hebrews is horizontal, from right to left. The writing of a few other nation-states is horizontal, left to right. It seems most logical, to Qi, to write vertically, like the fall of water into Lake Eternity." While Mari spoke, Qi demonstrated on a strip of hide with a half-burned stick dipped in fat. The writing was beautiful, evocative, and Zaccarias felt a surge of gratitude in his chest at the many ways *Deity* saw to their needs over the years. Qi was clearly a gift from *Deity* to the fledgling nation.

Zaccarias admired the written word as exquisite and felt the heft of *Deity* in each stroke, each symbol, every mark upon the hide, but he couldn't read it. He didn't think it likely he would ever read it. Amadore was learning the skill of reading and writing as if he required it to breathe. His brother Zacarian was only a little less adept. Zaccarias' own efforts to learn even the basics of the written word always ended in failure, and he eventually gave up. "Does Qi wish for me to observe the location of the archives?" he asked.

Mari shook her head. Her face had a mournful cast when she said with simplicity, "Qi believes you will not be able to admire his great work during his lifetime." She looked up at her spouse, her expression fond but shadowed. "But you will admire it during your own lifetime, Zaccarias. He is content to know this is true. He has had a vision that his creation – the written language of Estolia – will be used actively when there is nothing of his body left on this earth, not even the dust of his bones. There is a greater permanence in this world in having his creation survive longer than his physical body. And there is the promise of the life-after-this-life wherein his body will be whole, his voice will be recovered, and we will live as one into eternity."

Over the course of the years, Zaccarias frequently thought about the extraordinary blessings *Deity* granted both him and his people. The greatest blessing of all, he stated, was the soul-rich relationship he had with Estoliana. As his sons grew into maturity, he often took them riding to the top of Mount Estoliana, intent on teaching them the most important elements of what *Deity* whispered to him.

In all the years they lived there in the shadow of the mountain, Zaccarias felt a strange unwillingness to return to the interior of the temple mountain. He was considered a prophet by his people, and *Deity* did whisper to him many times over the course of his life, but he felt as if the spirituality of Mount Estoliana was more intense, and more focused than he could personally tolerate for very long. It was Amadore's great creation, his future place in life, and he, Zaccarias, would not taint his son's spirituality by dictating anything at all about the future home of the religion.

He shared with Amadore his misgivings, his concerns.

"You are the founder of a great nation, father," Amadore said to him, "and you have much that calls on your time. You were one of those who discovered Mount Estoliana and saw her potential. But it was always something Sebastian, Qi, and I had to develop. The day will come when you will be able to see what we are doing with the Temple. I hope you will approve."

"I believe you will bring more to Estolia than I ever could have," Zaccarias said to his son, his throat tight with the emotions threatening to swamp him. After a moment he pulled his son into his arms for a solid hug. He remembered the skepticism with which he received the initial promises of *Deity* and knew he had more and greater blessings than any other man in the entire world.

A few months before his oldest son's thirtieth birthday, Zaccarias and his two sons were touring the site of the future palace. "It sometimes surprises me how different the two of you are. I am proud of both of you, and yet I'm somehow closer to you, Amadore, than I am with you Zacarian. I wonder why that is?"

Zacarian was quick to shed light on the subject, "It doesn't surprise me, father. You've spoken directly with *Deity*. You've established both a faith and a nation. You're accounted a prophet." He smiled at his father and then put an arm around his brother's shoulders. "Amadore represents your spiritual side, your true nature. He will lead the nation spiritually, and if ever there is a need, he would always get the final word."

"It's clear that you love both of us equally, father," Amadore added to the conversation. "But you don't love us the same."

"I suppose I do not." Zaccarias smiled from one to the other. "The greatest joy I have, after Estoliana, is in knowing everything that blesses my life now will be there to bless yours and your sisters' lives, and the lives of your children, and their children."

The First Generation

690 BCE

Mari, as the midwife for Estolia, was probably one of my favorites of the first generation of Estolians. Her touch was gentle and sure, even when she was quite old. I was glad my fourth daughter was born under her expert guidance and ministration. I do not think I would have lived through the difficult birth without her being there.

~Ascelina; Ensayo 1

ZACARIAN, IN THE TRADITIONS Zaccarias established almost more than thirty years ago, discovered the woman who would keep his soul. A beautiful dark-haired beauty from Palmara. They sealed their union on the night of his thirtieth birthday. They spent a week in seclusion in the Spirit Grove, and then Sebastian performed the marriage ceremony for them, just as he once did for Zaccarias and Estoliana.

Ascelina was now showing the signs of pregnancy, just as *Deity* promised. All three of his daughters already found mates from among the descendants of the worthy men and women who came to Estolia over the years at the urging of *Deity*.

The festivities celebrating the pregnancy of the lovely Ascelina suddenly became blurred, as if they were no longer happening in the real world. Zaccarias felt a shiver of memory and he turned and saw the same *Deity* that had visited with him when first he set foot on Estolian soil.

"You have been very faithful, Zaccarias," she said.

"It is easy to have faith in a *Deity* who is able to keep her promises. In truth, I don't believe there is any other man in the world who is as blessed as I am. My wife had five children easily. We have had extraordinary health. You provided us with the spiritual guidance we needed." He gestured to Sebastian. "My sons listened to what Sebastian and I taught them. They are everything any man would want."

"Your nation will always flourish, so long as your son, and his first-born son and so on are willing to keep the promises you made to me."

She reached forward and touched his shoulder, and for just a moment he had a whirlwind impression of the future, of generation after generation doing the right thing and receiving the promised blessings.

He wanted to ask a question, but she held her hand up. "Zaccarias, there are many nuances to your future prosperity. Have faith in your son Amadore, he will have visions, and guide your nation solidly into her future."

A moment later time reasserted itself and *Deity* was gone in a familiar golden flash of light. His son's wife embraced him. "Yours is a blessed nation," she whispered to him.

Zaccarias said with simplicity, "No, Ascelina, *yours* is a blessed nation. You will be the Queen of Estolia. She is your nation as much as mine."

673 BCE

Zaccarias fondled the ears of the sturdy mare who held his entire world upon her back. He looked at Estoliana and marveled at the life he'd seen over the last nearly forty-seven seasons. Zacarian was King. Hieronymus was now happily established among the Acolytes. Amadore was guiding the nation spiritually better than he, Zaccarias, ever could have. He did not need to turn away from looking at his bride to recall the image of the busy construction on Mount Zaccarias, as his sons insisted it be called. Nor did he need to look to his other side to see the vast stone supply removed from the depths of the temple.

Estoliana grinned at him, and he was, as always, reminded of the extraordinary beauty of this woman as he first saw her. She did not seem to be nearing sixty-four years of age. She was still the exquisite woman who took hold of his soul and showed him how a man could live without his soul – so long as he did not choose to separate himself from the woman who kept it.

"I enjoy the delightful view from here, Zaccarias," Estoliana said softly, "however I will find it *more* pleasurable to see it from your side."

He helped her dismount, sighing heavily at the peace flooding his soul at her touch. He turned with her to look at the mountain named after him, at the foundation being laid with exacting precision to the plan specified by Amadore. They both turned then to look at the mountain their sons named after his beautiful bride. It seemed fitting to him the Soul of the nation was centered within the mountain named after the woman who held his soul so carefully.

"Will I ever be allowed to see within the Temple?" she asked.

Before he could respond, Amadore joined them. He heard her question and answered, "This is why I have asked father to bring you here today."

Zaccarias grinned at Estoliana and said, "It would never be acceptable to name it after you, if you were denied the chance to see it."

Her tone was arch when she asked, "And am I the *only* woman to be accorded the privilege?"

Amadore wasn't given the chance to respond. Zaccarias felt as if *Deity* gave his voice the resonance of absolute power when he said, "Never will women be denied the temple while the promises I have made to *Deity* are kept."

Amadore had opened his mouth to respond, but he closed it and looked to his father briefly before telling his mother, "The men of Estolia are nothing without the women to support and guide them. Everything that is within the Temple is open to the women of Estolia as much as the men."

"But?" she prompted, sensing he had more to add to what he already said.

Amadore's expression was full of love for the woman who gave birth to him. "But men are further from *Deity* than are women. Men require the guidance they will receive within this temple. Women can hear what *Deity* wants in a way that is natural for them, but difficult for men and as such, they will have less of a need for day-to-day contact with the guidance of the spirit. We are recording everything with great care. We have made it clear how pivotal the strength of the women of Estolia are to the future of our nation. Additionally, we have been clear in our records to explain that the men of Estolia will always require the guidance of *Deity* as second only to the need men will have for guidance by the women of our nation." Amadore's words had the strength of a vow.

"Well then, my son," she said in a tone colored by humor, "I would be most pleased if you would show your father and I the realization of the vision you have had regarding this temple."

Zaccarias was reminded of the time, nearly forty-three years previously, when he traveled to the mountain with Qi and Sebastian – both gone on into a spiritual realm now – and they discovered the temple and all within.

As they approached the entrance, Zaccarias paused to admire in awe the four stately columns holding up a roof over the entrance. On either side, carved out of the mountain itself, were feline statues, nearly twice the height of a man, guardians over the sacred contents of the mountain. They were reminiscent of the golden cat icon found in one of Pharaoh's crates. He knew that it was Qi's influence to add those two guardians.

He thought briefly about the man who, with his wife Mari, truly was one of the most critical founding members of his nation. In forty-seven years, he could recall only a handful of infant deaths, testament to Mari's influence as a midwife.

Qi was someone of high spiritual rank in Egypt before coming to Estolia. From the creation of a written language, to the inscribed words written on the walls within the temple, to several small details – like the two cat goddesses adorning the entrance to the temple, Qi's was an influence that would be permanent in this nation. He was a good man, and Zaccarias felt as if the loss of his quiet guidance was an aching pit of emptiness. After a moment he turned his attention to the here-and-now, allowing the memory of former friendships to drift back where they belonged.

They mounted the steps, seeing in the finished central region of the steps what it would be like when time and circumstances allowed the completion of the temple. He counted ten steps up to the entrance. The doors themselves were massive with carved wooden protrusions.

Once they stepped through the doors, Zaccarias had to pause again. Blindly he extended his hand to his soulmate and felt the sureness within as she moved against his side. He felt a surge of pride when he saw what they were doing, and what they would have when they were finished. The floor was paved with smooth rocks and a pathway was laid out to the right and left, as well as toward the room that had so awed him when he first viewed it.

For just a moment, he allowed the memory of that time to flow through him. He recalled the young firm flesh of his bride, as his oldest daughter suckled on her breast and she gave him permission to be apart from her for their explorations. A sense of destiny permeated their discovery. He pulled Estoliana close to his side, trying to contain the burgeoning emotions flowing through his system.

"To the right will be the office for the Keeper of the Soul of the nation. To the left it will lead towards some chambers that can be used for the instruction of the youth," Amadore explained. "Just beyond is a unique space, very long and narrow at irregular intervals. Qi and I both saw it as a perfect space wherein those gifted by *Deity* to be artistic might serve the temple and the nation. One of the first tasks that I've set for our Temple Artisans is to devise a tile that we can use within the temple."

Zaccarias turned to look at the son who favored him the most in looks, personality and spiritual calling. He smiled at the man, feeling a deep and abiding warmth within his heart. Zacarian was enjoying his position as the King of Estolia for the last sixteen years, but it was Amadore who understood him more than any other person on the island – aside from Estoliana of course.

"You will be most impressed, father, with the Ceremony Room," Amadore said. He inclined his head forward, clasping his hands together. Zaccarias recognized the posture. It was the one he himself adopted when he felt the push from *Deity* towards some conclusion. Or when he was thanking *Deity* for the many and varied ways *Deity* influenced him and his people, nudging them towards the pathway of greatest personal satisfaction.

Amadore led them toward the dark rectangle leading to the Ceremony Room. The aperture had been widened and shaped. A set of double doors would eventually be hung in the space created, enabling the Ceremony Room to be closed off from the rest of the temple.

Hundreds of candles illuminated the spherical Ceremony Room. Black charcoal lines were drawn around the periphery of the room – no doubt something Amadore could make sense of. The massive stalagmite was the biggest and most obvious change. It was truncated to just around midthigh on him. He remembered how it looked, climbing to more than four times his height and not quite meeting up with a nearly identical stalactite of similar dimensions. He wondered where the massive stone had gone.

"It occurred to me," Amadore answered his query, "that it will be important sometimes for me to meet the leaders of our various regions in a conference room of sorts.

Qi helped direct the Acolytes and Artisans to detach the rock to the level you see before you, he also instructed us in how we could take and shape the stone to form it into a large table. I will show it to you later."

Zaccarias stepped closer to the large base of the stalagmite. It looked to be about as wide as twice his height at its widest, but perhaps only one and a half times his height at its narrowest. Four wide stone steps led up to the oval dais. He could imagine how it would look when it was finished. The wide steps would surround the dais on all sides. Six individuals would be able to stand on the finished dais.

"This will be a ceremonial dais," Amadore explained. "Here some of our most sacred ceremonies will take place." He grinned at his mother when he added, "To which ceremonies, women of Estolia will *always* be invited."

Her tinkling laughter filled the chamber. Zaccarias was reminded of the time he met with *Deity* on the lonely rocky beach. "Did *Deity* plan everything you are doing with the temple?" he asked his son.

Amadore did not answer right away. When he did answer, Zaccarias felt as if the response itself was coming from *Deity*, "*Deity* shaped our land and populated it with creatures who would make it a paradise. We were given the Willowal birds and Tarssus snails; Maybury trees and Island Goats; bees, butterflies, and bats; so that we might find prosperity. Once you were washed ashore, father, you were the one who made our land what it is. *Deity* gave us the tools for success, but we were the ones who used the tools to make this land much more than it otherwise would be. I believe that *Deity* searched the four corners of our world to find one man worthy to beget this nation, and when you were selected it was because you had great potential. I am the man I am, and Estolia is the land she is, because of you and your belief. Because you were willing to make a Promise to *Deity*."

By the time he finished speaking, Amadore was flushed. He spoke with passionate intensity about Estolia, and Zaccarias felt as if no father could be prouder of their son than he was in that moment. He prayed that his descendants would always value this land and what *Deity* provided them.

When they left the Ceremony Room, they were almost blinded by the slanting sunlight permeating the steep sided crevice between the greater and lesser peaks of Mount Estoliana.

"What are these marks?" Estoliana asked as they reached the sunlight slanting over the rough floor. She pointed to a series of charcoal marks connecting small stacks of rocks about knee height.

"The greatest joy that any man will ever experience is that moment when he gives his soul into his future wife's keeping," Amadore said. "Once a man has discovered the woman who will be the keeper of his soul, he must seek her consent and make the exchange with her, and then wed her within a seven-day."

"Every Estolian couple should spend a seven-day period secluded from the tasks of normal life so that the connection between two souls will be solidified and become as permanent and unyielding as this mountain." Amadore spread his hands wide and said, "This area will be converted to a seclusion chamber for couples to give their souls into the keeping of their mates, they will be able to use this chamber to spend time in isolation." He grinned at his parents and pointed out, "Zacarian's oldest son Hieronymus will use it first, followed by his brother and my sons. It is my hope they'll all be able to use the seclusion chamber. It is perhaps many generations before the temple and palace are finished, but this chamber will be the very first room to be fully completed. In time for Hieronymus' thirtieth birthday." He gestured to the narrow space filled with a meandering stream and blooming Maybury trees. "Here will be a secluded garden where the couple can spend some of their time, speaking and dreaming about the future."

"I think it's charming," Estoliana said. "But is it only reserved for our immediate family?"

"No mother, we hope to build several seclusion chambers. Not all will have access to the garden, but they will all allow the couple a chance to be secluded from the rest of the nation. For now, there are several places in the Spirit Grove that are used for the same purpose. The first seven days of any alliance should include seclusion, for every citizen of the nation."

Throughout the tour, Amadore spoke with assurance on the wide variety of purposes that different chambers in the mountain would provide them. They continued deeper and deeper into the mountain, with a couple of Acolytes lighting the way with torches. Zaccarias could tell that Estoliana was tiring and was about to suggest they turn back when they got to the end of one long passageway and he had to halt in sheer shocked surprise. He remembered the labyrinth of passages they discovered the day they first explored the cave complex. On that day so long ago, Sebastian insisted it was time to retreat from their explorations. Qi had been reluctant to leave. Perhaps he had a vision then of what the labyrinth would become.

He felt a shiver of cold on his nerve endings as he recalled the prediction Qi made, that Zaccarias would not see the fruit of Qi's labors during Qi's lifetime. He paused to thank *Deity* yet again for bringing Qi and Sebastian to Estolia.

They faced the same part of the cave now. This time, instead of the vaguely threatening, low-head-clearance region from his memory, he saw the walls directly in front of him were as smooth as the surface of Lake Eternity on a cloudless, windless night. Upon the refined vertical surface, he saw the unmistakable touch of Qi's hand. He remembered Sebastian and Qi taking the time to create and refine their language, both spoken and written, in those early days. The initial script began as very similar to the language of Egypt. But it quickly became its own unique language. He could see the impression of the written word as being reminiscent of the Lake Eternity waterfall. A cascade of wisdom in written form.

He moved forward to the wall nearest him and placed his hand against the smooth vertical surface. It was a solid stone work of art. The language of the land of Estolia most likely transcribing his words and the words of Amadore. Zaccarias could not read it, but the extraordinary detail, the artistic flourishes, the sense of eternity and eternal purpose all permeating the effort took his breath away. "How…?" he began.

Amadore's voice was reverent as he shared, "Qi taught the group of Acolytes assigned to him the language of Estolia and how to write it and more critically, he taught them how to transcribe it in stone. They learned how to prepare the surface of the entire Labyrinth in the same way. The hope is we will transcribe the words of the leaders of the Nation onto the walls of the Labyrinth, so as to keep them permanently."

Estoliana crossed over to where her son was standing and embraced him. Zaccarias looked at the two of them and felt as if his heart would burst in pride. After a moment he cleared his throat so he could speak without the tears he knew were building inside – tears of pride, happiness, and love, "Will the words of all the kings be recorded along the walls here in the Labyrinth?"

Strangely enough, it was not Amadore who responded, but was instead Estoliana. "I had a vision, Zaccarias," she said. "I learned there will come a time when we will be able to record sentiments in a more convenient way. At that time…" She paused.

"What is it?" he pushed.

"I was thinking the transcription of each *Capitulo* of our history, from yours, Zaccarias, to yours Amadore, to those for all other leaders, would be one of the tasks set the young Acolytes as part of their training. This way they'll create their own copy and commit it to memory."

"*Capitulo?*" Amadore asked her.

"It would seem to me, Zaccarias, Amadore, our time together is but a single *Capitulo* in the great epic ongoing adventure of our nation. The opening *Capitulo* to be sure, but merely one in a long line of *Capitulos* detailing memorable events. Perhaps an Acolyte could even be tasked to transcribe a small *Ensayo* of my own, for Ascelina, and for your delightful wife Amadore. For, as with our nation, so it is with our record: it is as nothing if the women are not included."

Amadore asked a question of Estoliana, and Zaccarias watched their interaction with a smile. These two were the individuals closest to his heart.

The discussion ended and Zaccarias pulled his attention back to his wife and son.

"We will not see all there is to see today," Amadore said, "but I did wish to show you a couple more things."

They walked for a short time and then stopped when confronted by a pitch-black rectangle. "This passageway will take us to the upper level. There are four levels to the temple. The main level holds the Ceremony Room, my future office, and several rooms for instruction, along with the Seclusion chambers. There is at least one vast level below the main level, possibly more than one. Then we go up a level in the body of the larger peak of Mount Estoliana which is where the Labyrinth can be found."

"And the fourth level?" Estoliana asked.

"The fourth level is the highest level." He pointed to the black rectangle. "The access is quite narrow but it is worth it." He and one of the Acolytes entered the dark rectangular opening, followed by Estoliana and Zaccarias, and then the other Acolyte. The passageway switched back a couple of times. The darkness faded to a dim light as they progressed.

Zaccarias held his breath in awe at the view spread before them as they stepped out into the sunshine. They were standing at the elbow connection between the larger and smaller peaks of Mount Estoliana. To one side they could see the shimmer of the sea. To the other side they were looking down into the deep crevasse between the two peaks of the mountain.

Within the crevasse, he could see where it widened significantly in two distinct places, with beautiful plants forming an enchanting garden and providing a bold splash of green.

Once they had their fill of the view, Amadore led them forward into another dark rectangle. They had to move sideways as it, like the passageway, was quite narrow.

They followed Amadore in a sloping passageway until they reached another fantastical viewpoint. To one side was a large spacious chamber, but near the passageway leading to the chamber was another darkened square. It was about waist height and large enough to crawl through. When he looked through the opening, he saw that they were looking down into the Ceremony room. The charcoal marks along the periphery suddenly made sense. They would be carved into tiers for seating. Amadore then led them into the large chamber and across to the far side where sunlight slanted in and illuminated the large space. From the opening in the wall, Zaccarias saw that they were looking once again into the seclusion garden.

They were led to a shaft spearing vertically through the mountain. Along the perimeter a rough stone staircase was chiseled. Fixed along the narrow path was a thick rope that could be used to keep from plunging to the base of the shaft.

It did not take long to spiral down to the chamber below. He looked around with interest.

On the floor was the huge stalagmite lying on its side. The one removed from the Ceremony Room. *This* was the office of the Keeper of the Soul of Estolia. In that moment, he knew that the temple *was* the embodiment of the promises of *Deity*, and that his sons and daughters would be cared for throughout eternity. Amadore would keep the soul of the nation in concert with *Deity*, as would his successor, and so on throughout the ages. Zaccarias pulled Estoliana closer, holding her against his body as he thought about the spiritual promises he had been given.

"We are blessed, Zaccarias," she whispered. She leaned her head gently against his chest, wrapping her arms around his waist. He sighed in contentment, knowing it would be impossible to fit words to the feelings that filled their souls to overflowing.

His descendants would discover the blessings of *Deity* for themselves. He would describe everything he felt, and command that his descendants record their impressions also, but each new generation would discover for themselves that the words in the *Capitulos* could never describe the impact on one's soul that came with keeping his promises and feeling the sweet warmth caused by *Deity's* many blessings.

Part 2 – The Transition Year

✆ Cast of Characters ✆

Balthazaar Leopold Zacarian – (Leo) First-born son of the 86th Keeper of the Soul of Estolia: Zavier Archimedes Zacarian

Bethany Danielson – Melanie Andrews' best friend; photographer

Catherine Moravia Zacarian – 86th Queen of Estolia

Dr. Alan Wade – Doctor friend of Leo Zacarian

Gregory Annikaris Zacarian – (Greg) Second-born son of the 86th King of Estolia: Maximiliano Sebastian Zacarian

Harmony Zacarian – Wife of the 86th Keeper of the Soul of Estolia: Zavier Archimedes Zacarian

Jacqueline Renee Cathay – (Jackie) Daughter of Peter Cathay

Melanie Christine Andrews – Romantic interest of Sebastian Zacarian

Peter Cathay – Friend of Zavier Zacarian

Sebastian Guillermo Zacarian – Heir Apparent & First-born son the 86th King of Estolia: Maximiliano Sebastian Zacarian

Terrance Amadore – Personal assistant to Zavier Zacarian

Theobald Reginald Zacarian – (Theo) Second-born son of the 86th Keeper of the Soul of Estolia: Zavier Archimedes Zacarian

Zavier Archimedes Zacarian – 86th Keeper of the Soul of Estolia

9

Desperate Favor

1958 CE

Those who exercise faith in its truest sense will always reflect on their sacrifices and blessings and see how heavily the balance is and always has been in their favor.

~Alciderious Sebastiani, Capitulo 51

LEOPOLD ZACARIAN. Jackie looked at the name on the return address in curiosity. She heard a frantic bell ringing and sighed. Her father wanted her. She took the letter with her and ran up the stairs. He was sitting on the side of his bed, and she saw he'd made a mess. "Yes, father?" She pocketed the letter.

"Clean this mess up you damn spoiled girl," he demanded.

She was used to his outbursts. If he didn't have times when he was clear in the head, she wouldn't have been able to tolerate the more frequent times when he was demanding and unreasonable as well as verbally abusive. She cleaned up the mess he made and changed the sheets on his bed. He stood next to the bed, hanging on to the wall until the bed was ready for him. "Sorry Jackie," he said, his voice weak but clear-headed again.

She turned away from the made bed and hugged him, feeling how thin – almost skeletal he was. He couldn't hold on much longer. She would miss him when he was gone. When he went slack in her arms she turned with him to guide him back into the bed. He was almost fully under the covers when his face screwed up in pain and his legs jerked away from her.

She was unbalanced by his motion and before she could catch her balance, his foot hooked under her knees and she crashed backwards into the table. He tried to catch her but instead of keeping her from falling, his fist connected with her face.

When she landed on the table it shattered completely, shards of glass showering the floor. She lay where she fell, the hard metal base of the table pressing against her shoulder blade, listening to the roaring of her heart.

By the time she found the energy to pull herself to her feet her father was asleep, seemingly unaware of the disaster. She hoped he *wouldn't* remember it. He'd be appalled.

She looked at the sea of shattered glass and felt woozy. It was only when she saw several drips of blood, that she realized she was cut somewhere. Another drip brought her attention to her left arm. She had a deep cut from elbow to wrist that was steadily dripping. When she lifted her arm, she felt more pain from her rear. She didn't think any major blood vessel was injured, or she would have more than drips.

With every movement stinging, she swept up the shattered glass and maneuvered the heavy metal base of the table away from his room, stuffing it in the large space at the bottom of the linen closet. She couldn't leave it or he'd be cut up the minute he tried to get out of bed. She would have to mop up the blood later.

When she was done sweeping she went into the hall bathroom and looked in the mirror at the cut on her forearm. It looked deep enough to need stitches. Her father's ring left a long scrape along the top of her cheekbone. Her right eye was swollen shut.

Her father used to praise the bathroom mirror. He said that it was the perfect mirror for shaving. It wasn't, however, very useful for looking at what she was wearing or, in this situation, the damage to her rear. She got out a hand-mirror but couldn't get a decent angle to look at the cut or cuts on her rear; she had a feeling they would look much worse than her arm or her face.

She slowly went down the stairs, wincing with each step, while she tried to think through the options available to her. She wasn't sure how she would get her injuries looked at with her father so ill. She could just leave her father alone in the apartment and hope he didn't have any issues while she was gone. Unfortunately, he was more likely to need her and get in trouble without her than he was to sleep. But she had no way of getting her injuries seen to if she couldn't leave. She couldn't afford a house call.

Her thoughts drifted to the pile of bills she'd organized on her father's desk. They were going to have their phone disconnected in ten more days if they didn't pay, and other services soon after. Unless her father had money she didn't know about, she wasn't sure what they would do.

The last three or four times he was clear-headed, he hinted that he had some solution, some way of solving their financial problems. When she pushed him for details, he merely brushed her curiosity aside with a secret smile.

Her father's secret smile brought back dozens of wonderful memories. His playful nature, the way he often stopped, as if hypnotized by her mother's beauty. The way their eyes used to meet and they would seem to communicate – without a single word. But his smile now was only an echo of what it used to be. She wished she could somehow reclaim her mother's wonderful presence and balancing force. Everything good and wonderful about life seemed to leak away as the months passed and her home life became increasingly unbearable.

She reached behind herself, to try to judge how badly she was hurt. She winced as her finger was cut on a shard of glass still embedded in her flesh. Her hand came away covered in blood. She stared at the blood, uncertain how to get her injuries treated without money and with her father needing constant supervision.

In the middle of her indecision, the doorbell rang. She used her skirt to wipe the blood from her hands while she hurried to answer the door. The sound of the doorbell often set her father off. She winced as each step jarred her injuries.

Her first impressions when she opened the door were that her visitor was tall, broad, and vaguely foreign. He stared at her, slack jawed, his brow wrinkled. "You have injured yourself. Have you called a physician?" His accent was decidedly foreign, though he spoke with perfect clarity. She rather liked the way he put words together.

"Can I help you?" she asked him.

He shook his head, as if her response, along with her appearance, was incomprehensible. "My name is Leo Zacarian. I came to see Peter Cathay. I wrote to tell him of my arrival," he said distractedly.

She pulled the envelope out of her pocket and looked at it. "I'm afraid he hasn't seen your letter yet." The long gash in her arm was visible.

He grabbed her wrist, his hold gentle but firm. "You need urgent medical attention. Have you been attacked?"

She shook her head. Her brow wrinkled as she focused her attention on the hand on her wrist. As if in a trance, she responded, "I *should* see a doctor, but I cannot leave my father alone."

She looked towards her father's bedroom, thinking about everything she had to do. She still needed to mop his floor. She also had a load of laundry to run through from her father's most recent accident. She sighed, exhausted just thinking about everything she needed to do. She didn't have time for mystery guests or injuries or doctors.

She stepped back to allow him to enter the apartment, almost falling as she slipped on liquid on the hardwood floor. She looked down and saw a small puddle of blood. If she was bleeding that badly, she *needed* to see a doctor. At the thought of the amount of money in the bank, she felt despair.

"I have a friend in this city, a doctor, I shall call him," her mysterious visitor said decisively. "Do you have a telephone I might use?" He was quick to dial a number as soon as she showed him the telephone by the front door.

"Alan, it is Leo Zacarian. I had hoped to visit with you tomorrow, but I have a problem and wondered if you were free at this very moment." He listened for a minute before saying, "I am glad to hear it, Alan. A young acquaintance of mine has urgent need of stitches but apparently cannot leave her home. I believe she would benefit from your care."

He proceeded to give her address and then hung up. "My dear, you must sit down and rest, you have a serious wound."

She shook her head. The limitations imposed by her injury were starting to sink in. "I can't sit." She turned reluctantly away from him, allowing him to see the ruin of her mother's favorite skirt, and the torn flesh beneath.

He exclaimed something in his native language, before adding, "What has caused this?" He frowned, seeming to be at a loss. "Perhaps you should lie upon your stomach while waiting for my friend?"

The thought of getting off her feet was appealing. "I would like that," she said. She was appalled when she saw the amount of blood on the staircase. She had no idea she was bleeding *that* badly. The whole foyer looked like someone had been murdered there.

He saw her sway and, in a moment, she was being held carefully in his arms. He went up the stairs and pushed open the door she indicated, setting her gently on her feet. "Will you be self-conscious if I remove your lower garments?"

It was an absurd question to ask. Of course she would be self-conscious! But she was starting to feel light-headed and queasy from the pain and that was stronger than any embarrassment she was feeling, so she shook her head.

He saw a pair of scissors on her nightstand and picked them up. Showing them to her, he said, "If you do not mind?"

She shook her head again. The skirt and undergarments were both destroyed already. She tried to ignore the fact that it was her mother's poodle skirt he was cutting off her. She silently recited her times tables while he cut through her skirt and underpants. Once she was naked from the waist down, he went into the adjoining bathroom and came back with two towels. He laid one on the bed and assisted her to lay on her stomach, and then he lightly draped the second towel over her naked rear. Once she was decently covered he bent to remove her black and white saddle shoes, carefully setting them to the side. He was a very methodical, focused individual. He placed the shoes neatly side-by-side near the foot of the bed. He also carefully folded up her destroyed skirt with the shredded briefs tucked up inside.

Just as he finished a high-pitched bell started to ring. She tried to get up but he said, "I shall handle this."

"My father," she said hurriedly, "he's not himself."

He reassured her and then left. He was gone perhaps ten minutes when she heard the doorbell followed by the sound of him going down the stairs. The murmur of masculine voices preceded her door opening. Her swollen eye was towards the door, so she couldn't see who entered. "My father?" she asked.

"He needed assistance to use the facilities," he said for all the world as if it was a normal thing. "My friend here is Dr. Alan Wade. He will look at your injuries."

"How did you do this?" The doctor's voice was grumbly and old, with undertones of kindness and compassion.

"My father isn't well. I was helping him into bed when he had a muscle spasm and knocked me off balance. I fell against an old glass-topped night-table. I'm afraid it broke my fall and I shattered it."

"How long ago was this?"

"Perhaps an hour, maybe a little less."

The doctor used a damp towel to clean her lacerations; she winced as he found and plucked out numerous pieces of glass. He kept up a running commentary which helped her to keep her mind off the fact that the doctor and the stranger were getting an eyeful of her naked rear end.

Several more times her father rang his bell while the doctor was tending her. Each time the stranger went to see to his needs. Finally, the doctor said to her, "You've got three long gashes and four or five deep ones that need to be stitched. I don't think you lost too much blood. You didn't sever any major blood vessels, but you should take it easy for the next month or so. You may have a reaction to the trauma you've suffered, even if it seems relatively minor to you."

She didn't think the pain of having shards of glass picked out of her rear was minor. She winced as he proceeded to sew her up. Finally, he pronounced himself satisfied with his work. "You might have a few more shards embedded but I got most of it out. The rest will work its way out over time." He examined the long cut on her forearm. "This will need stitches too, though it doesn't look like you have any glass in there."

When he finished stitching her arm, he examined her face. "You'll have a really impressive black eye in the next few days, but otherwise I don't think there is any permanent injury." He gave her two pills and watched while she swallowed them.

The stranger stepped back into the room and the doctor repeated his prognosis for him. "Alan, if you could spare a couple more minutes?" With that, the two men left.

Once the two men were outside the bedroom door, the doctor said, "I gave her some heavy-duty painkillers. She'll be out like a light in the next few minutes."

"I am sorry to ruin your plans for the evening," Leo said. "I came at the urging of my father, who is unable to travel far these days. He received a letter from one of his long-time friends, Peter Cathay, which was impossible to fathom. As I was making plans to visit the States, my father begged me to check in on his friend. He was worried for him, and I wanted to ease his mind. I wrote to Peter to tell him I would be visiting. I received no response."

Leo led him towards the door at the end of the hall, before continuing, "From what I have gathered, Peter is phasing in and out of a state of senility or dementia. When he is lucid, he worries for his daughter, who has been left to care for him. He sounded almost suicidal in the letter my father received. I would value your professional opinion."

In the bedroom, an extremely thin man was weeping while he sat on the floor. "I can't keep on like this." He looked up at the two men. "I've got so little time left, and so much of it isn't even my time. I can't bear to think about my poor daughter."

Leo helped him to his feet and back to his bed. "You wrote asking my father, Zavier Zacarian to come and help you. He could not make it, but he sent me."

Peter gave a defeated sigh. "I knew it was a longshot. Why should he do it? Why should he take on a burden he doesn't deserve?"

"You mentioned you had very little time left," Alan said. "I take it you have a brain tumor?"

"Yes. I've already lived ten months longer than predicted. It can only be days left. Perhaps hours? I love my daughter, but she doesn't deserve this."

"What task did you want my father to undertake for you?" Leo asked him.

"Oh, well, take care of Jackie of course. But it's stupid. Why should he?"

"I am certain my father would wish to help you by taking care of your daughter. I can speak for him and agree to help you. It is the very least he and I can do."

"You're sure?" he asked. When Leo nodded the old man seemed to collapse in on himself, as if the tension of his worries about his daughter kept him rigid and taut. "I'm more grateful than you know, to have her future secure." Then he looked up, his expression altered. He screamed, "Who the hell are you? Get the hell out of my house." He started to slam the bed on either side of his skeletal legs and then he quieted down, slumping sideways and was asleep... or unconscious.

"Without his medical records I can't be certain," Alan said, "but I'd say days or even hours *are* all that is left. He might not have any more moments where he is clear-headed. Judging by his verbal abuse, I imagine he's dished it out in quantities to his daughter, and now she's injured. He needs professional care."

"Do you know of a place where we can get him care?"

"I can make a few phone calls if you like. I'm pretty sure that within the hour I can get him situated in a top-rated nursing home. You'll pay for it?"

Leo nodded. "I will stay here and help the young girl and be there for her when her father passes on."

The two men left the room and were chatting amiably in the hallway when they heard the unmistakable bang of a firearm. They returned rapidly to the bedroom, remaining in the room only briefly once it was clear what happened. He knew he was a burden for his daughter, that he was putting her through hell. When he was certain she would be cared for, he chose to take his own life.

"I am going to check on his daughter," Leo said.

She was sleeping on her side, a troubled frown between her brows. The pills the doctor gave her were doing their magic.

The knock on the apartment door was inevitable. The sound of the gun was quite loud. Leo went down the stairs to open the door. He was not surprised to see a police officer on the doorstep.

"Is everything all right here?" said the police officer. He was eyeing the blood-spattered foyer and the blood on the stairs.

"I was just preparing to make a phone call to the police," Leo said sadly. "I am afraid that my friend is dead. He accidentally injured his daughter, and then took his own life."

The police officer came in and Leo took him upstairs to the bedroom. Alan was standing outside the room. When he shared his identity, the police officer wanted to see the girl too. "Why weren't we called when she was first injured?" he asked after he saw the sleeping girl.

The doctor explained the effects of the brain tumor. "Until he killed himself, we considered it to be a matter for medical professionals instead of police."

Jackie slept on, under the influence of the pain pills while the coroner came and took her father's body away. Once the doctor left, Leo decided to clean the bedroom as best he could. The cold truth of her father's death could not be avoided, but at least he could assure that she didn't have the resulting mess to clean also.

Once he finished cleaning the bedroom, he went back down to the ground floor. He saw a neat stack of mail she had obviously been organizing to show her father. Out of curiosity, he looked through the envelopes. Several had ominous *Final Notice* in red stamped on them. He grouped together all the envelopes from different sources. Almost six months' worth of bills had been ignored. Telephone, water, gas, garbage, milk. The only bill not marked with a *Final Notice* was an electricity bill, which had been paid in advance. A well-used bank-book told him the rest of the story. With less than eighteen dollars in the bank, she was in dire financial straits.

Glancing at his watch, he added six hours to the local time. It wasn't too late in the day to call his father. While he waited for the operator to put through the international overseas call, he totaled the bills and had an amount that would be necessary just to keep her from bankruptcy.

When his call came through, he picked up the phone. His father sounded robust and healthy. Leo was thankful that his father's infirmities were not of the mind. Though he couldn't walk any more, he was as sharp as ever and likely to live another thirty years or more.

"Hello father," he said, and then proceeded to outline the events of the day, finishing with a summary of her finances.

His father was silent for several seconds before saying, "I am sorry son, I had no idea what you would be walking into. We must help his daughter. Get her affairs in order as she heals, and when she is recovered, bring her here. I will try to consider how best to help her out."

Leo hung up after speaking with his father. It was what he had expected but he wanted his father to know everything that was going on.

Pulling out a checkbook that would draw on an American bank, he systematically paid each of her bills with a request to close the account. For the rent and utilities, he paid until the end of the month and requested that services be terminated at that point in time. Finally, all the bills were paid, and her financial affairs were in order.

If he was going to bring her back to Estolia, she would have to travel via sailboat. There was no way she could tolerate the flight sitting in a regular airline seat.

He knew from his explorations that the apartment had only two bedrooms. In the living room they had a two-seater sofa with wooden arms unsuitable to sleep on.

Though he cleaned the master bedroom, the mattress was saturated and he couldn't sleep on it, even if he *could* bring himself to use a room that had known such a violent act. The only other choice he had was to sleep next to the sleeping beauty herself. He could not just leave her alone and return to his hotel.

She was still deeply asleep when he lay on the covers next to her. She would sleep for hours, he reasoned, which meant he could catch a few hours of sleep. Trying to find a comfortable position, he put an arm around her gently. Hopefully she would remain asleep, but perhaps, if she woke up, she would be comforted to experience some human contact and warmth.

As he began to nod off to sleep, He decided that they would use the sailboat *Last Resort* and sail home.

☙

Jackie woke to the feeling of pain. One injudicious move on her part and she remembered her stitches. She concentrated for several minutes on being as still as possible. It was only as the pain faded that she became aware of an arm around her waist. The stranger was in her bed. She held her breath, trying to figure out what was going on. In the silence she could hear how deep and even his breathing was. She relaxed and took a deep breath. She wasn't sure exactly what the story was, but clearly he didn't want to leave her alone with her father.

Once he decided to stay the night, however, he would have realized that he had only three choices. He was too long and large a man to sleep on their two-seater sofa downstairs. Her father was incontinent and often combative in the night, and it would be unpleasant to try to sleep in his bed. That left her bed as the only alternative.

She'd have to make up the couch downstairs to sleep in, she thought. While she considered the best way to deal with a sudden guest she drifted back to sleep. Her last thought as she fell asleep was that it was pleasant to wake up next to someone. It reminded her of stormy nights when she would climb into her parents' bed, held tightly by both while the thunder and lightning would rage outside.

☙

Leo woke stiff from remaining in the same position all night. He was glad the girl was still asleep. He did not relish the truth he would have to share with her. From what he could tell about her situation, it would not surprise him if she felt a sense of relief when she knew her father was gone. Likely her biggest pain would come from guilt over the sense of freedom she would end up feeling to know he was gone.

He slipped out of the bed and went into the bathroom to freshen up as much as possible. When he finished he went down to the kitchen and looked in the refrigerator. In no time he prepared a quiche and put it in the oven to bake. He sat at the table so he could make several phone calls to arrange the *Last Resort* to be prepped for a transatlantic journey. The captain of the *Last Resort* remarked that they would return to Estolia just in time for the Transition. He smiled at the thought. The girl might balk at the thought of traveling to Estolia, but when he considered the alternatives, and presented them to her, he hoped she would allow him to take charge of her destiny for at least a short time. He would explain that this *was* her father's dying wish.

His cousin would be starting to settle into the role of Heir Apparent, he hoped. Sebastian's trials must be a part of some grand scheme that would make perfect sense when looked back on from a historical perspective. If Sebastian didn't shape up, then Leo might be forced into the role of Last Resort, among other things, and he knew himself well enough – and hoped *Deity* knew him well enough – to know that his was not the correct personality for leader of the Estolian faith. No, clearly, Sebastian *had* to shape up for the position.

It *was* going to be a more interesting transition than usual because his father and the King were twins. Over the course of the entire history of Estolia, the King and First Consul were twins only four times, and in none of those situations had the firstborn son of the King been born a full week after the First Consul's first son.

Because of this unique situation, both his father and uncle felt that Sebastian, as the Heir Apparent, should give his soul into the keeping of his future spouse *before* Leo did so. Leo remembered his thoughts at the time. He didn't think that *Deity* would allow mere mortals to determine what would happen. Leo would give his soul into the keeping of his future wife the minute *Deity* wished it; the minute it was right for the two of them. But since he had no love interest in mind, he acquiesced.

His thoughts were interrupted when he heard a sound upstairs. He rose and went up the stairs. Jackie was quietly weeping. "What is it?" he asked her.

"I can't get up," she confessed.

Recalling that she was only half dressed he asked her, "If I get you a nightgown, will you be able to change into it on your own?"

She nodded. "There's a nightgown in the top drawer."

Five minutes later, he heard her call out to him to enter the bedroom. She was wearing a long cotton nightdress. It didn't take long for him to help her to her feet and to the bathroom. "I'll be right here in the hallway in case you need any help."

While he waited, he tried to weigh up the different ways he might tell her about her father. He couldn't figure out how he would tell her by the time she opened the door to the bathroom.

He was helping her to return to her bedroom when she stopped with a jerk. Her attention was on the open bedroom door at the other end of the hallway. From where she stood, she could see the bed – stripped of its bedclothes. She gave an inarticulate cry of despair and looked up at him. Her brown eyes were overflowing with tears and she said, "He's dead, isn't he?"

Not knowing what else to say, he nodded gently. "I am sorry."

She closed her eyes and then nodded in acceptance. Her eyes went to the stairs and he could interpret her look. She was thinking of the overdue bills waiting on her father's desk.

He began to guide her back to her room. "Your father called in a favor," he said.

"He has asked me to take care of you. You and your happiness and future security were his last thoughts. He loved you."

Her shoulders slumped. Once in her bedroom she got a puzzled expression on her face. "What was your name again?"

"Leo Zacarian. Your father and my father were great friends. At his request, I have arranged for you to sail to my country with me. You can recuperate during the journey."

"My name is Jackie," she said. Her eyes traced back to where the desk was. "I can't leave the country without settling my father's debts."

"I took the liberty of settling them for you."

Her eyes were wide as she looked up at him. "How will I repay you?"

"My father owed a debt to yours. I do not know all the details. By the time you have fully recovered we will arrive in Estolia and we will have the chance to ask my father to tell us the story. I am certain we will work something out that will satisfy everyone involved." He smiled and added, "Please do not let it bother you. It was not a hardship to settle your debts, and it was your father's dying wish."

She nodded. He could see the weariness in her expression.

"When you wake up next, we will discuss the future." He picked up the vial of pills Alan left behind and shook two out onto the palm of his hand. "Take these, Jackie." He held the pills and a glass of water out to her.

10

Abdication

Like a soul—my soul—aflame,
the woman who would
compass my world
was made known to me
in the purity and intensity
of her brilliant aura.

— Phineas Alistair Zacarian, Capitulo 81

JACKIE STOOD ON THE deck of the *Last Resort*, the wind in her hair, her eyes closed. They would be arriving in Estolia in the next couple of days. The deep exhaustion from tending her father's needs around the clock was nothing more than a memory.

Leo was perfect for the part of knight in shining armor. He swept into her life and, if he couldn't save her father, he at least saved her and was with her during the emotional trauma of her father's death and burial. She was lucky. If Leo didn't come when he did, she wasn't sure what would have happened to her. She gripped the rail. She had to face the truth. The reason she came up onto the deck in the first place.

Infatuation. It had to be that. He would never want her. He was almost thirty years old, and she was only just twenty. He treated her like she was his kid sister, indulgent, not romantic.

She consciously eased her grip on the rail and purposely smiled, focusing on all that was good about her life. She was crossing the Atlantic Ocean. She was the guest of Leopold Zacarian, the son of one of her father's friends. He was rich, with a whole crew on the large sailboat seeing to their comfort and serving them like they were royalty.

✦

Leo stepped out of his cabin and was surprised at the brilliance of the sun shining on Jackie. Then with a frown, he glanced at the sky and saw that it was overcast, the sun hidden behind clouds. He looked back at Jackie – she still looked like she was bathed in brilliant sunlight. He stared at her in fascination. He had admired her brown eyes and chocolate colored hair along with her beautiful willowy body. But he had kept her at a distance, treating her like he treated his sisters and female cousins.

59

He crossed over to where she was standing, drawn by the flame of what could only be her aura. She was looking out over the water.

When he reached her, he set his hands on her shoulders, feeling with an almost electric thrill the physical manifestation of the aura. His forebears were obsessed with their attempts to put into words the aura. As her brilliance bathed each cell in his body, he began to understand this obsession. Having felt the warmth of her aura, he wanted to be able to describe what he felt so his own sons might understand better than the existing texts, poetry, and prose were able to explain. Yet, how *could* he explain what it felt like to see a woman standing in shadows yet bathed in the warm glow of her aura? How could *words* explain the way *his* soul responded to *hers*?

Jackie turned and looked at him. The lessons from his year as an Acolyte came back to him in that moment. Warnings about the way it would feel when he finally met the woman destined to keep his soul. Once felt, once seen, his soul would begin to yearn to rest within her keeping. His earlier desire for her was explained. Now he wanted her more than any other woman he had ever known. He was looking at his future wife. "You are looking particularly lovely today."

She smiled before turning back to look out in the direction the ship was heading. "When will we arrive in Estolia?"

"We might get there tomorrow," he said. "The day after at the latest."

"Where will I live?"

"In the palace," he said nonchalantly. "I do not think I ever properly explained – my father has one of the highest-ranking roles in Estolia – he is First Consul to the King. My uncle *is* the King. It is a very small country. Please do not feel at all self-conscious. We are all just people."

"How did my father ever get involved in your family?" she turned to him to ask.

"Your father saved the life of one of my cousins, and my uncle – who was practicing as an orthopedic surgeon at the time, was able to treat the broken legs your father suffered because of his heroic act. He introduced my father to my mother."

"That's romantic." Jackie's cheeks turned rosy.

"There is a lot of romance built into the Estolian religion."

"Really?" she asked, "tell me about it."

He laughed outright, feeling suddenly free. "I *will* tell you *all* about it. Not today, however. You will learn much about Estolia. This next year is our *Transition* year. We only have one every thirty years. In fact, we will begin the *Transition* within a few days of our arrival."

"What is it about?"

"I shall explain the details over time. You will be lucky enough to see the bestowing of the title of Last Resort, the Heir Apparent's marriage, the coronation of a new king, and many other things. It is an exciting time in Estolia.

❦

Sebastian watched the sun rise from the back of his stallion Altair. He felt no joy in the familiar dynamic view. As with everything else over the last four months, there was only emptiness and unhappiness. He heard hooves behind him and knew either his brother or his father had joined him. They'd both been shadowing him for the last several weeks.

Altair's reaction told him it was his brother on his mare Tribecka. "I do not wish to exercise my duties as Last Resort," Gregory said without preamble.

"Has any heir abdicated before?" Sebastian asked. He knew the answer, but his brother would understand him.

"Only twice has the Last Resort been called on to act in his official capacity," Gregory said. "Both cases were different from this one. Alexandros begged Apollyon to abdicate, but he wouldn't do it. That's the only time it's even mentioned in the *Capitulos*."

Sebastian shifted his horse so he could look at his brother. "I've read every story of every ancestor. Read all there is on the topic, as you have brother. I don't believe it has ever happened this way. Has Uncle Zavier said anything?"

Gregory moved his horse closer and reached out one hand to his brother. The two brothers clasped forearms. "He's asked me to bring you to him. That's why I followed."

"Let's go then," Sebastian said. He turned his stallion towards the path leading to the base of Mt. Estoliana, following his brother. While they made their way, Sebastian studied his brother's wide shoulders, adorned already with the sash of Last Resort. His uncle turned the position over early, feeling the push from *Deity* to do so.

When they got to the base of the mountain a couple of Acolytes came up to them and held the bridles of their mounts. In moments Gregory and Sebastian were entering the temple. They turned and went down the hallway to the right. After only a brief knock, they entered the office of the Keeper of the Soul of Estolia.

Once inside the office, Sebastian saw that his father was also there. Between them, the four men were the highest ranking and most powerful men in all Estolia. To Sebastian that gave him a sense of bitterness. If he was honest with himself, he knew the reason. Melanie. She would not be, *could not be* Queen of Estolia.

Once he and Gregory were seated the door opened and one other person entered the room – Theo, Leo's brother. Once he was seated, Sebastian turned his attention to his uncle.

"What obstacle stands in your way?" Zavier asked.

"I believe the woman I belong with cannot keep my soul in the accepted traditions of Zaccarias. She cannot *be* Queen of Estolia. I don't believe there is another woman alive who *can* keep my soul." He thought of Melanie again. His entire body yearned for her.

"What do *you* say, Gregory?" Zavier asked.

With a grin towards his brother, Gregory turned to Theo and said, "Are *you* prepared to take on the duties of Last Resort?"

Gregory and Theo solemnly went through the prescribed words of the formal transferal of the burden of Last Resort. Sebastian's father took the role of Heir Apparent in Leo's absence, holding the ceremonial dagger as Gregory pinned the sash to their cousin's shoulder and hip.

Once the formal ceremonial words were over, Zavier turned to Sebastian and explained, "When your father and I were born it was never known which of us was the more rightful heir. The caesarian section made 'first-born' a mystery and nobody kept track of which child was removed from mother's womb first. When Leo was born a week before you, it seemed as if, perhaps, I should have been the one named King." He smiled at his brother before patting the arm of his wheelchair. "I believe, given the accident I had and the way *Deity* has whispered to me over the years, that I was *always* destined to be Last Resort, First Consul, and most importantly, Keeper of the Soul of Estolia."

Sebastian's father spoke then, "You haven't been happy since your return four months ago Sebastian. It would seem that *Deity* demands Leo is the one to take on the burden of the crown." He fixed his son with a stern look when he clarified, "Unless of course, you object."

Sebastian held his hands out rapidly, warding off the notion. "No! I don't object! Does he know he's the Heir Apparent yet?"

Gregory grinned at his brother. "He doesn't know, but I believe that, within moments of Uncle Zavier and I coming to the realization that the Promise of Zaccarias allowed for this change, Leo was confronted with the keeper of his soul."

"Doesn't this bother you, Gregory?" Sebastian gestured to Theo wearing the sash.

"No. Theo always attended the training with me. Leo was never interested. I rather like the idea of another year of freedom before I must start looking around for the keeper of my soul. I was never keen on being Last Resort, and even less interested in being King."

"After Leo's position is confirmed, you will be able to invite your Melanie here to Estolia," Zavier said.

❧

"What is it, Melanie?" Bethany asked her friend. "You've been moping around for the last four months. What's wrong?"

"I think Sebastian was going to ask me to marry him," she said.

"I thought so too. What happened?" Bethany asked.

Melanie had tears tracing down her face. "I lied to him," she whispered. "I couldn't force him to be childless." Her hand went to her abdomen.

Melanie fell in a cross-country competition. She landed softly, but her horse, Chastaine, did not land quite as softly, and with a broken leg she went berserk. The only permanent injury she sustained was to her reproductive tract. She ended up getting a hysterectomy. The loss of her beloved Chastaine was far more disturbing than the loss of children she may never want.

"What lie did you tell him?" Bethany knew her friend wasn't good at lying.

"I told him I was a wild child and had an abortion that went bad when I was seventeen."

"Why would you tell such lies?"

"I don't know." She frowned. "It just came to me suddenly that the only way to chase him away was to lie to him. He believed me. Wanted to sleep with me afterwards. I sent him away."

Her friend's unhappiness was of her own manufacture. "He didn't love you enough, then," she pointed out.

Melanie frowned heavily. "I don't know, Beth, I think what I told him was more profoundly disturbing than it should've been. He looked at me as if I'd just given him a death sentence." Her expression grew alarmed. "You don't think he'd kill himself, do you?"

Bethany snorted. "Mel, if he gave you up, just because you couldn't have a child, he's not likely to kill himself out of heartbreak."

Melanie's expression was still unhappy. "What did you need to see me about?"

As a photo-journalist, Bethany was at the Cross-Country competition when Melanie had her fall and touched the wrong setting on her camera, taking more than two dozen photographs in quick succession, accidentally capturing the entire tragedy. She'd felt compelled, after seeing the photos of the disaster, to visit with Melanie in the hospital.

The two girls became close friends, despite the three-year disparity in their ages. When Melanie saw Bethany's talented photographs of various equestrian competitions, she began writing the background information necessary to turn her photographs into coffee-table picture books.

Now that Bethany was nearly twenty and Melanie was twenty-three, they had five books to their credit. Somehow Melanie was always finding book deals for them through her wealthy contacts. For the first time, Bethany received a request to do a more substantial book:

> Dear Bethany Danielson, your talent as a photo-journalist has come to our attention, and we would like to offer you and your partner, Melanie Andrews, a year-long commission.
>
> If you choose to take the commission, you and your partner will be provided with transportation to and from the land of Estolia. While you are here, you and your partner would occupy a guest suite in the palace, and all your needs would be seen to. We have a fine stable of gifted Warmbloods from which your partner could select a mount to hone her riding skills. You may tell her that one of the horses – of Andestolian breeding – could be her bonus at the end of the year, including transport.
>
> Likely you wonder why it would take a full year. We have the desire, here in Estolia, to document our nation and our religion. Please call the phone number

below as soon as you receive this letter, and before you speak about it with your partner. Reverse the charges so that the phone call itself is not a financial burden. I will be able to share with you more of the details at that time.

> Yours, Faithfully,
> Zavier Archimedes Zacarian
> Keeper of the Soul of Estolia
> First Consul to the King.

The phone conversation was more enlightening than the letter. She spoke with Zavier Zacarian and he proceeded to explain that – while the job offer was valid, the need quite real – he had considered her for the job because of Melanie's relationship with Sebastian.

"I do not know, Miss Danielson, if Miss Andrews will patch up her relationship with my nephew Sebastian, or if there is no future in it. But I believe if you get your friend Melanie here to Estolia, then she and Sebastian will have the chance to iron out their difficulties and discover if they are, or are not, made for each other. If you wish to help your friend out, you should convince her to accompany you on this commission. However she is likely to refuse if she knows you are heading for Sebastian's home."

They spoke for some time. By the time she hung up, she knew she was going to convince her friend to go with her on this assignment.

ॐ

"Beth?" Melanie's voice cut through her thoughts. Embarrassed she grinned at her friend.

"I'm sorry Mel, I was just thinking about a job offer I got – it's a year-long assignment to create two books. It's a package deal, and they want us to fly out almost immediately." Bethany pulled out the photograph of three horses. "The person who wants us to come out will fly us in their private airplane. We'll stay in a medieval palace. He is, apparently, one of the breeders of..." She paused dramatically. "Andestolian warmbloods."

The two loves of Melanie's life were Sebastian Zacarian and horses. Beth could see immediately that she had captured her friend's interest.

"I was told to tell you that you'd be able to ride all of these three horses." Bethany added, "And you will be able to select one of them as your bonus at the end of the assignment."

With Melanie's eyes on the photograph, tracing the lines of the nearest horse, her question was almost asked in a trance, "When do we leave?"

"Tomorrow evening."

Allure

The study of modern and ancient religions was one of the most enlightening periods of my life. I was amazed at the man-made religious constructs designed to bring purpose and order to peoples' lives throughout the ages. I was baffled by the blind faith many people demonstrated when their Deity did not give to them the blessings promised to the faithful. In Estolia, Deity asks for very little and gives great rewards for our faith. Other faiths seem an inversion of the Estolian Faith asking much and giving little or nothing in return.

~Zavier Archimedes Zacarian; Capitulo 86

THEY WERE SEATED AT THE compact table in the dining area having dinner. "We will arrive the day after tomorrow in the morning. Not quite in time to be there at dawn, but before noon at the very latest," Leo said. His expression was full of happy anticipation.

Jackie smiled at Leo and sipped the wine he served her. "You really love your country, don't you?" He'd changed over the last twenty-four hours, though she wasn't sure how. She still had a monumental crush on him, but his attitude towards her had altered. His expression when he looked at her that morning on the deck of the *Last Resort* had an extra level of warmth. If she didn't lose her mother at a young age and wasn't isolated through caring for her father, she would trust the impression she kept getting – that he was exhibiting all the signs of romantic interest and attraction. Whatever it was, she enjoyed being with him and fantasizing that he had fallen in love with her.

"Yes, Jackie, I love my country. I am very excited to return. I did not expect to be away this long."

"I've inconvenienced you," Jackie said. "I'm very sorry for taking so much of your time."

"You have not inconvenienced me. Just delayed me a little. I will be turning thirty tomorrow. My cousin's birthday is a week after mine. He will be King, so there are festivities planned beginning with his birthday."

He got to his feet and crossed the room to the sideboard. He put a record on the turntable. Romantic music softly played in the background. He then picked up the bottle of wine and returned to the table so he could pour a little more wine in each of their glasses.

The song ended and another began. Leo bowed slightly before extending a hand. "May I have this dance, Jackie?"

She put her hand in his and he led her out of the dining alcove and into the more spacious lounge. He pulled her close to his body and she relaxed in his arms, enjoying the feel of his solid frame against her body. She closed her eyes so she could pretend they were on a date, and that he wanted to dance with her because he was in love with her.

When one song ended and another began, she became aware of a hot hard presence between them. She remembered some of her father's books she read over the last year, a guilty habit she had during the times her father was most distant. In those books, the characters did not merely kiss. They embraced, their kisses grew impassioned, and men's bodies reacted to women's bodies. She flushed and looked at him. "Leo...?"

"You are incredibly beautiful Jackie," he said. The expression on his face communicated his attraction to her more than his words could. He bent toward her, kissing her. His lips over hers were mobile, caressing, enticing, pulling a response from her she was incapable of hiding.

The brush of his tongue over her lower lip encouraged her to open to him, and his gentle persuasive kiss was quickly transformed into the flame of passion as he deepened the kiss.

His hands went to her hips, pulling her tighter against him so the outline of his aroused flesh was pressed against her.

"Jackie," he whispered against her lips, "you are intoxicating, extraordinary, perfection." He kissed her again, pressing his hard length against her.

He pulled back again and looked at her. "Jackie." His eyes studied hers and then after another long drugging kiss, he said, "I want to marry you, Jackie, give my soul into your keeping."

He meant it! He wanted to marry her. She felt like she could read his thoughts as she looked into his face. From the time her stitches were out she began to daydream about him falling madly in love with her.

His eyes searched hers, looking for any sign of acquiescence or rejection. She wasn't sure what he saw, but he seemed pleased when he started to kiss her again. Their earlier passion was multiplied, and she was rocked to her core by how it felt to have this man's body against her, to feel his hips softly thrusting against her, his mouth exploring hers, his hands on her rear, pulling her tight against his hard desire.

She felt like a volcano about to erupt; a balloon ready to burst. She wanted him, permanently, before he could change his mind. After several breathless moments, she closed the distance between them again and lifted her face to his, enjoying the alien sensations rushing through her body as his kisses grew in intensity. Not even realizing the implications of her actions, she extended her hand to his and once he took it, she turned and led him down the passageway to the door of his room.

Leo's hand on the door frame stopped her progress and he said, his voice lacking conviction, "No, Jackie."

She looked into his eyes, unaware how she looked with a flush on her cheeks, her lips swollen from his kisses, eyes dilated with desire. "We *must*, Leo," she whispered. She lifted her hands to the top button of his shirt and started to slip each button loose. At some point, while her fingers deftly dealt with each button, he pushed the door to his room open and stepped inside, pulling her with him.

His shirt parted under her hands and she caressed him. She enjoyed the sensation of his skin, slightly moist under her fingertips, rough with hair, warm, almost hot to the touch. His skin trembled at her touch. His scent was subtle, musky and rich.

He pushed the door shut and leaned against it. His head went back at the feel of her delicate fingers exploring his chest. Despite his earlier protest, his hands on her shoulders found the thin straps of her dress and he pushed them to the side until the dress fell off her body into a crumpled heap at her feet. She did not wear a bra, and he paused, sucking in his breath as he opened his eyes and looked over her body exposed to his view. She moved closer to him and allowed her fingertips to drift over his abdomen and down to the top of his trousers.

He tilted her face up towards him so he could kiss her again, passionately invading her mouth. When she fumbled in her attempts to unfasten his pants, Leo's hands settled over hers, as if he would stop her – and himself. She looked up at him and didn't know what to say or do. Her tongue explored the swollen contours of her lower lip and he watched it while he unfastened his pants and dropped them to the floor of his cabin.

Her eyes studied his, trying to grasp even the smallest sanity. She felt as if her actions were out of her control. She wanted to discover what was possible with this man. She led him the short distance to his bed and ran her hands up his chest to his shoulders. She pressed her body against his, her breasts against his chest.

"Jackie..." he again protested but then something within him snapped; his kisses escalated from passionate to elemental. In moments they were both naked, and he was pushing her back onto the bed.

Jackie was amazed at herself, at the wanton sensuality rushing through her. She never would have thought she'd be in a position of being willing or *able* to seduce a man.

She wrapped her legs around his waist and the last thread of his self-control broke as his body plunged into hers, possessing her as much as she possessed him. Their frantic, passionate coupling was elemental, ignoring how untried she was, as Leo's fierce driving need was matched only by her own. The rush of pleasure as their lovemaking reached its crescendo was something she would remember for the rest of her life.

🌺

What seemed like a long time passed before his breathing and heartbeat dropped back to normal. He held Jackie tightly against his body. He had no idea what would happen, but he knew one thing for certain: Jackie, this beautiful, extraordinary woman, had taken his soul into her keeping.

He would have to seek his father's counsel on this. The obligations were strictly delineated for the Heir Apparent. If he, Leo, was the heir instead of his cousin Sebastian, he would know exactly what would happen.

He lost himself for a moment in a vision of what it would be like if he and his brother were the Heir Apparent and the Last Resort. If that was true, he would be marveling at the strength of character of the future Queen of Estolia. He would know that his younger brother's function as Last Resort would be ceremonial rather than functional. He would be proud of fulfilling the prophecy for the eighty-seventh generation after Zaccarias and Estoliana. He would be prepared to take on the crown when, in nine months, Jackie gave birth to their son. He would be more certain than ever about the role of *Deity* in the lives of all Estolians. His actions this night, and over the next seven days would assure his nation of both safety and prosperity as they began the successful *Transition* to the eighty-seventh *Capitulo*.

Never, in all the history of Estolia, in eighty-six *Capitulos* and almost 2700 years, had the son of the First Consul been born *before* the heir to the throne. Never had the right of the Heir Apparent to bed and then wed his future wife prior to his cousin been an issue. He was third in line to the throne yet was the oldest boy in the rising generation. Once he saw Jackie's aura, he realized the enormity of the sacrifice he was being asked to make. And he couldn't do it. When faced with the temptation, he was unable to avoid placing his soul within her keeping at the earliest possible moment.

He sighed heavily. All he could do was move forward. With his lovely bride. And hope his action would be accepted.

12

Arrival

The greatest consolation Deity gives us when we must do that which is normally more than any one person should be asked to do, is the pure sweet guidance of the spirit telling us our choice is clear, our actions just.

~Lorenzo Delmont, Descendant of Zacarian; Capitulo 57

ZAVIER WOKE AND kissed Harmony. She smiled sleepily up at him and then turned over in her sleep. After thirty-one years of marriage, she understood the odd hours demanded by his role as Keeper of the Soul of Estolia. He quickly pulled on his robes and transferred himself to his wheelchair. Once he was ready to leave the bedroom he had to pause and fill his senses with the vision of his beautiful wife.

He knew that the Acolytes assigned to serve his needs within the palace would let those at the stable level know he was coming. His carriage would be ready to transport him to the temple. along with the Acolytes to assist him into the carriage. Others would be waiting to help him when he arrived. They, too, were always available to help him into the temple.

When he first had his accident, he'd been forced to decide whether they would install a ramp access to the temple, and to the inner dais. After some thought and prayer, he and his brother decided together that the service opportunities for Acolytes would suffice. It would not take much for Acolytes to bring him up the stairs in both locations in the temple. The integrity of their historic architecture mattered more than transitory convenience for one person. As it was, his brother converted one of the least useful towers in the palace into an elevator that made his life far more convenient.

Once he saw the elevator, he had to marvel at the innovation. One could almost imagine that Amadore, who designed both the palace and the temple, must have seen into the future and created the tower with the purpose of converting it into an elevator. The tower was the narrowest, most central tower in the entire palace complex, and was considered too narrow for a residence. It ended up being mostly unused over the course of the history of the palace. The only time it ever had anyone within it was when the thrice-per-*Capitulo* inspection was done on the design elements, to find and repair any deterioration.

Now the tower was fully functional as an elevator. Not only did it help Zavier to maneuver around the palace with ease, it also enabled the residents of the palace to descend all the way down to the Stables built into the side of Mount Zaccarias on the Zacarian Plateau. A few narrow staircases previously served as a connection between the two levels, but with more than eleven stories between the two, it was hardly a shortcut. Now the residents of the stable level enjoyed more freedom of access to the palace.

Zavier's thoughts wandered as his carriage made its way down the rest of the palace road to the valley between the two mountains and then through the rich agricultural region that filled it.

He recalled the story of Ulysses, who Kept the Soul of Estolia in one of the most turbulent periods of Estolian history. He broke his ankle and then the physicians of the times realized it was infected. In those days surgery was a matter of brute physical strength. His foot was detached by the blacksmith. When he recovered, the temple artisans devised for him a lightweight chair that the Acolytes of the era moved about the temple and palace. He did not even have the luxury of a wheeled chair for mobility.

At the temple, Terrance, his personal assistant, came out to the carriage and gathered him into his arms. It was only after Terrance settled him into the wheelchair at the top of the stairs that he realized Terrance was no longer the young Acolyte who saved his life after a near-fatal fall from the Elbow of Mount Estoliana. Zavier was sixty, closing on sixty-one. Terrance was now forty, and the father of three young men who were, like their father, extremely large.

He shrugged off thoughts of his assistant, the elevator, and his infirmity once he was at the top of the stairs. He wheeled himself into the temple and bypassed his office to go to the small room that was one of the few spaces that was almost exactly as it was from the inception of the temple. The floor was covered in the same tile as the two foyers. It was a small room – too small for any real purpose. Amadore declared it would be a perfect room to erect a small altar to *Deity*, wherein the different Keepers of the Soul of Estolia could commune with *Deity*. Not that they needed any special room or setup for that purpose. But it did help to focus his thoughts – and he knew from reading the writings of other Keepers that it helped them in similar ways.

The accident just after his youngest daughter was conceived precluded the ability to kneel at the altar, but *Deity* did not require obeisance or humbling of self like might be found in other religions.

He spent half an hour thinking about the upcoming week of festivities. If he understood the Promise of Zaccarias as well as he thought he did, then his son had already given his soul into the keeping of the young woman sailing with him to Estolia. In the meantime, Sebastian's woman was winging her way to Estolia. He hoped to encourage Sebastian to embrace the true Keeper of his Soul, even if she could not provide him with the most acute blessing promised by Zaccarias.

He heard someone joining him and turned to see his second son standing behind him. Together the two spent a little longer communing with *Deity* and then Theo pushed his chair out of the altar room and back into the office. Once Zavier was settled behind his desk, Theo sat in his customary chair next to the green and black marble statue of Zaccarias. It looked strangely naked without the sash of office that had adorned it for the last thirty years.

"This will only be the third time the first-born does not become Sovereign," Zavier said. "The first time the Keeper of the Soul of Estolia will have his sons be both Sovereign and Last Resort. I am a man blessed to have this privilege."

"Sebastian couldn't be Sovereign. Gregory didn't wish it. We both know that of the four of us boys, Leo is the best suited to be king." He grinned at his father, adding, "Besides, who would want it?"

Zavier chuckled. In the end, the position of King *was* a headache. He'd often thanked *Deity* that he'd been designated second-born, even though they would never know if he was first out of the womb. His brother filled the position of King perfectly.

"We've moved the festivities forward," Theo informed his father. "The more I have meditated on the issue, the more I believe that for Sebastian, it matters that he gives his soul into the keeping of his future wife on the day he turns thirty. Will his girl be here by then?"

"They should arrive at dawn," Zavier said. "It will be a most interesting day."

"I must greet my brother," Theo said, "And you and Uncle should also be there. Because he has abdicated, as has Gregory, it makes sense for Aunt Catherine to accompany her two sons to greet the airplane, while the rest of us go to greet the *Last Resort* as she makes her way into port."

Zavier looked at his son with fondness. The position of spiritual leader was the source of true power in Estolia. The Keeper of the Soul of Estolia had to be cultivated with the same care as the King. Of the four young boys raised so close together, he felt the selection of his own sons to fill the highest positions in the rising generation was the only logical choice. Sebastian found the Keeper of his Soul, but the Promises of *Deity* could never come true with her as Queen. Gregory, while having a lot of promise, had some time to go before reaching maturity. He would never have been able to fulfill the duties of Last Resort.

꒰ꘛ꒱

They were in the air about three hours before Melanie asked the question Bethany was hoping to avoid for the entirety of the flight. It was inevitable that Melanie's enthrallment with the horses presented to her would eventually wear thin enough so she would want to know further details. "Where, exactly, is this place?"

Zavier Zacarian had been adamant in that one phone call. "I do not believe your friend would agree to the commission if she knew you were coming to Estolia. Once the airplane is in the air, however, you are safe in telling her of your destination."

"Didn't I tell you already?" Bethany asked.

"Bethany... I know that tone." Melanie's attention was now sharp. She looked around the luxury airplane and then back at her friend. "What haven't you told me about this assignment?"

"You didn't really want to know the details once you saw the possible bonus," Bethany pointed out.

"Beth, Andestolian horses are like gold dust, there aren't many breeders, but they're divine in dressage, and gifted when it comes to jumping, and have superb stamina for cross-country competitions. You have no idea how valuable it would be to spend a year with a whole stable of Andestolians to ride and choose from. There was no way I was going to turn it down. But now we're on the way, I *do* need to know the details of the assignment."

Bethany said blithely, "This assignment is to do a photo-documentary of both a nation and the state religion. Apparently, it's a critical year and they'll be doing all kinds of things related to the religion over the year so they want us to document those events – that's why the job will last a year, with plenty of free time for you to exercise your passion."

"Yes, but *what* nation? What religion?"

"Estolia," Bethany said. This was the sticking point. Zavier didn't know, couldn't tell Bethany whether Melanie even knew Sebastian was from Estolia.

Melanie frowned slightly. "I think I've heard of Estolia, and fairly recently, but I can't remember where I heard of it. Is it one of the tiny European countries?"

Bethany was relieved. "Estolia is in the Mediterranean. It's a small island nation."

At dinner, Zavier said, "I've commissioned a photo journalist to come and document the *Transition* Year. The airplane will be arriving nearly simultaneously with the *Last Resort*." Zavier turned to Sebastian and Gregory. "I do not wish the photo journalist to arrive unheralded, so I figure it is best that the two of you, along with your mother, should greet the journalist. Your father, Theo, and I will greet the *Last Resort* and inform Leo of the changes that have taken place. If he's already placed his soul in her keeping we'll go directly to the temple."

"What suite has been prepared for the journalist?" asked Gregory.

"I believe the journalist is bringing an assistant. It might be a husband and wife team. I didn't get the details," Zavier said, "I've put them in the northwest tower suite. They will be with us through the birth of Leo's son, and his coronation, at the very least."

Leo pulled a large garment bag out of one of the closets in his cabin and went to Jackie's room. He paused outside her door, remembering the sweet sensation of her possession of him. Yesterday she wanted them to sleep together again but he had been forced to explain that – having given his soul into her keeping – he was constrained to wait for official sanction before he could touch her again.

He tapped on her door. When he heard her calling out to him, he took a deep breath and entered her cabin. "I have received word we will arrive at dawn. There was quite a brisk wind all night. This means we will arrive in less than an hour."

"My mother had the foresight to send a dress to Tenerife. When we docked there, we were able to pick it up. Visitors are rare, and the family are likely to be dressed up to receive you. Will you honor my mother's forethought and wear this dress she made sure to send?"

Jackie took the heavy garment bag and nodded. A blush colored her cheeks and he could imagine what she was thinking. He was thinking about it too. "I will be back in forty-five minutes."

❦

Jackie opened the garment bag. The dress inside was extravagant and beautiful. It was medieval, a light sage green with panels of violet purple on either side along with dark royal purple short sleeves.

When she was dressed, she looked at her reflection and her thoughts winged back to the despair she felt leading up to the day Leo walked into her life. She had less and less of her father's clear mind, most of the time he was an abusive stranger cursing at her. From near bankruptcy – injured and frightened – she was now hoping to marry him.

The previous day he explained that they would seek official sanction for their union. The only thing that stood in the way of their marrying would be if, for some reason, they didn't receive permission. She paused long enough to hug close the thought of Leo and everything she cherished about him.

She left her cabin and went up to the deck of the boat. The sky was a lighter gray to the east, and she could see the bulk of land obscuring the horizon.

Leo came over to her, leaning down to kiss her. She gave herself up to the kiss, reveling in the feel of his strong body, the warmth of his contours, the heat of a desire he couldn't contain, even if he could control it.

He pulled back when they heard a discreet cough. The captain was grinning at them. "I believe we will be at the dock just as the sun rises," he said. "Your father has commanded you to dress in full regalia. We have just enough time for you to change."

Jackie turned her attention to the approaching island. In the dimness of pre-dawn, she could not make out all the details. She watched, fascinated, as streamers of orange, red, yellow, peach, and cream started to festoon the skies. Shouts from the men on the dock preparing to secure the ship to its berth rang through the air. She heard the flapping of wind in the sails and the creak of the floorboards. The tang of sea-air was sharp, along with the scent of vegetation on the land. The air was cool on her bare arms.

A firm tread behind her had her turning to look at Leo. He wore a richly embroidered cape over a fancy shirt in purple and green. He had a sword strapped to his side and wore gloves on his hands. He had a hat under one elbow and held out his left hand to her. She crossed to his side and stood next to him.

As the captain had predicted, the boat was secured to the dock at the very moment the sun tipped over the edge of the world. For Jackie, it was as if the world went from a curious monochrome aside from the dazzling colors of the sky, to polychromatic splendor. She saw several horse-drawn carriages a short distance from the dock, and a group of three men approaching the boat. One was in a wheelchair.

🐚

Leo's attention as the sun finally tipped over the world, was on the lovely woman at his side. She was extraordinarily beautiful. He ached to join with her again; to have her as a permanent part of his life. Watching the enchantment on her face as the world gained color and depth brought him pleasure, the same pleasure he felt in knowing she chose *his* soul to take into her keeping.

He heard a shout and looked up, smiling with pleasure to see his father approaching. After he shouted a hello back, he extended his arm so he could escort his bride-to-be onto Estolian soil.

Once they reached the dock he turned his attention back to his father but the sight of his brother made him stop in pure shock. "Theo?" he said, his eyes on the sash his brother wore.

Theo inclined his head only slightly, the purpose – the *office* of Last Resort clearly at the forefront of his mind. He could not, if he was the Last Resort, do or be anything to Leo until the situation was resolved.

Leo's attention went from his father and his brother to his uncle. His uncle did not appear to be distraught in any way. He was smiling, relaxed. It was clear that something monumental and unique had taken place during the time he was away from his home. There could be only one conclusion since his brother was now Last Resort. This meant Leo was now the Heir Apparent.

Theo stepped forward, one hand gripping the dagger in his sash, the strength of purpose in his face was clear and evident. "As Last Resort, I Theobald Reginald Zacarian, must ask your intentions, Leo. Have you given your soul into the keeping of this woman?"

Leo drew himself up proudly, gently positioning Jackie in front of him, his hand resting over her abdomen, as he said with great dignity, "I, Balthazaar Leopold Zacarian, have taken this woman, Jacqueline Renee Cathay, and in so doing, *have* placed my soul securely within her keeping."

Theo turned his attention to Jackie. "My brother claims that he did take your purity. Did you willingly give this to him?"

Leo could only squeeze her tight in reassurance. She raised her chin. "I did willingly give him my heart, my soul, and my body."

"Do you accept Balthazaar Leopold Zacarian, along with his soul which already rests within your keeping? Or do you reject him?"

"I accept everything Leo is, and everything he will ever be," she said.

Zavier wheeled closer and said, "Do you, Balthazaar Leopold Zacarian, accept she who keeps your soul, or do you require your brother to exercise his role as the Last Resort?"

"I accept the Keeper of my Soul. She is a worthy Daughter of Estolia. Without her, I cannot live."

"This morning you will both enter the temple to complete your seven days of seclusion which you began on the *Last Resort*, thereafter to have your union sanctified by the spirit, the church, and the state, on the eve of your cousin's birthday," Zavier rolled closer to where Jackie stood and placed a hand over Leo's hand resting on her abdomen. He closed his eyes for a moment and then opened them. "You will continue to fulfill the Promise of Zaccarias, a son will be born to you, the future King of Estolia. *Deity* smiles upon your union."

13

The Celebrations

A week of seclusion following the exchange brings strength to each couple. His soul settles within her keeping, and she, in turn, learns how to gently keep and nurture his soul and the son that completes the exchange.

—Ignatius Siderious, descendant of Zacarian; Capitulo 33

T HE AIRPLANE sat on the tarmac for several minutes. Bethany felt her heart racing in her chest. She knew it wouldn't be long before Melanie would realize what she had done. She could only hope that in the end, she'd done the right thing for her friend. If nothing else, she reasoned, her friend would get the type of horse she'd coveted for years.

A set of mobile stairs was pushed up to the airplane. "Your luggage will be transported to the palace, to your rooms there," one of the unobtrusive stewardesses said.

They descended the stairs and saw two carriages waiting. Next to them were two men and a woman. Several other equestrians were standing nearby. Melanie was so entranced by the sight of the horses she didn't even notice the three individuals moving forward to greet them. Bethany, however, saw that Sebastian had eyes only for Melanie. The look in his eyes embarrassed her, and she looked away. Her eyes were caught and held by the warm amber eyes of the man standing next to Sebastian.

"Melanie!" Sebastian exclaimed.

Melanie's attention was swiftly centered on the man standing looking at her like she was the beginning and the end of his world. "Sebastian!" Her voice carried the same tone of longing and love as his.

He shook his head, as if in a daze, and then seemed to regain his equilibrium. Drawing himself up he bowed briefly and said, "Melanie, Bethany, may I present my mother, Catherine Moravia Zacarian, Queen of Estolia and keeper of my father's soul. Mother, this is Melanie Andrews and Bethany Danielson."

The exquisitely dressed woman stepped forward and embraced Melanie, kissing both her cheeks and then she did the same with Bethany. "Thank you," she whispered in Bethany's ear.

"Bethany, Melanie, may I present my brother, Gregory Annikaris Zacarian. Gregory, this is Bethany and Melanie."

Once the introductions were over, Sebastian pulled Melanie over to one of the carriages, leaving Bethany to travel back to the palace in the other one. She could only hope, based on the clear love the two of them showed, that they would patch up their differences.

"My uncle told us, after you were on your way, what he had done," Gregory said. "He hoped that if your friend came to Estolia, she and my brother would overcome whatever caused them to separate. I think they will."

"I believe you're right." She turned her attention to the beautiful woman and said "I had no idea his mother was the queen of anything. Does that make him a prince?"

Gregory was the one who answered, "My brother was to be the next King of Estolia. He believed your friend would not meet the requirements for Queen of Estolia. He abdicated so he would be free to pursue her."

She would never have guessed that the man who was such a constant companion to her friend was a Prince or planned to be King. She wasn't sure how Melanie would feel when she learned what he had done. Her eyes were troubled when they met those of the man across from her.

His smile was gentle as he explained, "He abdicated because he knew it was impossible for him to fulfill the requirements of being King. For him, the joy of making that decision was knowing he was free to pursue the only woman on the planet whom he could ever love."

She hoped Sebastian could reach through the wall that separated them. "She can't have children."

"I thought it would be something like that."

"She loves him."

"I do not doubt it," he said. "I am glad you brought her here."

"Oh!" she said, as realization hit her.

"What is it?"

"Then *you* will be King someday?" she asked.

"No," he said, smiling broadly. "I chose to *also* abdicate at the same time as my brother."

"You also love a woman who cannot be queen? The requirements must be tremendous."

He laughed outright. "No, Bethany, it is not that complicated. Your friend could not be Queen because she cannot have children. Those who have become Queen have been serving girls, slaves, stowaways, nannies, heiresses, and simple country girls. The requirement to be Queen is fertility and..." he paused. "Well, that is enough of that."

"What were you going to say?" She had to ask. He'd flushed slightly.

His mother spoke then, "Virginity, my dear. If a woman has been loose with her favors, she cannot fulfill the requirements of Zaccarias, and would never be seen to be the correct woman for the heir to the throne."

It was Bethany's turn to blush. She looked at Gregory and wondered if he was in love with someone impure.

He correctly interpreted her unasked question. "In my case, I simply knew, at a deep gut level, that I was not the right man for the position of King. I also knew, at the same level, that my cousin Leo *was* the perfect man for the job. He is returning to our nation today, and learning he is the Heir Apparent." His smile was broad. "The pressure for me is off. I can move forward happily without the burden of the crown."

Speaking to her son, the Queen of Estolia said, "You will assist Bethany when her friend is occupied with your brother." She had a slight smile on her lips.

"I would be delighted to help you, Bethany," Greg said.

❦

Sebastian stared at the woman who held his heart. Even if she couldn't hold his soul. He didn't care. There would never be another woman for him. He would forego the blessings associated with placing his soul in the keeping of a woman rather than live without her. She was everything he needed in his life.

"Sebastian," she whispered, "I didn't know we were coming to your country." Her face was white and her hands were trembling.

"I am *glad* you are here," he said firmly. "It is a good year to learn about my people, my faith." He picked up both of her hands, holding them tightly. "I can think of nothing more destined to bring me happiness than having you here, in my country, at this time."

Her eyes searched his, looking for answers within. "I haven't changed from the person I was when last we met," she said stiffly.

"I have not been happy a single day for the entire time we have been apart. I should never have left you."

They traveled in silence for a time before she tilted her head to the side and asked, "Your mother is the Queen? Does that make you a Prince?"

"Yes, I am a Prince. You should see me in my full royal outfit. Actually, you *will* see me all dressed up. I am sure your friend will take many photographs. Will you consent to partner me at the celebration ball?"

"I will *not* consent to a casual tumble in bed, Sebastian Zacarian," she said, "I value myself too highly."

"Melanie, I also value you highly. I respect you, and your boundaries. *Will* you partner me to the ball?"

She inclined her head before asking, "What is being celebrated?"

"My cousin is spending a week in seclusion with his bride-to-be. At the end of the week, they will marry. The celebration is something like a wedding reception. That will also be the eve of my thirtieth birthday, so it is dual purpose."

"Do you have an older brother?" Melanie asked.

"No. I have a younger brother."

"You will be King someday?"

He shook his head. "I was disqualified, the most I will ever be is Prince." He grinned. "I have never been so relieved. When I abdicated, my brother did too. My cousin, the one who is in seclusion with his bride-to-be, is now the future King."

She frowned. "It doesn't bother you?"

"I am not disturbed at all. I could not be King without the woman I wanted for my Queen."

Melanie's eyes widened as she took in his meaning. "Are you saying you abdicated because of me?"

His expression was gentle, his thumbs rubbing the back of each hand that he still held. "Melanie, I knew when I met you there would never be another woman for me. The requirements for our future Queen are very minimal, but you could not hold that position. To be King I had to be married and if I could not find a woman to marry who was acceptable, I could not be King. In a way, it is because of you, but it was more about the requirements being out of your reach. I would rather be with you."

"You shouldn't have done that," she said sharply. "You should have found someone else. Why would you do that? I'm not worth giving up a crown!"

"Melanie, you *are* worth it to me. Perhaps after this celebration month is over, you and I can discuss exactly why this was literally the only choice I had. Please, remember that I am happy with my choice. My father the King is happy with my choice. My brother – who also abdicated – is happy with my choice. My younger cousin and my uncle – our spiritual leader – are also happy with this decision. It was the right decision."

She dropped the topic. "Was all that information about Andestolians just a ruse to get me here?"

"I did not know you were coming here if you will recall. I do not know what you were promised. Andestolians originate in my country. In fact, one of the things I was thinking of doing, now that I will not be King, is work in the Royal Stables, specifically with Andestolians."

"Bethany and I are supposed to be here a year," Melanie said. "Will that bother you?"

"Not a bit. It saves me from choosing to forego the celebrations. I was trying to figure out which ones I could afford to skip so I could find you and convince you to come and visit Estolia."

❦

Jackie was tracing patterns on Leo's chest, thinking about everything that took place since they arrived. He brought her to the seclusion suite and told her they would use the suite for the first few days of their union, as part of the marriage process.

"We will be officially married when we are done with our seven days?" she asked.

He smiled at her. Enjoying the freedom to do what he wanted with her. "There is a formal ceremony after the seven days, a confirmation that the spirit does accept our union. It is a formality. But is special nonetheless."

"What exactly happened at the dock?"

"When my cousin decided it was impossible for him to become the King, he abdicated. If he was not capable, normally it would be his younger brother who would become the new Heir Apparent. However, Gregory, Sebastian's younger brother, turned it down instantly. He knew himself well enough to know he was not suited as King. If none of the King's sons are suitable to become the new King, then next in line for the throne are the sons of the King's younger brother. I am his oldest son. When Sebastian and Gregory abdicated, I became the Heir Apparent."

"That means you are to be King?" she asked.

He leaned towards her and kissed her for some time before answering, "Yes, Jackie, in nine months, when you give birth to our son, a week later we will become the King and Queen of Estolia."

"I don't know that I'll make a very good Queen," she said reluctantly.

"You will make a *superb* Queen of Estolia." He sighed deeply in contentment. "Both of my cousins were unhappy with their future roles. My younger brother and I, on the other hand are both quite happy with the way things turned out. In truth, the burdens are greater for those who take on those roles. But it is an accepted axiom, or proverb, here in Estolia to say that he whose burdens are greatest is given the greatest blessings in recompense. I consider you the greatest blessing in my life. By extension, you will bless all Estolia with your wonderful personality and fine compassion."

"Am I really pregnant?" she asked. Her hand lay over her abdomen.

"Zaccarias, our founder, was promised by *Deity* that he, and his descendants would always be blessed. If the heir to the throne always waited until his thirtieth year to marry, if he always chose a virgin, and married her within seven days of taking her virginity, and remained true to her, then Estolia would always know prosperity. In addition, as a mark of the benevolence of *Deity*, and to demonstrate *Deity* is still with us, each Estolian couple will have a son born to them, conceived during the exchange of her purity for his soul. You will always hold my soul within your keeping. I have taken your purity. You will give us a son as part of the exchange. As *Deity* has already shown the depth of our connection is inspired, I have no doubts whatsoever that you are pregnant with our son. The future King of Estolia."

❧

Since she arrived in Estolia, Melanie spent nearly all her time with Sebastian. Every time she looked for her friend, she saw her with Sebastian's brother.

The celebrations were worthy of getting in a photographer of Bethany's skill levels. She was imagining what the photos would look like. Especially in the beautiful cathedral for the solemn Sanctification Ceremony for Jackie and Leo. The couple glowed with their love. Melanie hoped fervently that somehow, she and Sebastian would come together. She wanted to experience a love as profound and moving as the love of the newlyweds.

She and Sebastian traveled back to the palace, with the rest of the entourage, after the ceremony, in an open topped carriage. Sebastian pointed out that white horses were always reserved for royalty. For their carriage, they had four dapple-gray horses.

The celebrations were hard to pay as much attention to as she should have. She was enjoying being with Sebastian too much. Over the previous week, they'd spent a lot of time together, but they had also been constantly in the company of others aside from that first carriage ride. They were dancing together when she asked Sebastian, "Is it my imagination, or have we been unable to spend any time alone since I got here?"

He laughed. She had missed the rich vibrant sound of his happiness slipping through her nerve endings during the four months they were apart. "My family have conspired to force me to wait until my thirtieth birthday prior to being allowed to be alone with you."

"Why?"

"Because, Mel, in Estolia a man does not marry before he is thirty, and he does not consummate the union with the woman he plans to marry before the eve of that birthday."

She wondered if he meant what she thought he meant. He must have sensed the stillness within her because he clarified, "In case it is not clear, Melanie, I plan to marry you just as soon as I am able to do so." He stopped dancing and cupped her face with both hands, looking at her, searching her eyes. "Will you marry me, Melanie, be mine for the rest of our lives together, be my *everything*?"

"Oh yes, Sebastian. Once you left I stopped living. You are *my* everything."

14

Rewards of Sacrifice

The riches to be found in the greater world can never supersede the riches found within the arms of Estolia, in the bosom of the temple placed securely within Mt. Estoliana.

~Fernando Gilmar Zacarian; Capitulo 75

MELANIE DANCED with each of the Zacarian men. Theo danced with her after Sebastian's proposal. He smiled at her fondly. "Has my cousin made his intentions known to you yet?" he asked her.

She nodded, a blush on her cheekbones. "He's asked me to be his everything."

"In Estolia, Melanie, a man is blessed if he consummates his future union upon the eve of his thirtieth birthday with a virgin. Seven days later he marries her, and his are the greatest of all blessings."

Her blush deepened to hear a man talk so openly about consummation and virginity.

"Sebastian believes you are no longer pure, and therefore cannot keep his soul in the traditions of Zaccarias. He will *still* attempt to seduce you tonight."

Melanie didn't know how to respond to this man.

"I speak with you about this not to cause you embarrassment, Melanie," Theo said, "but because it is important for you to understand his frame of reference, and the beliefs that are a critical part of his self-identity. Each Estolian is given great peace when difficult decisions are made and the result is pleasing to *Deity*. Sebastian felt profound peace when he abdicated. He knew there was no other woman who walked the planet whom *Deity* had available to keep his soul. It was you or no woman at all."

He stopped dancing and placed his hands on her shoulders, looking her directly in the eye, he said, "Sebastian will only know happiness if you consent to be his – both tonight when he seduces you, and at the end of the seven-day seclusion, when you promise to walk through life as both his partner and his wife. Have faith in him and in yourself."

Before she could respond, Theo stepped back a pace, bowed to her, and then turned and left her side. A touch on her elbow caught her attention. It was Gregory, Sebastian's younger brother.

Gregory said, "My brother is a very lucky man to have you."

"But he abdicated because of me."

"And I shall be grateful to you from now until my dying day. If he did not abdicate, I would have been forced into a role for which I had no aptitude. The only thing I was less suited for was the role of King. When he abdicated, I was given the freedom to do the same. You will never know how profound the peace from *Deity* that washed over me upon making that monumental decision."

Bemused, she said, "Your family is peculiar."

"Ours is the most blessed nation in the world. I *know* you will bring my brother the happiness he deserves."

The celebrations were almost over when Leo asked her to dance. He was very pleasant to her, praising her for coming to Estolia, for her attachment to his cousin.

"Does it bother *you* that I've made him abdicate?" she asked.

"No, Melanie. I did not grow up expecting to be King. But I firmly believe that it was always my destiny."

The clock started to chime the midnight hour and Sebastian cut into his cousin's dance, saying firmly, "This is *my* dance, cousin, go back to your lovely bride."

Melanie melted into Sebastian's arms. They felt so *right* around her, holding her. She was disappointed when the music ended and she saw the musicians packing up.

Was he really going to seduce her? When he walked with her back towards the tower guest suite she felt disappointed. But just before they got to the hallway that would lead to her suite, he led her down a different hallway and through a doorway into a bedroom. Her heart was leaping in her chest when she turned to look at him.

"Will you be mine, Melanie, heart, body, and soul? Will you give yourself to me?"

That was the moment when she realized she would never be happy apart from him. The misery of the four months apart from him told her that. She reached up to her hair and pulled it to the side, turning and presenting him with her back, and the fastening to her gown.

She felt his cool fingers on the nape of her neck fumbling with her zipper and then pulling it down. He pushed the dress off her shoulders and then unfastened her bra. Once he freed her breasts, she felt a shiver of loneliness when his hands left her entirely. She turned around, wondering if he'd decided to reject her after all, but she was stopped in her tracks by the sight of him swiftly unbuttoning his shirt, unfastening his pants, pushing his clothing off his body, until he stood in front of her dressed only in his underpants.

"Your soul entices me. I love you, Melanie. I will always love you." He stepped towards her and his lips covered hers. Their kisses went from subdued passion to red-hot inferno. Within moments they were on his bed and he was pulling her briefs down her legs before removing his own.

"Will you be mine, Melanie, forever?"

"Sebastian there will never be any other man for me. I love you."

He kissed her again, his body coming over her, merging smoothly with hers, pausing only when he heard her small sound of pain as he took her innocence. Her legs locked around him, and together they experienced the most profound blessing that came with the Promise of Zaccarias.

Afterwards, Melanie rested against his chest realizing he knew now that she had lied to him about her wild youth. She wondered if he was going to reject her for that lie. Especially if, somehow, it was the lie *itself* which caused him to give up his crown. Had she deprived this man of a crown because of her lie?

His voice was thick with emotion when he said, "I thought to forego the most profound blessings that *Deity* promised to the sons of Zaccarias when I knew you were the only woman on the planet I could ever love." He crushed her close to his body. "But the most significant blessing ever made to Estolians has *not* been denied me. The sweet sensation of your soul taking mine into its keeping will never be possible to explain. In all the *Capitulos*, not one Estolian has ever properly explained what it meant to give one's soul into the keeping of their spouse."

Melanie didn't understand. "I never should have lied."

"No, Melanie, *Deity* inspired you to tell me the one thing I needed to hear to know I could not be King. I was never meant to hold the office. But I was always meant to give my soul into *your* keeping. Had you told me you were pure, I might have tried to defy the Promise of Zaccarias and install you as the future Queen. No, we have been guided by *Deity* so our choices would be clearly defined."

"You aren't mad at me?" she asked in a small voice.

"No, I am not mad at you. I could never be mad at you. I am grateful you were so receptive to the promptings of *Deity*. Our historians will always look upon this event as further evidence of the extraordinary continuing presence of *Deity* in our lives, guiding us to the most profound future possible." Sebastian looked at the clock in the bedchamber. "If I know my uncle, he and Theo will be visiting us in about five minutes."

He kissed her before climbing out of the bed. He opened a chest to pull out a robe. After he shrugged into the robe, he then handed her a long nightgown.

While she slipped into the nightgown he went to the rumpled clothing on the floor near the door and scooped everything up so he could create a tidy pile on one chair. Once the clock started to chime, he returned to Melanie's side, sliding behind her, and putting his arms around her. She leaned back against him even as the clock finished chiming and the double doors to the room were opened.

Melanie couldn't help the rush of color to her cheeks when she saw Sebastian's father, the King, was holding one of the doors open, while his cousin Theo held the other, and his uncle Zavier wheeled into the room.

All three men had solemn expressions, and Melanie wondered if she misunderstood the things these men communicated to her earlier.

Zavier halted in front of them, the other two men standing even with his shoulders. "Sebastian?"

"I have placed my soul securely within Melanie's keeping," Sebastian responded.

Zavier looked at Melanie. "My nephew claims that he has taken your purity, and in return, you keep his soul. No woman is constrained to remain unwillingly. Do you accept Sebastian Guillermo Zacarian, or do you reject him?"

"I could never reject Sebastian!" Melanie said, shocked at the question.

He rolled closer and set his hand over Sebastian's hand, resting on her abdomen. He looked up at the two of them sharply.

"Sebastian, bring a couple of pillows over here," Zavier commanded.

Melanie felt bereft for a moment when Sebastian moved away from her. He picked up two of the ornamental pillows and set them in front of her.

"It is critical, Melanie, that I give you a blessing. Will you consent?"

Melanie looked at Sebastian and he smiled and nodded. She turned to the man in the wheelchair and said, "What do I do?"

"Kneel on these pillows. Theo and I will place our hands upon your head. We will say a type of prayer over you."

Melanie followed their instructions, her eyes meeting Sebastian's and feeling reassured by the love shining out.

Zavier's accent was more pronounced as he spoke, his blessing was in English.

Melanie Christine Andrews, Deity influences our lives in subtle ways. Since the beginning of our nation, we have felt the gentle push to fulfill the promises Zaccarias made to Deity so we might feel the blessings Deity promised him. Sebastian, having been born 87th in line for the throne, was never destined to wear the crown, nor to bear the burdens of being the King of Estolia. In meeting you, Melanie, Sebastian recognized you were the only woman capable of keeping his soul.

It is accepted as truth that the greatest sacrifices lead to the most profound blessings. Your life together will be filled with joy. You will work with Sebastian to refine the Andestolian breed, and ultimately this work will serve the purposes of Deity. You will discover a peace in your decisions and will know always that your joy in life is your reward for the willingness to sacrifice.

While you leave no children here upon this planet, know that your actions will have a lasting impact on both this nation, and on the greater world. Deity smiles upon you. I say these things in the light and sight of Deity.

When Melanie got to her feet, she was moved by the heartfelt hug the King gave her. Only in that moment did she really believe that this family was glad she was with Sebastian. Regardless of the impact on his role in this nation.

"You will spend a week in the royal seclusion suite," Zavier said. "When you are finished with your seclusion, and the spirit confirms your alliance, Sebastian will study in the temple for his elder year. Afterward, you'll both be apprenticed to the Stable master, to take over his role when he retires."

The squall of young Isaiah punctuated the words of the ceremony to transfer the crown from Maximiliano to his nephew. Zavier looked out at the various participants in the living drama that was the ruling family of Estolia. His heart surged with pride and love. He was proud of his son, Leo, as his brother placed the crown upon his head. Young Jackie was transformed from the isolated young girl kept at home caring for her father, battered emotionally and psychologically. Now she was every inch a Queen of Estolia, the glow of love, motherhood, and happiness colored her features and gave her the presence every Queen was described as possessing.

His attention then turned to Sebastian. *His* joy was transparent and sincere. While the role of King was what he grew up expecting for the first thirty years of his life, it was clear he had no regrets as he watched the crown being placed upon Leo's head. Zavier felt privileged to not only have his son be made King, but to witness everything about the young man who would never be king, and never be a father. It was not surprising to Zavier, but it was fulfilling to know *Deity* was still watching out for the Sons and Daughters of Zaccarias – bringing them extraordinary happiness and profound joy.

He looked from Sebastian to his second son. Taller than average and somewhat awkward, he would make a fine Keeper of the Soul of the nation. He did not know every element of his second son's future, but he sensed his pathway would hold both profound happiness as well as true heart-wrenching sorrow. He closed his eyes, knowing that in some way, *Deity* would teach his second son a lesson he, Zavier, did not personally have the strength to learn. Perhaps, he thought, perhaps there were *some* lessons better not learned. He reached up and wiped away a tear as he turned his attention away from his son.

The next individual his attention turned to was his nephew Gregory. He knew Gregory was in love with Melanie's former partner Bethany. He frowned when he saw the kiss Gregory bestowed on her. If Zavier did not act, Gregory was at risk of taking Bethany's purity well in advance of his thirtieth birthday. He was about to turn away, to look at some of the other members of the family, but there was something about the couple that disturbed him. After a couple of moments, he forced himself to look away.

His eyes then focused on the one person guaranteed to distract him.

Harmony.

He felt the impact of her sweet presence in his life. The woman who had exchanged souls with him. No other son of Zaccarias was given the privilege and obligation of holding the soul of another. And, in holding her soul, he knew it was but a proxy to represent the souls of every Estolian who embraced the Promise of Zaccarias and lived their lives in accordance with the faith.

Harmony was the only woman asked to give up her soul. With the sweet strength her soul gave him, he was able to meet the needs of all Estolians. No other Estolian was given a gift as profound as that shared by the Keeper of the Soul of Estolia and his wife; and no other Estolian was asked to make so great a sacrifice in the day to day running of the nation.

Part 3 – Witness Protection

༄ Cast of Characters ༄

Balthazaar Leopold Zacarian – (Leo) 87th King of Estolia

Cassiopeia Zacarian – (Cassie) Daughter of the 87th King of Estolia

Eduardo Lestalt – Professor at Fresco University in Alabama

Isaiah Monterrey Zacarian – Heir Apparent and First-born son of the 87th King of Estolia

Jacqueline Cathay Zacarian – (Jackie) 87th Queen of Estolia

Lazarus Ezekiel Zacarian – (Zeke) Second Son of the 87th King of Estolia

Morgan Luc-Dumaine – Distant relative of Harmony Zacarian (Wife of 86th Keeper of the Soul of Estolia) from France

Randolph Smythe – Former Associate of Lily Elaine Tirane

Taryn Lilaine – aka Lily Elaine Tirane, Student at Fresco University

Theobald Reginald Zacarian – (Theo) 87th Keeper of the Soul of Estolia

Exploration of World Religions

1989 CE

With eighty-six generations of Capitulos and Ensayos, I believed there would be nothing new to write about for the modern generation. Then the Heir Apparent and the Last Resort abdicated and it was clear in all things Deity is as close – and as necessary – to us now, as he was to Zaccarias and Estoliana.

~Balthazaar Leopold Zacarian; Capitulo 87

LILAINE LEANED BACK against the cement column. This was her favorite place to study. She could look out on the other university students but did not have to mingle. Her years with Randolph didn't make mingling easy. Thinking about Randolph had her snapping her book shut. She had an appointment with her faculty advisor. In moments her school bag was packed and she was striding briskly towards the building.

She knew he was going to advise her to take a lighter load next semester. She couldn't explain to him *why* she wanted to keep so busy. Once in the building she paused to take a deep breath and do her best to shed the memories that threatened to swamp her.

She knocked on Dr. Long's office door and entered at his invitation. She liked him. He was several inches shorter than her own modest height and his features looked like he had a variety of ethnicities in his pedigree. He had a way of lecturing that caught the students' attention and laughed as often at himself as at others.

"Taryn, one of the requirements of your scholarship to this university is that you take one of our *Explorations* courses. After looking over your information, I'd like to encourage you to take the *Exploration of World Religions* course. We have one small section of the class and you could take it and get it out of the way."

Every time she heard the name she was using, she had to control a desire to shudder in distaste. She wasn't given a choice regarding her name. The only thing that made it tolerable was that she could ask to be called by her last name, Lilaine. The courtyard clock started to chime, so she didn't bother to correct him or the name he used.

She had to fulfill the requirements this university placed before her, and the

Explorations classes were one of those elements they built their reputation upon. As Dr. Long stated, it was best to get the requirement finished, rather than wait and possibly take one of the less desirable courses later.

They discussed her schedule of classes and at the end of their meeting, he signed off on it. While she took the completed form to the main office, she realized how blessed she was to be given the chance to discover herself here in this tiny private university.

⚜

"Over the four months of this course," droned the professor, "each of you will select a different unique religion to *explore*. We will meet once a week to discuss the aspects of world religions to guide you in your explorations. Some of you may have chosen this university *because* of our *explorations* courses, so you may all know that the purpose behind the class is to help each of you become lifelong independent learners, willing and able to explore whatever topic grabs your interest throughout your lives." He stopped to cough, his eyes shut and his face contorting in pain. When he finished, his voice was wheezing, whistling in his chest. "During this course you will each explore the religion assigned to you. I will make the time to meet with each of you once every week or two."

Lilaine looked at the list of esoteric religions. She had only heard of one of them, and that one had already been selected. When she'd been urged to take the course, she didn't realize they had allowed her to be in the class even though it was already filled to the normal capacity with nine students. A tenth religion – Estolian – was penciled in to the bottom of the typewritten list and was the only one not yet selected. She wrote her name next to it.

Over the course of the two-hour lecture, the professor gave them tips on how to proceed in their explorations as well as some information on what their finished term project would be like. After the class let out, Dr. Lestalt requested that she remain behind.

"Do you mind walking with me back to my office?" he asked her. "We can speak while we are walking."

They slowly walked across the small campus. Dr. Lestalt asking her how she was settling into the university, what she thought of her first semester. Once they were in the spacious office he set his books down and gestured for her to have a seat.

"Tell me a little bit about yourself, my dear," he encouraged her. His breathing was labored.

"I grew up in a very remote area of Alaska," she told him her cover story, still uncomfortable with lying. "Because we were so far from others, my mother homeschooled me. I finished my graduation requirements and applied at several universities. My father thought a small university would be easier to attend as compared to a large one. When I was offered a scholarship here at Fresco University, he wanted me to accept it."

"Do you have brothers and sisters?" he asked her. He was no longer wheezing, and seemed to be doing much better overall.

She thought of the brothers and sisters she grew up with but shook her head. She was grateful her cover story had her as an only child. "My parents didn't expect to have any children. They were in their early fifties when my birth parents were killed in an airplane crash near their place. They took me in and raised me. I didn't have any other relatives."

"Did you go home and visit your parents during the recent holidays?"

She shook her head. Truthfully, she related the demise of the couple who were part of her cover story, "Once I left for school, my parents decided to take a trip they saved up for over a lifetime. They planned to do it earlier, but when I came along they postponed their trip nearly fifteen years for my sake. They were on the Gambian Queen." The notorious ship had come aground and capsized, with nearly two-thirds of the passengers killed in the ensuing disaster. "They would have been happy to go together, and to know they died only after they saw me situated in life." The one time she met the elderly couple, she liked them, and she had to blink back tears at the thought of their death.

"I'm very sorry to hear of your loss," he said solemnly. "If I or anyone else on the faculty can help you in any way, you must share with us your needs."

"Thank you." She paused and then shared, "Strangely I felt more peace than grief. They lived a long and fulfilling life, and I know they felt as though they had accomplished their major life goals. I was in college, they were together, it was a blessing for them and just exactly what they wanted out of the end of their lives – no loose ends, the chance to go together."

He was silent for several minutes, perhaps in tribute to her parents, and the loss she was reliving. "I wanted to speak to you about your assignment. Normally I have only nine students in the class, but Dr. Long asked me to take on one further student. I agreed, but whenever I do take on a larger class than expected, I give Estolia as the religion to investigate. That is why I asked you to come to my office. Estolia is perhaps the hardest assigned religion because there is very little about it available in reference books. I happen to know a couple of individuals who are Estolian, and I wanted you to know that I will arrange for you to meet with one or both if you wish. I think you will find it an interesting religion to study. Especially as every member of the little-known country of Estolia is also a member of the faith."

❦

Four weeks later, Lilaine was working on her homework and trying to quell the feelings of frustration that kept welling up. She finished her English and her math homework. She closed her math book, picked up her English and math notebooks and pushed them both into her satchel.

She looked at the final notebook. With a slight sigh she reached for it, pulling it towards her slowly. When it was in front of her, she ran her fingertips over the cover.

She took a deep breath and then flipped it open. The first three pages in the notebook were filled with all the questions she had come up with to ask about the religion.

She ran her finger down the list, pausing only a couple of times at the few questions she was able to answer. She closed the notebook abruptly. She went to the local library, and even made the journey to the larger library at nearby Collings University, but there was almost no information at all about the country and even less about the religion.

She learned that Estolia was an island nation with about ten thousand inhabitants. The language was like Spanish but considered unique – and almost extinct. It had an inherited monarchy and had enjoyed prosperity since 720 years before the current era. That meant the nation was more than 2700 years old. It seemed incredible that there wasn't more information. No other nation existed that long.

She followed that idea, thinking that she might discover more information if she focused on its longevity. But when she tried to look up Estolia by researching the nation with the longest life-span. She made no progress. According to what she could uncover in the library, the nation that existed the longest was the Roman Empire – lasting a little more than 1500 years. There was no mention at all about Estolia.

She found one obscure reference in a society newspaper from San Francisco, in 1905. The source was Quincy Lucullus Amadore. "Men of Estolia are brainwashed to believe that they'll be impotent if they don't marry before they turn thirty-one. Yet another piece of evidence that the Estolian religion is really just an elaborate cult."

Aside from that one reference, she couldn't find anything else negative about the religion in any of her research. She even researched the man who *did* make the one derogatory comment, but the information about him was sparse and ended with a short obituary following the earthquake in San Francisco.

For a religion so dominated by men, she expected to find at least a few grumblings from women, but there didn't seem to be any.

During one of her private meetings with Dr. Lestalt, she expressed her frustration with the assignment. The other students in the class had all discussed their assignments and remarked upon the abundance of information that was available for them to choose from. In her case, it was the opposite.

Dr. Lestalt admitted, "This is why I don't put Estolia on my list, and why my class size is limited to nine. However, I would not give you an impossible assignment. As I mentioned in the beginning of the semester, I do know a few individuals who are, or will be in the States who are members of the Estolian faith. I can arrange a meeting for you, and you can get the information directly from the source."

"When would I meet with them?" She wanted to be successful in college after her interrupted high school years. If she failed this course, she'd have to take another *Explorations* course.

"Let me make a call and find out," he said, pulling his desk telephone towards him. He had a jovial expression on his pudgy face as he dialed a phone number and leaned back in his chair. He winked at her while he listened to the phone. After a minute he left a message, "Cassiopeia, this is Eduardo Lestalt, and I was looking forward to speaking with you. I know your schedule can be difficult to pin down, so it may not be possible, but if you can spare the time, I have a student who is learning about Estolia, and I was hoping you could share with my student the perspective of women in your country. Please give me a call back. I will also see if Isaiah can spare her the time. For the record, I know your uncle Theo would consider her an ideal Daughter of Estolia if he were to meet her."

After he hung up he saw the puzzled expression on her face. "They use some of the most flowery language as a matter of course," he explained. "Women are both peripheral to the religion, and the central tenet if you can imagine the dichotomy. They both love and revere women but feel that spiritual guidance is necessary only for the men of Estolia. A Daughter of Estolia is one who would fit in well in their society, and who would not need religious guidance. In truth, few women from our culture could – or would – be a Daughter of Estolia." When she still looked confused, he clarified, "I was complimenting you on your character."

"How do you know so much about it?" Lilaine asked him, fascinated by what he was telling her.

His expression was shadowed and he said with sadness in his voice, "I had the opportunity to marry a woman from Estolia. I did not cherish her or value what she had to offer, so I ended up being the one to lose out."

Lilaine felt like there was something he wasn't saying in his response, but before she could fully analyze it, he was calling another number. Once again, he leaned back and an unruffled look of affability replaced the sadness that had colored his features.

"Isaiah, my good friend," he said into the phone. "I call you to beg a favor. I have a young student who has been assigned to learn everything that she can about Estolia. There is no person more qualified to share Estolia's secrets than you." He paused to listen. After a minute, he frowned slightly and said, "I see, yes, of course, I realize now that the timing is difficult. We do have a week-long vacation commencing in two days, but I cannot be sure if my young student has specific plans. I shall enquire and call you back." He paused again for some time before telling the other person good-bye.

Leaning back the professor grinned at her. "It appears that there is to be a ceremony in Estolia over the coming holiday. Because of this, my friend Cassiopeia will be journeying to Estolia on Friday, with plans to return by Sunday a week later. Isaiah will also be similarly busy in Estolia." He smiled gently towards her. "Would you be willing to travel to Estolia over the vacation? There can be no greater way to learn about the land and the religion than by visiting."

"I couldn't possibly afford the cost of the flight," Lilaine demurred.

"Is that the major objection you have my dear? The cost of flying out? Or is there another reason you cannot go? A boyfriend perhaps?"

She could feel the heat of a blush. Discussion of her love life was somehow embarrassing. Probably, she thought wryly, because her love life was nonexistent. "I have no boyfriend. I've never had a boyfriend." Randolph didn't count. He'd never taken her on a date, kissed her only once in all the time she knew him. "But I have very little aside from the full-ride scholarship. I don't have a job to pay for extra things."

"So, it is merely finances that keep you from being able to journey to Estolia?"

She nodded.

"Excellent," he said, "Then you *can* go to Estolia. You see, Cassiopeia's father is a man of some import in Estolia, and for this reason, he is going to send the family jet to pick her up. They can bring you my dear, and it won't cost them or you any money."

Lilaine was tempted. But she pointed out, "I couldn't afford a hotel."

"My dear, there are no hotels in Estolia. In truth, tourism itself is prohibited. It is a very insular nation that holds its secrets very close indeed. However, my good friend Isaiah knows what I do here at this university, and he will cut through the red tape to make it possible for you to visit. You will not be able to bring your camera or any recording devices with you, but they will allow you to visit. You will be a guest and will be provided with a guest room. This invitation is extraordinary. It is, perhaps, a testament to my friendship with the members of some of the elite families of that great nation, that they will allow me to send one of my students to visit. It's an exceptional opportunity. I would consider it a great honor if you would be willing to attend this ceremony – they only have it once every thirty or so years. It is a changing over of the religious mantle to a new leader of the religion."

Lilaine was infected with the enthusiasm of going to an exotic location. Before she could have second thoughts she agreed to spend her spring vacation in the small country of Estolia as Cassiopeia's guest.

⁂

Isaiah looked at the dossier as it printed out, studying the features of the young girl who would be flying out to Estolia with his sister. Once the printer stopped spitting out papers he dialed the number of the American University professor who once had the chance to enjoy the richest blessings of Estolia but who, in his ignorance, spurned the opportunity.

"You received the information?" the professor didn't waste words.

Isaiah looked again at the eyes of the girl in the photo. "Yes, though the information is quite sparse. What makes you think this girl could be a Daughter of Estolia?" Few women from the United States had the necessary temperament – much less purity of body, self, and soul – to find happiness in Estolia.

"I cannot say why I am convinced of this, it is something I cannot personally fathom. I was having lunch with Cassiopeia and when I saw Taryn Lilaine, I was amazed at the imperative I had to assure she learned of Estolia, and if possible met – with you."

The door to Isaiah's office opened and he smiled at his uncle as he entered the room. Isaiah turned his attention to his friend, yielding up the photograph when his uncle reached for it.

"Once I had this feeling that she must learn about Estolia, go there if possible, I thought fate would intervene and keep me from following up on this most extraordinary impulse I have ever had. Before I could even begin to find out who she was, she boarded a bus and was gone." The professor paused before saying, "When I was asked the very next day if I would be willing to allow another student to take my *Exploration of World Religions* class, I was amazed to learn she was a student at my university and would be – if I were to allow it – a student in my class. *Deity* was not willing to be denied."

"She will travel with Cassiopeia?"

"Yes, I was able to convince her to make the journey."

Isaiah looked up at his uncle in amazement when he took the phone and spoke into it, "Eduardo, it is Theo, you must tell me about this young girl."

Isaiah studied his uncle's face as he listened to the American professor. He had seen his uncle in the grip of a vision numerous times. As the man in charge of the soul of Estolia, his was a great burden, and a wonderful gift, to see into the hearts of men and women. It was clear there was something uniquely compelling about the young woman.

While his uncle discussed the young woman, Isaiah looked through the papers that accompanied the photograph. He saw that she lost her parents as a toddler and was raised by an elderly couple who had recently passed on. She was considered extremely gifted based on her standardized test scores, though quite sheltered. During her first term at the university, she took a heavy load of classes and received top marks. This term she'd been encouraged to take a slightly lighter load, with the *Exploration of World Religions*. From what he could tell, she'd been raised without any specific religious influence.

"We will receive her visit with great delight," Theo said. "If she is, in fact, a true Daughter of Estolia, we will expect you to help out on your end."

Once he hung up, Theo turned to look at Isaiah. "I have never, in all my time as Keeper of the Soul of Estolia, felt as strongly about any woman. Even when I met the Keeper of my own Soul the sense I got was not as strong as I have for this young woman – for you. You are prepared for this?"

Isaiah nodded. He grew up knowing what his duties and obligations were. He had the opportunity to enjoy his freedom, spending four years going to college in the United States, partaking of the casual relationships that so permeated that society.

Since he returned to Estolia those pursuits seemed shallow and meaningless, and he focused his attention on learning everything that would be necessary to pilot his nation through the uncharted waters of an increasingly complex world. He expected to spend the next several months searching for the one woman who would make it possible for him to assume the mantle of leadership and provide his father with the freedom from duty each monarch looked forward to. Having met, at one time or another, each of the young women on the island who were likely to be a soul-mate, he had grave doubts that he would be able to find her within the boundaries of his country. Few of the ruling class discovered their soul mate within Estolia. He was certain the upcoming visit would clarify many things for him regarding his future, and that of Estolia as a nation.

He didn't notice the frown of concern on his uncle's face as his uncle looked at the photograph one last time.

Heir Apparent

Glorious Estolia. A hidden paradise where dreams come true, where the soul rejoices. Where love at first sight is normal, and family relationships are the foundation of faith.

~Yuliana Maria Zacarian; Ensayo 84

LILAINE PAID THE TAXI driver and then looked at the small building. The main terminal at the airport was more than a mile away. She'd been directed to come to the smaller auxiliary building. She wasn't sure exactly what to do from this point on. When a vivacious woman around her own age came up to her smiling, she smiled back shyly.

"You must be Taryn." the woman said. "I am Cassiopeia Zacarian. It would please me if you would call me Cassie. My family calls me that. The other is quite a mouthful anyway. My family is quite fond of long complicated names."

While she was speaking a couple of somber men in suits came and picked up Lilaine's luggage.

"I actually prefer to be called Lilaine."

Cassie hooked her arm in Lilaine's and steered her towards the main building. "I can already tell that we shall be great friends," she burbled on, happily guiding Lilaine through the building and out another door that led to the tarmac. A small private jet stood near the building, with a set of mobile stairs leading up to the open door. Cassie blithely led Lilaine up the stairs and into the airplane.

"I am sorry to hustle you up like this," Cassie said, "but when it is time to return to Estolia, I am always most anxious. The sooner we are boarded, the sooner we are on our way. You will love my country!"

***

Over the course of the flight, Lilaine learned a lot about the country of Estolia. Cassie had a bubbly personality and the ability to talk endlessly. Lilaine did more listening than speaking.

She learned that the island nation had been in existence longer than any other. "You will not find that information in encyclopedias," Cassie confided. "We like our privacy much too much to be a curiosity. We have been able to remain shielded from scrutiny because of our lack of resources. No gold, or diamonds, or oil. No major exports. Self-sufficient and unimportant. We like it that way."

"Even atlases don't seem to have much information on Estolia," Lilaine pointed out.

Cassie giggled, explaining, "They need to have permission for more than the most basic information, and my father refuses to give it."

"Your father?" Lilaine asked, curious. "Dr. Lestalt told me that your father was a man of some import in your country."

"Of course, you could not know, but yes, he is one of the most important men in the country. My uncle has three titles. He is First Consul to the King, Last Resort, and the Keeper of the Soul of Estolia."

"What does all that mean?"

"Being the Keeper of the Soul of Estolia means," Cassie said slowly, as if gathering her thoughts, "that he is the leader of the Estolian religion. He receives inspiration from *Deity*; gives special blessings; and oversees the religious and historical education of the young men of Estolia. It is considered the most powerful position in Estolia. Even more powerful than the King."

"Is every inhabitant of your nation also a member of the religion?" Lilaine was fascinated by the intricacies of the tiny nation.

"Yes, of course," Cassie said as if there was never any doubt. "Nobody is accepted as an immigrant who is not a member of the faith. Those who are not members of the faith would be unhappy and uncomfortable in our nation. There are perhaps as many as five, maybe even ten adherents to the religion who live off the island for every one adherent who lives on the island. We do not, however, seek converts."

"What does Last Resort mean?"

"If the Heir to the throne, the Heir Apparent, cannot fulfill his obligations, it is the duty of the Last Resort to be the one to step in and do so. It is a very important role, but it does not last long. My brother Isaiah will be able to explain to you more of this, as it has to do with the obligations imposed by our faith, specifically regarding the royal succession."

"And what was the third thing you said about your Uncle?"

"He is the First Consul. This means he is the first man the King goes to when he needs advice. If something terrible were to happen to the King, the First Consul would take over until the Heir Apparent was ready to be King."

Lilaine asked later in the flight, "Why do you live in the States?"

Cassie flushed, looking momentarily unhappy. "There is no man in Estolia who has moved me. Not all women born in Estolia are true Daughters of Estolia, with but one soul worthy of their Keeping. Those who cannot find a soul mate tend to leave Estolia and search in the greater world. Despite the great blessing my Uncle gave me seven days after I was born, which he repeated when I turned eighteen – that I was indeed a true Daughter of Estolia – I fear that the man whose soul I could keep does not exist, or will, like my family's good friend Eduardo Lestalt, reject the Keeper of his Soul."

"I don't understand this Keeping of the Soul stuff."

Cassie brightened, saying, "A man's soul is unhappy until it finds its true home – in the keeping of his wife. When he meets the woman who is destined to be his, he will know it and must act on it. If he hands his soul into her keeping, he must choose to marry her. No man can live without his soul. If he spurns the woman who has charge of his soul, he will not survive."

The explanation didn't exactly clear everything up. "Dr. Lestalt mentioned something about that, but I thought it was a long time ago that he loved and lost," she pointed out.

A sad expression settled on Cassie's face; she explained, "In his case, he met the woman who would keep his soul, but he never gave it *into* her keeping. The soul knows its home and having found it, it will never settle any other place. So, he lives without the love that he spurned."

"What happened to her?" Lilaine asked.

"She was thrown from her horse and died," Cassie said. "My aunt. Eduardo has always been a great friend of the family; his loss was even more extreme than our own. I do not remember my aunt, as she died before I was born. But Eduardo has been like an uncle to the three of us. My brothers and I that is. Likely he would have seen the truth and come to entrust her with his soul, but he was denied that chance."

"It sounds like you have an amazing country and an even more amazing set of beliefs," Lilaine said thoughtfully, wondering if it would be possible to properly understand a faith without in some way living it.

The intercom in the airplane suddenly came to life, and Lilaine listened to the foreign words with curiosity. This was the first time she heard the actual language of Estolia. She found it exotic, fluid, and evocative. When the announcement ended, Cassie unbuckled her seatbelt and jumped to her feet. "The captain says there is just the right amount of time for the two of us to dress for our arrival!"

"Dress for our arrival?" She'd handed over her suitcases when she got to the airplane. "I don't have a change of clothing available in my carry-on bag," she explained.

Cassie grinned at her. "Eduardo knew, as a man with great perception, that you would feel awkward if you were not properly dressed during this visit. He shared this concern with me, and I have remedied the situation. We are exactly the same size, so you will be able to use some of my own items of apparel. I will have a special gown commissioned for the celebration, of course, and they will make one for you at the same time. It will be extraordinarily exciting!"

Lilaine knew an irresistible force when she met it, realizing it would do no good to argue. She followed Cassie to a room at the tail of the airplane with two gowns hanging from hooks. One was a deep purple with a tracery of gold and green accents, while the other was deep green with purple and silver accents. Cassie crossed over to the green gown and said, "This color is not flattering on me. It would be absolutely splendid with your red hair."

Forty minutes later Lilaine was staring at herself in a full-length mirror in amazement. The dress was off-the-shoulder, exposing more cleavage than she felt comfortable exposing, and was absolutely the most extravagant thing she had ever owned or worn. She looked over at Cassie, whose darker beauty was absolutely stunning in the purple and green gown. The flight crew were all wearing outfits that were purple and green. "Are these colors special in some way?"

"They are the state colors. Purple and green. Our flag is mostly purple and green."

Lilaine followed Cassie to their seats and about five minutes later the jet began its final approach. Cassie reached across the aisle and took Lilaine's hand, smiling happily at her new friend as if they'd been friends for years instead of only the duration of one long transatlantic flight.

✦

Shortly after the airplane taxied to a halt the door was opened and Cassie was eager to disembark. Lilaine felt a sense of adventure to be visiting this strange land with such peculiar customs. She decided as they approached the door and her first real glimpse of Estolia, she would enjoy every minute, store up every impression, and not worry about fitting in.

Lilaine saw several horse-drawn carriages, as well as an assemblage of individuals who looked very much like they must be members of the ruling class. She began to realize that Cassie might be more than simply the niece of the Last Resort. Remembering her vow to enjoy every element of her unusual vacation she lifted her chin slightly and smiled more broadly. Cassie grinned at her and began the descent of the stairs – carefully due to the voluminous skirts that both girls wore.

At the bottom of the stairs, Cassie grabbed Lilaine's hand and led her towards the man at the head of the small group. He was wearing a richly embroidered elaborate cape, a ceremonial sword, and a crown. He looked very much like he could be a prince or a King.

Cassie launched herself into his arms, receiving a loving embrace. Then she turned with her arm around his waist and said, "Lilaine, this is my father, Balthazaar Leopold Zacarian, Duke, Sovereign, and King of Estolia. Father, this is Taryn Lilaine, a protégé of Eduardo Lestalt. She prefers to go by the name of Lilaine."

Lilaine was just processing the implications of the introduction when she was pulled into the arms of the man she was just informed was the King of this nation. He hugged her tightly before kissing her on both cheeks and smiling into her eyes. "I hope I may call you Lilaine," he said to her, "and I would be pleased if you would do me the honor of calling me Leo."

Lilaine nodded shyly in agreement, seeing genuine pleasure in his eyes.

With his arm around her shoulders, he guided her to a man who looked very similar to him, with slightly longer blonde hair, a goatee, and wearing purple and green robes that looked vaguely religious, something like the robes of a monk. A black sash went from his right shoulder down to his left hip. "May I present my brother, Theobald Reginald Zacarian, he who Keeps the Soul of Estolia, my First Consul, and my Last Resort. Theo, this is Taryn Lilaine."

Both of her hands were taken in his and he looked down at her silently for an extended length of time, his eyes searching hers. Finally, with a strange note in his voice, he said to her, "I am pleased to meet you, Taryn Lilaine, I see now why our good friend Eduardo felt you should visit Estolia. You could easily be a Daughter of Estolia. In truth, you honor us by your presence in our tiny country." He smiled at her before asking her, "As the leader of the Estolian faith, I ask if you will do me the greatest honor and allow me to give you a formal blessing during your visit." He paused and then as if he sensed her reluctance to agree to something without further details, he added, "You would be required to sit in a special chair, and I and my Acolyte would place our hands upon your head. We would then say a special prayer in the Estolian language. As a further gift to you, you would be presented with a scroll containing the words of the blessing, in both Estolian as well as the best possible translation into English. It would not take more than half an hour of your time, but it would give me great pleasure."

Lilaine nodded acquiescence.

"I should like, now," he said, "to introduce you to Lazarus Ezekiel Zacarian, my nephew, and Cassie's younger brother. He is my Acolyte and will soon take on the role of Last Resort. Eventually, he will take over my positions as First Consul and Keeper of the Soul of Estolia. Zeke, this is Taryn Lilaine."

He was in his late twenties with light brown, almost blonde hair, and amber colored eyes. He pulled her into his arms for a hug and then looked at her with the same intensity of purpose, if only for a moment before he grinned at his uncle. "I see what you mean, Uncle Theo."

The last person to greet her stepped forward. Whereas Zeke was dressed reminiscent of the monk, this man was dressed in the style of the King; with a similar cape and ornamental sword. He didn't have a crown. His hair was a deep mahogany with incongruous light gray eyes. His eyes met hers with a peculiar intensity.

The King stepped forward again and said to her, "This is my oldest son, heir to the throne, he whose burdens and blessings are the greatest in the service of Estolia. Isaiah Monterrey Zacarian. Isaiah, may I present the delightful Taryn Lilaine who comes to us as a visitor, but who is worthy to be called a Daughter of Estolia."

He smiled and leaned forward to press his cheek briefly to her own. "I am delighted to meet you, Taryn Lilaine. Welcome to Estolia. We are truly blessed by your visit. You light up our nation with the radiant beauty of your aura."

He turned and smiled at his father before holding an arm out to Lilaine, "I would be delighted if you would ride back to the palace with me in my carriage."

Lilaine took his arm, feeling the lean strength of his flesh beneath the trappings of civilization. She felt inexplicably shy and knew there was a blush on her cheeks as she climbed into the foremost open-topped carriage. Once she was seated, Isaiah sat across from her and the carriage started out with a couple of men on horseback leading the way.

For a while they traveled in silence, Lilaine looking around at the beautiful countryside. Her attention then turned to the handsome man seated across from her. "Your family is very generous," she said. "Cassie seems a most extraordinary person. I'm glad I had the chance to meet her."

"Eduardo is a great family friend. He has never recommended any person to our family who was unworthy of our friendship. We are grateful you have allowed us to share our country with you."

"What is this ceremony that is taking place this week?"

"I will be turning thirty in four days. The day before my birthday my Uncle Theo will pass the position of Last Resort to my brother Zeke. This is what we will be celebrating. Uncle Theo will instruct Zeke in giving a royal blessing. Did he make you uncomfortable with his request?" One of his eyebrows quirked upward in query.

"Not really. I don't mind receiving a blessing." She decided to share with him, "I plan to enjoy every minute of my unexpected vacation. I might not want to leave at the end of my stay."

Isaiah's eyes were warm on hers as he said, "I have no doubt that you will feel as though this *is* your home by the end of the week. You will always be welcome in Estolia."

Turning slightly, he gestured ahead of the carriage. The carriage was now traveling down a narrow valley. To one side was a beautiful structure that looked like a cathedral. On the other side she saw the road they were on was heading up the side of the mountain. She followed the meandering road with her eyes and when she reached the end her breath left her in a long-drawn-out sound of appreciation. Atop the mountain was an immense turreted palace with a pyramid-like peak. From their vantage point it looked enormous, larger than life.

"I have lived my entire life in the palace," he said to her. "I often forget how magnificent it is. It is only when we have visitors like yourself that I am reminded of how truly unique it is." When they arrived in the forecourt he climbed out of the carriage and then turned to offer her a hand so he could help her out. Once they were out of the carriage, it was driven away and the other carriage arrived.

Isaiah put an arm around her shoulders and turned her attention towards the front of the palace. It was too much to take in at once. Arches, columns, towers. Extraordinary. In addition, it was pristine, as if it was only just constructed. They were standing near a set of stairs that came together where they were standing. About a dozen or so steps up, the stairs split in two, one set going to the right, one to the left. Where they split was a remarkable carving of a flag with strange alien writing beneath it.

The dual staircase climbed for some distance and then doubled back, meeting up just as the stairs reached the third level in front of the main entrance to the palace. While they were climbing out of the carriage, a beautiful woman descended the stairs. She reached them just as the others joined them.

Isaiah placed a hand between Lilaine's shoulder blades and urged her towards the woman. "Lilaine, this is my mother, Jacqueline Cathay Zacarian, Queen of Estolia, Keeper of my father's Soul. She prefers to go by the name of Jackie. Mother, this is Taryn Lilaine, who, as I understand it, prefers the name Lilaine."

She was beautiful. She had thick chocolate brown curly hair with only a few strands turning silver with age; a willowy body; and warm brown eyes. "Lilaine, it's such a pleasure to meet you. Eduardo was most impressed with you, and we're delighted to show off our tiny country to you." While she was speaking another individual descended the staircase, and she turned to him. "This is a distant relative from France, Morgan Luc-Dumaine. Morgan, may I present my daughter, Cassiopeia Zacarian, and her friend Taryn Lilaine."

"Enchanté," he said in French, before adding in English, "It is a delight to meet two lovely young ladies."

They all began the climb up the many steps leading to the grand entrance of the palace. Lilaine's hand on Isaiah's sleeve, Cassie's hand on Morgan's.

Lilaine was enthralled by the extraordinarily fine architecture, the intricate stone carvings and beautiful statues. She smiled at Isaiah, saying, "It's marvelous!"

"I am glad you like my home."

17

Ceremony

*Each of the descendants of Zaccarias receives a blessing at seven days and a coming-of-age bless-
ing eighteen years later. It is a test of faith to believe in the words bestowed, both the mundane
and the fantastic, the seemingly impossible and the expected. Deity guides and tests each generation in this way*

~Thaddeus Makarios Zacarian; Capitulo 79

OVER THE NEXT THREE days, Lilaine, Cassie, Morgan, and Isaiah spent almost all their time together. When Lilaine admitted that she'd never ridden
a horse, she ended up riding double with Isaiah on his massive Andestolian
stallion, Zareth, a white horse she admired as being perhaps the most dynamic animal she'd ever been in contact with. The others rode their own mounts. He told her
that if she was going to be on the island longer, he would give her riding lessons. But,
he explained, it didn't make sense to waste the time she had with lessons when Zareth
was strong enough to carry both.

Lilaine leaned backwards against Isaiah's chest, feeling Zareth take a deep breath.
They were on a promontory on Mount Estoliana, and the first streaks of dawn were
starting to lighten the gray of pre-dawn. Cassie and Morgan were some distance
away, talking softly. She sighed heavily, thinking about the last several days, and the
time she'd spent in this man's company.

As the sky turned to a fiery red, Isaiah's arms around her waist pulled her closer,
silently sharing with her the beauty of the sunrise. Without thinking she rested her
hands on his hands, absently stroking them.

"Tonight is a special night," he said once the sky lost the last hint of rose. "Uncle
Theo has decided that his last formal act before the ceremony to turn over the role of
Last Resort will be the blessing he will give you." Isaiah turned Zareth away from the
precipice and started down the pathway they climbed an hour earlier in near total
darkness. Cassie and Morgan followed on their horses.

"I understand you and Cassie have special gowns you will wear," Isaiah added. "I
am looking forward to seeing what the dressmaker was able to create for you."

"If it is your birthday tomorrow, do your family have any special plans?"

"Indeed." his voice rumbled in his chest. "There are some special plans in the works. Perhaps tonight I will share some of those plans with you. You did, after all, venture to Estolia to learn about the religion, yes?"

"Your birthday celebrations have a religious element?" Over the last several days they didn't spend much time talking about the religion. She enjoyed their activities so much she didn't want to remember that her reason for being in Estolia was an assignment for a class.

"Indeed," he said again. "For Estolian men, the most pivotal year of life is their thirtieth year." She could hear the smile in his voice. "As I am to be King, it is more momentous for me than for any other man in our nation."

At the mention of his place in Estolian society, the half-formed notion, that he might come to care for her as much as she already cared for him, came crashing to earth. This man, no matter how human and approachable, was going to be a King someday. He wouldn't want a little nobody like her permanently in his life. Even if he did, she had her own insurmountable barriers.

She suddenly wished she had never come to this nation. She couldn't imagine ever finding any other man as interesting or vibrant as this man. She would store up the memories and pull them out to cherish them throughout her long, lonely life.

At the base of the mountain, Isaiah reined the horse to a halt. "This is the Royal Cathedral and beyond it, built into the mountain itself is the Temple," he said to her. "Your blessing and the other elements of the ceremony will be held here in the Cathedral tonight. Then we will travel back to the palace for the celebration in the grand ballroom."

"I'm looking forward to it."

"I, too, am looking forward to it," he said. He reined Zareth away from the temple and then pulled the horse up abruptly at the sight of Morgan leaning across the gap between his horse and Cassie's horse to kiss her. She noticed her brother watching them and pulled her horse away from Morgan's horse, cantering back towards the palace. Morgan glanced towards them and then set out after Cassie on his horse.

"I shall have a discussion with Morgan," Isaiah said, his tone dark and forbidding. Lilaine felt as though he could as easily be warning her off as planning on warning off Morgan.

In the late afternoon, Lilaine and Cassie spent time getting ready for the gala evening. "What do you think of Morgan?" Cassie asked.

"He seems very handsome, very nice," Lilaine said, not sure what Cassie wanted.

"I think if he had the chance," Cassie said, "he would seduce me." She laughed wickedly. "I do believe, Lilaine, I would let him seduce me." She sighed adding, "But my brother will warn him off."

Lilaine had no idea how to respond to that. She thought about the time she spent with Isaiah. He'd never given the slightest inclination to kiss her or otherwise seduce her. She would not have minded a little bit of seduction, she thought.

"Has any man ever seduced you, Lilaine?" Cassie asked.

"Me?" Lilaine asked in astonishment. "I've never been that close to any man. I grew up quite isolated and haven't been asked out since I've been at the university." She thought about the one man who had been close enough to possess her repeatedly and was grateful for the hundredth time that his peculiar drives hadn't included what she had available.

Cassie laughed at her expression. "You are quite beautiful." She paused before adding, "I am sure if you gave my brother encouragement, he would seduce you."

"Cassie!" Lilaine said, turning bright red.

"Lilaine!" she said back. "Tonight, my brother will monopolize your time. I am glad. This way I will be able to take all of Morgan's time."

✦

By the time they left the palace, the sun was dropping rapidly toward the horizon. They traveled again in the open-topped carriages from the palace to the Mount Estoliana Cathedral. Both Zeke and Isaiah helped her out of the carriage. They were dressed more formally than they had been when she and Cassie arrived. Isaiah was wearing a crown that was less ornate but no less official than the one worn by his father. Both men wore heavily embroidered capes and had swords in scabbards. Zeke was wearing a green and purple outfit which showed off his religious future. He looked solemn, serious, and somber.

The Cathedral was packed to capacity, filled with Estolians who had come to witness the ceremony. Isaiah led Lilaine up onto the platform and had her sit on a gilt stool. She had been told she should sit with her hands settled on her knees, her head bent, eyes closed.

She felt strangely confident as she sat there. Zeke and Theo placed their hands on her head and she listened raptly to their rich language. She often forgot English wasn't the language of Estolia since they spoke mostly in English around her. While Theo's rich voice echoed through the silent cathedral, she tried to get a sense of the language. It was like Spanish but she thought it had its own unique style and flavor. Melodic and exotic. If she could have understood the blessing, she would have heard:

> In this transcendent period of knowledge without wisdom, it is not enough to keep the Promise of Zaccarias, nor partake of the blessings promised by Deity. This Daughter of Estolia will have a pivotal role in Estolia's future. Three sons will bless her womb, one to rule Estolia, one to safely Keep her Soul, and one to act as a Catalyst of Change in the greater world. This woman is worthy to Keep the Soul of the King.

> Only through the salvation of the planet, will Estolia remain safe. This flame-haired woman will have a lasting impact on the nation. As a Catalyst of Change, her son will be instrumental in the rebirth of a golden era.

Though her trials have already surpassed those experienced by any other Queen of Estolia, she has come out of those tribulations pure and able to hold within her the soul of a King. She is worthy of the blessings promised to Zaccarias and Estoliana. She is worthy of the soul that will come into her keeping. The strength she will bring to Estolia cannot be measured. Her compassion and empathy will bring solace to many.

Through her place in Estolian society, she will enrich all who touch her life. This gentle woman is a worthy successor to Estoliana. Through her impact, the Keeper of the Soul of Estolia will discover within himself a greater power than any other Keeper including Zaccarias.

This worthy Daughter of Estolia will be remembered among the greatest of all the Queens of our nation. The blessings of Deity upon her, and her posterity, are as bright as the aura that confirms each Keeper, as bright as her fiery hair. She will try the faith of many in the crucible of their inner convictions and strengthen their faith through that trial by fire.

Deity commands that all remember above other considerations that this Daughter of Estolia is indeed worthy.

In the light and sight of Deity, we proclaim these blessings upon this woman who will keep securely the Soul of the King.

Zeke gently urged her to her feet and Isaiah escorted her to sit between his mother and sister before returning to stand next to his brother. Lilaine was enthralled by the emotion Theo communicated as he spoke before pulling an ornate gem-encrusted dagger from inside the black sash crossing his chest. He held it aloft and spoke briefly. Isaiah held both of his hands out, palms upward and Theo placed the dagger on them.

The King unpinned the black sash from Theo's outfit, bowing before handing it to Theo. The two older men smiled at one another before Theo carefully pinned the sash to Zeke's outfit. He then bowed and gestured Zeke toward his brother. Zeke walked over to where his brother held the dagger. The brothers spoke to each other before Zeke took the dagger, held it aloft, said something, before slotting the dagger within the black sash.

Zeke sat on the same stool Lilaine occupied a short time ago, and Isaiah left the stage to sit next to her. He put his arm around her, and gave his attention to the events on the stage.

Theo placed his hands upon Zeke's head, and gave another blessing. The blessing was as long, or longer than the one she received, and she could feel Isaiah tensing up slightly as it went on for some time. She wished she could understand the blessing.

When the ceremony was over, Isaiah helped her to her feet and escorted her out of the building ahead of everyone else. She was aware of all eyes on them and was grateful that she was wearing the beautiful dress the dressmaker designed for her.

During the carriage ride back to the palace, Isaiah explained, "In our faith, the first-born son of the King becomes the next King seven days after the birth of his oldest son – his heir."

"What if your wife couldn't have children or didn't live long enough to give you a son?"

"In the history of my lineage there have been a couple of times when the Heir Apparent could not fulfill the duties of his role. In each case there was a second son, or the son of the First Consul – the Last Resort – to take up the mantle of duty and become King. There has never failed to be a son born to each King. It is one of the promises *Deity* made to us."

"If one woman keeps the soul of a man, what happens if the marriage is dissolved, or the woman dies?"

"Coming from a culture so entirely different from my own, you might find it strange to hear that divorce is unheard of in Estolia."

"And if the wife dies?"

The carriage came to a halt and a footman opened the door and placed the stool for them to alight. Isaiah escorted her up the stairs so the long line of carriages following their own could disgorge their passengers. Once within the foyer, he led her to a small breakfast room instead of the ballroom.

He picked up both of her hands, his grey eyes meeting her green ones. "A man cannot live without his soul, Lilaine. No man gives his soul into the keeping of a woman without realizing he is tied to her in life and in death."

She searched his eyes, seeing that he believed what he was saying. He leaned forward to kiss her, his lips warm on hers. Before she had a chance to react, he smiled down at her and then led her from the room, down to the ballroom.

Isaiah was commanded to begin the dancing, and he escorted Lilaine out to the floor. In no time, the dance floor filled up. Over the course of the evening, she danced with all of the men she'd met in her time in Estolia. But most of the time she was paired up with Isaiah.

As the evening wore on the crowd thinned out until it was nearing midnight and only the family remained. Cassie was dancing as close and as often with Morgan as Lilaine danced with Isaiah.

Theo came up to where they were dancing and put one hand on each of their shoulders. "The orchestra is packing up after this number is over," he informed them, "I shall see you tomorrow, Isaiah."

Isaiah smiled at Lilaine and said, "Come, I enjoyed our earlier conversation in the carriage. I should like to explain more about the significance of the Keeping of the Soul." He extended a hand to her.

She went with him easily, following as he led her to a part of the palace unfamiliar to her. When he entered a bedroom, she paused, shocked. His bringing her to his or any other bedroom seemed out of character – and improper.

He escorted her to a group of chairs opposite the large bed. Once she was seated, she tried to ignore the bed behind her. Rather than sit in the opposite chair, he sank to his knees in front of where she was sitting. "In my faith," he said, his hands on her thighs, stroking her skin through the fabric of her ballgown, "the Keeping of the Soul is irrevocable. Once a man turns thirty, it is his duty to find a woman into whose keeping he can place his soul." He leaned towards her, his lips caressing hers, one hand warm on her face.

He pulled back slightly. "You are so lovely, Lilaine. I wish to place my soul within your keeping," he whispered.

She thought she understood what he was saying but wasn't sure. She wanted to know this man in a way Randolph never once inspired. She wanted to give herself to him. He touched her lips with his own. After several blissful minutes, he climbed to his feet and pulled her up and into his arms, one hand going to caress the side of her face, the other exerting gentle pressure on the small of her back, pulling her body up against his.

His mouth over hers was mobile, alive, nibbling, tasting, teasing. He deepened the kiss, and she was enthralled, caught up in the sensations building between them. When she felt a hard pressure against her abdomen she pulled back, shocked. He was aroused.

"Lilaine," he whispered. His eyes were dilated as he looked at her. "Oh, Lilaine," he said again before his mouth settled once more over hers in a kiss that was no longer restrained. She returned his kiss with equal passion, feeling intoxicated by how close he was, the feel of his strong body against her own.

Just how they went from standing and fully dressed, to lying on his bed in their undergarments she did not know. She became aware of where they were when he pushed the edge of her bra down and took her nipple into his mouth. She moaned at the sensation, her hands running over the skin of his back. "Isaiah, we should stop." She was distracted by the feel of his hand under her dainty briefs.

"No, Lilaine, we should not stop," he said, cupping her, feeling the heat of her arousal. "There has never been anything in my life more right than this is, right now. Say you will be mine."

Logic and sense fled. She wanted him, his possession. "Yes, Isaiah."

The clock began to chime the hour as he pulled the last of her garments off, divesting himself of his own. The reverberations of the final chime of the clock were still echoing through the palace when his body merged with hers. The momentary discomfort hardly registered before she felt a fullness that seemed to extend from her body to her soul. She surrendered her body and soul up to him as they enacted the most elemental of dances. When he finally called out to her, she felt as though the universe itself came to a halt in tribute to the fundamental beauty of their union.

A Lesson in Theology

The recording of the pinnacle moments in the life of the Sovereign and his First Consul in the Capitulos is one of the critical duties of the First Four of Estolia. Lessons learned in one lifetime will enhance the decisions of future generations in profound ways.

-Cristoforo Alexius Zacarian; Capitulo 64

THEY WERE BOTH breathing heavily when he pulled away from her, tucking her body tightly up against his, her head on his shoulder, his hand stroking her hair. She listened to the beating of his heart, feeling transformed in a way she never would have, or could have imagined. It was only as his heart settled down to a steady even rhythm that she realized exactly what happened.

"My soul is in your Keeping," he said to her. His voice was solemn. His eyes studied hers. His hand settled over her abdomen and he asked her, "Lilaine, will you cherish my soul? Bear our children? Share my burdens? Be my Queen?"

Overwhelmed she closed her eyes, processing all he was saying, all they had spoken about over the course of the monumental day. She could hear his heartbeat start to race as she processed all the information she'd gathered in her time on the island. She realized then that he was unsure of her response. "Isaiah, I want nothing more out of life than to stay with you here in Estolia, by your side for my entire life." If only it was *possible*. But, she reasoned, perhaps it was? The barriers weren't insurmountable. Perhaps Isaiah would understand. She allowed herself to hope, to dream.

He pulled her close in a crushing embrace. A moment later he glanced at the clock. He kissed her briefly on the cheek before rising to walk to a chest at the foot of the bed. Opening it, he pulled out a white silky nightgown and a purple and green bathrobe. After shrugging into the robe. He walked over to where she lay and handed the nightgown to her. "Put this on."

She slipped the nightgown over her head, watching as he crossed to pick up and neatly fold the items of apparel that littered the floor in a near straight line from the chair to the bed. He was just settling her elaborate ball gown over the back of the chair when the clock struck the half hour. He crossed the room swiftly to where she stood next to the bed and pulled her close against his body in a hug.

The door opened and Isaiah's father, Theo, and Zeke entered the room. Isaiah slid behind her and pulled her body up against his, one hand resting lightly on her abdomen.

All three men approached, but Theo was the one who appeared to be in charge. Lilaine remembered that nobody married in this nation without his approval. She wondered if she would be found wanting.

Theo's eyes never left Lilaine's. "Isaiah?"

"I have placed my soul in Taryn Lilaine's keeping." Isaiah's voice was rich and satisfied.

Theo was silent for so long Lilaine became uncomfortable, especially when it became obvious that his silence was unusual. She could feel Isaiah tensing up behind her, and both the King and Zeke looked at Theo curiously.

Finally, he asked her, "Have you accepted his soul, his burden, his seed?"

"I have," she said, not sure if that was the correct response.

Again, the silence was uncomfortable. The large standing clock by the door was the only noise, ticking in the background. To Lilaine, it was like a doomsday clock, ticking down the last of her happiness.

Theo's expression was inscrutable, unhappy. He looked like he was preparing to tell someone they lost a member of their family in some dreadful accident. When she was certain she would be unable to live through any more silence, he turned to Zeke and asked, "When we blessed this woman, what one thing did you note above all other things?"

Zeke stepped forward. Against the beautiful green, purple, and gold of his robes, the black sash was stark, punctuating his role. He looked from his uncle to his brother and father before his focus turned to Lilaine. "You never once spoke her name. You merely referred to her in different ways descriptively. I remember thinking at the time that it was extraordinary. I have never once heard a blessing that did not, as a central element, include the name of the recipient. I recall your instruction on this matter. You made it clear to me that every blessing, large and small, had several elements that were critical. The first on the list was the recipient's name.

"The blessing did, however, have all the weight of being direct from *Deity*. The power that permeated each word was more than I have ever felt. I would swear every word was inspired, and know, therefore, that the lack of name had to be a part of that inspiration. You did not *forget* to use her name."

To have Theo giving what appeared to be a lesson in theology in the middle of the night seemed incongruous. Judging by the expression on the face of the King, he was equally puzzled.

"Tell me, Zeke," Theo said, "why was her name not included?"

His eyes widened and he looked at Lilaine in shocked disbelief, before looking at his uncle and blurting out, "because her name is not Taryn Lilaine!"

She felt as if her future, so brilliant and beautiful ten minutes ago, shattered in that one moment. With Isaiah still standing behind her, holding her, she had no idea what she would see on his face if she turned around and looked at him.

Theo had a faint smile on his face as he looked at Zeke. "I believe you were gifted with a deeper spiritual connection and perception than I was ever granted. When it is time to pass on the Keeping of the Soul of Estolia you will guard her well." He turned and looked at her and said, "Your name?"

In a nation with no divorce, she knew she was likely unacceptable. "I was born Lily Elaine Tirane. Lilaine to my closest friends." If she was going to lose her heart, lose the man who still held her tightly, she didn't care about keeping the secret, didn't care that she was opening herself up to those who would silence her permanently.

"Your age?" Theo asked.

"Twenty-four," was her rapid response.

"You have never been to Alaska," Theo asserted. His eyes rose to Isaiah's. "Your soul is in her keeping? You have no doubts?"

Isaiah's arms were warm around her pulling her closer. "Orlando Maximiliano was most eloquent in his description of that moment, putting his words in the language of his beautiful bride from England:

> When with my body to her wed,
>> The exquisite pleasure
>>> Of that virgin marriage bed;
>>>> Could none compare
>>> The stark cessation
>>>> Of my soul's departure
>>>>> With that sweet sensation
>>>>>> Of coming home?
>>>>> No, nor can I,
>>>>>> For words are weak
>>>>>>> When used to explain
>>>>>>>> This indelible link.
>>>>>>> What agony of mind
>>>>>> Swept o'er me in that time
>>>>> 'Twixt yielding soul
>>>>>> And consent.
>>>>> Ne'er more will I wonder,
>>>> Ne'er more doubt divinity
>>> When with the soaring of my soul,
>>>> The searing of my heart,
>>> I yielded up my soul to her,
>> And safe
> She took it in her keeping.

"She was pure, and as I took her purity, she took my soul as recompense." Isaiah's final words were as poetic as those he quoted.

Lilaine was touched by the beauty of the words Isaiah quoted from memory;

moved by the throbbing intensity of his emotions. She could not doubt that this man had fallen in love with her.

"Randolph Smythe is dead," Theo stated. His words were incongruous enough to have all but Lilaine look at him in utter bafflement.

To Lilaine it was as welcome a message as any she could imagine, though if Isaiah wasn't holding her, she would have crumpled to the floor at that amazing pronouncement.

"Who is Randolph Smythe?" Isaiah asked predictably.

She pulled away from him and turned so she could see his face. She owed him the truth, and her eyes met his steadily when she stated, "My husband."

She'd shocked him. He stepped backward and looked at her as if he couldn't stand to touch her.

Zeke stepped forward and said, with authority, "Your soul is in her keeping Isaiah, married or not, she came to you pure. She is also free to knit her life to yours."

The King, who had remained silent throughout the entire drama, asked, "Why did you come here as Taryn Lilaine?"

She realized how fond she was of this entire family. She was terrified they would now send her away, and afraid that her actions would result in harm coming to Isaiah. She wished desperately that his arms were still around her. "Randolph wanted an ornament, not a wife. My family," her words were bitter, "sold me to him when I was fourteen."

She looked away from the three men and her thoughts returned to the day she was participating in a car-wash for the local high school. The stretch limousine pulled in to the wash and the man inside offered a staggering sum to the teenage car washers to clean the already immaculate vehicle. Stuart, Randolph's flunky, climbed out, and within minutes he gathered the necessary information. Lilaine, washing the windows in a damp bare-midriff top, was oblivious to Randolph's interest.

Three days later Stuart showed up at her crumbling house that struggled to contain the seven kids and five adults who called it home. The money he offered Harold Tirane was enough to overcome any scruples her father might have had at the request – to give permission for Randolph Smythe to marry his fourteen-year-old daughter. Her father leapt at the chance, and two days later, baffled, she was exchanging vows with the large blustery man who saw her and wanted to possess her. By the end of the day, she was in New York, learning she was to be the ornament to decorate Randolph Smythe's arm. The prize virgin he might, someday, choose to possess. For eight years she lived under the threat of his eventual possession. She learned within a few hours to put on an act of docile stupidity. He came to believe in her basic simple nature after a time. Keeping her with him always, even when he took part in the business that kept him rich.

She remembered the sense of unreality she experienced when agents for some government agency bustled her into a black van. "I gave evidence against Randolph, and they gave me a new identity. They were certain he'd try to have me killed."

"Randolph Smythe," Theo said, "was arrested. Apparently, he found it *amusing* that the ornamental wife who decorated his home for eight years gave evidence against him. He, in turn, gave evidence that would imprison many men. Having obtained his freedom, he refused protective custody. He was shot and killed twelve hours after his release. His last words were: 'Elaine will probably never know how deeply she affected me. The sweet purity of her spirit reformed me.' You are now a very wealthy woman."

Lilaine knew what she wanted out of life, and it was the man looking at her with great solemnity. "None of the wealth of the world matters to me. The only thing that matters is Isaiah."

Theo stepped forward and took her hand in his left hand, and Isaiah's in his right and placed her hand in Isaiah's. He then rested his hand gently over her abdomen and closed his eyes briefly. "Isaiah Monterrey Zacarian, as heir to the throne of Estolia, your burdens are great, your freedoms few. Having given your soul into the keeping of Lily Elaine Tirane, your union will be blessed with a son, born in the waning moments of this year." He looked at Zeke. "Lazarus Ezekiel Zacarian are you prepared to exercise the duties of Last Resort if your brother, the future King, rejects the Keeper of his Soul?"

Zeke looked extremely grim but his voice was clear and sure as he said, "I am prepared to fulfill my role as Last Resort if my brother, the future King, chooses to reject the Keeper of his Soul."

※

Isaiah never felt the burden of his role in life, nor of the religion, as he did in that moment. He looked into the eyes of the woman who possessed his soul and knew with a depth of certainty that no man could understand what it meant to have his soul possessed until it took place. If he could not accept her his brother would be forced into the one act of barbarism that was part of the religion. Only twice, in eighty-eight generations, was the Last Resort called on to exercise his duty. If Isaiah rejected this woman who kept secrets, who believed herself married to another when she gave herself to him, then his brother would be forced to take first her life – and the son she was conceiving – and then Isaiah's.

His eyes locked onto hers, and he realized the burden of this decision. He would not be able to choose her merely to spare her life, nor to spare his own. He could not choose her just because she kept not only his soul but his heart as well. He could not even choose her to spare his brother the most heinous of duties. He had to choose based on what was right for his nation.

He knew his brother's hand was even now upon the ceremonial dagger strapped to the inner surface of the sash of office of Last Resort.

The only way Isaiah could accept this woman was if he knew it was right for his nation, for his lineage, and for himself. The sordid tale of her life made him doubt her suitability as Queen. He felt the inevitability of his decision and closed his eyes. Even as he opened his mouth to make the most difficult, and the final decision of his life, his uncle stopped him. "Consider the blessing," he said softly.

Isaiah closed his mouth and opened his eyes, noting Zeke's hand was at his side again and his uncle – First Consul and in this moment never truer as Keeper of the Soul of Estolia – was urging his memory to take in the words of the blessing he heard shortly before the sun set on Estolia only hours ago. The blessing his brother proclaimed to be inspired by *Deity*. In part, the words he recalled included:

"...This worthy Daughter of Estolia will be remembered among the greatest of all the Queens of our nation. The blessings of Deity upon her, and her posterity, are as bright as the aura that confirms each Keeper, as bright as her fiery hair. She will try the faith of many in the crucible of their inner convictions and strengthen their faith through that trial by fire. Deity commands that all remember above other considerations that this Daughter of Estolia is indeed worthy..."

There was more to the blessing, but the part he needed to remember came back to him. The three words kept echoing round in his head. "She *is* worthy," he reiterated, pulling her up tight against his body.

He felt in that moment why it was married couples so often touched. His body yearned after his soul, but he could only have it when they were in contact and in accord. He knew in that instant he would never be complete so long as he was separate from this woman. They would be together until time and age pulled one to the grave swiftly followed by the other.

His brother's blessing was as powerful as Lilaine's, proclaiming him to be one who would have visions of equivalent power to those received by Zaccarias. If he demanded that Zeke exercise his role of Last Resort, it would have nullified the blessing he received less than six hours ago.

19

Coronation

Coronation in Estolia always takes place upon the heels of the blessing of the Heir Apparent, seven days after his birth. This has not changed in sixty-six generations. The details of the actual ceremony are, however, subject to the whims of the First Four of Estolia.

~Malachi Tobias; Capitulo 66

ZEKE MOVED BACK TO the chest at the foot of the bed and pulled out a more feminine version of the robe Isaiah was wearing. He handed it to her. "Come," he said, "Our obligations are not yet at an end."

She shrugged into the robe and after tying it around her waist she looked at Isaiah. He was again looking grim, though when he glanced at her he smiled. He was now grim about something entirely different. He extended a hand to her, and they followed the three other men.

While they moved through the palace, she thought about Zeke. When she first met him, she thought of him as a less powerful personality next to his older brother, a sort of pale copy. Now, in the four days she knew him, he seemed to have grown into his own identity. Especially after the strange episode in Isaiah's bedroom. She thought he would only gain in power throughout his life. She looked forward to watching him mature.

A few minutes later they were at Cassie's room. They didn't knock before entering the room. Morgan was in bed with Cassie.

The King said, "Monsieur Luc-Dumaine, do you care to explain yourself?"

Morgan smiled at Cassie before saying, "Cassie tells me she has captured my soul and we are bound for all eternity together."

Zeke was the one to respond, his words clothed in steel. "She cannot *capture* your soul. But she can keep it for you if you gift it to her. The one thing she cannot do, Morgan Luc-Dumaine, once you give your soul into her Keeping, is give it back."

Morgan did not look at all disturbed. "I do not want it back. I knew if I touched her I would be tied to her for all eternity." He turned and smiled fondly at the woman in bed with him.

The King spoke again, "I cannot countenance my daughter leaving Estolia. Many do leave, to keep the island from over-population. But she must remain."

"When I was a boy, my great-aunt visited the family several times. She very quickly became my favorite relative. Father told me his Aunt lived in Estolia, a magical land where she fell in love and was living happily ever after. I was enthralled with the story of the wonderful woman who I only met three times in my life. I wanted to go to Estolia, find love, and live happily ever after too. Eight months ago, I turned thirty, and the desire to visit my Great Aunt Harmony became overpowering, until finally I could not avoid acting on it. I wish only to live here, embrace the Estolian faith, and remain forever with Cassie."

"At dawn tomorrow," Isaiah said, "a double ceremony?"

Leo smiled at his oldest son and then at his daughter. "Your brother has placed his soul in the keeping of your friend Lilaine."

Cassie smiled brightly at her brother, extending one hand to him. "The blessings of Zaccarias come thickest to those who honor his vision most completely," she quoted an Estolian proverb. "I am honored Morgan and I will be able to share in the blessings of your union."

"Come," Leo said, "There is much to prepare if we wish to celebrate in less than six hours." He went to a chest at the foot of Cassie's bed and opened it, pulling out another robe identical to the one that Isaiah was wearing. He handed it to Morgan. And tossed a nightgown to his daughter. Lilaine closed her eyes until she heard the men moving towards the door. When she opened her eyes, she saw they were leaving the room.

Cassie smiled at Lilaine, patting the bed at her side. Lilaine didn't need a second invitation. She removed the robe and climbed into the bed with her best friend. "I knew you would not be returning to the United States. Eduardo has never sent someone to Estolia who has left. He has a very special perception."

"Did you think I would marry your brother?"

Cassie nodded. "Eduardo was specific that Isaiah should be the one to 'instruct' you on the Estolian people and faith. He has never sent someone with so specific a message before. Uncle Theo had concerns about you, but his blessing was everything any woman would want. He said multiple times throughout that you were worthy of the honor."

"Your brother almost rejected me," Lilaine pointed out.

Cassie sat up at that, staring at her in shock and horror. "Before or after you took his soul?" The natural color in her cheeks was gone.

Lilaine admitted, "After. Your Uncle Theo asked if Zeke was willing to exercise his duty as Last Resort if your brother rejected me." She felt a shiver of remembered fear as she recounted, "I think he *was* going to reject me until Theo reminded him of the blessing."

Tears began to trace their way down Cassie's cheeks. "What is it?" Lilaine asked.

"The position is called Last Resort for a reason. When the Promise of Zaccarias was recorded, the future of our nation was linked to the willingness of the heir to fulfill his part of the bargain." She looked away as she admitted, "The requirement was any

Heir to the throne should find the Keeper of his Soul in his thirtieth year, place his soul in her keeping, and wed her within seven days. If he was to reject the keeper of his soul and not wed her, our entire nation would crumble and become as nothing. For two thousand seven hundred years this promise has been fulfilled. Only twice has the Last Resort been called upon to do what is necessary to ensure the heir to the throne would always wed the Keeper of his Soul." She shook her head at the images visible only to her mind.

"He could not marry me if he was dead," Lilaine whispered.

"Nor could you marry him if you were also dead," Cassie added. "It is the most brutal aspect of our faith. Twice in our history, in over eighty-eight generations, has the Last Resort been called on by duty to our nation to fulfill his obligation and murder his own brother."

"Your Uncle Theo saved my life."

"Yes, he is a very wise man. He keeps his finger on the pulse of the greater world." Cassie cocked her head to one side to ask, "Why would my brother reject you? He was taken with you the moment he met you."

"He found out I have already been married," Lilaine admitted.

"Extraordinary, and yet you keep his soul? Did your husband die prior to the consummation of your marriage?"

"No, I didn't even know he was dead. I don't think I would've come here if I understood the implications. However, he died two days after I was placed in witness protection. That is why you did not know my name. Instead of Taryn Lilaine, my real name is Lily Elaine Tirane, but I prefer to go by Lilaine."

"I like the name Lilaine, it is beautiful."

"What will happen in six hours?"

Cassie's smile grew wide, her bubbly nature reasserting itself. "We shall begin the process of getting married. Once a man of Estolia gives his soul into the keeping of the woman he will wed, they must spend seven days in seclusion. In seven days it is determined whether *Deity* sanctions the marriage, and then an actual wedding takes place."

"It seems to me," observed Lilaine, "that in Estolia things are sort of backwards when compared to the rest of the world. To wed someone here, it begins with intimacy, followed by a honeymoon of sorts, and then finally the actual wedding."

Cassie's laugh was musical. "Oh, Lilaine, you and I will be the best of friends! Consider – to an Estolian it is inconceivable to marry someone who has not already shared intimacy with their spouse. The rest of the world does things most backwards compared with the logical way it happens here in Estolia."

Lilaine gave Cassie a spontaneous hug. "I believe I shall enjoy living here."

The two girls were quiet for several minutes, thinking their private thoughts. Then Lilaine asked, "Theo said I would have a son by the end of the year. Do you think he's right?"

"If he said it, Lilaine, you can be certain it is going to happen. Hopefully I, too, will have a baby. They can be raised together." Cassie paused before adding, "Your blessing actually mentioned you would have three sons." She grinned. "I keep forgetting you do not even know the content of your blessing! You will find it most enlightening to see the translation."

JANUARY 7, 1990

Lily Elaine Zacarian. I, Theobald Reginald Zacarian, eighty-seventh Keeper of the Soul of Estolia, confer upon you the title of eighty-eighth Queen of Estolia after Estoliana, Keeper of the Soul of Isaiah Monterrey Zacarian, eighty-eighth King of Estolia, and Mother of Leonidas Agamemnon Zacarian, Heir Apparent to the Throne of Estolia. You enrich our nation with the strength of your character and the progeny you will bear. I urge you to place the needs of Estolia over the needs of self. Always remember that unto those who are given great burdens, are also given great blessings. As Queen your life is wholly given over to the citizens of Estolia.

This blessing I give you in the light and sight of Deity.

When Theo finished, he settled a crown upon her head. Isaiah urged her to her feet with a hand at her elbow. She looked into his dear face and knew the peace and happiness filling her heart, mind and soul was greater than any one person had the right to possess. When Isaiah cupped her face gently, she sensed he felt the same. He wore the crown she saw his father wearing many times before. Together they turned to Zeke, who was holding their son in his arms. He passed the baby over to Isaiah and then stepped off the dais.

Isaiah settled their son in her arms carefully, and then put his arm around her shoulders, pulling her close against his side. Lilaine looked at the man who was sharing her life and knew beyond any doubting that they would be together forever – fulfilling their place in Estolia. She would have two more sons and maybe even a daughter. Most important of all – she would have this man by her side – always.

Part 4 – A Nudge Towards Destiny

❧ Cast of Characters ❧

Calista Teare – (Cali) Sister of Orion Teare. Lives in Phoenix, Arizona, attends Mariposa University

Isaiah Monterrey Zacarian – 88th King of Estolia

Kedarin Zacarian – Wife of Zeke, the 88th Keeper of the Soul of Estolia

Lazarus Ezekiel Zacarian – (Zeke) 88th Keeper of the Soul of Estolia

Leonidas Agamemnon Zacarian – (Leon) Heir Apparent, Son of the 88th King of Estolia

Lilaine Zacarian – 88th Queen of Estolia, mother of Leon, Nico and Zeb

Nicodemus Luciano Zacarian – (Nico) Second son of the King of Estolia

Orion Teare – Former roommate of Nico Zacarian at Harvard; Professor at Mariposa University

20

Misdirected Mail

2019

Deity will always guide the sons of Zaccarias to find the one true Keeper of their Soul. All Deity requires in return is faith in this promise.

~Montavius Geronimo Zacarian – Capitulo 84

CALI TURNED THE large bulky padded envelope over to see if there was a return address on the back, but there wasn't. The only thing written on the envelope was her address but with the name Leonidas Zacarian. Without a return address, it would never get to its destination. It might even be a Christmas gift. She wondered briefly if she should open it, but then decided against it. She would leave it on her entryway table in case another letter or package with more information showed up.

Early on Christmas Eve, three days later, Cali was pulling the mail out of her box when she saw the apartment manager, Trent. He was wearing a fuzzy red and white "Santa hat." She remembered the mysterious package she received. If someone lived in the vast apartment complex, Trent would know. "Is there a tenant in the complex by the name of Leonidas Zacarian?"

He wore his usual jovial expression as he greeted her. Setting his chins to wobble uncontrollably, he nodded. "Indeed, we do." His expression took on the overdramatic mournful look he often wore. "However even for a tenant as lovely as you I can't give away personal information without permission."

She laughed. Trent was so delightfully absurd. She learned over the last eighteen months to respect the apartment manager as one who would jealously guard his tenants and their rights to privacy. She considered giving Trent the bulky envelope, but his sense of honor was contagious. She didn't want to pass the envelope through an intermediary.

"The next time you see him, could you ask him to stop by and see me?"

"I'll text him." He pulled his smartphone out of his pocket and stated the contents of the text while composing it, "Calista Teare in Apartment Q11 would like you to visit her." He quirked an eyebrow at her and when he saw she approved, he hit "send."

Leon heard his phone chime. He had a text message. He ignored it, his eyes on the painting on the wall in his spacious living room. It was one of Kedarin's paintings depicting the sun slicing through ominous storm clouds over Mount Zaccarias. He missed Estolia at the cellular level. When he was in college he was homesick then, too, but it was nothing like how he felt now.

In a week, he would be thirty. The birthday that would define the rest of his life. Yet, despite his faith, and deep-seated belief in the customs of his people, he was pessimistic. It seemed unlikely that some woman would just magically materialize in his life.

For the last eleven months, he lived here in Phoenix, Arizona on the advice of both his brother and his uncle. His *Blessing-at-Eighteen* stated he would find the woman who would keep his soul safe and place it within her safekeeping a full week before his birthday and that it would be sanctioned *on* his birthday.

He stood up and crossed the room to where he kept his car keys and cellphone, his movements were jerky, his carriage rigid. He closed his eyes and took a deep breath. Then a second and third. When he felt a measure of peace seep into his soul he opened his eyes and looked at his phone to see who was texting him.

Why was the apartment manager texting him? Reading the message, he frowned. He didn't know anyone by the name of Calista Teare. Though there *was* something familiar about her last name. With only his dark thoughts to keep him company, he opted to visit his neighbor to find out what she wanted. The walk would do him good.

He was halfway across the vast apartment complex when it began to pour. Within seconds he was drenched. He started to walk faster, punctuating his steps by swearing in every language he knew.

Cali had every conceivable financial document laid out on her dining room table. She would have to move in six months. But long before six months were done she would starve to death without some form of income. She grimaced at her left ankle. The doctors did a splendid job of making it *look* normal. But it still couldn't withstand the rigors of a job where she stood all day long. So far, her search for a job where she could sit rather than stand yielded nothing whatsoever.

The loss of her scholarship would only hasten the financial ruin she was heading towards. The university granted her a waiver when her grades suffered a year ago after the loss of her family. But she was left with a financial tangle after her hospitalization and the funerals. Only her brother's habit of always paying the rent in advance and her scholarship kept her afloat, barely. But without her scholarship, she was heading for complete financial ruin.

The doorbell chimed. She dropped the bank statement she was glaring at and gratefully left the muddle of her finances for the mundane of answering the door.

It was pouring outside and the man standing on her doorstep was soaked. There was a particularly nasty broken drain pipe that would continue to drench him as long as he stood on her doorstep. "Come in, please," she said, opening the door wide. She went to her linen closet and grabbed a couple of towels and brought them back to where the man was standing on her linoleum entry tiles, dripping.

He took the towels gratefully. He was tall and lean, with dusky skin, dark hair, and light eyes. When he finished drying himself she told him, "Just leave them on the floor."

He dropped the towels onto the puddle he created and then stepped over them towards her. "I apologize for arriving in such a state. One of your recent unpredictable storms caught me as I walked over to your apartment." He spoke with a lilting melodic accent. Cali thought it was familiar but couldn't recall where she heard it before.

"How can I help you?" she asked him.

He looked surprised by the query, and for the first time seemed to really notice her standing there. She was wearing a silky ankle-length caftan printed with the pattern of a giraffe's hide. Her bronze-colored hair was loose and flowed halfway down her back. He stared at her with a frown, as if he didn't understand English. Cali repeated, "Can I help you with something?"

"The apartment manager sent me a message asking me to contact Calista Teare at this address..." he faltered to a halt, his brow wrinkling in a troubled frown. He continued hesitantly, "My name is Leon Zacarian."

"I asked Trent to contact you," she said. She moved over to the table and picked up the bulky envelope. "I received this in my mailbox, but it's addressed to you. I didn't know how to contact you, and without a return address, it would never get back to the person who sent it, so I asked Trent if you were a resident of the complex. I didn't want it to go astray if it was a Christmas gift."

He took the envelope from her. "Do you mind if I open this immediately?"

"Oh, feel free. Come on in and have a seat," she invited. She frowned and then offered, "Would you like me to put your outer clothes in my dryer or anything? Your clothing is soaking wet."

"I would not want to put you to any trouble."

"It's no trouble," she said. "Follow me." She was afraid he would catch a cold if he sat around in soaking wet clothing. She also didn't think it would do her furniture any good to have him sitting on it soaking wet.

She led him to the bathroom and said, "You're the same size as my brother. I'll bring you his robe." He didn't need to know her brother was no longer alive.

She stepped into Orion's bedroom, noting the small stack of presents from the previous Christmas. She was instantly transported back in time to that day...

It was a week before Christmas. Orion was talking non-stop about how much their parents would love the Mediterranean trip he was going to give to them next

Christmas.

"How did you get us tickets to the show? I thought they were sold out," she asked Orion as they left their apartment.

"Nico sent them to me," he said. Nico was his former college roommate.

Together she and Orion picked up their parents and drove into town, parking some distance from their destination. They discussed school, Orion's new job, and Christmas on their walk to the concert hall.

When the concert was over, they went to a fancy restaurant. Her parents worried about her, and she knew it was because she was so shy, even timid, having difficulty meeting people and making new friends. It helped that she was sharing the apartment with her brother. She could honestly tell them that she was settling into her life as a college student with ease.

That night the concert and meal that followed were some of the sweetest, most precious memories of her life.

They left the restaurant with plans to spend an hour sightseeing some of the more memorable neighborhoods decorated for the holidays. They were waiting with a large group of shoppers to cross the busy road when everything went dreadfully wrong. The high-pitched screech of metal scraping metal, combined with the lower-pitched rumble of metal crushing metal all seemed to happen in slow motion. She saw Orion almost horizontal in the air, leaping towards where she was standing. Then several impacts shattered everything for her.

Orion had jumped into the path of the vehicle, to shove her out of harm's way. Orion, their parents, and two other shoppers were killed in the horrendous accident. She suffered a crushing injury to her ankle, and it took several operations and a long hospital stay before she could be released.

It was almost Valentine's Day when she was released from the hospital and she stared at the dead Christmas tree in numb disbelief. The presents underneath that she and Orion had wrapped with joyful anticipation of the holidays were now littered with dead pine needles. Unable to face dealing with the reality that she was all alone in the world, she took the presents and stacked them in Orion's bedroom, shutting the presents, and her memories, away.

She picked up the largest gift bag, pulling out the red and green tissue paper, and then holding the thick robe to her body briefly before turning and leaving the room. Perhaps it was time to look back and remember the joy and happiness of that last day, rather than the trauma and loss.

She went to the bathroom and knocked on the door. "Here's a robe you can wear while I dry your clothing."

He opened the door and took it from her, passing her the sodden bundle of clothing. She went to the compact launderette closet at the end of the hall and opened the slotted folding doors, exposing the small washer and dryer stacked vertically. She pushed his clothing into the dryer and set it for a full cycle. By the time his clothing was tumbling in the dryer, he was leaving the bathroom wearing the plush robe.

"Thank you for your kindness," he said to her. His smile caused her heart to lurch. She looked away, knowing her cheeks had a rosy blush. "Your apartment appears to be laid out exactly like mine," he said, putting her at her ease. He caressed the quality fabric of the plush robe. "I hope your brother will not mind my borrowing his robe."

She led him back to her living room. He followed her, sitting in a chair covered in faux leather. He picked up the bulky letter and opened it, drawing out the contents: a dark purple-blue colored ring box; what looked like a passport in the same color; and a letter written in a beautiful flowing script she couldn't read:

Leon, I hope this letter reaches you in time. Since I first met Calista I felt as if she was likely to be the one to keep your soul. Originally her brother and I planned to bring her to Estolia for the holiday, but she lost her family in a tragic accident a year ago and I knew I would have to approach it differently. By the time you read this letter you should know whether she is the right woman for you. Remember that your Blessing-at-Eighteen explicitly states that you should wed the woman who keeps your soul – on your birthday. This means that Deity sanctions your union as much as seven days in advance of the date of your birthday. Go gently brother, she's fragile. With the trauma of her grievous loss a year ago, she needs understanding and care. Remember all that rests on your choices. I've anticipated your success and provided her with the necessary passport to travel internationally. If you discover that she is not the woman to keep your soul, I have enclosed a letter for her extending an invitation to visit. Please bring her to Estolia.

~Nico

21

Aura

The Aura is one of the intangible gifts provided by Deity to guide the Sons of Zaccarias to make the right choice in their selection of a bride. One of the peculiarities noted early in the history of Estolia was the fact that each man who was gifted with the aura described it differently. From the shimmer of rainbows, to the mist of Arrow Falls. From the glow of sunrise to the glimmer of sunset. Pulsing, swirling, expanding and contracting. The consensus opinion has always been that the differences are as simple as the unique characteristics of each of the Sons and Daughters of Estolia – as each citizen of Estolia has their own unique appearance, it is only natural that the substance of their souls should be as uniquely individual as the outer appearance.

–Balthazarius Keifer Zacarian – Capitulo 78

LEON TOSSED the letter onto the table in front of him and leaned back to look at the girl he'd been deliberately sent to meet. She was exotically beautiful. Especially with the aura surrounding her. Her aura was the first thing he noticed once he dried himself on her entrance tiles – a pulsing bronze-gold shimmer surrounding her, causing him to lose his train of thought entirely. It was only her repeated queries about what brought him to her door that pulled him out of the trance caused by the exquisite view of the substance of her soul.

"Am I keeping you from anything?"

She grimaced slightly and glanced over at a table covered in paperwork. "Nothing I want to return to," she said.

"What do you do, Calista Teare?" he asked her, smiling. He had been told often enough that his features weren't classically handsome, but that when he smiled, some alchemy of genetics transformed his features into a compelling and attractive whole.

She was not looking his way, so the smile did not perform any of the magic he'd been told it would perform. In fact, she looked distressed.

"Please call me Cali. I don't do anything anymore."

"Tell me about it." If he was going to win this woman over, he had to gain her trust. Something was dreadfully wrong in Calista Teare's world.

Unshed tears darkened her lashes, making them spiky. She pulled her feet up onto the couch in front of her and clasped her legs in a way that made him realize she was feeling vulnerable – not to him, but to whatever was bothering her. "I've lost my scholarship." Her jaw jutted out mutinously. "But I couldn't do what was necessary to

126

keep it."

"Surely keeping a scholarship is merely a matter of keeping your grades at a certain level?" Whatever was disturbing her, he had a feeling it was one of his keys to winning her.

Her dove gray eyes met his and a flush colored her cheeks. "Yes, but Dr. Halloran said..." She looked away, gulping on her emotion. "He said I could convince him to give me an A, but otherwise I would get a B." She rubbed at her forearm, at a bruise there, faintly in the pattern of a hand.

Leon felt a flare of fury at the implication. "You are saying your instructor required sexual favors in order to bestow the desired grade?"

"I can't prove it," she said, forlornly. "But yes, that was his implication. The scholarship was a full-ride one, for academics, but without the required grades, I lost it."

"What will you do now?" he asked. If she was having financial difficulties, she might be easier to woo – but he wanted to win this woman over due to her feelings for him as a man, rather than because she was desperate to be saved from some financial riptide pulling her under.

She rested her forehead on her knees. She was crying. He felt each sob, each jerk of her shoulders as if a knife was turning in his gut. He wanted to eviscerate the man who did this to her, and at the same time, he honestly did not know if his own advent in her life would leave her just as disturbed, or if she would respond positively to his interest – his *intent* to make her his Queen.

She remembered Dr. Halloran grabbing her breast and shuddered in distaste at the memory of the confrontation. He had greasy skin and a large rounded belly on an otherwise slender body with narrow hunched shoulders. There was no way she would allow him access to her body.

It had been the family joke that she was never going to leave home unless she married. But it really wasn't a joke. Everyone in the family understood her reticence. She was shy around strangers and disliked being alone. Only her academic prowess gave her the courage to accept the full-ride scholarship at her brother's university half an hour away from her parents' home, and then only because she could share her brother's apartment. She was not emotionally or psychologically well-equipped for the real world. The year she spent alone since the accident left her feeling frightened and insecure.

"Did your professor take your innocence?" he asked her gently, eyeing the bruise on her arm.

"He tried," she whispered. She was grateful at the time when another student knocked on his office door, wanting to talk to him. She stifled a sob of emotional anguish, wishing fiercely her parents and brother were still alive.

A warm arm coming around her shoulders had her head jerking upright. She looked at the stranger, who settled next to her, her eyes studied his. "I'm sorry, I'm not very good company at the moment," she said, ashamed of what the professor did to her.

"You are distressed, little one, it would seem you need a shoulder to cry on. I happen to have very broad shoulders. Perhaps you will make use of them?" His voice was gentle on her ears, sincere, soothing.

He pulled her into his arms and she allowed herself to be held, giving in to the emotions she kept at bay for the last year. First the horror of losing her entire family, then the grueling surgeries and therapy to reconstruct and rehabilitate her ankle, and finally the disgusting confrontation with Dr. Halloran. She snuggled into the plush soft fabric of the robe she purchased for her brother and allowed the emotions free rein.

Leon held the girl as she cried. After a time, she fell asleep. It felt peculiar to have her in his arms, as if his soul had already taken up residence within her, feeling a happiness that contact alone would bring him over the entirety of his life. He wished he could render the man who injured her incapable of repeating the performance. Finally, there was a part of him that felt guilty. He planned to possess this woman, make her his, bring her home to Estolia, and keep her. If he used her distress to fulfill his own needs, would that not make him just as sleazy as her professor? He was uncomfortable as he thought over the ramifications.

Once she was asleep he pulled out his cell phone and proceeded to make detailed plans. The jet would be fueled and waiting for his arrival at the nearest airport. His brother was going to send him the information he had on Calista so he could understand her situation more fully.

He would proceed cautiously, carefully, doing everything he could to make choices that were not only right for him, but also right for her. He believed his plans for her, ultimately, were in her best interests, but he knew it was important, even vital that the things he did from this point forward were always clearly the right choice for *her*, regardless of his own wants and needs.

He would also employ a young woman to take a class from the disagreeable professor. If Dr. Halloran made a habit of propositioning his students, then she would obtain proof of his evil intentions and see that he lost his job as a result. Leon felt a thrill of satisfaction when he thought of stopping the professor from preying on young women. The bruises on young Cali's arms infuriated him; he had to stifle the desire to have him maimed so he would never force another unwilling young woman into his bed.

His phone vibrated as a text came through with an attachment. He opened the attachment and read the information his brother sent on Calista Teare.

For two years, his brother was roommates with Orion Teare. The two men had become the best of friends and Orion expressed a lot of interest in Estolia. Especially as concerned his sister. She was very shy, sweet, self-effacing, not well suited emotionally or psychologically to the culture of the United States. Nico met her and felt, with the strength of his future calling, that it was a good idea to introduce her to Leon when he was nearing his thirtieth birthday.

Five months after Nico returned to Estolia, just over a year ago, she was involved in a dreadful accident with her family. Nico felt the tragedy acutely, to learn that his best friend had died. Orion's last action had been to protect his kid sister before a truck plowed into the crowd, killing her entire family. Calista had her ankle crushed, while it had been successfully reconstructed, it had a permanent weakness that made it impossible for her to get a job on her feet.

The report indicated that she was incredibly intelligent, doing very well in all academic disciplines. She didn't yet have a specific subject she was studying, having enjoyed every topic she studied. She was twenty.

The one thing the report couldn't say was whether she would be the one woman above all other women to capture his heart, ensnare his body, and keep his soul safe. It could not say whether he would see the glimmering beautiful aura that was the visible manifestation of her soul.

About an hour after she fell asleep there was a loud buzzing from the end of the hallway, followed immediately by the cessation of the humming sound of the dryer. He felt her begin to stir.

Cali couldn't believe she cried all over the handsome stranger, and then fell asleep in his arms. She pulled away from him and looked at him, her eyes searching his. "Please forgive me for my emotional outburst," she said softly. "I didn't mean to take so much of your time."

"There is nothing to forgive," he insisted. "I can only hope I have done you a service in being available for you."

She sighed. The release of emotions did help, but they didn't solve her money problems. She stood up and walked over to the table strewn with her financial documents. She looked again at her bank statement. By the end of the week, she would be overdrawn. She knew only part of her problem was the loss of her scholarship. The mismanagement of money following the death of her family was her biggest problem.

He followed her over to the table and stood next to her, looking at the paper in her hand. She knew he could see how dire her financial situation was.

"Do you have any family to turn to, to help you out?" he asked her.

She shook her head. "No. My family died in an accident a year ago. I'm alone in the world. I'm hopeless at coping with this." She indicated the pile of financial documents. "I don't have the slightest idea what I'm supposed to do."

"In my country a woman as beautiful as you are would have made an advantageous marriage. Arranged by your family and the family of the man fortunate enough to be acceptable."

"Even in this modern era?"

"Especially in this modern era," he asserted. "I am obligated to marry. In fact, the letter mistakenly sent to your mailbox is a command that I return to my country and, if unmarried still, I am to marry whomsoever my father has decreed." He paused for a moment before saying, "Perhaps you would do me the honor of marrying me?" He smiled at her.

Her eyes widened and her pupils dilated as they searched for the joke or sincerity within his amber eyes. After a time, she looked away, confused. "Why would I do that?"

"You have a financial crisis that requires a solution. I quite like the idea of choosing my own mate rather than having one thrust upon me."

She suddenly imagined this man intimately entwined with her on a bed and blushed. She should be refuting his suggestion, but the echo of his voice and compelling accent reverberated through her mind. Finally, she said, "it's stupid to even consider it." She could hear the hesitation in her semi-refusal. She wanted to say yes to him, allow him to take over her concerns and problems, and rely on him to keep her safe.

He took the bank statement out of her hand and set it on the table. Taking her hand, he led her back into the sitting area. Guiding her to sit on the sofa, he reached for the ring box. His eyes met hers and he said, "No, Cali, it is not stupid. I meant my proposal. Will you do me the honor of marrying me?"

She was mesmerized by his eyes, by the intent within them. She was only barely aware of nodding her head, agreeing to marry him. She felt the cold of metal and looked down at the beautiful ring on her finger; what he asked began to sink in.

22

Acceptance

Estolian history demonstrates the profound impact the writings of earlier generations have on the righteous choices made by the Sons of Zaccarias, especially in adversity or when faced with the unusual.

~Erramun Zeladon, Descendant of Zacarian; Capitulo 44

LEON STARED at the ring on her finger and for a moment her aura shone more brilliant than ever, confirmation, if he needed it, that she was the one *Deity* decreed would be the Keeper of his Soul. He cupped the side of her face in his hand before he leaned forward to salute her lips with his. He felt her hesitant response and brushed her lips with his tongue before invading her sweet recesses, escalating into passion.

The feeling of her response, sweetly innocent, to his mouth on hers quickened his breathing. With his physical response reverberating through his body, he knew he would do anything for the woman in his arms. He needed to make the right choice for her. For them.

His hand on her breast through the thin fabric of her caftan brought a gasp to Cali's lips. Her hand settled over his but did not try to push him away.

He felt the incredible heat of her body against his own. She was wearing *only* the caftan, and he felt every contour of her body. He lifted her hands to his chest and in moments she was sliding them under his borrowed robe, caressing his skin.

After what seemed like hours of kisses and caresses, he urged her to her feet and guided her towards the back bedroom. Once there, he kissed her again, seducing her senses, reveling in the feel of her body through the thin silky fabric of the caftan.

She explored his body, speeding his pulse considerably. She pushed the robe off his shoulders and then her questing hands fumbled with his briefs until he assisted her to push them off his body. He kissed her again, hiking her caftan up, caressing her thigh. She moaned against his lips.

"I want to solve all of your problems, Calista Teare. I want to rescue you from poverty and loneliness. I want to make you mine, and in turn, I want you to brand me as yours. From the moment I saw you, I knew we were destined to be together." He pulled her to her feet and back into his arms. "Marry me, Cali," he whispered.

His words were seducing her mind, as his hands touched, seduced her body.

She felt his hand on her naked thigh. Somehow, they'd gone from her living room to her bedroom, and he wasn't wearing anything at all. When he pulled the caftan off her body and discarded it, she whispered half-heartedly, "we shouldn't." He pushed her backward onto her bed. Her hands continued their exploration of his shoulders, his body, urging him closer.

"We should," he countered, "Say yes, Cali. Say you'll be mine." He kissed her, and she was torn between objecting to the pace he was setting and agreeing to his crazy proposal.

"Yes," she said in response to the pleasure he was giving her. Before she could conjure any objections, she felt his body come between her legs, burying his length in her sheath.

As his body moved over her, within her, she felt as though they were somehow two halves to a single whole, as if there was nothing more elemental and basic on the planet than the fact that they belonged together. She felt a deep power and strength coursing through her body as they experienced the fusion of two souls, even as he called out something in a foreign language and came to a halt over her. The rush of pleasurable warmth flooding her body was nothing like any description she ever read. So exquisite that she felt emotionally overwhelmed, tears rolling down her cheeks at the beauty of that one infinitely long moment in time.

He kissed away the tears before rolling with her, tucking her body close to his. When their breathing quieted her eyes grew heavy and in moments, she fell back to sleep.

He contemplated the experience he shared with the exquisite woman. How could the *Capitulos* he studied as an Acolyte leave out the profound sensation of connection between two souls? How could the writings of Zaccarias not include the extraordinary fulfillment he would feel upon completion of the conditions demanded of each of the Heirs of Zaccarias? In what way was this requirement ever a burden to the Zacarian male line? He could not comprehend the lack of expressive poetry and prose designed to encourage men like himself to comply with the exacting requirements. Perhaps the lack lay in the abilities of the men blessed to be a part of his lineage? He understood now why the Elders insisted on certain exercises for the Acolytes.

His hand settled over her abdomen, and he imagined how it would feel for her body to swell with a child, bringing forth their first son. The gift she was, even now, preparing to give them. He had much to accomplish. First, he must convince her to accompany him to Estolia. Once there, they would present their union to his Uncle Zeke, the Keeper of the Soul of all Estolia, and to his father, the King, seeking the sanction of both the body and soul of his nation.

They would then finish their first week together in seclusion in the Mount

Estoliana Temple, receiving the blessings, learning whatever was taught new couples.

He knew his impressions of this monumental day, from his trek through a downpour, to his sweet seduction of the woman who now kept his soul would all be memorialized to the very best of his abilities. If he could only express half of the exquisite ecstasy, one fourth the joy, an iota of the sense of rightness, no other Estolian would ever doubt the requirement to pay heed to the Promise of Zaccarias.

How could any man, knowing what he would find in compliance, choose to do anything other than accept this fate? He looked forward to the discussions he would have with his father, brothers, cousins, and Uncle in the Temple.

He could now return to Estolia. Leon had no intention of remaining separate from his land a moment longer than was required. He would not have remained away for this long but for the recommendation by both his uncle Zeke and his brother Nico. Knowing how close their connection to *Deity*, how critical their communion, he followed their suggestions. Spending time in the greater world was an important preparation for the time he would lead his nation. He sighed deeply in contentment. He may have had his doubts, but he knew now how important this time apart from Estolia was to him.

Cali woke and for a few moments, she felt a level of peace and satisfaction that dwarfed any similar feeling she ever had. She stretched in an excess of physical and mental well-being and then came down to earth with a thump. She felt the warmth of a human body next to her own. She was in the arms of her enigmatic neighbor. A man she'd barely met, and whom she had allowed to access her body. Her behavior was inexplicable. She rolled over so she could look at him, sure she would see indifference and impatience to be gone.

The look in his eyes was warm and proprietorial. He smiled. "It is to be hoped that your sleep was refreshing."

She blushed bright red and looked away from him. "I've never done anything like this before," she admitted.

"I could tell you were a virgin. A gift received with pleasure so exquisite, there are no words in your language or in mine to express it adequately. A memory I shall treasure every day of my life."

She wondered if that was his quaint way of telling her the memory was all he expected to get out of it. She felt bereft at the thought that this was his flowery way of beginning the process of saying goodbye.

His hand settled over her abdomen, "I believe the conception of our firstborn son could not be any more momentous or memorable. In truth, I consider the pleasure and extraordinary fulfillment of our union to be a most convincing sign that our lives will be fully blessed."

She frowned, having trouble following his convoluted method of speaking.

He added, "Come, we must dress if we are to leave for Estolia."

"Estolia!" she exclaimed. "What is Estolia?"

"Estolia is my homeland. It is one of the Balearic Islands south of Barcelona."

"Barcelona? Spain? As in *Europe*? I can't go to Europe!"

"You do, after all, have a boyfriend from whom you cannot bear to be parted?" he asked, his voice clipped and no longer loverlike.

"Of course not," she said. "It's just that it seems a bit crazy to travel to a foreign country at a moment's notice. I can't afford to fly to Europe!" He already stated his need to return to his country. She felt an acute emotional pain at the thought that he would move on with his life and forget her.

"The King of Estolia has sent his personal jet to fetch me back," he admitted. "The flight crew will wait until we are ready to depart. However," he looked at her steadily as he added, "I should not like to be the one to explain our tardiness to the King. I refuse to return to Estolia without you."

She was torn between demanding some breathing space, and the chance to take this wild suggestion and travel to a country she had never heard of, with a man she didn't know a day ago.

"Cali," he said, his voice persuasive, "I meant it when I proposed to you earlier." His thumb rubbed over the ring on her finger. "I knew the moment my ring was on your finger there was no doubt we were meant to be together. Having consummated our union and in so doing declared before *Deity* that our souls are inextricably attached the one to the other, we must marry. It is considered a grievous sin – even a crime punishable by death – for any man of Estolia to take the purity of a woman and not marry her. It is the worst of all crimes. I must present you to the King and our highest religious leader to gain their approval and make you mine."

He climbed out of the bed and then pulled her upright and into his arms. "Come, if we leave within the hour we will arrive by dawn." he kissed her, his kisses soft and persuasive, pulling a response from the depth of her soul. She agreed to his urging that they visit Estolia.

Less than an hour later they were pulling up at a private airfield. She was apprehensive at the thought of just leaving and traveling to some foreign country. But the thought of being separate from this man gave her a physical pain. He also stated frequently his conviction that she was pregnant with their son.

The attendant on the airplane approached Leon and spoke to him softly, telling him they would be landing within the next half hour. He thanked her. "Is the outfit ready?" he asked.

She nodded. When they'd boarded, the dressmaker took Cali's measurements so she could create the perfect dress. Cali deserved to look and feel like the princess she didn't even know she was. He grinned at the thought of *his* princess, the Keeper of *his* Soul, the woman who was literally as necessary to him as oxygen. When he felt a tightness in his loins, he realized he would have to contain his thoughts. It was not the right time to experience again the feeling of her body wrapped tightly around his, or to think about her voice raised in pleasure along with his. He closed his eyes and recited the Twelve Postulates of Inner Peace until he felt an easing in his loins.

He mentally thanked his brother for being so receptive to the Spirit, for knowing two years ago that this woman was right for him, and for sending the jet, complete with the dressmaker, to make sure that her arrival was everything she deserved.

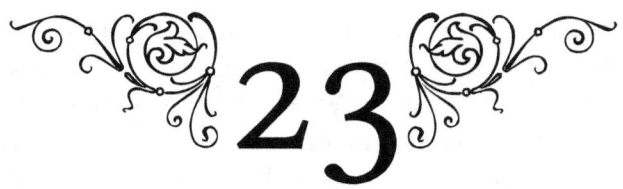

23

Princess

The first time one of the Acolytes called me Princess I wondered who he was addressing. How could I be a Princess? I spoke with Quedaro about it, and he explained that the oldest son of the King is the Heir Apparent, confirmed to that position on the day he is wed to the keeper of his soul. Once wed he is most properly addressed as Prince, and his new bride is Princess. On the seventh day after the birth of the future King, the baby receives a blessing and his parents become the King and Queen of Estolia.

-Fleur Broussard Zacarian; Ensayo 80

THE WARMTH of a hand cupping her cheek woke her, and she sat up in her seat, looking around in confusion. As the mists of sleep withdrew, the memories of their passionate interlude returned. She met his eyes and couldn't subdue the rush of heat to her face as her cheeks reddened, especially as she recognized the desire to experience their intimacy again. She *wanted* to feel his body over hers, inside of hers, the driving force of their mutual passion pulling from her the most intense of sensations.

"We will be landing soon," he said softly. He gestured to one of the flight attendants. "Annika is going to take you to a compartment at the back of the jet and help you change into a dress. You may be presented to the King, so I wanted you to look your best."

The dress looked like it was made for a different, more elegant period of human history. It made her feel like a princess. The bodice was close-fitting with a light sage-green base color covered in gold-edged lilac-paisley designs. The skirt had horizontal layers in alternating green and purple. The sleeves were very short, leaving her arms bare. She wore white gloves. A necklace with amethysts and emeralds adorned her neck. Her hair was pulled back away from her face, a clasp holding it back on the crown of her head. From the clasp, it flowed in waving splendor down her back. Aside from the necklace, the only other jewelry she wore was the exquisite ring he slid on her finger back in her apartment what seemed a lifetime ago.

Once the airplane landed she rejoined Leon. He was wearing a formal outfit like something worn by royalty. He sported a dark forest green cape with an inner surface of purple, and extensive, intricate embroidery in gold, purple, and green. In addition, he wore a black long-sleeved dress shirt and black slacks. Strapped around his hips was a scabbard with a sword. On his head was a lightweight crown. He wore black gloves.

The jet taxied towards a carriage with four white horses standing at the edge of the airfield. There were no buildings. "How do they handle tourists?" she asked, curious.

"No tourists are allowed on Estolian soil," he said. "We value our privacy and our way of life too much to allow ourselves to be the subject of speculation, judgment, and photojournalism finding all the wrong meanings in the motives and methods of our people."

"If tourists aren't allowed, how can I visit?"

He admitted, "My brother believed that if I were to meet you, I would fall in love with you. As such, he deliberately misdirected my mail to your home, and had a passport created in your name so you could freely travel to and from Estolia. There is a more formal, if quite small airport in Pequeño, to the northeast, but I asked the pilot to bring me to the Amadore Airport, which is nearest to my father's home." He pushed a rich purple passport into her hands.

Cali opened the passport and saw her photograph. The script was impossible to read. The letters were nothing like anything she'd ever seen before.

"How would your brother know anything about me?" she asked.

"He told me he was friends with your brother Orion. Nico Zacarian. Do you remember meeting him? He told me the day he met you was the day he vowed to himself that he would introduce us when it was nearing my thirtieth birthday. Estolian men do not marry until they are thirty years old."

"Nico!" she remembered him with great fondness. After the accident that took her family, she received the nicest of condolence cards from him. She felt as though he truly understood her loss. It was *Nico* who first exposed her to the delights of the accent that so intrigued her.

He led her down the stairs to the tarmac and over to a man standing next to an opulent carriage. To Cali, the deference shown by the people on the private jet, and now here on the ground, screamed out 'important' to her. Leon was clearly someone of high station in this land. She admired the rich colors on the uniforms. The green was not quite forest green, perhaps a shade or two lighter. The purple was a deep rich royal color. Throughout the mesh of color was elaborate embroidery with a pale gold thread.

"Welcome back, highness. The King, his First Consul, and your Last Resort will meet you in the Ceremony Room inside the Temple."

Leon inclined his head slightly and assisted Cali into the carriage before he climbed in and sat across from her.

"My father intends to determine immediately if you are acceptable to Estolia."

She felt inadequate. While the carriage left the vicinity of the airfield, she asked, "Why did he call you 'highness'?"

His eyes met hers steadily as he admitted, "Because I am my father's son; my father is the King of Estolia."

"I don't think he'll find me at all acceptable, I don't know how to act around royalty." She could hear the edge of panic in her voice. Once she agreed to accompany him to his land she was committed. She didn't want anything to ruin it for her – for them.

"Do not worry. My father is just a man. He would not expect you to act in any manner other than that which is natural for the person you are."

"But, you told me he was going to select your wife for you. What if he prefers her to a penniless orphan?"

"Calista Teare," he said her name with obvious pleasure, "I will have no other woman, *touch* no other woman but you. *You* are the Keeper of my Soul, as such, there is no other woman on the planet who could be my wife. The only person who can decide that we do not marry is *you*. I hope *you* will accept *me*."

She was digesting that information when he called her attention to two mountains. One had what looked like a cathedral at the base, next to another structure that looked like it was the façade for a structure built into the mountain itself. It reminded her of pictures of Egyptian temples. The other mountain was broad and shorter, and a road twisted around the base leading to a palace on the summit. "On the right," Leon said, "is the palace on Mt. Zaccarias. On the left is both the Mt. Estoliana Cathedral as well as the Mt. Estoliana Temple."

At the top of the mountain, the palace was impressive. It looked like a peculiar mixture that combined the type of Fairy-Tale palace common in Disney movies with the ancient archeological artefacts of Egypt. Rising from the center of the palace was a pyramidal shape, giving the truncated mountain a sort of artificial peak.

The carriage pulled to a halt in front of the temple. Leon climbed out and then turned to hold his hand out to her, helping her down out of the carriage. He settled his hands to her bare shoulders, smiling at her warmly. After a moment of looking at her, he leaned forward to whisper, "You *look* like royalty, Calista Teare, you *will be* accepted." His lips settled over hers, the familiar touch doing its part to chase away her misgivings.

He pulled back reluctantly and extended his left hand. She took it with her right hand and they began walking slowly together towards the broad steps leading to two massive doors. They were opened by two men in their early to mid-twenties, wearing green robes.

Inside, the floor was a mosaic of brown, black and gold tiles. As Leon guided her straight down the hall to another set of smaller double doors that, it occurred to her that, for a religious building, there was a curious lack of decoration commemorating the holidays. As they neared the next set of double doors, she wondered what new surprises Christmas would bring this year.

Inside the second set of doors was an oval-shaped chamber with a raised stage-like area on the far side. Steps wrapped all the way around the small stage, four steps leading to an elevated surface. The stage was big enough to accommodate the three men standing there along with a large pillow in purple and green with thick gold embroidery.

Leon led her directly up the steps. "Kneel on the pillows," he whispered to her.

Cali followed his instructions, grateful for both his guidance as well as the feeling of his hands settling on her shoulders. Once she was kneeling as instructed, she had time to study the three men standing facing them. In the center was a man wearing robes like those worn by the men who'd opened the doors for them, but richly embroidered; a tapestry of green, purple, and gold. Rather like something a monk might wear. A man of power.

Standing on his right was a man who was clearly King. He wore a thick elaborate crown more imposing and impressive than the one Leon wore and a similar sword. He looked austere and forbidding. Cali felt her legs trembling in fear that, despite Leon's words, these men would find her unacceptable.

The third man, on the other side of the central monk figure, was also dressed in monk's robes. He wore a black sash pinned at shoulder and hip. His right hand gripped the handle of a dagger, with the blade resting lightly in the palm of his left hand. It was Nico! He saw her eyes on him and he winked at her, before turning his solemn attention to the man in the center.

"My name is Lazarus Ezekiel Zacarian. I am the Keeper of the Soul of Estolia, First Consul to the King, and former Last Resort. I understand your name is Calista Teare, daughter of Raymond and Estrella Teare?" the man in the center spoke to her. When she nodded, he smiled. She thought it was a strangely gentle expression for a man whose appearance was so forceful. "Welcome to Estolia, Calista." He smiled briefly before adding, "I would be pleased if you would call me Zeke."

"Thank you," she said, unsure if it was okay for her to speak.

He turned his attention from her to Leon and his expression grew cold, austere. "Leonidas Agamemnon Zacarian, firstborn son of Isaiah Monterrey Zacarian, he who is Duke, Sovereign, and King of Estolia, to fulfill your hereditary role in our nation, from the time you were conceived, you were always constrained to give your soul into the keeping of a woman worthy to be Queen of Estolia, and to do this no more than seven days prior to your thirtieth birthday. What have you to say?"

Leon squeezed her shoulders and caressed her skin with his thumbs as he answered, "I, Leonidas Agamemnon Zacarian, firstborn son of the King of Estolia, have given my soul into the keeping of Calista Teare. A woman more than worthy to hold the soul of a King. In so doing I have kept the promise made by Zaccarias to *Deity*."

"Rise, Calista Teare," Nico said.

Cali got to her feet with Leon's help. One of the younger men wearing robes approached and took the pillow away from the stage. Leon climbed one step so he was standing directly behind her. He pulled her backwards against his body, one large hand on her abdomen while the other was on her shoulder.

Nico stepped forward. "I am Nicodemus Luciano Zacarian, second-born son of the King of Estolia. I have taken on the office of Last Resort. I stand ready to exercise my sacred duty if I am required to do so by Estolian custom and law to uphold the promise made by Zaccarias to *Deity*. I wish to also extend to you, Calista, a heartfelt welcome to Estolia."

The King stepped forward and said, "Calista Teare, I am Isaiah Monterrey Zacarian, Duke, Sovereign, and King of Estolia. My son claims you as the Keeper of his Soul. Did you yield your purity to my son?"

She felt a blush rushing to her cheeks. "I did." She was grateful for the squeeze Leon gave her shoulder.

"Do you wish to reject the man who has taken your purity, or do you accept him as the other half of your soul?" Zeke asked.

She wasn't sure what to say. "I choose to stay with Leon so long as I have that right. I will only leave his side if forced to do so." When the expressions on the faces of the three men did not change, she added forcefully, "I do *not* reject Leon!"

Zeke turned his attention to Leon, "And you, Leonidas, do you accept the Keeper of your Soul or do you require your Last Resort to exercise his sacred duty?"

Leon didn't hesitate. "I accept the Keeper of my Soul and believe she is *worthy* to keep my soul, and that she is *perfect* as the future Queen of Estolia, and mother of the future King. Calista Teare is my *everything*."

Nico tucked the dagger in a hidden pocket on the inner surface of the black sash.

Zeke, his expression transformed to pleasure, said, "You will spend a week in the temple. If the spirit sanctifies your union, you will be married when you have finished your time within."

Several hours later Cali was walking with Leon in the small garden outside the seclusion suite. Even though it was winter, it was still pleasant, with only a chill in the air. She looked at the man who transformed her world so quickly. They had spent some time asleep in the beautiful bedroom and were wearing matching green and purple robes.

"Will you really be King some day?" she asked him.

"I will, Cali. And when I am King you will be my Queen."

"Nico used to call me princess all the time," she said. "The way he said it gave me goosebumps."

"My brother was convinced, from the moment he met you, that you and I would be perfect for each other." He led her back into the seclusion suite, bringing her to a small two-seater sofa. Once she was seated, he went to the small refrigerator and pulled out a carafe of juice, pouring both a glass.

"My brother was so convinced that you were right for me, he planned to bring you, and your brother and parents, here to Estolia this Christmas. But then your family suffered that tragedy."

She sipped at the juice, remembering her brother's plan. She met his eyes and asked, "Do your people even celebrate Christmas?"

"Your people now, too, Cali," he reminded her. "And no, we do not celebrate it the same as your country. We honor many religious traditions of other faiths. Those teachings from other faiths in line with our own are often found in our religious texts."

The things he was telling her about Orion, about his land, and about their future were swirling through her mind. She felt as if it all solidified into one shining, glorious truth. She lived in fear and loneliness the last year, but now that was at an end. More than that, she realized, she was loved and in love. She had a future here.

Part 5 – According to Prophecy

✎ Cast of Characters ✎

Calista Teare Zacarian– (Cali) 89th Queen of Estolia

Cassiopeia Luc-Dumaine – (Cassie) Daughter of 87th King

Isaiah Monterrey Zacarian – 88th King of Estolia

Kedarin Zacarian – Wife of the 88th Keeper of the Soul of Estolia

Kenzie O'Rourke – Customer Service Representative, lives in Anaheim, California

Lazarus Ezekiel Zacarian – (Zeke) 88th Keeper of the Soul of Estolia

Leonidas Agamemnon Zacarian – (Leon) 89th King of Estolia

Lilaine Zacarian – 88th Queen of Estolia, mother of Leon, Nico and Zeb

Lyre Leilani Langham – Girlfriend of Maximilian Icarus Luc-Dumaine

Maximilian Icarus Luc-Dumaine – 2nd son of Cassie and Morgan Luc-Dumaine

Morgan Luc-Dumaine – Distant relative from France; Great-Aunt is married to the 86th Keeper of the Soul of Estolia

Nicodemus Luciano Zacarian – (Nico) Second son of the King of Estolia

Rheannon Zacarian – 4th child of the 88th King of Estolia

Zebastiani Zacarian – (Zeb) third Son of the 88th King of Estolia

Zhare Amadore – Distant descendant of Zaccarias

Circus Freak

2022

The quality of a woman's soul is reflected in the brilliance and colors of her Aura. Deity promised, from the time of Zaccarias, that guidance would be provided to grant clarity to the Sons of Zaccarias and confirm the suitability of their chosen mate.

~Alessandro Octavius Zacarian; Capitulo 72

K ENZIE DEFTLY slipped her shoes back on her feet and then picked up her carry-on luggage. Pausing for a minute, she got oriented and then moved in the direction of the gate for her flight. She ignored the various looks being cast her way. She'd grown used to the way people looked at her.

She remembered what Mark said when he saw her, "You look like a goddamn circus freak." She focused in on the supercilious curl to his lip as he terminated their engagement and summed up everything she was lacking.

He said that having two different colored eyes was proof that nature hated her. Even before her hair was dyed all the colors of the rainbow, he said it was an insipid dishwater blonde, falling like a child's to just below her waist. He added that her blubber at hip and bust, above and below a very tiny waist, made her look like a caricature of a woman.

She was only a few inches shorter than his five-foot ten-inch frame. He called her an amazon that no man would find cuddly or attractive. "A man wants to be needed, to feel as though his woman needs to be protected. He doesn't want a woman big enough to protect him instead."

She arrived at her gate and found a convenient place to sit. She continued to remember that last conversation, especially the sneer on his face as he denounced her personality as too flamboyant, her intelligence as lacking, and her singing voice as too shrill. In all things, he basically summed her up as coarse, unattractive, lacking in proper femininity and, once a man got to know her, unworthy of marriage.

Most of what he said didn't bother her. But she *had* always felt too tall, too fat, and too strong a personality.

She should have seen the writing on the wall once Mark met Shayla. Yet it was still a shock when he dumped her.

When Leila begged her to take part in a before-and-after hair styling and coloring competition Kenzie agreed. She thought back fondly to the extraordinary competition. Mark used the change in her looks as his primary reason, but she knew he planned to dump her and would have used any excuse available.

By the end of the competition her hair was a glorious rainbow, and she had ten outfits designed to mesh perfectly with her extraordinary coloring, and an all-expenses paid trip to Paris – her part of the prize for having the prize-winning hairstyle. And Mark was using her new look as his reason for dumping her. One of his reasons, anyway.

Kenzie shrugged off her memories and thought ahead to the new chapter in her life. With her new wardrobe and the ten-day vacation, she felt as though her future would hold some great new *solo* adventures. Mark's denouncement solidified her belief she was not marriage – or girlfriend – material. No, she thought to herself, she would not seek out romance in her future. There were plenty of things she could do in her life that didn't include men. She would get a new job when she returned. Possibly even move to a new city or a new state.

For now, she decided, she was going to enjoy Paris. All other decisions would wait until she returned.

She glanced at a clock and saw there were still two hours before her international flight would begin boarding. Across the busy concourse was a lounge. She decided to get a drink.

Ten minutes later she was standing next to the concourse sipping a rainbow concoction the bartender insisted she *had* to try. She idly watched the stream of humanity flowing back and forth in the busy airport. People were arriving from far distant places and heading either for the exits, or for connecting flights. People were also arriving from the city to board their flights and begin their adventures. Old people and young people. Women with babies. Affluence and poverty. Businessmen. Newlyweds. Solo fliers and large families. Pilots and flight attendants. People working at the airport. Humanity in all its raw sizes and shapes.

She amused herself by speculating on the lives of the people she saw. Especially the men. One man had a roll of fat like a spare tire around his middle almost perfectly emulated by the brown fringe of hair around a shiny bald head. His face seemed to settle naturally into smile lines. She imagined that he was a father of three, with a little eight-year old daughter grinning adoringly at him with one tooth missing. His wife would be sort of dull and uninspiring to others, but he would not see that, he'd see her as beautiful and desirable.

Kenzie turned her attention to another man who was probably in his mid to late fifties. His tank top showed off a long expanse of skinny sinewy tattooed arms and parts of his tattooed torso. His hair fell to below his shoulders and was a bit lank and greasy, dark brown with more white and gray than the original color. She imagined him going to head-banging rock concerts in his younger years and waiting for his music career-ship to come sailing in and bring him glory, riches, and women – only to have it sail right by the pier of life upon which he was standing.

A slender man with receding red hair and lots of freckles looked around like he was lost until a musical shout caught his attention. Before Kenzie could dream of what his life was like, a small blonde woman raced up to him and kissed him – oblivious of where they stood in the airport. With a blush, Kenzie turned her attention away from the couple. She wished some man would care for her as much as the redhead seemed to care for the petite blonde woman.

The next person she noticed was a man in a business suit. A high-powered executive, she decided. Coat slung over one shoulder, briefcase in his hand, walking slowly towards where she was standing, his thoughts clearly centered inward. He was looking directly at her but didn't seem to see her. She decided that his thoughts were troubling him. He probably had some critical business decision he was faced with and didn't know whether he should make a leap of faith or do something conservative instead. He had very dark hair, dark eyes, and she thought he would sport dimples if he ever bothered to smile. He looked like he was in his late twenties or early thirties. Tall, well over six feet, with very broad shoulders, slender hips, large elegant hands and overall the sort of build Kenzie found attractive. Mark had a similar build, but compared to this man, Mark fell far short of her ideal. This man *was* her ideal. For just a moment, she had an erotic image of the man approaching her in bed with her, their limbs intimately tangled, their bodies joined, and she had to look away with a slight blush.

She glanced at her drink and sipped some more of the concoction. It *was* as good as the bartender promised, and it matched her hair and her dress. She smiled whimsically at her thoughts and looked up, ready to continue her people-watching. Except now, standing in front of her, was the sexy man she had fantasized about. He did have dimples.

"Hello," he said to her. His eyes ran over her outfit and hair before returning to her eyes. "I saw you from a distance, and I thought to myself that I have never seen a more incredible looking woman in my life."

He spoke with a rich accent and sexy voice, delivering an amazing compliment she never expected to hear. His words were a balm for her injured soul after Mark's denunciation of her. "Thank you. You're pretty incredible looking yourself."

He laughed. The sound trickled down her spine and lodged in her core. "Do you mind if I have a drink here with you? It is some time before my flight, and I should enjoy having the chance to relax for a moment with a beautiful woman."

She shrugged in acquiescence. Five minutes later he was back with a drink, asking if she would sit inside the establishment instead of sitting on the edge of the concourse. She followed him to an isolated booth.

He sat across from her and smiled at her again. "My name is Nicodemus Luciano Zacarian. Please call me Nico."

She smiled and offered, "I'm Kenzie. O'Rourke." She felt a thrill to have this handsome man spending time with her, even though they were just two strangers who would never meet again.

"It is a true delight to meet you. Tell me a little about you Kenzie. It is obvious that you have a fascinating story." His eyes lifted to the rainbow blast of color that was her hair.

She had to laugh at that. "I'm not, really," she demurred. When he just waited she said, "I'm twenty-two. Single. On my way to France for a vacation with only myself as company. I'm between jobs, and when I return I will look for another job. I might move someplace else and find a job there. I work in customer support."

"Is there not some extraordinary story about your marvelous look?"

She shared with him the contest she volunteered for and how hers became the winning hair style, resulting in the vacation to Paris.

"Have you recently divorced?" He touched the circle of lighter skin on her left ring finger.

She frowned at her hand, at where he was rubbing the lighter skin with his thumb. "No, my fiancé decided I looked like a fat circus freak and he traded me in for someone better-looking."

He shook his head sadly. "A man singularly lacking in taste to so malign a woman as incredibly beautiful as you." He raised her left hand to his mouth so he could kiss the circle of lighter skin.

25

Abduction

The sons of Zaccarias will encounter the woman who will keep their soul in the most unlikely of places. The key ingredient that must always be at the forefront of their minds is that when Deity provides the aura, they must be willing to see and act upon it.

-Johnathon Tethys Zacarian; Capitulo 83

THE WAITRESS PAUSED by them and asked if they wanted another drink, or something to eat. Her companion ordered another of the rainbow drinks for her and a drink for himself. He was charming and personable to the waitress, and Kenzie's opinion of him went up. She was always impressed by people who could treat those in the service industry with respect and dignity.

"So, tell me about you, Nico."

"I am from the island nation of Estolia. I am returning to my land to be married. It is a family and religious obligation to marry during my thirtieth year; I will be thirty at the end of the week, so I must needs fulfill my destiny and marry."

"Your bride-to-be is waiting for your return then?" she asked. She felt a little let down to discover this man who was so flirtatious with her was already taken.

"No indeed. When I began this journey, I had not yet met the woman who could keep my heart and soul safe. I simply knew that the sooner I could find the woman who would fulfill my needs, the happier I would be." His expression grew intense. "I should like to ask you two questions, Kenzie. Will you promise to answer them truthfully?"

She nodded and took a long sip of her fresh rainbow-colored drink.

"I found myself wondering, the instant I saw you, if my first overwhelming impression of you could possibly be correct." His eyes searched hers, as if seeking answers in their multicolored depths. "From the moment the thought came to me, I knew it was essential I determine if my impression was in fact truth. It seemed so unlikely in this era, in your country for a woman of such exceptional beauty, such exquisite presence to be untouched, and yet, Kenzie, that was the thought that came to me when first I saw you. Will you confirm that you are, in fact, untouched?"

Kenzie felt a flood of warmth rise to her face. She wasn't sure if he was asking what she thought he was. After a second, when he continued to wait, she sought clarification, "You're asking if I'm a virgin?"

He nodded and waited.

Raising her chin slightly, remembering Mark's words on the topic – how men didn't want all the tears, blood, and inexperience of a virgin in their bed – she admitted, "I am a virgin. Do you make it a hobby to go around trying to figure out whether women have had sex?"

He shook his head in response to her question. "In truth, I have never once actively entertained such a curiosity about a woman before now. I felt it was something I had to know – about you."

"Why? We're strangers. In an hour, I'm getting on an airplane headed for France."

"I suppose the main reason was that if you were, as I suspected, untouched, then I would be able to ask you my second question."

She took a long drink of her rainbow beverage before asking, "And what is your second question?"

He grabbed both of her hands and locked his eyes with hers before asking, "Will you marry me?"

She was left speechless. Here was a man who was an eleven on the Richter Scale of male good looks somehow asking her to marry him.

"You're serious?" she clarified.

"Never more so," he said. "I knew, from the moment I saw you, that you were in fact the one woman on this planet I could marry. Once I recognized you for the woman destined to keep my soul, I was faced with the task of somehow convincing you it was true."

She knew she should be telling this man she couldn't possibly marry him. But there was something compelling about him. Alluring. She had the strongest urge to just tell him she *would* marry him, on the strength of that one question. "I'm intrigued," she said, "how *could* you convince me?"

"I believe if you saw my home land, you might be more easily convinced. Would you be willing to accompany me to Estolia? It is a beautiful land. We do not allow tourists, but it is a rich nation, and every invited visitor we have ever had has told us how fine and inspiring our land is. I could give you a most delightful vacation, treat you like a princess, and you could decide there."

"My mother taught me to not take rides or candy from strangers. I'm not sure it would be wise to just allow you to take me to your home land."

"Alternatively," he said, "I could follow you to France, court you, seduce you, and thereby convince you." His voice was low and sexy, and when he spoke about seduction, she felt he was already seducing her nerve endings into compliance.

"I don't know why I'm tempted to accept your proposal," Kenzie said, feeling as though the mental clarity, she normally enjoyed was missing. She glanced at her drink. Two tall exotic alcoholic beverages were likely chiseling away at her inhibitions. "What would you do if that didn't work?"

"I could simply abduct you, bring you to Estolia, seduce, entice, and ensnare you."

"I should say no. It's crazy. How do I know I can trust you? You've admitted to plans to seduce me or abduct me."

"Tell me, Kenzie O'Rourke, what enticement might find favor with you? How might I convince you to at least explore the possibility? I believe firmly that if you came to Estolia, you would discover my proposal meets with your favor. So, if I cannot entice you to agree to marry me, can I entice you to travel with me to Estolia?"

The more he spoke, the more tempted she was. "I have a ticket to France. I do *not* have a ticket to Estolia. Even if you could buy me a last-minute ticket to Estolia, what if I choose not to marry you? I'd be giving up my all-expenses-paid trip to France."

"I have an acceptable solution. Allow me to convert your ticket to an open-date ticket in first class. You will be able to request travel on any date, via Estolia Airlines. This will clear up the airfare. I am certain your hotel accommodations can be likewise shifted. If they cannot, I shall supply new ones for you."

"My luggage? I can't do without my luggage, and it's going to France." Earlier she explained to him her wonderful wardrobe that was created specifically to look good with her hair.

He chuckled. "So, will you accompany me to Estolia if I can miraculously acquire your luggage?"

"You haven't addressed the one other thing I mentioned. How do you know I can get tickets to Estolia?"

"That, my dear, is the easiest of all hurdles. If you will give me your tickets, your hotel information, and your claim tickets for your luggage, I will return within fifteen minutes with new tickets to Estolia."

She handed over the requested items and watched him leave, wondering if she was crazy to just hand over her tickets to this handsome man who proposed within an hour of meeting her.

She sat back in her seat and closed her eyes, trying to keep thoughts of the handsome man out of her mind. She kept imagining his body entwined with hers in the most erotic positions. After a minute, she decided to use her smartphone to look up his country. She'd never heard of it. The information available online was minimal. Barely one page:

> Estolia. One of the Balearic Islands situated between Mallorca and Ibiza in the Western Mediterranean Sea, southeast of Spain. Sometimes referred to as Pequeño. 2020 census data puts the population at 13,293.
>
> Founded in the year 720 BCE by the prophet Zaccarias and his wife Estoliana. They established both the nation and a religion at the same time. The nation has a hereditary monarchy but is primarily a theocracy. The current monarch is Leonidas Agamemnon Zacarian.
>
> In the Estolian religion, men are constrained to marry at the age of 30, and there are restrictions as to whom they can marry. All

marriages must be approved by the leader of the religion – usually the younger brother of the King.

Desiree Andora of Barcelona won the gold medal in dressage in the 2020 Tokyo Olympic Games. Her horse, Cimitarra de España, is an Andestolian warmblood. These talented horses originate in Northern Estolia.

The Wallard Swan is indigenous to the Balearic Islands but can now only be found in Estolia.

Tourists are not accepted. travel visas are strictly limited.

She stared at the picture of the King. He was very similar in looks to Nico. Perhaps a couple of years older, and not nearly as handsome. She tried to look up further information but got the same few paragraphs on multiple websites. She'd never heard of any country having so little information available on the internet.

"I was able to finish the tasks you set me in under ten minutes!" Nico said, sliding back into the booth, breathing heavily as if he'd been running. "I could not, however, bring your suitcases into this region of the airport, as they do not allow this due to security screening. I do promise to demonstrate to you my success prior to boarding so you will have no doubts."

"You were able to get my luggage... what about the hotel, the airplane tickets?"

He smiled, his dimples showing again. "I must confess that I decided my true quest to win your agreement to visit my nation was to find your luggage. I was able to do that easier than I anticipated. I shall simply pay for hotel accommodations in Paris if you do not choose to remain with me in Estolia. And the airplane tickets were easiest of all, as I merely had to secure tickets on Estolia Airlines."

"How will I obtain a travel visa? Google says they are strictly limited." She was going to do this crazy thing and go with this stranger to the land of Estolia.

"I have not mentioned that my father and uncle are men of some importance in Estolia. I, too, have a position of some power. I am the one who issues travel visas. It is easy for me to invite anyone I wish to come to Estolia."

"And the next flight to Estolia?"

"They are ready for boarding, even at this very moment." He slid out of the booth and extended a hand to her. She wondered if she was crazy to go with this man. After a minute, she extended her hand to him and allowed him to pull her to her feet.

While they walked she reviewed again the information she got from her internet search. "The internet says all marriages must be approved by the religious leader of your nation." She stopped abruptly before pointing out what, to her, seemed to be an important consideration, "I can't imagine them accepting someone who looks like a circus freak."

He stopped when she did, and at her reference, he looked at her, his eyes traveling over her colorful hair and mismatched eyes. He shook his head slightly and said, "I believe you will find favor with the leader of the Estolian religion. You are truly an exceptionally beautiful woman."

"This is crazy," she said, her eyes meeting his. "I don't know anything about you."

"But you are tempted. That means it is right that we marry." He put his hands on her shoulders and leaned forward to kiss her lightly. The kiss wasn't demanding or taking, rather it was reassuring with a hint of future passion. When he pulled back he smiled into her eyes before heading for their gate, she followed him without question.

Fifteen minutes later they were at a little-used gate where a woman in a fancy uniform of green and purple stood next to the open door waiting. She smiled at them both. "We are ready to board." Her attention turned to Kenzie and she said to her, "We were able to retrieve your luggage from the Air France flight. It is on the tarmac awaiting your inspection before we stow it properly."

Kenzie followed Nico down a ramp and out a door. She wondered how they knew it was her luggage specifically. Once they were outside, she saw her suitcases standing on the tarmac near the stairs for boarding a small unmarked jet. She opened one of them and saw the items she'd packed away. The other was also her suitcase. They even had her garment bag with the exquisite ballgown. Straightening she looked from Nico to the stairs. She had a sense that if she were to climb those stairs she would end up marrying this man. Was she becoming complicit in her own abduction?

Nico stared at her. Kenzie O'Rourke. She impacted his senses the moment he saw her. Even before the colors of her hair melded into the colors of her aura, making her look like the living epicenter in a vortex of rainbow insanity. He shook off the memory and focused on her. She was looking at him with concern, and he realized she needed to be convinced to get onto the airplane.

He closed the distance between them, pulling her slowly into his arms so he could kiss her again. He put his heart, soul, and mind into using the kiss to convince her to accompany him. When he pulled away she looked bemused. He tucked her arm beneath his own and led her up the stairs and into the airplane.

Once inside the airplane she looked around curiously. It didn't look like any airline she'd ever frequented. The padded seats and other furniture looked more like luxury furnishings in a sitting room. There were no other passengers. "I thought you said they began boarding already."

"They were ready to have us board. Estolian Airlines is a convenient name for the small fleet of private jets used by the government of Estolia for matters of state."

The door to the jet was secured and it began to back up. She was kept from asking the next question dancing in her mind by an announcement over the intercom. She listened in fascination to the lyrical foreign language; the fluid symmetry of consonants and vowels; and the inflections on different syllables. She recognized the influence of the language on Nico's exquisite accent.

Once the announcement was over, Nico said, "I have been informed we will be stopping twice to refuel, but it is anticipated we will land before dawn in Estolia."

"Have you abducted me?" she blurted out.

"That is an interesting question. Mostly because the answer is not clear. I could answer your question with perfect honesty by saying you have not been abducted, but I could also answer honestly and say I have abducted you."

Before she could respond to his peculiar multi-faceted answer, the intercom came alive again and the person spoke this time in English. "We are next in line for takeoff. Please buckle your seat-belts. Once airborne we will be serving refreshments and a little later we will have a meal."

Shortly after the announcement, the airplane took off. Kenzie looked at Nico, seeing pleasure and satisfaction on his face. She sensed that this was the short-term objective he was aiming at. To have her completely within his power.

Once the airplane was no longer climbing, she was served a glass of wine. Only then did she have the chance to question Nico's assertion, "In what way have I *not* been abducted?"

He sipped at his golden wine and seemed to be considering his answer. "When you were given the courtesy of an invitation that you chose to accept and you came aboard of your own free will, you could hardly be considered the victim of abduction. In addition, there are no shackles that hold you captive. Nobody will make you do anything you sincerely object to doing. You will not come to any harm while on this airplane or within my country. You will be an honored guest at all times."

While he spoke, his eyes met hers and delivered an equivalent message of sincerity. She sensed some undercurrents, but she believed she was safe. "If all that is true," she asked, "then how *have* you abducted me?"

"If I wish it, I could keep you in Estolia indefinitely."

"And is that your wish, Nico, to keep me indefinitely?"

"Kenzie O'Rourke, you knew before you came aboard this airplane that I want the chance to convince you to marry me. It is my hope that you *will* marry me and remain with me forever in Estolia."

Their conversation became more general after that when they were brought a meal. Shortly afterwards the two rainbow drinks, along with three glasses of wine had Kenzie drifting off to sleep.

Nico thought about his brother; Leon was behind him fully in his semi-abduction of the colorful woman. He had no doubt that she would marry him. It would be impossible for the future Keeper of the Soul of Estolia to meet the woman who was meant to keep his soul and have her truly reject him. No. Fate, the Promise of Zaccarias, and pure chemistry dictated that this woman was the one woman who would keep his soul, complete him, and hand to him the final mantle of power that he could not obtain without her.

In his case, becoming the Last Resort was only a matter of helping his brother find the one woman worthy of him, and then making sure his brother followed the dictates of Estolian law by wedding her not more than seven days after bedding her. He would gratefully retire the sash of office to its normal location in the Mount Estoliana temple once his first-born child received his birth-blessing. It would adorn the statue of Zaccarias in his office until a year before Leon's son Tiernan turned thirty.

What would he learn in the days ahead about this woman who called herself a fat circus freak? He recalled the ring of white flesh on her left ring finger. His heart flipped when he saw the circle of untanned flesh. Could the aura be mistaken? Had some other man deprived him of the Keeper of his Soul?

Uncle Zeke would be surprised by how flamboyant this woman was. Certainly, she was nothing like the women he dated in college. Yes, Kenzie would surprise his relatives. But appearances were unimportant when compared to the character and soul within, and on that score, he had no doubts about this woman.

He felt the subtle push from *Deity* and realized in that moment that Kenzie would never be *his* if he pushed her, seduced her, without telling her everything she needed to know beforehand. He could never take any woman without consent, but just having her agree to intimacy wasn't enough. She had to know *what* she was agreeing to. Her recent break-up left her soul slightly bruised, but he had no doubts that she was a strong woman, with a powerful sense of self

No, for the woman who would keep his soul safe and enable him to Keep the Soul of all Estolia, it mattered that she understood who she was marrying. He had a week to acquaint her with the most important aspects of Estolian religion, custom, and law. A week to gain her heart. A week before he would claim everything that she was, inside and out. A week before the most pivotal moment of his life, when his soul would find its home, comforted, cared for, and kept gently and securely.

The blessings bestowed upon his people, when they were willing to keep the Promise of Zaccarias were impossible to enumerate. He looked at Kenzie – he had absolutely no doubts about her.

He hoped he would be able to convince her as soon as possible. She might not have really understood what he meant when they joked about abduction, but he was determined that she would never leave Estolia except by his side, as his wife.

26

Technicolor Dawn

The hardest part of being a daughter of Estolia in the modern world is in accepting the patrilineal model of succession and the misconception that women are somehow lesser in this model of government and religion... Once I took the soul of my husband into my keeping, I realized that the opposite was true. If anything, women are given more control over our world than the men. We keep their soul and influence their actions from the age of thirty onward.

~Ensayo of Rheannon Zacarian

KENZIE FELT A WAFT of fresh sweet-smelling air on her face and opened her eyes. Sitting up, she saw the airplane was on the ground, and the door into the jet was open. Through the windows and through the open door she saw that the sky was a rainbow of colors, from deep indigo night all the way to an incandescent yellow white near the eastern horizon. Nico changed while she was asleep. He looked like a prince. His outfit was crisp and almost military in its precision. He had white gloves on and what seemed to be a ceremonial sword strapped to his side. He had shaved and looked refreshed. He even had a slender but unmistakable crown on his head.

"You are awake, Kenzie. Good! We have arrived in Estolia. If you will follow Lauretta, she will show you where you can refresh your appearance."

Fifteen minutes later Kenzie was wearing another of the outfits she was given as part of the contest. It was a bold rainbow color. The bodice was a creamy pale yellow in almost a peasant style, with a low neckline showing off plenty of cleavage. The skirt was the whimsical feature. There was a mid-thigh-length underskirt in the same color as the bodice. She felt like it gave her the appearance of walking in a frothing roiling seafoam of rainbow. When she joined Nico, she knew she was looking her best.

"I believe no Estolian has ever brought home a bride as exquisite as you."

She looked at him sharply and said, "I haven't promised you, Nico." She knew when she said it that it wasn't true. They both knew she was probably going to marry him. But she didn't want him to make assumptions.

He inclined his head before saying, "Welcome to Estolia. I hope your promise will brighten both of our futures – when you are willing to give it."

At the top of the stairs leading out of the jet, she paused to look at Estolia. The sun had not yet crept over the edge of the world, but the sky was more brilliant than before. At the base of the stairs were three men dressed very formally. Behind them were several carriages. One was closed, the other two were open-topped. The open-topped carriages were each pulled by four identical horses. White horses for one carriage. Brown horses for the other open carriage, and the closed carriage had what looked like the horses from beer commercials.

They descended the stairs together and when they reached the pavement the sun spilled over the horizon, bringing the world of Estolia into bright technicolor relief.

The three men who were there to meet them were impressive. One man, a few years older than Nico, was familiar to her – his picture had been on the internet. He dressed fancier than Nico, with a thick crown on his head. Seeing him in person like this made it obvious that Nico must be related to the King.

The other two men looked to be around the age of sixty. One wore a sort of monk's robe in rich purple and green. He looked related to both the younger men. He had a goatee and looked very sharp, very intelligent.

The third man wore a slender crown, and dressed very reminiscent of the two young men, with a cape and sword. All four men wore, like an invisible cloak, a sort of ultimate confidence. Like they knew their place in the world and the world knew them. Authority and leadership.

Nico halted next to the youngest man and bent at the waist briefly before turning to her, "Kenzie, I should like to present to you my brother, Leonidas Agamemnon Zacarian, Duke, Sovereign, and King of Estolia. Leon, this is Kenzie O'Rourke, the woman I hope will consent to Keep my Soul."

He said he had relatives in high places, so Kenzie shouldn't have been surprised by the revelation that his brother was the king. She had no idea how to properly greet a king. He solved her difficulty by pulling her into his arms in a solid hug.

"Kenzie, you are welcome here in Estolia. Please call me Leon."

His arm around her shoulders, the King turned to the other man wearing a crown and said, "This is our father, Isaiah Monterrey Zacarian, King Emeritus, and my Third Consul. Father, may I present Kenzie O'Rourke, the woman destined to Keep the Soul of my First Consul."

She got an even more solid hug from the former King. "Kenzie, I can see you are truly a special woman. It is my hope that you will choose to bring my son the happiness he deserves." His voice was gruff with emotion.

Nico grabbed her hand and pulled her over to the man with the goatee. "Kenzie, this is Lazarus Ezekiel Zacarian. He is the current Keeper of the Soul of all Estolia, Former First Consul, and Former Last Resort. He goes by the name Zeke. Uncle, may I present Kenzie O'Rourke. By the light of her aura, I knew she was the one who could Keep my Soul."

He stepped towards her and took both of her hands in his, looking at her intently. She had the strange sense that he was looking into her soul.

"Kenzie, it is more of an honor than you can possibly guess for the three of us to meet you, here, this morning." His eyes flicked to Nico before returning to her. "I see my nephew has selected a woman with a rare and extraordinary strength of will. I've only ever known one other woman with a similar strength, and she it is who keeps my own soul safe and dear. My nephew has probably not had the time to share with you much about himself. He is a humble man. He is also First Consul to the King. I can say now he has chosen wisely. You are worthy to Keep his Soul. You have the sanction of the Church."

Kenzie didn't know what to say to this man, but she was amazed at the way all three men accepted her despite her crazy circus-freak hair and clothing.

Nico took her hand and led her to the carriage with the brown horses. Once she was comfortably settled, he sat across from her.

"What did your uncle mean, when he said you are the First Consul?" she asked.

He looked more relaxed, more handsome than ever. "It is traditional for the first-born son of the King to become the next King. The second son of the King has, in many ways, the position or positions of most authority in Estolia. I would not want to be King, and he would not want my position." He paused for a moment to take a deep breath and smiled broadly. "It is great to be home again," he said. "When my brother was ready to turn thirty, when it was time for him to marry. I took my first of three separate roles: the Last Resort. If he was unwilling to fulfill his duties to become King, then as a Last Resort, I would be the new Heir Apparent. To eliminate the possibility, I made *certain* he met and married the perfect girl."

When he seemed disinclined to continue, she prompted, "And First Consul?"

"I was getting to that. The way succession works here in Estolia, when the Heir's wife has her first son, seven days later, the Heir is coronated. Once he becomes King, the First Consul steps down and the King's younger brother takes his place. It means that if something happens to him, I become King. When important decisions must be made, I am the first one he goes to for advice and counsel, though often he seeks simultaneously the counsel of our father and our uncle. We are called the First Four of Estolia, the four most powerful men in the nation. In many ways, the First Consul is the most powerful."

"Your uncle sounded like he was also speaking for the church," she pointed out.

"Being second in line to the throne, and counselor to the King would not place my power above that of my brother. I have a third role I will take on when I marry: Keeper of the Soul of Estolia. This means I will take over and run the Church of Estolia as the spiritual leader. I cannot become the Keeper of the Soul of the nation if I have not first given my own soul into the keeping of my wife."

"This whole Keeping of the Soul stuff sounds weird."

"Our faith revolves around several ideas unknown in any other religion. We believe a man is compelled to set aside all women but one – once he turns thirty. Then he must find a woman who is pure and untouched – a virgin – and have an exchange of like value with her. If he takes her purity, he takes from her something of great value. It is impossible for a man to take something of that value and not give something of like value in return. To us, that means that the man gives to the woman his soul. Once he has found the Keeper of his Soul, a man cannot find sexual desire or pleasure in any other woman. *Deity* takes a strong hand and guides us to the right woman, guards us from making wrong choices, and for our willingness to yield up our lives and futures to these beliefs, we are provided great rewards far beyond anything those who are not Estolian will ever experience."

She remained silent, absorbing everything he said.

"It is not typical to share so deeply the nuances of our faith," Nico said solemnly, "but mine is a peculiar role, as he who acts for the spiritual good of the nation. I did not propose to you lightly Kenzie O'Rourke. I knew you were the right person to Keep my Soul, that you would be acceptable to the church, and that your unique presence would provide something my nation needed."

Before she could respond to that the carriage came to a halt and she looked up. She'd been so intent on what he was sharing that she didn't pay attention to the world outside. The carriage was standing in the forecourt of a fairytale palace. On one side of the carriage was a huge pond with a fountain and on the other side was the palace. They were next to a grand staircase with a mirror image set of dual steps leading up three floors to a grand entrance. "How enchanting!" she said.

"I agree, even though I think of it as the family home, it is also the seat of our government. We will continue to live here in the quarters set aside for the next Keeper of the Soul of Estolia." He climbed out of the carriage and guided her over to the fountain and then pointed out to her a mountain not far distant. "There is Mount Estoliana. At its base is the Temple and the Cathedral. I will spend most of my working time in the Temple. I am certain that you never once thought to marry a man who spent his life in religious pursuits."

She looked from the mountain back to the man who brought her to this peculiar nation. Her eyes searched his, trying to see her pathway forward. She knew, as she looked at him, that she couldn't say no. She wanted him, no matter how insane it was, how crazy to meet someone and so clearly imagine and crave intimacy.

She doubted, if all he said was true, that he would allow her to say no. She took a step closer to him and put her palm on his chest. No matter how calmly he spoke of his religion, keeping of souls, palaces and temples, his heart was beating rapidly.

Whatever he saw in her eyes seemed to communicate something. He leaned forward and kissed her, pulling her body closer to his. She could feel his desire and knew it matched her own. She'd been sexually attracted to this man like no other man she'd ever known. When he finally brought the kiss to a close, he pulled her closer to hug her. "I believe you will find great happiness here in Estolia."

❧

Nico lay on his bed in his room, staring at the ceiling. After they arrived, his mother and sister-in-law took Kenzie under their wing. If he had been of any other calling, he likely would be regretting not following her to France and seducing her away from Estolia. Now that he'd been given official sanction, and now that she'd told him – nonverbally at least – that she was going to marry him, he'd be kept away from her until the night before his birthday.

The thought of the sweet seduction on that night heated his blood. He rejected the notion of anything sweet or seductive. He had a feeling they would ravish one another. She struck sparks off him in ways he'd never read about or spoke about with his father, uncle, or brother. Kenzie O'Rourke was a passionate, vibrant force to be reckoned with. And he looked forward to the reckoning. Oh yes, he looked forward to the moment when her soul would consume his.

A light tap on his door preceded it opening. He looked over and saw his brother coming into the bedroom.

"She's amazing," Leon said, laughing. "You might have warned us though."

Nico laughed with his brother. He knew the flamboyance of his choice would bemuse his family. "*Deity* had a hand in choosing her," he reminded his brother.

"Certainly true, brother, certainly true." His face took on the familiar look of remembering that so frequently fascinated Nico. All the men had it, once they were solidly wed. Estolians were simple people, their religion not at all complex, more spiritual than anything. But the blessings seemed to be uniformly great for those who heeded the message the religion spoke to their hearts.

"How are Cali and Tiernan?"

Leon sat in one of the chairs by the bed and leaned back, a bright smile on his face. "Tiernan is doing very well. Cali is enjoying motherhood. I believe we might try to provide your son a playmate of the same age."

"A true hardship, I'm sure," Nico said dryly.

"Cali likes your Kenzie. I think she'll appreciate having someone else closer to her age to keep her company."

"I thought Rhea just moved back to Estolia?" Nico said, thinking of one of the reasons he journeyed to California in the first place.

"You're right of course. And Lyre. She and Max are also staying at least a year. Cali won't want for company. Nor will your Kenzie."

Kenzie. Every conversation drifted back to the woman who would keep his soul. Nico closed his eyes to savor the visual memory of Kenzie standing surrounded by the pulsating glow of her aura.

Kenzie was grateful for the chance to be by herself. She would join the family for the mid-day meal in a few hours. It was important to take some time to absorb the impact of the last twenty-four hours.

She sat in front of an ornate vanity mirror and brushed her hair while she pondered her impressions of all that took place since she arrived.

If she could believe Nico, adultery was unknown here in Estolia. Faithfulness was built into the religion. Was it really true? Mark was full of the concept of faithfulness when they started to date. He wanted to impress on her how special he was, how close to her ideal *Prince Charming*. One of the things that hurt the most, once she realized that he was spending time with Shayla, was that his protestations of faithfulness were without substance. Once he found someone smaller, thinner, prettier than Kenzie, he ignored everything he ever said about being faithful.

When she called him on it, he blamed her lack of allure. "What the hell did you expect?" By the time he was done denouncing her character, appeal and femininity, she had grave doubts she could keep the attention of any man for an extended period. Nico might be attracted to her now, but she knew from experience that it could – probably would – wear off.

She set the brush down on the vanity table and looked at her reflection. If she could just believe everything he told her about his faith, she would marry him. Marry him and remain in his country.

She looked at her rainbow reflection and grinned, feeling a sudden lightness of spirit, knowing she wanted to marry the marvelous man she had fallen in love with.

Suddenly she felt her skin prickling, and she realized the thoughts filling her head. Had she really fallen in love with Nico? She'd barely known him twenty-four hours. She recalled the mental exercise she indulged in to amuse herself, thinking about some of the more notable individuals she saw walking by her table in the airport. When she saw him, she recognized him as a man with great personal power and, within moments of seeing him, imagined herself intimately entwined with him. Never before had she entertained such erotic thoughts.

She never thought about Mark the way she thought about Nico. He had the ability to energize her imagination. If she was honest with herself, he did more than that. Nico walked into her life and tilted it on its axis. He enticed her with his exquisite accent and captured her with his charm. If what she was feeling was *not* love, then she didn't know what was. Because for certain, her emotions were more involved with Nico than they ever were with Mark.

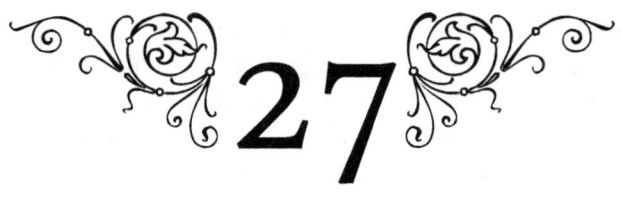

27

Decision

Deity chose the Estolian people to bestow great blessings upon – but like day follows night, all things have their price – and the price for our great blessing, as a people, is to keep the promise Zaccarias made to Deity.

~Antonio Seton, descendant of Zacarian; Capitulo 35

A DISCREET TAP ON HER door roused her out of her thoughts and she rose and went to open the door. She was glad it wasn't Nico. She wasn't sure, in the mood she was in currently, that she would be in the right place mentally to see him. At least, she thought, not without exploring if intimacy with him was as earth shattering an experience as her instincts said it would be.

It was Nico's uncle. "Do you mind if I come in my dear?"

She stepped backwards, allowing him to enter. They walked over to the small arrangement of chairs.

"I sensed your need to have a few more questions answered," he said.

"I do have questions," she admitted, "Nico said it is not typical to be so forthright about your religion, but it is a little bit different in a situation like mine."

"Nico's future was set before he was born. Before his parents were married. He was always slated to be the man to take my position in the fullness of time. It is not, however, an easy job he will be taking on. Keeping the Soul of the nation, as I am sure he mentioned was his future, requires much more from both the man filling the position, but also from his spouse. You. We believe that *Deity* – our God – has a way of guiding us to the woman capable of filling this most critical position. When the right woman comes into his life, he knows it because he sees her aura."

"Nico was walking in the airport, and he saw my aura, and that was it, he was stuck with me, even though he didn't speak with me before he saw it?"

"We have been a successful nation because of our great faith in the promises and blessings of our founder Zaccarias. Not every generation has the same level of faith. We are as human as anyone else on the planet."

"From what Nico told me, he makes it sound like being unfaithful is either impossible, or at least uncommon. That sounds too good to be true."

He smiled softly, as if reflecting on something pleasurable. After a moment, he shared, "Estolians are not perfect. There have been a few limited situations where a couple have anticipated the correct timing, have come together outside the accepted time-table. I have known of three couples in my nearly thirty years of being the Keeper of the Soul of Estolia. I knew, in every case, that they had given up the greatest blessings available to a man or a woman for the transient sensation of physical attraction. In all three cases, the couple did not last. None of them chose to live in Estolia once it was clear their choice was known to me. My heart breaks every time this happens."

"So those who do wait until the marriage is sanctioned they never stray? Ever?"

"The Promise of Zaccarias is such that it is impossible to feel desire for another woman once I give my soul into the keeping of my wife. You could, if you were so inclined, strip naked, but nothing you did would entice me, *could* entice me to desire you."

He meant it. He didn't believe he could be tempted by another woman.

"What about if your wife died? Would you be able to have another wife?"

His expression was solemn. "No man can live without his soul. One of the great trade-offs the men of Estolia make in embracing the faith is the way they become tied to the woman who keeps their soul. Some women who lose their spouse will live on. Often it depends on how much they are needed in this world. Typically, a man and his spouse pass away within a week of one another." He leaned forward to grasp her hands. She felt as if he was communicating more than through his voice and body language, his touch itself seemed to be transmitting information. "When a man's wife – the Keeper of his Soul – passes on, then he will die within one week. He has time enough to finalize any of the loose ends of his life, but no man can survive without her. The joy we experience in life makes this a sacrifice we are willing to make."

"I guess that means Nico really does need to be sure I'm the right one for him." Kenzie said. She felt a shaft of physical pain at the thought he might re-evaluate and choose someone else.

"No, my dear, it is not that simple." He frowned slightly before explaining, "Once a man is gifted to see the aura of his future mate, his future is sealed. Nico has two futures available to him at this point. Only two choices. He will do everything in his power to convince you to consummate your union, preferably on the day of his thirtieth birthday, and then marry you after." His eyes were shadowed for a moment before he continued, "If you are not sure, he does have a full year, until he turns thirty-one to try to convince you."

"One of his choices is to marry me, either sooner or later, so long as he is thirty when the marriage takes place?" she asked.

"Correct." He smiled with a look of fond reminiscence. "Once he marries, seven days later, the spirit is consulted, and if the marriage is sanctioned by the spirit, then you are tied together until time ceases to be. This is merely a formality so long as the union is sanctioned beforehand. For the First Consul, he is made Keeper of the Soul of Estolia on the eighth day after his marriage. A very solemn and sacred ceremony."

"And if he doesn't marry me, you select his bride for him?" Kenzie guessed.

Zeke lost some of his color. "No, Kenzie, this is not what will happen." He stood up and walked away from where she was sitting, going to look in the vanity mirror. He had a dark frown on his face. Turning he swiftly walked back to where she was and pulled her to her feet, holding both of her hands, his eyes meeting hers. "I fear for Estolia, even for the planet itself, if you do not choose to marry my nephew. It is not typical for the King to have three sons. Nico has an older and a younger brother, and there was a prophecy made about all three. The fate of our entire world is dependent on your choosing to take Nico's soul into your keeping. It was prophesied that the three sons of Lilaine would be the future King, the First Consul, and a Catalyst of Change for Planet Earth. Zeb must be allowed to fulfill his destiny.

"If Nico does not marry you, then he will never marry, never know the joy of having a woman keep his soul. Once he saw your aura, he had no choice as to whom he would marry. He would likely live to a ripe old age, as we are a long-lived bunch of people, but he would not marry, and would not stay the First Consul. Zeb, his youngest brother, would be forced to take his place, and when he married, he would take over the Keeping of the Soul of Estolia. A position for which he does not have the appropriate temperament."

"I don't understand," Kenzie said, "if the Keeping of the Soul is linked to virginity, can't Nico find another woman?"

"No, Kenzie. Once he saw your aura, he had no more choice."

She studied his expression, despite his deep alarm at the thought of her rejecting Nico, he didn't believe she would reject him. Feeling self-conscious at the way this man could so easily see into her soul, she asked, "Is there no room for *love* in this religion?"

"Kenzie, I can see you will be a delightful addition to our family. To answer your question, *yes* love *is* a part of our religion. In the secular, non-Estolian world, the viewing of the aura is akin to love at first sight. When Nico saw you, and your aura, he fell in *love* with you. As you, I think, fell in love with him."

"Has anyone ever rejected the woman whose aura they saw?" she asked.

His face grew serious again. "My aunt Anastasia attended university in Alabama. She fell in love with one of the young associate professors at the university. Even though he was not Estolian, he saw her aura. She invited him to visit Estolia, in hopes that her brothers and father and uncle could explain the faith to him. Unfortunately for him, he was disturbed by what he heard. He told her he would not accept the Estolian faith. They argued. She rode back to the palace but her horse spooked and she was thrown. Her neck was broken and she died instantly. Eduardo was devastated. He never had another woman in his life. He remained a good friend of the family. His loss was felt by all who knew him."

She looked down to where her hands were still clasped in his. All the Estolian men she met seemed to feel things acutely. "It is strange that so much of your religion is centered around the actions of the men. I haven't heard much referencing the obligations of the women."

He chuckled, squeezing her hands before leading her to sit back down. "Women who are Daughters of Estolia, those who embrace both the faith, and more importantly, those who take the soul of an Estolian into their safe keeping are considered to have all the attributes of godliness. They do not need to do more than guide their spouse on the road of life. The rewards are impossible to enumerate. As a unit, a man and the keeper of his soul have great promise as to their eternal nature. The essence is felt here in this life. The details of what it is like in the *life-after-this-life* are not given to us to know. We are simple, our religion is simple."

They were both silent for some time. Zeke finally stood and bowed at the waist. "I believe that is enough information for now. Please know I am always available to you. You might also wish to speak with Nico's father, or his brother Leon. None of us doubted you were the woman destined to Keep his Soul."

He pulled her into his arms for a hug and then left while she was still mulling his words over.

❧

Over the course of the week Kenzie spent time with many of the individuals in the palace. She knew she would marry Nico, yet there was something that held her back from agreeing outright. They were relaxing in one of the elaborate sitting rooms. The Queen, Cali, played softly on the piano while conversation drifted from subject to subject.

Nico sat next to Kenzie. "The day after tomorrow, I turn thirty."

"I know."

"Are you willing to watch the dawn with me tomorrow morning?" Nico asked. "It is tradition that, if possible, the men of Estolia climb Mount Estoliana to watch the sunrise on the last day we are twenty-nine."

"I will come with you," Zeb volunteered. He grinned, knowing that this would make him an unwanted third.

Zeke responded, "I believe it *would* be ideal if Zeb did come with the two of you."

"Perhaps when you have finished, the two of us could have a chat," Lilaine, the former Queen of Estolia, suggested.

❧

Circumstances were starting to build a momentum of their own. The ride to the top of Mount Estoliana was far more emotionally and spiritually moving than she anticipated. The horses seemed to know the pathway, as it was very dark when they began the trek. Kenzie rode double with Nico to the top of the mountain. She worried about the burden on the horse but was reassured that Aristotle – Nico's proud stallion – was extremely powerful.

The time spent with her back pressed to Nico's front, his arms around her waist, was special; it felt like a banquet for the senses, the warmth of his body, his unique scent. She was aware of his arousal, and her own.

She wished she'd opted to fly to France. His stated intention to follow her and seduce her seemed simpler than the reality of being in Estolia surrounded by his relations and his religion.

The sunrise did not disappoint. The rising sun came up behind Mount Zaccarias, throwing the turrets of the Palace into bold relief for several moments before the sun peeked over the edge of the central pyramid and suddenly it was transformed, like a black-and-white photograph turned to color.

Later that morning, she was invited to the private sitting room of the former King and Queen. She and Lilaine, as she insisted on being called, enjoyed a cup of tea together.

"I've heard," Lilaine began, "that you are torn in making your decision. I felt I might be able to clear up at least one or two things that might be bothering you."

"You're very kind," Kenzie said.

"No, Kenzie, I'm *not* kind. I'm a *mother* and I desperately want my sons to be happy. I know you, and *only* you can bring my second son happiness. I want you to know your own mind when you allow him to seduce you tonight."

Kenzie blushed bright red.

"What barrier stands in your way, Kenzie?"

"I want to believe," she said. "I just don't think it's nearly as good as they make it sound. It's too good to be true. Men are men, how can they be faithful to one woman for life? I mean to say…" She paused to gather her thoughts before continuing, "I know some men can be faithful to a single woman for life, but every member of the faith, that just sounds like a fantasy to me."

Lilaine smiled in comprehension. "I've lived here in Estolia for thirty-three years, as Queen for thirty-two of them. I've never seen any man stray who has given his soul into the keeping of his wife." She grinned at Kenzie before adding, "They don't even have a word for adultery in the Estolian language."

"Don't you feel like women are sort of superfluous in the Estolian faith. Almost as if there was no reason for them to be a part of it?"

"Oh no!" Lilaine was definitive. "No, it's not like that at all. Think how it was more than 2700 years ago. Life could be brutally short for a woman. Here comes this faith that gives women unheard of reassurances. It's common for a man to see his oldest grandson wed. The way things are done here, that means the man has lived to be ninety-three, or close to it. Women in this faith get longevity, a spouse who can't cheat, and they share something immeasurable. You cannot know how it feels to take your husband's soul into your keeping. The connection is intimate, exquisite, extraordinary. There is no way I could explain it, though many women have tried."

She paused to sip her tea before expanding, "The men of Estolia have their *Capitulos*, the novella that tells everything about the life of each King. They spend a year of education sometime between the age of eighteen and thirty learning about the lives of each former King. Women may read the *Capitulos* if they wish. They're frankly erotic. The women have their *Ensayos* where they take the time to share their thoughts."

"It seems to me," Kenzie said, "that most of the time the selection of a man's bride must be easy. Why is it so hard for me, for Nico?"

"*Easy?*" Lilaine laughed. "My dear, I'll tell you someday just how easy our union wasn't. Or you can read my *Ensayo*. No, my husband decided to reject me and was on the verge of requesting that his brother exercise the office of Last Resort, when he was reminded of something and realized I was right for him and for the nation. No, it is not always easy."

Kenzie felt no nearer deciding.

"I believe I know, Kenzie O'Rourke, what will help you to decide. And the beauty of it all is that it's quite easy to do."

"What must I do?"

"Tonight, at the small party we are having, dance with my son. Give him all your attention. Let him convince you that you are the very center of his universe. I think you've spoken with everyone but the one person most qualified to help you really make this decision. You need to speak with him. I think you'll feel like you've discovered a clarity of thought that has been missing up until now."

28

A Perfect Fit

The longevity of Estolia can be directly attributed to the strength of the promised blessings. No Estolian man, having yielded his soul up into the keeping of his spouse, can do so without experiencing the compulsion to raise each child steeped in the teachings of Zaccarias so that they, too, will have the same wondrous experience in their time.

~Francisco Feliciano Zacarian; Capitulo 77

KENZIE WAS DRESSED for the evening's celebrations early. She left the delightful room she'd been given. As far as she could tell, it was about an hour before the evening meal. She went out to stand by the fountain, and gaze at Mount Estoliana. Her eyes had been drawn frequently to the cathedral and the entrance to the temple.

She sat on the side of the fountain nearest the valley between the mountains. It provided her an uninterrupted view of the two holy buildings. She had been fascinated by both since she came to Estolia.

"There comes a time when you do have to make a leap of faith," said a firm voice behind her.

She turned. It was Nico's brother Leon, the King of Estolia.

"Why is it hard for me?" she asked him.

"My guess is that you have grown up in the absence of any guiding faith or religion. You are not comfortable yielding yourself up to *Deity* in any form, and probably you have felt a certain level of contempt for those who have a belief based on something so ephemeral as faith."

She felt as if somehow this man, whose job description wasn't about matters of the spirit, understood her better than Zeke did.

"If you yield yourself up to faith, it feels like you are rejecting a love and belief in science and the scientific method. It is hard to accept there can be *Deity* who can influence your life."

How could some *Deity* know her, choose *her* as the one for Nico?

"Tell me, Kenzie, if you were to remove religion from the equation, would you be more or less tempted to marry Nico?"

She didn't have to think about it. "More."

"You would marry him if the faith was not a part of this," Leon asserted. "It is the religion *itself* standing in the way. It gives promises you are not willing to believe – because you worry you will discover that they are not true. You worry you will be promised Nico is yours for eternity, only to find he has strayed, and you were a fool to believe this silly religion and the assertions within it. You do not want to believe if believing makes you a fool. You feel strongly that the promises are too clear, too specific. Not nearly as vague as Christian religions you may have learned about."

"You understand me better than I understand myself."

"I felt moved by the spirit to reassure you, help you to see a few things clearly from a new perspective. I believe there are strong forces at work here in Estolia." He was silent for a short while. "I could take you to visit every family in Estolia. *Every* family. You would find a sort of universal happiness in marriage. I believe it is *because* the promises of *Deity* are kept, that there is so much faith in our religion. We believe, because we are given proof that there is a reason *to* believe."

Her eyes returned to the temple. Nico knew what his purpose in life was. What would her purpose be?

"If you *would* marry Nico in the absence of his faith, you *should* marry him in its presence. I ask you, Kenzie, as Sovereign of Estolia, and as Nico's brother, to exercise faith in only *one* thing... yourself. You are right for my brother. Have faith that you can hold him. Trust in *yourself*."

He pulled her into his arms and hugged her. "Save at least one dance for me tonight."

After he left, she turned her back on the temple and looked instead at the pond. Immense Koi swam lazily in the water. She sat on the edge and trailed her fingers in the water, watching as one gold and red fish surfaced and tried to swallow one of her fingers. She giggled at the sensation. In front of her was the palace spread out in all its wondrous glory.

Suddenly she felt carefree, as if her soul was a hot air balloon and all the ballast was jettisoned. She wasn't sure, not entirely, how the evening would go, but she sensed everything was coming clear to her. She was glad that the waiting was almost over.

Hands crept around her waist. Kenzie knew instinctively that they belonged to Nico and she leaned backwards against the strong bulk of his body. The erotic dreams warming her nights came back to her, as his body pressed against hers. She put her hands over his and sighed.

"It is just about time for dinner."

She nodded and when he stepped away she turned and looked at him. He was the most attractive man she had ever met. She remembered back – was it only a week ago? – to when he proposed to her. After Mark's brutal denunciation of her, it seemed impossible to believe anyone would find her attractive.

His eyes met hers, studied them, perhaps trying to decipher the message within. Whatever he saw spurred him to step closer and take her into his arms. She returned his kiss passionately, wanting to do nothing more than skip the celebration and explore everything this man had to give to her, for as long as he could.

She felt the hot prod of his desire just before he pulled back, easing his body away from hers and smiling. "Kenzie, I would love to have you for my wife. What I do not want is for you to answer right now. Let us enjoy the festivities."

The meal was convivial; the family as pleasant as ever. They all used English, for which she was grateful. She had already picked up some of the Estolian language, but it would be a while before she would be fully comfortable with it.

After the meal, Nico escorted her to the ballroom, and they were the first on the dance floor, dancing to a chamber orchestra set up to one side of the ballroom.

The evening was magical, with beautiful music and the sense of an occasion. She learned over the course of the evening that it was typical in Estolia to have celebrations on the day before rather than the day of the birthday. It was the aim of every Estolian man to spend his thirtieth birthday alone with his future wife.

She danced with each of the men, Nico's father and uncle, his older and younger brother, Rhea's husband, and Nico's cousin Max. But most of the dances she spent in Nico's arms, reveling in how matched their bodies were.

During one long slow song, Nico said to her, "I think I never really took much notice of where you were coming from emotionally when I met you."

"I had a lucky escape," she said.

"That you characterize it as an escape tells me there is trauma involved. No matter how lucky you were to escape, and especially no matter how lucky I was to have you free, it cannot be easy to wear a man's ring and then have him call it off. You told me he called you a fat circus freak."

She didn't want to think about what Mark called her. Which meant his words still had the power to wound.

Nico stopped dancing and pulled her closely into his arms, hugging her tightly. The other dancers swirled around them, leaving them like an island in the middle of the dance floor. She reveled in the feeling of his strong arms around her, holding her tight, making her feel as if she was precious and protected. The feel of his body against her own set her heart to hammering.

He pulled back slightly so he could cup the side of her face before tilting her chin up slightly. "I need to tell you what I see in you – what you are to me." His eyes searched hers.

"You don't really have to." Mark had extolled her virtues frequently enough in the beginning – until he met Shayla.

"One of the greatest delights I have, Kenzie, is how close you are in height to me. I do not wish a wife who is so small I worry about breaking her when I make love to her, so short I suffer from back ache just because I like kissing her. From our very first kiss, I have marveled at how perfectly you were constructed to be the correct height for me, and hopefully you feel the same: that I am the correct height for you. We are so well matched!"

She didn't expect him to comment on her height.

"In fact," he said, "I believe you wear your height better than any other woman I've ever known of a similar height. Most tall women hunch over, or they fail to show off their glorious long legs. I have been falling asleep at night thinking about your legs, and how they will feel wrapped around me."

It was her turn to blush. She had the same fantasy: dreaming of her legs wrapped possessively around his hips, his torso, his thighs, holding him tight while his body claimed hers, and she claimed him.

He laughed, and she liked how carefree he sounded. "We are making a bit of a spectacle of ourselves," he said. "We should sit so we can continue this fascinating conversation."

He led her to an alcove on the opposite side of the ballroom from where the small chamber orchestra was playing, in view of the dancers.

"Kenzie, I want you to know how I see you. You are not required to reciprocate. I just feel a deep compulsion to share with you what has been with me since I met you."

Leon and Cali interrupted them. "We brought you a bottle of the Danieli Vintage," he said, "we thought you would enjoy it while you are chatting."

He and Cali moved a small end table closer to them, so they could place an ice-bucket on it to keep the wine cooled. Once the wine was poured, the King and Queen of Estolia melted away again.

Nico handed Kenzie a glass of the wine, cautioning her, "This is incredibly potent wine, so be careful."

She took the wine from him, marveling afresh at his thoughtfulness. She learned that occasionally an Estolian seduced his wife-to-be to tie her to him. But regardless of what was typical, Nico was set on winning her over rather than simply storming her defenses. His comment about the wine proved his intentions. He would not get her drunk to achieve his aims.

"Do you know if your eye color is genetic?" Nico asked her. "Because I am really hoping it is. I think the one thing that fascinated me the most, when I first looked into your eyes, was how your hair color seemed merely an extension of the rainbow you were born with."

"It is genetic," she admitted. "My father, grandfather, and aunt all had one blue eye and one green eye. It's entirely possible we'll have at least one child with two different colored eyes."

"I shall cherish all our children, but those with different colored eyes will hold a special part of my heart."

She sipped at the wine. His words were like a healing salve applied to the wounds Mark inflicted upon her soul.

"Zeke believes the times we are moving into are very difficult, even for those of us blessed to live in Estolia. When Zeb marries, he will be a catalyst of global change. Because of the prophecy, it is critical that both the Keeper of the Soul of Estolia, and his wife are individuals with strong personalities and depth of character. Zeke states it is critical to the success of Zeb's mission that I have chosen a woman who has a strong character."

"What will Zeb do?"

"It is not known. He went to Harvard at sixteen and has been living separate from Estolia since he concluded his Acolyte year just after getting his degree in international business. In fact, he attended Harvard at the same time as Leon, Max, Darin, and I. He is brilliant. In five years, he took a legacy from our mother Lilaine and has multiplied it more than a hundred times. Zeke believes at least one part of the prophecy might relate to the power that comes from an obscene level of wealth. We may never know, in this life, exactly how Zeb will influence the minds and hearts of world leaders."

"He's been here since I arrived," she noted. "I thought he lived here."

"Not to alarm you, but he returned home for my wedding. He does not plan to return again until after he himself marries at the age of thirty."

She frowned. "After he marries? I didn't think Estolians married away from the island."

"It would be impossible for every Estolian to marry here in Estolia. There are Estolians all over the world. In Spain, California, and British Columbia there are *Designates* who have been granted spiritual leadership of those communities. If possible, every couple sanctioned by the *Designate* will visit Estolia to receive sanction from the Keeper of the Soul of Estolia. In Zeb's case," Nico added, "he has a most peculiar blessing."

"Zeke mentioned something about it."

"Yes." He looked away from her, seeing something in his minds' eye. "When our mother first came to Estolia, the Keeper of the Soul of Estolia asked if she would allow him to give her a blessing. In the blessing he gave her she was told she would have three sons. One to be King, one to be Keeper of the Soul of Estolia, and a third one to be a Catalyst of Change."

Nico looked around the ballroom until he spotted his mother and he smiled at her. "Then Zeb got further clarification in his seven-day blessing, and his *Blessing-at-Eighteen.* He was told in both blessings that he would not be gifted with the aura of his future wife. The implication was that he would have to forego the greatest blessings of Zaccarias so he might fulfill his destiny. He was told he would marry at thirty, but he would not meet his wife prior to the hour of their wedding."

"That must be hard for him to deal with," Kenzie observed.

"It is hard to deal with, but I hope he will not miss what he has never experienced. He will not really know what he has given up. Therefore, it will not be as painful as it might otherwise be." Nico did not look satisfied with what he said. He looked mournful, as if he could imagine how empty his brother's life would be compared with his own life, and their older male relatives.

"It sounds like he'll need a lot of support from us when the time comes for him to marry." Kenzie's voice was gentle, her heart went out to Nico's youngest brother. She liked Zeb, even if he did seem to be a somber, serious sort of person, rarely smiling.

"Yes, Kenzie, he will need every bit of help we can give him. Here in Estolia, we believe that those whose burdens are greatest also have the greatest blessings to offset and balance it all out."

It occurred to her that she was, once again, blithely speaking with Nico as if they would be a married couple trying to comfort his youngest brother at some point in the future.

29

Keeping of the Soul

She who Keeps the Soul of the First Consul is, and always shall be, the most critical, pivotal, and significant role for any person in Estolia.

~Coming of age Blessing given to Lazarus Ezekiel Zacarian.

SHE HAD TO choose what she was going to do, and it felt as impossible now as it was the moment Nico-the-stranger proposed to her. She knew beyond doubting that she could not reject him. Her heart would break if she left him. And yet, she wasn't sure she could accept him. His brother urged her to have faith in herself above all other things. But that did not change the internal argument raging within her.

"What will I do?" she blurted out.

He got to his feet and pulled her slowly into his arms. "As the wife of the First Consul and Keeper of the Soul of Estolia, yours is truly the position of greatest importance. I cannot keep the soul of Estolia if my own soul is not safely in your keeping."

"It's not that I don't think you have a critical role here in Estolia. But I just feel like I'll be an unimportant cog in the machinery of Estolia. Perhaps it's selfish, but I want to matter Nico, I want to do more than just be some awesome support to help you be great."

"I cannot explain how it works. I believe you will discover that your role will be much more than you anticipate. Perhaps, Kenzie, you need to understand how much faith I have in you."

"Your brother told me the only faith I really needed was in myself." She moved towards him, her body in contact with his, her arms going around his waist. "Perhaps the time for convincing me with words is past, Nico."

He dipped his head down to kiss her. When he pulled away he looked at the clock on the wall. It was nearing midnight. He picked up the bottle of Danieli wine and topped off both of their glasses. Handing her glass to her, he grabbed her hand and led her away from the ballroom.

Soon they were in a part of the palace she'd never visited. "This wing is set aside for my tenure as Keeper of the Soul of Estolia." He explained. "It is my home. I eat most often with the family, but sometimes I feel like a quiet night at home without worrying about family."

She looked around curiously as he led her through the different rooms. This was her future home.

She looked at Nico, realizing she was alone with him for the first time since they met. Every angle and plane of his face was known to her. She'd memorized his features, his accent, his dimples, his beautiful eyes. Everything about him was etched in her memory. The true barrier keeping her from fully agreeing to be with him suddenly occurred to her. She had fallen in love with this handsome man, she wanted him, and more than that, she wanted him to love her. She didn't want their union to be demanded by tradition, or religion, or peculiar rules. She wanted the only reason for him to be with her, to marry her, was because he loved her to the exclusion of every other woman he'd ever known. She needed to matter to him as much as he mattered to her.

"What is it, Kenzie?"

She couldn't contain the feelings racing through her. "I love you Nico. I need you to love me the same."

He took the wine glass from her and set it carefully on the desk next to him. Taking both her hands in his, he squeezed them and said to her, his voice thick with emotion, "Kenzie O'Rourke, I have been in love with you from the moment I first saw you. I was terrified my heart would break. How was it possible that a woman so sophisticated and extraordinary could be chaste? How could my heart be involved with a woman who would not fit in Estolia? How could *Deity* let me down, by allowing my heart to be stolen?

"But then, on the tail end of those thoughts, Kenzie, I recognized your extraordinary beauty was enhanced by the glow of an aura. I was frightened then that you would somehow, some way, not only steal my heart, but also prove my faith was misplaced. How could a woman as wonderful as you, from your society be pure? I was jealous, deeply jealous of all the men who knew you intimately, and who had stolen you from my great need! I could not believe everything going through my heart and soul in the short time between first seeing you, and actually speaking with you."

She could not doubt his words. Could not doubt he meant everything he was saying. "You asked if I was untouched," she reminded him.

"My heart was in my throat when I prepared to ask you that question. I knew, in that moment, if you were not chaste, not pure, I would never be able to fulfill my destiny and remain the Keeper of the Soul of Estolia. If you had known one or more men, I was going to forego the deepest most intense spiritual connection that exists for men of Estolia. I would not seek another woman. I would do everything I could to win you. I fell in *love* with you, Kenzie, and I would leave my nation and my faith if that was what was necessary to remain with you."

While they were talking Nico was guiding her out of the library. He paused to kiss her briefly before he turned and led her rapidly to a set of double doors. Once through them he turned to look at her.

"As a rule, men in my country tend to be very romantic, focused in on the sensation of giving our soul into the keeping of our mate." He smiled one of his quirky dimple-enhanced smiles. "Part of the Acolyte Year we spend time discussing the romantic turn of phrase the most erotic *Capitulos* use. We discuss how to express ourselves best when we experience the extraordinary moment when our soul leaves our body and takes up residence next to the sweetly wonderful soul of our wife."

Kenzie began to unbutton the shirt he was wearing while he spoke.

"What most of my forebears have said, universally, is how little the *Capitulos* helped them, how little like reality the accounts of yielding of the soul really are. How one must experience it to be able to discuss and describe it." He brushed her hair away from her face, cupping both sides and staring into her eyes. "I realized how true that was when I met you. My heart was so fully involved, I knew in a moment that there would never be a woman I would be able to love other than you. No way for any other woman to rouse me."

"You really love me, Nico?" she asked. She slipped her hand under the shirt, feeling the hair-roughened chest.

"Kenzie, your sweet self has taken hold of me. If I did not know the exchange had not taken place, I would insist you already took my soul into your keeping. I do not know if I could continue to live if you did not accept me."

She pushed his shirt off his shoulders and leaned towards him, bending her head to taste the warm salty skin of his neck. The unique heady scent of his body filled her senses.

He tugged at her zipper for her ballgown, dragging it down her back with one steady sure motion. The cool breeze on her back raising gooseflesh. In moments, he pushed the dress off her shoulders so it could pool in a brightly colored puddle at her feet

She dropped her hands from his chest to the belt holding his pants up. She unfastened both belt and zipper before pushing his pants down over his hips.

He bent down and slipped his shoes and socks off, stepping out of them. When he straightened he surprised Kenzie by sweeping her up into his arms. She met his eyes with an uncertain expression. He smiled at her as he crossed the room to the large bed, laying her gently down on the soft surface.

"I love you, Kenzie. You matter more to me than anything else. More than my family, my religion, my nation." He climbed onto the bed next to her, his mouth covering hers, escalating from small nibbling to deeply passionate kisses. While he kissed her, he began to caress her breasts through the fabric of her camisole. Her hands explored his chest, his shoulders, his stomach, and encountered the fabric of his underpants.

He teased her nipples through the material of the camisole before finally tugging it upwards. She sat up and he removed it and her bra, leaving her wearing only the silk and lace briefs. His eyes remained locked to hers for several heartbeats before his gaze dropped and took in the sight of her unconfined breasts. He leaned towards her, his mouth on the tip of one breast while his hand teased and inflamed the other.

While he was rousing her nerve endings, she felt as though she was aflame herself. She caressed the firm rear end she'd admired multiple times over the last week. She couldn't help the mewls of pleasure as he teased and tormented her nipples to firm awareness.

She slipped one hand under the waistband of the briefs, caressing the skin and rounded contours of his rear. Soon her second hand joined the first. Her senses were alight, and she felt like she wasn't getting or giving enough. She pushed at the waistband, freeing his erection and pushing his last item of clothing down his legs.

After a moment, he paused in what he was doing to finish removing his briefs, dropping them on the floor. When he returned to her, his lips were on hers, one hand on her breast. She caressed his silky skin, tracing the contours of his aroused flesh, enjoying the contrasting textures of hot taut skin, crinkly hair, and loose cool skin. He mimicked her explorations; his hands first delving under her briefs to caress and cup her rear before he pushed them down her legs. When he dropped them on the floor and returned to her, they were both completely naked.

He explored her breasts again before one hand trailed down her torso to her hips, exploring and caressing her nerves. She was doing similar things to him. After a short time, his hand stilled hers, pulling it away. His knee came between her legs, joined swiftly by the other. He kissed her passionately but did not complete the union her body was screaming for.

"Nico," she said his name, her hands going from his shoulders to his rear end. She was going crazy, needing, wanting his possession.

"Kenzie," he repeated her name, his eyes meeting hers. The large grandfather clock in the room started to chime. Nico rubbed his body over hers in time to the chimes. It was only as the last chime reverberated through the palace that he cupped her face and locked his eyes onto hers. He surged forward, crying out with her as he broached her barrier, both experiencing a momentary disorientation before the feeling of pleasure and the deep sensation of how right their union was overtook them.

For seven days, they'd danced around the reason for her visit to the strange foreign land. She felt as if she was in a wondrous land more marvelous than the most extraordinary fairy tale land of her childhood. His body fit perfectly within hers, just as she felt like their hearts melded, their minds met, and her soul consumed his.

She locked her legs around him emotionally consumed by the feeling of possession. She couldn't contain the inarticulate cry of pleasure as waves of warmth coursed through her system. His voice joined hers, the lower pitch supplementing the musical sounds of pleasure she was making.

They both stilled in mute testimony to the truth neither could avoid – that Deity was responsible for bringing them together, for helping to merge two souls that always belonged together. She felt satisfaction in having his body on hers, over hers.

For a moment she had a vision of the future, his warm eyes still clear and full of life and intelligence, surrounded by the wrinkles and marks of age.

Her eyes met his as he shifted his weight off her. He pulled her close and tucked her body against him, pillowing her head against him. The sound of his heart augmented her vision of the future, and she imagined how it would be to fall asleep with the sound of his heartbeat in her ear – every night for a lifetime. She felt as if there was more happiness and peace filling her soul than any one person could possibly contain or feel.

When his pulse rate dropped off she looked at him and knew, in that moment, that everything he told her about the Keeping of the Soul was accurate. It was as if she could feel his soul along with her own, a deep elemental connection, like Siamese twins of the soul. It also seemed like the love she'd felt for him had been two-dimensional before but was now three-dimensional.

His eyes met hers. He smiled at her and the look of infinite pleasure emanating from him was unmistakable. "I love you, Kenzie, with every particle of my Soul, every ounce of my Body, every iota of the Self within me."

"In about eight minutes," he warned her, "we'll be visited by my brother, my father, and my uncle."

She looked at the scattered clothing on the floor. With a smile to Nico she slipped out of the bed and picked everything up swiftly.

"Lift your arms," he whispered.

She did so and he settled a beautiful nightgown over her. She turned and looked at him. He was wearing a bathrobe. The clock began to chime the half hour. It had not yet finished its chimes when the door opened and Zeke, Leon, and Isaiah all came into the room. While they approached, Nico pulled Kenzie back against his body, his hand splayed over her abdomen.

"What say you, Nico?" Zeke asked.

"Kenzie O'Rourke has taken my soul securely within her keeping." Nico stated.

Zeke stepped closer, looking at the two of them. "My nephew claims he has taken your purity and as a result he has placed his soul securely within your keeping. What say you, Kenzie O'Rourke?"

She frowned, not quite sure what to say. Her eyes met Zeke's and she got a sense of peace from him. "I was pure, and Nico did take that purity and in exchange I took his soul into my keeping. I hope to never be parted from the man to whom I've given my heart and body. I may possess his soul, but he possesses all of me."

Zeke smiled at her, and she sensed how pleased he was. "I believe it is in your best interests to go now, tonight, to the seclusion suite."

She shrugged into a robe like Nico's, and Zeke led them towards the end of a long hallway. "When my grandfather shattered both of his legs," he explained as they went along, "his brother – the King – had our smallest tower converted into a combination elevator, library, and staircase. Very little work was necessary. This will take us to the stable level and cuts the journey to the Temple almost in half, since the stable level is halfway down the side of the mountain."

Kenzie only barely heard what Zeke was sharing with her. She felt like everything she was seeing and feeling was done for the first time, as if there was a close connection between Nico and herself growing in strength and durability. What mattered was that she was with Nico now, and would be with him for their entire lives. Until time ceased to be.

Part 6 – Catalyst

⊱ Cast of Characters ⊰

Brant Kinsey – Karis' employer in East Lake Tahoe (Nevada)
Calista Teare Zacarian – (Cali) 89th Queen of Estolia
Isaiah Monterrey Zacarian – 88th King of Estolia
Kenzie O'Rourke Zacarian – Wife of the 89th Keeper of the Soul of Estolia
Krissandra Taylor-Smythe – (Karis) Daughter of Marsden Taylor-Smythe
Leonidas Agamemnon Zacarian – (Leon) 89th King of Estolia
Marsden Taylor-Smythe – Father of Krissandra
Melody Cormick – Plastic Surgeon and wife of Reardon
Natasha Kinsey – Brant Kinsey's wife
Nicodemus Luciano Zacarian – (Nico) 89th Keeper of the Soul of Estolia
Reardon Cormick – Lawyer. Married to Melody
Sloane Danvers – One of the richest men on the planet
Zebastiani Zacarian – (Zeb) third Son of the 88th King of Estolia

30

Power Games

2026

Zebastiani Zacarian was the catalyst that brought together the many different elements neces-
sary to save the planet.

~Orion Zacarian, Capitulo 91

KARIS YANKED A BRUSH through her thick orange-red hair. She ignored the pain of her protesting scalp, wanting only to produce the look Natasha Kinsey required of her housekeeper. It didn't take long to tame the wild mass, twist it into a knot, and secure it with a hair-tie.

She slipped on her undergarments and closed her eyes, running her calloused fingertips over the expensive fabric. After a moment she pulled her hands away. She turned her back on her reflection and picked up the dull blue-gray overalls. The clock over the door to her tiny quarters always ticked loudly. She was once four minutes late. The blistering dressing-down she received from her employer discouraged her from ever arriving even a minute late.

The last item of apparel she tied around her waist was the heavy white apron with a variety of tools of her trade tucked into the pockets. It was one minute before eight.

She left the tiny room and stopped only long enough to pull the vacuum out of the closet next to her room. She pushed it towards the parlor. It was Tuesday, and she was to vacuum every inch of the carpet every Tuesday morning. The large grandfather clock in the hallway just began to chime when she switched the vacuum on and began to vacuum.

While she vacuumed, she remembered the expression on Natasha Kinsey's face during the interview. Her nostrils kept flaring, as if she smelled something rotten. Combined with the way her brows twitched toward one another like love-sick caterpillars, Karis had the hardest time keeping her expression blank.

"Your hair," Natasha informed her, "must either be cut or severely restrained. Makeup is unacceptable. You must strive to be invisible."

At the time of the interview, she was desperate for a live-in job. Her employer's next commandment almost had her rethinking the job.

"Eye contact, Ms. Smith, is going to be a problem." She proceeded to explain that she and her husband, and their visitors would not want to be forced to acknowledge her in any way. Eye contact was to be avoided always. It would give all of them a greater level of comfort. "I'm certain you can understand my point of view."

A door slammed somewhere in the house and Karis upped the tempo of her vacuuming. She didn't wish to be accused of idleness. The thick pile white carpet picked up the slightest smudge of dirt or strand of hair. One of the parlor doors opened behind her; she trained her amber eyes on the carpet in front of her.

While she vacuumed she repeated the one set of facts that made it possible to live and work in this atmosphere: "Five hours a day, six days a week, good money, and only a few more months until my birthday."

This was her second week in this job, and she understood now why they paid so much. Even the least sensitive person on the planet would realize quickly that Brant and Natasha Kinsey would never treat her like she was a human being with actual self-worth. She could only be treated like that for so long before the thought of rebellion would start to set in.

She took a deep breath and reminded herself it was only five hours a day, six days a week, and she would be twenty-four soon enough.

A masculine grunt sounded behind her and she looked up. Brant Kinsey. She didn't meet his eyes, following the rules his wife set. She switched off the vacuum cleaner and waited to hear whatever he had to say.

"Natasha has gone to stay with her sister for the week," he said with relish, "I thought this would give us an excellent chance to get to know one another."

Rules notwithstanding, her eyes snapped up to meet his watery blue eyes framed by jowly yellowed cheeks and a sloppy jawline. Stepping backward, she said clearly, "I think not."

His face grew hard and mean. His narrow mouth tightened and a white line showed around the edge of his thin lips. "You don't have much of a choice." The edge to his voice held the tone of the natural bully. "It's not like you'd get another job if we have to give you a negative referral."

In the current financial climate, the threat was real and substantial. She wondered how many of her predecessors chose starvation over the slack corpulent body of this man? How many chose to sleep with him and realized later that starvation was preferable? She had no doubt over which one she would choose.

She let the handle of the vacuum go. "If you try to touch me, I'll break your arm." Stepping behind the vacuum she waited to see what he would do.

After a moment of indecision, his jaw firmed while he took in her tiny frame and fine-boned features. To a bully, she probably looked like a perfect target. It was clear he didn't think she could win in a fight with him. He was more than a foot taller than she was.

He reached for her with an ugly expression on his face. A moment later, he was yelping in pain. She was using a submission hold she learned in a self-defense class.

Not to be used for a sneak or surprise attack, but it worked exceptionally well for this sort of incident. He yelped again and realized quickly that any movement on his part resulted in pain. Most individuals faced with this hold would yield. Some would take further persuasion. She realized her mistake in categorizing him in the group that easily yielded when his fist connected with her face, knocking her backwards onto a delicate antique table, shattering it completely.

He shook his right hand a moment or two before advancing on her. "We'll be taking the price of that table out of your paycheck. Or you can pay for it now..."

His meaning and intention was clear. The words of her instructor came back to her. "Sometimes, you have to make a strategic withdrawal. You generally don't want to run, don't want to show fear, but some of the male hunters out there are too dangerous, and ultimately your best bet is to elude them long enough to make them grow weary of the chase."

The doorbell began to chime, the long sequence to *Für Elise*. Brant turned his attention towards the front door, and that was all she needed to dart past him, and out the open back door. She could gain the dense forest upslope above his property quicker then he could, and her own explorations of the surrounding territory gave her a familiarity he might lack.

Twenty minutes later she limped down the drive towards Reardon Cormick's house. Her only other employer. She'd been hired by a firm to tend his home, stay there, feed the animals, and ride the one horse on the extensive private grounds and public lands adjoining Reardon's land. That job ended when the temp agency told her that Reardon's wife was returning from an extended out-of-town trip.

She was halfway down Reardon's drive when reaction set in and she felt the entire world fade in and out. She fell to her knees and was sick, once, twice, three times until her stomach was empty and the black void surrounding her began to take on familiar shapes again. When she tried to rise, her legs were weak. She subsided onto the drive once more to wait for her strength to return.

The squeal of brakes needing a bit of attention broke into her personal misery. A car was turning into the drive. She would be virtually invisible in her absurd cleaning outfit. Too wobbly to rise, she did the next best thing and crawled out of the way, hoping they would not crush her.

The car was driven so slowly, tentatively almost, that the driver had plenty of time to see her and stop. She heard the application of a parking break and then a car door opening and closing.

A cultured foreign voice said, "Are you okay? Have you been in an accident?"

Gentle feminine arms came down around her shoulders, and with the woman's support, Karis was able to get to her feet. Swaying, she looked at the woman who seemed a match for Karis in build and height.

Taking a deep breath helped Karis feel more stable, though she was conscious of the unpleasant smell of vomit. "I just had an altercation with my employer."

The woman looked incredulous. "You have? Not Reardon, of course, he is in Antarctica. But if not him, could you be speaking of Brant or Natasha Kinsey?"

In as few words as possible, she summarized what happened, finishing with, "I'm Karis Smith. I'm afraid he'll have my car towed, throw out my purse, try to have me arrested. I just don't know what he will do."

"I think not." Spoken with her accent, it sounded humorous. Karis sensed that this woman was very tenacious given a motive. She pulled a cellphone out of her purse and dialed a number. "Brant? Melody Cormick here. I understand my cousin Karis has been working for you. It appears she left her car at your home. You may drop it off at Reardon's if you like."

Karis could hear what sounded like angry shouting. Melody waited for him to quiet down before saying softly, "I understand she could bear testimony against you. While you can afford a top lawyer, keep in mind that Reardon is due back soon, and nobody is better than he is. He will represent her. If there is a need."

Karis was awed at the way this woman was managing Brant's blustering bullying behavior.

"I believe she is owed her wages, plus the extra two weeks for early termination of her contract and a bonus of a similar amount for her trouble and medical expenses." More vociferous words she couldn't make out spluttered over the line. When he came to a halt Melody said, "I misspoke. *Four* times what she is owed for two weeks will be enough. Her face is cut up, she will need a plastic surgeon." A smile played about her lips during the silence before she added, "in cash, Brant, in her purse, and her car and purse brought to Reardon's within the hour."

When she was done, the woman said to her, "It is probably best if you ride with me to Reardon's house."

At the house, Melody had Karis sit in the kitchen and she examined her face. "I can stitch that up for you." She offered.

"You're a doctor?" Karis asked.

"I am a plastic surgeon, and faces are my specialty. If you would prefer I can take you to your own doctor."

"I haven't any health insurance," Karis admitted. She had been promised that upon successful completion of three months of work for the Kinsey family, she would receive health care benefits, but that wouldn't happen now. In eight months... she broke off that line of thinking. It was unprofitable.

"Then you are in luck," Melody said.

Karis closed her eyes, trying to ignore how grim her situation was. She should have known that the simple would become complex. In eight months Sloane would have no power over her. But if she could not remain hidden and inaccessible until then his power over her would be complete and irrevocable.

An hour later Karis looked at her face in the mirror. The cut was not very large. A small right-angle tear from the ring on Brant's pinky finger. It would scar, but she didn't think it would be notable. Her face was numb from the local anesthetic.

They heard a ring at the door and Melody went to answer with the droll comment tossed over her shoulder, "That will be Brant with your car. I promise to not invite him in."

She could hear Melody and Brant speaking in the foyer. The conversation was short and shrill. Something about the indecipherable words made her uneasy. She turned around when the door opened, half afraid that Brant – or even worse Sloane – would be entering the room. But it was just Melody returning. She had a strange expression on her face. She looked like something awful happened. "What is it?" she asked, stepping towards her.

Melody handed her purse to her and then backed away with a look of faint disgust on her face. "You are Krissandra Taylor-Smythe?"

"Or Karis Smith for short."

"Sloane Danvers is looking for you."

"I'm sure he has quite the reward out for information about my whereabouts," Karis admitted. If this woman knew who she was, it was probably because Brant Kinsey snooped in her purse. It wouldn't take much time for him to tell Sloane, and for Sloane to get there. Or to send a minion.

Fleeing, at this point, was futile. Bleakly, she turned her attention to Melody to ask, "Why such animosity towards me?" Was it just the connection to Sloane, or was it something else?

"Danvers is a monster," Melody asserted, "and anyone who would marry him for his money." She shook her head, shuddering delicately.

Karis held up her hand. Her voice was rock-hard as she explained, "My father stipulated I marry a man with the wealth to match my inheritance, dollar-for-dollar. He wanted me to marry Sloane. But he couldn't stipulate my groom in the will. He couldn't force me to marry Sloane any more than he could force anything else. But if I marry a man with less wealth, the inheritance will go towards the Parity Group." The political machinations of the Parity Group were legion, and she had no desire to enrich them significantly. She met Melody's eyes steadily when she added, "In eight months, if I'm still unmarried when I turn twenty-four, the conditions of the will change. If I'm pregnant before I turn twenty-four then the estate goes to the child." And Sloane would still have control of the money. He would do everything he could to ensure it was his own child.

"It would seem," said a deep masculine voice, "that you're looking for a man to outbid Sloane Danvers."

"Reardon!" Melody said, rushing to throw herself into his arms.

He smiled at the vivacious blonde and kissed her passionately while twirling her around the room. "I thought I would surprise you," he stated.

"Darling, I am so glad you are home early," she said. "I am, as you noted, in a peculiar position."

"Indubitably," he said. He turned his attention to her and the expression on his face was clear - he wasn't sure whether she was worth his notice. "Do I understand the situation," he asked her, "you're in a position to deny Sloane Danvers the opportunity to double his current net worth, and deny the Parity Group a similar influx of capital?"

She nodded slowly. "But if Brant Kinsey has communicated my whereabouts to Sloane, it's already too late."

"I think the situation can be redeemed," he said. "Depriving him of that money is, of course, imperative." He looked at his wife with a tender smile and then bent to kiss her again. "I'm sorry to so immediately indulge in business."

"Just having you home matters more than anything," she said.

He pulled his phone out and dialed a number. "Zeb, I'm calling to find out what you would do to keep Sloane Danvers from doubling his net worth." His eyes met Karis's eyes. "You'd have to marry his fiancée." After a moment, he added, "Today."

He hung up and kissed Melody one more time before saying, "I must draw up a legal agreement. I'll be back."

Once he left, Karis went with Melody back to the spacious kitchen. She could tell that the other girl was still unsure whether she was worth knowing.

Melody set to work in the kitchen cooking something, leaving Karis alone with her thoughts. She wasn't sure who Reardon called. Was it possible he called the wealthy financier Zebastiani Zacarian? He was more than capable of meeting the requirement. She didn't know of anyone else in the same financial bracket who was free to marry her or who would be inclined.

The scrape as a plate was set in front of her brought her attention back to where she was. "Thank you."

Melody inclined her head, sitting across from her. "Will I curse this day?"

Karis considered the question carefully before answering honestly, "If Sloane Danvers and the Parity Group are as evil to you as they are to me, and your husband's effort to get me married falls through, then I believe you will indeed curse this day." She looked away and whispered, "I curse the day my father was made to believe Sloane Danvers had my best interests at heart."

At this point, Reardon came into the kitchen. He smiled gently at his wife and said, "My dear, it's time for you to put on your other hat." He dropped a piece of paper onto the table in front of Karis and saluted his wife's mouth briefly with a kiss.

"You are sure about this?" Melody asked. She looked into her husband's eyes anxiously.

"I'm certain this is the only way," he said. "Zeb will be here soon." He caressed her face briefly before turning his attention to Karis.

Once Melody left the room, the warmth in Reardon's face seeped away, leaving his expression cold and austere. "I have no idea, Krissandra Taylor-Smythe, if I'm doing a grave disservice to my best friend or not. I can only hope you are not the cold mercenary bitch you are reputed to be."

Karis lifted her chin. "Money is power, Reardon Cormick. Power is merely a force that can be used in many ways. I am tied to the reins of power. Will your friend use the money for good or for evil?"

"You act as if he will have power over the money."

"The money reverts to my husband with the requirement that it be passed on to the child that I will have." She quirked a brow at him. "It's written into the will that the DNA must be tested, and the child be the confirmed genetic offspring of myself and my husband."

He tapped the contract he had placed in front of her. "This is a prenuptial agreement. It states that..."

She pushed it back to him, having taken in the salient points. "It's insufficient."

He looked offended. "How? I must warn you that you can expect no more from your husband."

"No," she said, "it must be written that if we dissolve the marriage he will maintain control of my financial interests, and if he dies, then you, Reardon Cormick, *you* take over my financial interests. At least until my child is thirty."

"That's one-sided. I don't think it would stand up in court."

She shrugged her shoulders and said, "Then give control of my finances to the injured party. If he seeks a divorce, I am once again in control of my finances, and if I seek a divorce he will have this control. Put in a clause that we must seek mediation prior to any divorce, to include your presence. Whatever will protect your friend."

He looked at the contract and tapped it several times. "I believe I could come up with something. I'll be right back." Ten minutes later he presented her with the revised contract. She read it through and nodded. "I consider this exceedingly fair." She signed it and then pushed it towards Reardon.

She noticed the name for her husband-to-be was indeed Zebastiani Zacarian. She tried to picture him. Black hair, dark eyes, not running to fat. Quiet and broody, his name wasn't a target on social media sites because from all she read about him, he did not indulge in sexual liaisons with anyone of any gender.

The doorbell rang and she stood slowly, wondering if it was Zeb or Sloane.

Melody rushed into the room and pulled her out, dragging her to a large master bedroom. Within ten minutes Karis was dressed in a medieval gown. Melody left her in the bedroom and Karis felt weak-kneed at the thought that she was supposed to marry a total stranger. She shuddered to think what would be happening to her if she didn't have that option open to her. She would be safe only when Sloane lost the chance to control her.

Reardon stepped into the room and asked, "Are you sure you want to do this?"

"I've never wanted anything more in my life than this," she said truthfully.

"Sloane is here."

She tensed, but there was no place she could run or hide.

Reardon led her out the back door and towards a fern grotto she admired when she was house-sitting. She wasn't at all surprised to see Sloane or Brant Kinsey. Her attention brushed over them and fastened on the man who was doing exactly what she was doing – marrying a total stranger.

Her eyes met his and she walked forward steadily, smiling into his beautiful warm brown eyes. He looked at her like she was precious.

Melody was the one who was doing the officiating. As soon as she started the service, Sloane objected.

Zeb pulled her close, his arms around her, one hand splayed across her abdomen, as they faced off against the man who would do anything to possess her, and the money that possession would bring him.

Two older gentlemen who were quietly observing from the background stepped forward and began to query Sloane, asking for details and substance to his claims of breach of promise. Finally, one of the two said, "I am satisfied Zebastiani Zacarian and Krissandra Taylor-Smythe have a sincere desire to wed and see no evidence of a breach in promise. The wedding can go forward."

Karis knew this was the moment when Sloane would have to decide how much her wealth mattered to him. If she died before she married, he would inherit the entire sum.

Sloane started to move forward, but before he moved more than a few feet the second witness spoke, "I should like to take a moment prior to the nuptials to interject one additional fact."

Sloane shifted from one foot to the other like an uncertain rhinoceros preparing to charge. After a moment the old man continued, "I was with Marsden Taylor-Smythe multiple times over the final days of his life. I believe my testimony, should I enter it, could quite easily result in his entire will being overturned. But even if it stands, I should like to acquaint you with one final codicil he added to his will just prior to his death. He included the provision that if Krissandra were to die prior to the bearing of a child, especially in suspicious circumstances, then her wishes were to be honored, and the entirety of the assets of her father are to go to the Galaxy Collective."

31

The Blessing

Amadore, the second son of Zaccarias, is often overlooked when the history of Estolia is under discussion. Among his many significant accomplishments is the design of our three most critical historical buildings. The palace on Mt. Zaccarias, the Cathedral next to Mt. Estoliana, and the Temple within it.

—Antonio Cordero Zacarian; Capitulo 85

ZEB LISTENED AS THE TWO Elders argued and dithered with Sloane Danvers, but his thoughts were on the substance of his *Blessing-at-Eighteen*. As the third son of the King, his blessing had a different set of priorities than his brothers' blessings:

Estolia is of little interest to any other country. This is one of the Promises of *Deity*. Despite the lack of covetous eyes being cast in her direction, she is threatened by the actions of other nations that court planet-wide disaster. As such, it is time for Estolia to exercise influence over the nations of the world. The burden of this requirement is more than any one Descendant of Zaccarias should be made to face. And yet, it is placed upon your shoulders, Zebastiani Alexandros Zacarian, to meet this extraordinary need. The blessings that will come to you will be more than you can imagine, even as you will feel like the sacrifices you are asked to make are more than any son of Estoliana and Zaccarias should be forced to endure.

Your influence in the greater world will come at a great price, and that is to forego Estolia as your home for much of your life. You will also be given to marry a bride for whom there will be no aura, no advance sanction by the church. You will marry a woman in your thirtieth year who you have never met, never touched prior to the hour of your wedding. The secular inducement, when the rewards are counted in terms of the good of the planet, and thus the good of Estolia, will be impossible to reject. Your willingness to meet the needs of the planet, and by extension Estolia, will result in rewards that cannot be numbered, but if you have the faith to meet and accept your destiny, you will, ultimately be filled with the sure sense of right.

Peace in all your decisions will be one of the greatest blessings bestowed upon you – a peace that will provide you further guidance...

He held the girl in his arms who would take away the greatest joy any Estolian was given to know in this world. But the sense of sureness when he received the phone call had been immediate. Marrying this woman was a part of his destiny. Denying Sloane Danvers and the Parity Group made the reasons obvious.

He left Estolia after his Acolyte year. Returning only for his brothers' weddings. He would have to see if he would be allowed to use the Seclusion Suite in the Temple, or if he would be denied.

The arguments dried up, and Quinton was sharing additional information. When Zeb heard her preference of the Galaxy Collective, he hugged her slightly closer. Whatever the reality behind this slender girl's appearance in his life, it reassured him to know she would go with Galaxy over Parity.

Once the objections – as well as the motive for murder – were behind them, Sloane and Brant left, and they were able to get on with the wedding. In almost no time, it seemed, he was married to a woman whom he had never met, never spoken with.

Karis couldn't believe the threat of Sloane Danvers was finally removed from her life. She relaxed in the spacious living room, seated next to her new husband. The older gentlemen discussed nuances in the legal situation with Reardon. Melody somehow conjured up catered delicacies and was acting the perfect host.

Shortly after the two older gentlemen made their excuses and left, her new husband said, "I believe it might be in our best interests to absent ourselves while the seismic impact of our marriage in the business world runs through its paces. In a week to two weeks, the dust will settle, and we will see our pathway forward."

"Where will we go?"

"Estolia," he said. "One of the few places on the planet where we can be certain we are beyond the reach of Sloane Danvers and the Parity Group. I have not seen my latest nephews or my niece, and I am anxious to visit with my family."

Reardon asked to speak with Zeb privately and Karis was left alone once again with Melody. "Thank you, Melody. You saved my life today."

She still didn't look like she believed it was a good thing. "Will you divorce right away?"

Karis' troubled eyes met Melody's. "Was that the real understanding, that this whole thing was window dressing?" Karis looked away, swallowing on the emotions welling up, fighting back tears. Her voice was monotone as she continued, "If Zeb wishes his freedom, he knows what to do. I don't want to be free. I'll stay with Zeb as long as he can stand me." She clasped her hands together to quell the trembling. Her knuckles were white and her breathing was shallow.

"Are you really as genuine as you would like me to believe?"

"You should delay any character judgements about me until you get to know me, at least a little." She heard the men leaving Reardon's study and rose to her feet. The way Reardon wrote the prenuptial agreement made divorce a disaster.

"You will take care of our friend Beau?" Zeb was asking Reardon.

"It's done already," Reardon assured him.

When Karis saw the serious looks on the faces of the two men, and the suspicious expression on Melody's face, she felt compelled to clarify, blurting out, "For the record, I don't ever want a divorce. But..." she broke off at the looks of surprise on their faces. Clearly divorce wasn't the subject of their conversation in the study.

"But...?" Zeb prompted her.

She met his eyes and said, "If you want out, please let me be the one to request the divorce." Her eyes flicked over to Reardon before returning to her new husband and she clarified, "Reardon wrote the pre-nuptial contract so that it's best for me to be the one requesting it. Otherwise I get control of the money back, and I don't want it."

Zeb's voice was gentle, "I do not intend to divorce you. I pledged the entirety of my future to you, Krissandra. I do not believe in divorce, and I will never ask it of you."

She blushed, feeling like a fool for bringing it up.

"We'll see you back here in ninety days," Reardon told Zeb.

Karis followed Zeb out to his helicopter. "Where is Estolina?" she asked once they were in the air and heading towards the airport.

"Estolia," he corrected, "is an island nation south of Barcelona. Near Mallorca."

"Estolia," she said, getting the pronunciation correct in her mind. "Is it a territory of Spain?"

"No, it is an independent nation. It is very small, and few people really notice it exists." When he finished speaking he turned his attention to landing the helicopter near a sleek private jet.

She climbed out of the helicopter and followed Zeb over to the jet. A handsome man in a uniform came striding up to where Zeb and Karis were walking towards the jet and started speaking rapidly in a foreign language she never heard before. A third man joined them, speaking to the others in the same language.

They seemed grim, and Karis wondered what they were discussing. While they spoke in their foreign language, Zeb pulled her close to his side, holding her against his ribs.

Whatever they were discussing seemed to be upsetting to all three men. The third man left their side and walked over to another airplane that looked like a military jet, complete with what looked like bombs or guns strapped to the wings.

When they finished their discussion, Zeb placed a hand under her elbow and hustled her into the jet. "Strap yourself in, we are being moved to the top of the queue for immediate takeoff."

In no time, they were climbing into the sky. Once they leveled off she saw the military jet was shadowing them. She turned to Zeb for clarification.

"Power takes many forms, Krissandra Zacarian. I believe you are more well-acquainted with power than the average wealthy young woman. However, few there are who can comprehend and make use of the type of money and power Sloane Danvers and I possess." He glanced out the window at the military jet. "Sometimes it is all about a demonstration of power. Many animal species have the genetic imperative to breed with the most successful male. When the male red deer with the most impressive rack of antlers shows up, the lesser males give way rather than joust over the females. They see his power and realize they cannot win in a fight. As a result, the male with the greatest longevity nearly always passes on his genes.

"The same basic structure is seen in the type of power struggles surrounding you, Krissandra, in that men of great power wish to be the winner, and to possess you and your money. It is not as obvious in the beginning, without antlers to demonstrate genetic superiority, which man is the one predestined for victory. What I am doing is showing my power, so Sloane will realize his best course of action is to forget everything to do with you, your power, and the ill-conceived will your father was strong-armed into writing."

She looked from his eyes to the jet outside. "Thus, it remains to be seen whether Sloane is willing to give up, or whether he'll try something more extreme." She tried to predict what he would do but couldn't quite figure it out. "He's a coward."

"I diagnosed him as a bully from the beginning. If he is, as you say, a coward, I believe he will not sink any further resources into his pursuit of you."

Turning her back on the window, she focused her attention on Zeb. "What is our itinerary?"

"We will refuel twice. Because of the need to demonstrate my power, but not set either of us up as targets, we will not spend any significant time at either stop."

"Why *would* we have stopped for any length of time?"

"I was thinking you would want to increase your wardrobe significantly." He said with a smile that reached his eyes and seemed to be saying more than she could interpret.

"Oh!" she blushed. For months she'd been living on a tight budget, needing to keep off the grid so Sloane couldn't find her. "I didn't even think about that."

"We have a very skilled dressmaker who will make you a wardrobe. And Melody gave me several outfits to tide you over."

"That's very kind and thoughtful of you, and of Melody," she said. "Other than stopping for a quick refuel, we're heading straight to Estolia?"

"Yes. We will hopefully land by dawn."

"What happens when we get to Estolia?"

He relaxed slightly and smiled in genuine pleasure. "I am pretty sure my two brothers, father, and uncle will meet us at the airport." He paused and the pleasant expression dropped off his face. "As an Estolian, normally all marriages must be approved through the church. We may have some religious constraints put upon us when we arrive."

"Like what?" she asked, wondering what sort of religion Estolians practiced. Nothing she read about this man mentioned religion. It occurred to her that he might be a member of one of the more restrictive middle-eastern religions. The unanswered questions swirling through her mind made her realize the enormity of what she had done – tying herself to this man she did not know – for life!

"Do not be too disturbed or concerned," he said with a smile. "Nothing truly bizarre will be asked of us. The Estolian faith has its peculiarities, like most religions, but nothing that you would find onerous or difficult. You would be surprised at the one thing I have done that is contrary to our teachings and for which I might receive censure."

"What did you do?"

He grinned. The expression transformed his face and made him seem much younger than her first estimate. "The most egregious thing I did not do was consummate our union prior to the wedding."

"That is a peculiar inversion." She grinned back.

"The Estolian faith is unique, it has no analogs in the greater world."

"It is a sin to not – consummate – the union prior to marriage?" She stumbled over the word, but was grateful for the chance to use his word instead of the vernacular terms that were all too common.

"Sin is a western word. I do not believe that there is an equivalent word in the Estolian language. However, I have broken with tradition. For this reason, I do not know what the leader of the religion – my brother Nico – will have me do as a response. Other young people who have strayed have been banished permanently from Estolia."

"You expect to be banished?"

"No, not really. I do not live in Estolia and have no plans to live there permanently. Thus, being banished would be immaterial." His expression grew more somber. "I simply do not know how the leadership will respond." His hand reached for hers and his thumb rubbed over the skin on the back of her hand for several moments. The flight attendant poured them both a glass of wine before moving unobtrusively away from them, giving them privacy.

"They may require us to spend a week in the temple. That is not unusual, in fact it is typical. I am hopeful we will be asked to do this thing." He sipped his wine pensively. "Alternatively, I might be informed I am to be banned from the temple. This is a very real possibility as well." His eyes locked with hers, "There is even the possibility we will not be welcome in Estolia. This could easily be the last time I will set foot on Estolian soil."

Karis could sense the emotions roiling beneath his somber exterior and wanted to cry out at the pain she sensed. She leaned towards him and set one hand lightly on his thigh. "I hope, Zeb, I don't end up costing you your religion or your home nation. I can't regret our marrying. I needed you to save me, but I hope you don't find the sacrifices you've made are beyond bearing."

He set his warm hand over hers on his thigh and looked at her, studying her face. "I believe, Krissandra, on balance I will feel as if the actions of this day were both in-valuable *and* inevitable."

She nodded faintly, hoping it was true. "I feel as though this has been so unfair for you, Zeb. I get to be saved quite literally from a fate worse than death – or from death itself – and you get nothing, or worse than nothing, if you're banished from your faith and possibly your home land."

He quirked a grin at her, pointing out, "You forget, you have, if Reardon's math is correct, nearly doubled my net worth."

She shook her head. "Not yet. First, I must conceive, and give birth, and then we must do a paternity test. Once it comes back that you are the father of the child, then you lay claim to my inheritance."

His eyes were warm on her as he said, "Which, of course, leads to the sweetest reward for me, and that is to have an extraordinarily beautiful wife and children. You are not the only one who benefits from this alliance."

The flight attendant unfolded a table between them. "I will be bringing dinner out in the next five minutes," she said.

Over their meal they discussed a variety of topics. Their earlier intensity passed, and they focused on less volatile and emotional topics. Zeb told her about Estolia as a nation, shared some anecdotes about his two cousins and two brothers and himself. The trouble they got into, and the brief time they were all at Harvard together. Being the youngest of the five, he said he was the 'pest' they barely put up with – tagging along all the time. Reardon was one of his best friends at Harvard, and he studied law with Reardon more out of friendship than interest, finding an aptitude for the law exceeded only by his aptitude with money. Melody was one of Zeb's Estolian cousins.

She had a hard time imagining him as a young insecure boy hanging on to the activities of older boys. He seemed very self-assured, as if he was always in control of the situation and events surrounding him. She believed implicitly that in any high-stakes power game, he would always come out on top.

"You mentioned that you have a home in Barcelona?" she prompted.

He proceeded to tell her about his home in Spain. His hobby was raising Andestolian warmbloods and he sponsored one promising young equestrian every three years.

"I was blessed to be able to sponsor Desiree Andora. You likely heard of her. She works in my stable now. Her horse, Cimitarra de España, won the gold medal in dressage during the Tokyo Olympics. It is not often that a person is able to compete and win against the moneyed elite who normally dominate that sport."

Being a financier and entrepreneur meant he did not have a nine-to-five job. He seemed pleased to be able to tell her that he would never leave her side. "What good is money if one does not use it to make certain to maximize happiness and contentment all the hours of the day? I do not mean the hedonistic selfish pleasure of some, but rather focus instead on being with my family as my primary obligation."

Karis wasn't quite sure she followed whatever point he was trying to make. The emotional trauma of the day began to take its toll on her, and after her third attempt to stifle a yawn, he encouraged her to put the seat back and close her eyes. It would be many hours before they arrived at their destination.

Zeb went over the blessing he'd been given regarding the woman he would someday marry. He was promised peace with each of the decisions he would make. The same peace that flooded his soul when he decided to marry this woman. Clearly he was receiving the guidance of *Deity* steering him down the pathway of life. Every decision he'd made since he received Reardon's phone call that morning felt like he was in an impossible labyrinth with the spirit whispering in his heart which way to go at every split in the road.

He would never live in Estolia permanently, but that was knowledge he'd been given from the start. He hoped he would be able to partake as fully as possible in the blessings of Zaccarias. He wanted to be able to share his experiences with his brothers and cousins. He wanted to hear the guiding cadence of his uncle's voice as he shared insights into the experiences that Zeb already had. He wanted to see Nico's power grow as the newly appointed Keeper of the Soul of Estolia, as he, too, shared his interpretations of all that had taken place around him on this fated day.

At some point in his musing, Zeb fell asleep next to his bride.

32

A Marriage Sanctioned

We muſt make a change in this world. If we remain sheltered from the nations of the planet, Deity has proclaimed that the forces at work will deſtroy our ecoſphere. What victory is it if we remain unknown to moſt of the world, but are deſtroyed by the attitudes of those who put profit over progeny? We muſt make a change, and to do it, we muſt be more visible. Deity will provide for Eſtolians, when they are willing to keep the Promise of Zaccarias, and receive the promised blessings in return.

~Nicodemus Luciano Zacarian, Capitulo 89

NICO TOUCHED THE SCROLL in front of him. For a moment he was distracted by the feel of the paper. It was manufactured using an ancient technique, with cotton, wood pulp, sea grasses, and crushed Willowal eggshells. The edging was thick with the purple and green sea-grass found only along the Purple River. The artisans who created the paper in ancient Estolia were true geniuses.

He snorted softly as he recognized one way he procrastinated – he would focus on irrelevant details to sometimes avoid the relevant details that required his attention. He rubbed the bridge of his nose between thumb and forefinger and then opened his eyes and focused on the content of the blessing rather than the medium it was written upon. The scroll was written by Kedarin in the elegant calligraphy for which she was known. It was his brother's *Blessing-at-Eighteen* and was lengthy but subtle.

"What does Zeb's blessing tell you?" Zeke asked him.

"Zeb told me he felt the confirmation of the spirit from the moment he was presented with the opportunity. He described it as 'A deep and abiding peace,' once he decided to marry the woman. *Deity* approves the match."

"If *Deity* approves the match and proclaimed from seven days after his birth that this would take place; we would be going against *Deity* if we were unwilling to sanction the union after the fact."

Nico closed his eyes and thought of his younger brother. "It's essential that they spend seven days in the temple. He may not be able to give his soul into her keeping, but he will need the spiritual nourishment that comes from the seclusion."

"You're right. It's a peculiar situation, to have him married to someone he has spent no time with. There are no precedents. But I recall the day I laid hands on your mother's head while my uncle blessed her, it was clear then that her third son had a holy calling that could not be quantified, and as a result he would have greater burdens, perhaps, than you or your older brother."

"The blessings are always greatest for those whose burdens are heaviest," Nico quoted. Suddenly his head came up and he looked at his uncle sharply. "I believe, uncle, there..." He broke off as he realized what his role would be. "I know now, uncle, exactly how I am to handle this. Has the Seclusion Suite been prepared?"

"Yes, Nico, it has. I'll let your mother know. She'll be disappointed to have to wait for a week before seeing your brother. But she knows her family well enough to realize that *not* being invited to the temple would be devastating for Zeb."

Karis felt a hand on her shoulder and she yawned and sat up. It was Martha, the flight attendant. Zeb was asleep in his seat next to hers. He looked vulnerable. "We will be arriving in Estolia soon." Martha whispered, "Come with me."

Karis followed her to a separate compartment towards the tail end of the jet. A beautiful dress was hanging from a hook on a closet door. Martha helped her dress from the skin out. The dress was silver gray matte-colored fabric with elaborate embroidery in purple, gold, and green. It was off-the-shoulder and had gauzy translucent strips of fabric that trailed like streamers, making her feel like a fairy princess. White gloves completed the outfit. Once she was dressed Martha styled her hair.

The captain made an announcement in the Estolian language. Martha translated, "We will be landing in about ten minutes or less."

She followed Martha back to the main lounge but halted when she saw how Zeb had been transformed. From white gloves, an embroidered cape, a ceremonial sword, to a slender crown, he looked extraordinary. "You look like royalty," she said after a moment.

He held out a hand to her, and she moved forward and took it. Smiling at her he said, "I am royalty." He bowed theatrically with a swirl of his cape. "Prince Zebastiani Alexandros Zacarian, at your service." He gestured for her to be seated and then sat next to her. "Luckily for me, I have two older brothers, so I never had to worry about becoming King."

"I had no idea," she said, her eyes wide as they met his.

"That is why you have been dressed in that enchanting gown. By extension, you are now a princess. When we meet my two older brothers, my uncle, and my father, we will be meeting the four most powerful men in Estolia."

While the jet descended rapidly towards the runway, Zeb felt an overwhelming peace wash through him. The same peace he felt when Reardon asked if he was willing to marry this woman. A woman characterized as a money-hungry harpy, willing to marry one of the most amoral men on the planet so she could double her riches. The feeling of peace increased when he saw her approaching him in that pleasant fern grotto. A peace that spoke to his soul and proclaimed that this woman was the one who *Deity* wanted him to marry. He hoped fervently that there would be compensations for his willingness to forego yielding his soul up into her keeping.

During his Acolyte year, every time he read another account of that pinnacle moment in the lives of his forebears he felt bereft. It was hard to stomach the thought that he would be forced to forego that experience. The only thing that made it bearable was the realization that his willingness to fulfill his birth-blessing would save the planet and preserve Estolia for millennia to come.

He turned his head to look at her and the same sweet peace stole over him again. *Deity* was telling him that this alliance was the correct one for him. *This* was where he was supposed to be. Krissandra was the woman *Deity* proclaimed would be his spouse, his lover, his companion, and confidant. Perhaps, he reasoned, he would find a depth of pleasure, joy, and even love with her and he would never really know what he was missing. He could only hope that this union would fulfill the needs of his soul.

The airplane was almost to the ground when he reached over to her and grabbed her hand tightly just as they touched the runway. No matter what his forebears had, what mattered the most was what he had right now, and that was this woman.

Karis held Zeb's arm as they descended the stairs. Just as they stepped onto Estolian soil, the sun burst over the horizon, and Estolia was thrown into sharp colorful relief.

Zeb led her to the nearest of four men standing at the base of the steps to greet them. He looked a little older than Zeb and wore a thick ornate crown.

Zeb bowed before turning to her. "Krissandra, I would like to present you to my brother, Leonidas Agamemnon Zacarian, Duke, Sovereign, and King of Estolia. Leon this is Krissandra Zacarian, my wife."

His nod was solemn and his words were stiff if not quite unwelcoming, "I look forward to having the opportunity to get to know you better, over time." His eyes searched hers, taking in her orange red hair and short stature, seeing the black eye and stitched cut on her face.

The second man Zeb introduced her to was a little younger than the first. He had the classic tall-dark-and-handsome look. "Krissandra, this is my other brother, Nicodemus Luciano Zacarian, Last Resort, First Consul, and Keeper of the Soul of Estolia. Nico, this is my wife, confirmed by no less than *Deity*, Krissandra Zacarian."

His expression was as inscrutable as his older brother's. He took her two hands in his and drew her slightly closer, looking into her eyes. He nodded sharply twice before turning to look at one of the two older men, her hands were still clasped in his. When he turned back, he said, "Forgive me, my dear. You are extraordinarily beautiful, nothing like your reputation on social media sites." He pulled her into his arms and gave her a solid hug. Once he let her go he bowed towards her and then held up one hand. "Brother, it is essential that you and your new wife go directly to the temple, there to spend seven days in the royal Seclusion Suite. At the end of the seven days, the spirit will speak to me and tell me all I need to know about your marriage. Then, and only then, will we know for sure if the marriage is sanctioned."

Zeb's eyes met his brother's and for a moment they shared some silent communication. He let his breath out, as if he'd been holding it, and started to turn towards the two older men. He stopped when Nico said, "As Keeper of the Soul of Estolia, *all* other introductions and interactions, beyond those prescribed by your time in the temple, must be curtailed. You will have time to greet everyone once your seven-day period is at an end. Go now, direct to the temple. We will have our interview after seven days." He gestured to the other carriage. "You are expected at the temple. May the Promise of *Deity* come true and permeate your life, your marriage and your future. May you fulfill the blessing given to you at your coming of age."

Knowing she would not be living in Estolia, and that she might never return, she chose to focus her attention on her husband during their journey, rather than on the countryside. It was the first time she really looked at him.

He was perhaps an inch or two shorter than six feet, which still made him tall compared to her five-foot-nothing frame. He had black hair and warm brown eyes; a firm determined chin, thick eyelashes, and high cheekbones. His shoulders were broad, and she recalled the lean strength of his body when he pulled her against him during Sloane's challenge to their marriage. He was the supreme male animal. The deer with the most impressive rack of antlers – to use his peculiar analogy. He was her mate. She felt the prickling of her nerve endings when she realized she would be on intimate terms with him.

He broke the silence to ask, "Do you use contraceptives?"

"No." She was short in her response. What else could she add to that one word?

"I hope we will begin a family when you are ready, Krissandra."

"I would like that." She added, "I normally go by the name of Karis. I don't mind Krissandra, but I thought I would let you know."

"Thank you, Karis. I think both names are delightful."

The carriage had been following a road around the base of a tall mountain. Soon they were travelling in a narrow valley between two mountains. The one they had been circling had two structures that caught her attention. One looked like a medieval cathedral, while the other looked like a façade to a temple of some kind, against the face of the mountain itself.

"This is Mount Estoliana," Zeb explained. He gestured to the building standing near the mountain, "Estoliana Cathedral. Normally a wedding is a private affair focused only on the two people joining their lives, nothing like the world at large. But the children of royalty have a special ceremony here in the Cathedral after their seclusion to allow the citizens of Estolia the chance to get to know the newest member of the ruling family."

His expression was wistful as he looked at the Cathedral, as if he was uncertain whether he would be allowed to have that royal ceremony. She hoped, for his sake, that they would be able to have the ceremony in the cathedral.

"The temple is within the mountain. At the heart of the temple are several Seclusion Suites where we will spend seven days. Not all Estolians who marry use it. Some create their own. It is, however, expected that royalty, sons and daughters of the King and First Consul, spend the first seven days of their union together there. At the end of that time we will have an interview with the head of the Estolian faith – my brother – and we will find out for sure what our future will be."

"Are we completely isolated for the entire seven days?" she asked him.

He shook his head. "As I understand it, there are a variety of rituals we will be learning about. We will spend the first 48 hours together to the exclusion of all others. Beyond that, I am in as much ignorance as you. What happens within the Seclusion Suite is a topic for Elders – men who have married and are spending an additional year in religious study. It is supposed to be a spiritual experience of some magnitude, and I was willing to forego this time if necessary, if *Deity* asked it of me, but it appears we will be blessed to have this time together."

The carriage pulled to a halt near steps leading to an immense set of double doors. Two young men in monk-type robes opened the doors of the carriage. Zeb smiled at her before leading her towards the double doors which were also opened for them.

Inside they faced a foyer with brown and gold tiles. Another smaller set of double doors were at the end of the fan-shaped foyer, and there were halls to right and left.

She held his arm as they walked slowly towards the double doors. As they approached them, he explained. "Normally, I would bring my prospective bride here to the temple, to this Ceremony Room, and we would then be sent to the Seclusion Suite for seven days. We are not considered married in Estolian law until after the seven-day period and the ceremony that follows."

Another set of somber-faced young men opened the doors they were approaching. The room inside had a raised dais towards one end with an elaborate gold, purple, and green pillow resting on it. Several young men created an aisle, making it obvious they should climb onto the dais.

Zeb looked at his bride, as they approached the dais, and he wondered if he was being given silent instructions. She looked at him, and he realized in a blinding moment of clarity that he was *glad* he married her, glad for the trials they were currently faced with, and he accepted with a level of deep peace the place he inhabited in this and the greater world.

He halted her and instructed her to kneel on the pillow. While it was not his place to give blessings, he felt the need to lay his hands on her head and take a moment to thank *Deity* for giving him so much guidance in his life, much more than the average Estolian received.

She looked up at him, and in the moment before she knelt, he took in her appearance a little more closely than he had before. She was barely five feet tall, with long orange red hair, large amber eyes, and a curvy figure. Her face was swollen and she had stitches on a right-angle tear near her left nostril from where she'd been struck prior to his meeting her. She had a black eye.

Once she was kneeling on the pillow he placed his hands on her head lightly. Speaking aloud in the Estolian language, he offered up his thanks to *Deity*, to Zaccarias, to Estoliana, and to more than eighty generations of Estolians who always did the right thing in the interests of preserving the paradise of Estolia for all time. He accepted his role in the greater world, of somehow influencing world events and helping to turn the tide of power-hunger so they might, as a planet, move forward on a quest for peace and mutual beneficence. His time away from Estolia, and the knowledge he would never call it home again, led him in different pathways, bringing to him the extraordinary wealth through which he was able to secure this woman to his side. He felt the same wash of peace come through his body and his soul and knew he was given an extraordinary role. He took a deep breath and then helped Karis to her feet.

Karis got to her feet at Zeb's urging. His expression was thoughtful; he looked more at peace than he had up until this moment. Something deeply personal took place during the five minutes his hands were on her head and he spoke in his native language. Personal and peaceful. She took the arm he proffered and they descended on the back side of the dais towards yet another set of double doors. Those were also held open for them.

On the other side of the doors was a larger foyer with the same tiles. Several doors and hallways led off in many directions. They walked towards the only set of double doors. When they reached them, they were opened and Karis gasped in delight at the sight that met her eyes. In front of them was a wall of glass and on the other side of the glass was a garden, with beautiful trees climbing into the sunlight festooned with large pinkish-white blooms. A meandering pond wandered around the garden with numerous large fish swimming lazily within.

Inside the Seclusion Suite to their left was a seating area where one could admire the beautiful courtyard from inside. To the right was a large half-moon shaped table that looked like it could seat six. Beyond the seating area to the left was a lustrous tapestry-like wall hanging fringed in gold, with elaborate designs in purple, gold and green. It was held back by a thick golden velvet rope. On the other side was an enormous bed. She could see a bathroom just beyond the bed. The glass wall facing onto the natural courtyard continued from the small sitting room to the bedroom.

Zeb's voice was quiet when he said, "I think, my dear, the best plan right now is for the two of us to have a nap, get some sleep. It has been a very long 'day' for us."

He led her into the bed-chamber and asked, "Do you wish to use the restroom first?" He handed her a long silky white nightgown.

She nodded and took the nightgown from him.

When she was finished taking a shower, she felt curiously vulnerable stepping out of the bathroom wearing only a nightgown.

Zeb came up to her as she stepped out of the bathroom and handed her a glass of golden sparkling wine. Holding his own glass up, he said, "To our alliance. May we make something truly wonderful out of it."

She raised her glass to his toast, and then sipped the wine, stopping to savor the delightful flavor. He topped her wine off and then stepped into the bathroom for his own shower.

She sipped at the wine a little longer before moving to the bed and slipping under the covers on the side that was already turned down. She felt awkward knowing she was going to sleep with this man. He probably knew her reputation for promiscuity. What he couldn't know was that it was all manufactured out of thin air.

For just a moment, she allowed her memory to flow back to the two years after her mother died. Her father understood money and high finance but was lousy at parenting. She asked to move into an apartment of her own once she was eighteen. She thought he was secretly grateful for her taking herself out of his home. Shortly after she moved into the spacious apartment in the Carpathia building, she invited Charles to live with her. Rumors were rife on the internet about their relationship, especially when a few photographs were 'leaked' by Charles.

In retrospect, she wasn't sure what she hoped to get out of the sham relationship. Charles had his own motives and she knew he benefitted greatly from their time together. Nobody in his family circle suspected his interest was in men. Her father told her that she would be written out of his will if she were to marry Charles, or any other man, without his approval. She had a few uncomfortable conversations with her father, but for the most part, so long as she didn't marry Charles, he ignored her.

She had hoped to explain the situation to any man she became seriously interested in – if that ever happened. Once her father's plans for her were made known to her, she'd been fighting against the clock to remain single and not become pregnant. Marriage to Sloane, or single motherhood were both disastrous.

When the door opened, she saw he was wearing pajamas in a chocolate brown. He crossed over to where his glass was resting and took a sip of the wine, before topping his glass up. He carried his glass and the bottle of wine over to his side of the bed. "A little bit more?" he asked, proffering the bottle of wine.

She extended her empty glass to him, and he filled it with the last of the wine. She watched as he went to the thick tapestry wall hanging and loosed the velvet rope. Once released, the tapestry closed the bed-chamber off from the rest of the suite. He moved over to the floor-to-ceiling window and pulled another sash, bringing down similar wall hangings to cover the windows. The bed-chamber was thrown into darkness with only the light from the bathroom shining into the bedroom.

When Zeb slipped into the bed, Karis wasn't sure what he was planning. Did he really mean sleep, or did he mean to go about consummating their alliance now?

"It will take a couple of days to get adjusted to this time zone," he said. Then, after a pause, he asked, "May I hold you, Karis?"

She didn't answer verbally. She just scooted closer to him and into his arms, her head pillowed on his shoulder. She could hear his heart beating rapidly, which told her more than anything else that he wasn't nearly as relaxed as he tried to appear.

He stroked her hair almost like she was a cat in bed with him. "I am looking forward to introducing you to my family. It is important to me they get to know the real you, rather than the caricature that has been bandied about online."

She set her hand on his chest, feeling his heart thumping against her hand. "Zeb," she whispered.

He looked at her, and whatever he saw in her eyes must have told him something. He tilted her chin upward and leaned over to kiss her. She knew in that instant the only right thing to do was to give herself over to this man, everything else seemed secondary. Nothing was more important than becoming truly attached to the man who was her husband.

He pulled back slightly to look at her in the dim light of the bedchamber, and then his lips were on hers again, his tongue lightly brushing over her bottom lip, encouraging her to open for him.

She touched his chest and she felt a rush of heat at her core as his hands explored her breasts. His mouth left hers, and moved to her neck and the back of her ear before whispering, "May I take your nightgown off?"

She nodded. The touch of his mouth on the crown of one breast had her calling out in pleasure. She ran her hands over his back. When her questing hands encountered his pajama bottoms, she slipped her hands under the waistband, caressing his buttocks, enjoying the sensation of skin twitching and muscles tensing in response to her touch.

His hand cupping her intimately brought a rush of heated desire to her, and she felt as though her nerve endings were being dipped in pure sensation. She pushed the pajamas down, encouraging him to be as naked as she already was. He needed no further invitation, and in moments the warmth of his skin was pressed against her, the heat of his arousal against her thigh.

"Zeb," she said again, her hands urging him to kiss her, her legs urging his body over hers.

His lips claimed hers as his body merged with hers.

Karis couldn't help the mewl of pain as he took her purity from her. She knew he didn't expect it. What she didn't expect was for it to hurt quite so much. His tempo changed from undisciplined passion to gentle persuasion.

Afterward, he pulled her close against him, almost crushing her in an embrace, comforting and soothing her.

The emotions of the last twenty-four hours, on top of three glasses of wine, and the physical trauma of her altercation with Brant Kinsey all contributed to her weariness, and she fell asleep to the sound of his heartbeat in her ear.

Zeb couldn't believe where his faith led him. Regardless of the reports on social media. Regardless of her unsavory reputation... she was pure!

He'd been willing to forego the most extraordinary gift from *Deity* – the feel and sensation of having a woman gently take his soul into her keeping – the knowledge of how safe it would be, how nurtured and cared for – the chance to experience vicariously through that close connection what it was like to nurture a child from conception to birth. But it was the most difficult sacrifice he ever made.

With thoughts of a child, his hand covered her abdomen, and he realized that, if the promises of Zaccarias were to be believed, she would conceive a son. Their son.

His thoughts centered on the extraordinary woman who had given him the gift of herself. Selflessly. Having felt what it meant to place his soul in her keeping, he now understood what he had been asked to give up. He willingly gave up this profound blessing in light of the need of his nation and his world. But he had been rewarded for his willingness by having this woman take his soul and show him the profound joy felt by those who came before him.

Nico knew, somehow, that Karis was pure. He would ask the time-honored question and he, Zebastiani Zacarian, would be able to answer honestly that his soul *was* in her keeping. The union *would* be sanctioned after-the-fact, he would *not* be denied his land or his religion. His major sacrifice was in not living in Estolia, a future he'd known his entire life.

He looked forward to the conversations he, his brothers and his uncle would have. He anticipated the marriage blessing they would receive would be powerful, perhaps giving some further clues as to how he would make a major difference on their beleaguered planet; a planet sick to its very soul of the pestilence of power hunger.

33
Saving the Planet

Our isolation from the squabbles and petty bickering of the rest of the planet has kept us out of many conflicts that would otherwise have torn us apart. There will, however, come a time when as a nation, Estolia will have to step in and take a greater hand in the events shaping the world. At some point, a leader will emerge who will be able to bring together the factions of this planet and procure a secure and lasting change in the deep enmity driving mankind to war.

~Maximiliano Sebastian Zacarian; Capitulo 86

KARIS WOKE TO THE feel of a hand on her breast. She rolled over and smiled at the man who possessed her a few hours earlier. The memory of their intimacy was with her. "Hello." She knew she was blushing.

"I hope you are feeling well-rested." He moved closer to her, brushing the hair out of her face. He kissed her gently. He pulled back slightly to look at her before kissing her again. His tongue brushed against her lips, seeking access and then taking advantage of her yielding to him.

His kiss grew more passionate, she felt the heat of his arousal growing between them. As his mouth danced with hers, she explored his body with a greater sense of sureness. Her fingertips enjoying the tactile sensation of his silky skin over firm muscles. The way his body reacted to her touch was fascinating. He was so reactive.

When his body joined hers, she was moaning at the buildup of sensations within her. While there was a twinge of pain, she felt pleasure from his possession, and knew as they made love that she had discovered something far more profound than a mere means to an end in rescuing her from her impossible situation. She felt her nerve endings pulse with the heat of the pleasure he was giving her. Her legs locked around his body, taking him as deep as she could.

For the first time she was grateful for the absurd will her father wrote. She never would have been brought into Zeb's orbit without her father's incentive. And Zeb had declared himself to be hers for all time.

Later he got up and held out a robe for her and then donned a similar robe. Both were in the royal colors of Estolia. Green and Purple, with golden accents. He took her hand and guided her out to the small sitting room and then to the tiny dining room. When she opened the refrigerator, she saw a note. It said simply, "meals are provided. Open the door to make a request for your meal."

Zeb chuckled when he saw the note. "I knew those who entered this suite would receive pampering. I was not sure exactly how it would manifest."

He went to the double doors and pushed one open. She heard him exchanging a few words before he closed it.

"We will have a meal delivered in less than fifteen minutes."

As they prepared for bed on their last night in the Seclusion Suite, Karis couldn't believe the way the last seven days had gone. After forty-eight hours they'd been visited by several different teachers. Each time they were visited by a pair of Elders and they had discussions about Zeb's ancestors.

They'd been given seven separate blessings between them. After the last one, they were told the blessings would be transcribed and for her sake, translated and presented to them. They were also told during the blessing itself that it was necessary that they be given the blessings, no matter how out of the ordinary it was to be given so many. As the Catalyst and Conduit of Change they were both instruments of fate and *Deity*. Guidance was the one thing *Deity* planned to give them in abundance.

"What will happen tomorrow?" she asked.

"Tomorrow, my brother will ask me about the consummation of our union." He smiled at her wryly. "From an outsider's perspective, it might seem bizarre that such a personal topic would ever be asked openly, but if you consider it, we have been reading some of the erotic exploits of my forebears in the *Capitulos* and *Ensayos*. Our culture is very open about these things. One of the things I was not promised was that my wife would be a virgin. To an Estolian, foregoing that is a sacrifice of tremendous proportions. I was asked to give that up, in the interests of my nation, and of my world. I was willing to fulfill my destiny, marry the woman that fate would decree to be mine, and by doing so I was willing to give up the most exquisite connection any human being can ever experience." He broke off what he was saying, and Karis was surprised to see the glimmer of tears on his lashes. "I was willing," he repeated in a whisper.

"I don't understand, Zeb."

He closed his eyes and took several big breaths of air before finally continuing. "I shall explain more fully at another time. Share with you some of the most critical teachings of our faith. If a man is willing to embrace the teachings – and the Promise of Zaccarias, he can expect his connection with his wife-to-be will be deeply spiritual. There is a deeply profound spiritual and physical connection between them that cannot be severed."

"I'm still not sure I understand."

He rolled away from her and she felt a shiver of loneliness. "What are you feeling right this moment?"

She responded promptly, "I don't like it when you move away from me. I feel lonely."

He moved close to her, holding her tightly against his body. "And now?"

"When we touch I feel extremely close to you. It brings me happiness."

"You keep my soul, Krissandra Zacarian. As such, you connect with it and know what it wants. It knows its rightful home is with you, but it still wishes contact with me. When we touch, my soul is happiest. This will never change. I will never wish to be apart from you for any substantial length of time."

He smiled at her and then reached for the *Capitulo* they'd been reading. He flipped it open to one page and said, "what does this say?"

She looked at the lines he pointed out and read from it.

> *Faith,*
>> *To the sons of Zaccarias*
>>> *Is in believing*
>>>> *The Promise of Zaccarias*
>>>>> *To Deity*
>>>>>> *Will result in the blessings*
>>>>>>> *Deity proclaimed*
>>>>>>> *Would be their reward.*
>>>>>> *Faith rewarded to each*
>>>>> *Estolian with tactile,*
>>>> *Spiritual, extraordinary*
>>> *Precision.*
> *Faith!*

She looked at Zeb and smiled, somewhat puzzled.

"Look again at the page and note the placement of my hand," Zeb said.

She looked at the book he held. Like all the books they'd been reading, it was a dual-translation copy, with the text on the right in English, and the text on the left in the Estolian tongue. Zeb's hand was placed over the English translation. She'd been reading from the Estolian.

"How is that possible? I have only been studying the Estolian language for a week." The words in Estolian just made sense to her when she didn't think about it.

"Because, my dear, you keep my soul. When you relax, you discover my soul helps you in this *Transition* to living with me in a foreign nation. We will not live here permanently of course, but we will visit. Our children will grow up bilingual."

He picked up the book and set it on the bedside table, turning off the light at the same time. "I no longer worry about our coming interview. I look forward to it with an acute sense of joy. However, my wonderful Karis, I think tomorrow will come soon enough. For now, the two of us should enjoy the last night of our seclusion."

The next morning, she donned the dress that was brought to her. A beautiful confection in gold, purple and green. When Zeb was dressed, he again looked like the

Prince he claimed to be. After he was dressed, he came over to where she was brushing her hair and he placed upon her head a tiara. "As a princess, you must dress the part." He grinned at her in the mirror.

When it was time he extended one gloved hand to her, and she took it, feeling again a diminishing of loneliness that always happened when she touched him. They approached the double doors and when they opened for them walked through. They returned to the oval chamber she barely remembered from when they entered the temple. She remembered that he had her kneel and he laid his hands on her head, very much like the many blessings they'd received.

This time standing on the Dais were the same four men who greeted them when they landed on Estolian soil. Two of whom she'd met – Zeb's two older brothers, and two who had not been introduced to her. She and Zeb climbed the dais and stood in front of the four men. Zeb pulled her to stand in front of him, and he settled one hand over her abdomen, his other arm wrapped around her just beneath her breasts, holding her close.

Nico, she remembered his name, stood wearing his elaborate robe, looking somber. All four men were dressed in, she guessed, the full regalia of their office and station. He stood slightly forward of the other men.

"As the Keeper of the Soul of Estolia, I ask you, Zebastiani Alexandros Zacarian, to provide cause for the spirit and the nation to sanction your union with a woman whose aura was not visible to you, and to whom you wed without intimacy, specifically for secular reasons. Why should your union be sanctioned, when you scorn many of the precepts of Zaccarias?"

Zeb pulled her tight up against him for a moment before easing his hold. "I, Zebastiani Alexandros Zacarian have placed my soul securely within Krissandra Zacarian's keeping. Having been commanded by *Deity* to marry a woman unknown to me, without aura, possibly without purity, I was willing to fulfill my obligations to my nation, my family, and ultimately this planet. Having followed the demands of *Deity*, I ask now for the sanction of our union to be declared openly so that it might be so recorded."

Nico looked at her. "And you, Krissandra Zacarian, did you willingly give up your purity and take his soul in recompense?"

She didn't know what to say to that. "I was pure and untouched until Zeb made me his."

"Do you wish to remain with this man, or by the teachings of Zaccarias, would you prefer to reject the man whose soul you keep securely?"

"I shall never reject Zeb, never!" she said with vehemence.

"Kneel." Nico commanded.

Karis knelt on the pillow, recalling yet again the first time she was in this oval chamber. This time it wasn't her husband's hands on her head, but Nico's, and a second set of hands. She could feel Zeb's hands on her shoulders.

The blessing was in the Estolian dialect. She knew she would receive a translation. If she tried very hard, she might understand some of what he was saying. Instead she chose to feel the moment, absorb the spiritual impact of his words. When he finished and Zeb helped her to her feet, she realized that she was now Estolian. In her heart and soul, she embraced the faith. The peace that washed over her was different than the peace that came with touching Zeb. This was deeper, more profound. She wasn't sure if *Deity* was what she was feeling. But she was certain of one thing. Being with Zeb, keeping his soul, *loving* him was her true destiny.

Zeb handed his bride into the carriage, looking at Estolia with a fresh sense of purpose. He understood now why the Seclusion Suite mattered so much. The time spent mostly alone, together, was like the time spent allowing cement to dry. The focus was on the connection between the couple. Now that they had the solidity of their union they could look upon the greater world with a new perspective. He had never appreciated his world and his nation so much as in that moment, when he stepped out of the cathedral, formally married to the woman at his side, with all his life spread before him and the enchanting reality that she would be with him every step of the way.

This nation was worth keeping and preserving. Much of what he'd read made more sense now than it ever had before. He would do everything in his power to promote the future prosperity of his nation, and by necessity he would promote the future prosperity of the planet.

He glanced at his wife and was shocked at her brilliant aura. It was blinding in its intensity. She looked at him and he thanked everything within himself that he was gifted with *this* woman. She was everything any Estolian would want. He had the courage to listen to the guidance of the spirit so he could fulfill his destiny as the Catalyst of Change and somehow save the planet.

The End

Acknowledgements:

I want to thank McKennzie Patton & Hannah Cayer for being my two most staunch supporters, for listening to a lot of "Estolia" talk, and for encouraging me to reach out for my dreams. I literally could not have found the courage to publish my work without them. I also must thank the many people on the internet who gave advice, support, answered questions, and otherwise helped me to make my books, both print and eBook, successful.

Thanks especially to Kelsey King Lecky for allowing me to use her photograph on the cover of my book and another of her photos for the title page.

In addition, I must thank Aubrey Say, who has an absolutely amazing talent for photography. I've only know a few photographers who have that spark of true genius, and Aubrey is one of those individuals. In fact, I must thank the many individuals who came together one *extremely* hot July day to convert me from my normal slightly zany appearance into a beautiful woman. Chasity Rasdal owner of the Pretty Drama Salon in Klamath Falls was incredible in the way she came in early and answered about twenty anxious text-messages leading up to the big day. She, and the people she has working at her salon are true artists. Chasity did my eyebrows and my nails, while Dezzi Anderson colored and styled my hair. I'm grateful for the time Dezzi took away from her gorgeous baby Paisley to make me look my best. The entire day was magical and will always be one of my fondest memories of the day I realized my most cherished dream – of becoming published.

In addition to all of this, I wanted to thank Gregory Shipp for his invaluable work on the Map of Estolia. He was able to take a photo of a sketch, and a Google map image of the sea-floor and *create* Estolia. Whenever I look at the Balearic Islands, I think something must be missing because they always skip Pequeño. Gregory created a cartographic wonder, and he did a truly wonderful job of it.

I also must thank my Beta readers, Dad, Lucy, Don, Paul, and Abi for their willingness to read my book and give me feedback. Estolia is a much finer nation because of their feedback.

I should also thank the feline furballs who "helped" me to write, warmed my toes in winter, purred in encouragement, and occasionally interfered due to differences of opinion as to what their "pet human" should or should not be doing when they are demanding love and attention. Jynx, Tigger, Blackie, Lucy, George, Jack, Fang,

Kamoki, Daisy, and Tortellina all deserve a mention, for tolerating the usurpation of their lap by my laptop computer.

And of course, none of this could have happened without my husband. He is always there to support me, love me, and encourage me.

Afterward

On August 21st, 2017 we had a total solar eclipse in Southern Oregon. For the summer vacation, I was spending time writing stories and editing them and dreaming of someday being published. It occurred to me on the day of the eclipse that I didn't have to write a traditional novel. If short stories were my strength, I could always write a book with connected short stories. But the next question was – which stories? I'd written literally hundreds of short stories. But it didn't take more than a moment to realize that I would want to write about Estolia. I already had fifteen short stories written – I could easily pick out a few and make a novel.

It was harder than I thought. I had to use a time-machine to change the date for the sequential stories. It's harder than I thought to eliminate the internet and smart phones from stories infiltrated by such things. As things progressed, I eliminated five of the original ten stories from my initial outline and wrote the first part of this book to establish the original story of Zaccarias and Estoliana. On November 9th, 2017, during National Novel Writing Month (NaNoWriMo), I finished my first draft. And I already had the five "rejected" short stories organized into Volume 2 and outlined so I could dive right into the next volume.

By December 31st, I finished my first draft of Volume 2, and by March 10th, I finished my first draft of Volume 3. I was also refining, editing, and otherwise working on Volume 1, but I was so caught up in the stories that kept pouring out, that I became quite prolific. During the April Camp NaNoWriMo, I set myself a goal of writing 50,000 words and picked up Volume 4. I ended up writing nearly all of Volume 4 during one nine-day period of April... when I declared it finished and began to work on Volume 5. I worked steadily on Volume 5, but also kept thinking about things that I had to add to Volume 4. By the beginning of May, Volume 5 was half-done and Volume 4 was bursting at the seams and I needed to split it in half. I was suddenly faced with the fact that I had 3 volumes finished, and three volumes 'in progress'.

Planned Release Schedule:
Volume 2: The Promises of *Deity* – Fall 2018
Volume 3: The Estolian Way –Early Winter 2018
Volume 4: The 5ᵗʰ Set of Twins – Earlier 2018

The original intention was to write seven volumes, with Volume 7 already planned out including the title: Saving the Planet. But once I split volume 4 into two parts, the series is now likely to extend into 8 volumes – at least. Volumes 5 and 6 are already more than half-way complete. It is my hope to release those two Volumes so that the release date of Volume 6 is no later than one year after Volume 1 was released.

Read more about my novels on www.estolia.com.

Summary of Volume 2:

1 *Brotherly Love* – 413 years before the current era (BCE). The first set of Twins born to a King of Estolia. The dagger for the office of Last Resort is introduced in this story. We also learn about the two women who are as different as night and day and how they are able to tame the hearts of the two identical princes.

2 *Gentle Rebellion* – 1990 years into our current era (CE), we explore some of the double standards relating to gender which are prevalent in the modern world, particularly in Estolia. Virginity is considered critical for women, and optional for men. In this story, we meet Gregorio and learn of his decision to gently rebel against this double standard. He must resist the subtle pressures of his cultures – a process he considers simple – until he meets Wraith.

3 *Kidnap of Kedarin* – 1991 CE – In this story we learn about the darker side of jealousy and acquisition. A horrific accident keeps the second son of the king from seeking out a woman to keep his soul until it is almost too late. Estolian men must marry before they turn thirty-one, or remain single for their whole lives. With barely three weeks remaining before his birthday, he discovers Kedarin, only to have her kidnapped!

4 **Rejecting the Estolian Way** – 1992 CE – The flip side of the coin of rebellion is rejection. Gregorio's younger brother Dominick agrees with him about the double standards of Estolia. He plans to thoroughly reject the Estolian Way. The seeds of his rejection began in his youth. Dominick was thirteen when he read the story of Quedaro, one of his ancestors. He was alternatively fascinated and appalled to read about how he abducted his bride from her brother's estate in France, taking her aboard his sailboat to bring her back to Estolia. During the journey, Quedaro wrote, he seduced his unwilling bride, and forced her to marry him. Dominick rejects Estolia and plans to defy his birth blessing and live his life celibate. As part of this goal, he left Estolia and purchased a subterranean home in Northern California. He plans to hide away from his nation, his faith, *and* eligible young women until he is thirty-one years old.

5 **Confluence in California** – 2022 CE – Max has plans to travel to California to attend the wedding of his former college roommate. He and his cousin Nico are both nearing their thirtieth birthday, and both have had no luck finding a woman to love in their search within Estolia. Nico chooses to travel with Max so that they can travel to a large population of Estolians in Canada in hopes of finding brides. The surprise comes when their uncle, the Keeper of the Soul of the Nation opts to travel with them to Northern California.

Shortly after the three men arrive in California, a confluence of circumstances envelops them. Depending on how they grab hold of the opportunities being presented to them, they may in a way that will, inevitably, result in three unique couples coming together. It begins with the bridesmaid that Max is supposed to partner to the wedding. His friend apologizes that he will be stuck with a woman who is somewhat uglier than a gothic gargoyle. Complicating this situation is a case of mistaken identity, when Nico's sister Rhea is confused with a call-girl. Zeke is forced to commandeer the Zacarian Jet so he can bring two couples back with him so he can heal any rifts and untangle the snarled relationships. Nico, abandoned in California, is told he'll have to fly to Los Angeles International Airport so he can meet up with another of their jets. Though he grumbles about the inconvenience, he forgets it immediately when he is nearly bludgeoned by Kenzie O'Rourke's prismatic aura and falls in love instantly. (Volume 1, Part 4).

6 **Apollyon's Heresy** – This section of the book gives some background into the Acolyte year that each young man is asked to serve. A year of service to the nation, coupled with intense instruction in both their history and their religion. We begin in 2015 CE, followed by a flashback to the time of Apollyon – 417 CE – the first Heir to the Throne of Estolia who holds the Promise of *Deity* in contempt. We learn what his Last Resort does to resolve the situation. The final chapter of this section we move forward in time to the point when the Acolyte from this story (in 2027 CE) is

introduced to the woman who holds the keys to his future happiness.

Volume 2 in the Tales of Estolia will be released in September, 2018 as an eBook, in October in Print.

Note on Historical Accuracy

As a math teacher, with a Master's degree in Education and a Bachelor's degree in Statistics, you might realize that my personal strength is not History. In fact, it is one of my weakest subjects. The only thing I am weaker on is math.

That said, I did want to make a note about the historical and geographical elements to my Tales of Estolia. First – the three communities that will be mentioned in detail in the series: Estolia, Hath, and Halloween County, California are all fictional. Every aspect of those three locations is a construct of my imagination. Some of the outlying regions – Mallorca, Ibiza and parts of the United States used to flesh out my Tales are of course not fictional. However, it is entirely possible that there are historical inaccuracies that will crop up in these stories. I beg your forgiveness, reader of my Tales, for taking clear liberties with the known historical facts and changing them to fit my story. I eventually decided that I could either spend all my time researching all these little details – and never really have the time to write my stories, or I could spend my time writing, and make up most of the details, knowing that there are many things that do not mesh with reality. But, then again, this is the Earth of the Grand Design, so perhaps, on that Earth, these things are all true...